LAST CALL

Joseph Anthony Weber

DEDICATION

This book is dedicated to all of those who work tirelessly to help people they do not know find their way out of addictions and into a life of purpose and peace.

And... to those who are still lost and suffering in the depths of addiction and alcoholism. May you find your way to a loving God and begin to walk the path that He had intended for you and a life of true freedom.

"If the Son sets you free, you shall be free indeed."

JN.-8:36

ACKNOWLEDGMENT

I would like to thank my wife of 51 years, Teresa, for the abundance of love and patience, the tireless prayer, and her hope against all hope that one day I would find sobriety.

To my Mother, Catherine Teresa Weber, who never stopped praying for me.

To my Father, James Joseph Weber, who taught me more than I had time to thank him for.

A special thanks to Marie Huffman, who spent many hours, days, and years showing me how to live a sober life. Whose constant encouragement instilled in me the belief that I could, in fact, finish this project and that it was worthy of the effort.

To Doctor William Edward Lowe, who wanted to see this work published in life but was called home. His friendship and generosity in death have helped to make this possible.

The 12-step program leads me into a deep spiritual relationship with God.

Above all, I thank my Lord and Master, Jesus Christ, who heard my cry and lifted me out of my despair.

Table of Contents

ABOUT THE AUTHOR

Joseph Anthony Weber is a Husband, Father, Grandfather, and Great Grandfather. A Chaplain and a Pastor, a writer and a musician. Currently living in a small rural town and enjoying a life of peace and sobriety. Walking in a joy that surpasses all understanding, an unmerited gift from a loving God.

PROLOGUE

My name is Joe, and I'm a… well, I'm not sure what I am. I can tell you what I used to be. I was just a guy who wanted to get along. I was just a guy who wanted to do what he had to do in life. I had a wife and a couple of kids, a really good job, and everything was going ok, you know. Sure, there were some problems in my marriage, and it seems as though the last few years, I have been getting some bad breaks at work; mostly with asshole bosses but on the whole, everything was okay. I enjoyed going for a few after-work with the boys and having a laugh. Is that too much to expect? A little pleasure in an otherwise boring and practical existence! I work hard, and I provide, and all I ever wanted was a little space to unwind at the end of the day. All I ever wanted was to be left alone. Well, I guess I got that last part. I am alone.

I am staying at this guy's place at the moment because my wife has lost her mind. She has pretty much always lived on the edge of two worlds, but now, she has stepped completely over into the abyss. I blame those nut jobs she has been talking to, the ones who are telling her she needs to kick my ass out. The ones who say some crazy shit about detaching with love. Well, I can tell you that I did not feel a lot of love in the room when I was detached. She tells me that I crossed a line. She says she can't deal with the uncertainty I bring into her world. I guess she means the uncertainty that comes with every pay cheque I bring home, every bag of groceries my money provides, every gallon of gas she puts in the car, I PAID FOR while she is shopping for her spring wardrobe! She also says she is sick of my sarcasm and my anger. She may have a point there about the anger, I mean.

I told her she would be angry too if she were me. Suppose she had a boss who did not appreciate her or, for that matter, a wife who didn't! If everyone on earth depended upon her for their existence, she might take a drink once in a while. But she did not buy any of that, even though it is the truth. She only uses the truth to hurt me and to blame me because she is jealous of my life. I have friends and people who like me and respect me! I am going to places in my life, and I can tell you that for sure! This thing at work is just a temporary setback, just some bad luck with a bad boss. I know it will blow over after the suspension. Anyone would drink for a couple of days after the week I had. I told her I didn't see any line let alone cross over any, but she kicked my ass out anyway, typical.

I'm lucky I got to know this guy at work, Bill. Well, I don't really know him all that well. He only comes into the bar with the guys once in a while and never stays too long. A real up-and-comer, you know what I mean. Kind of a dick, really, but he told me I could crash at his place while he was out of the country. I was kind of surprised that he was so concerned, to be honest. He has probably been screwed over by a wife as well. Maybe he is not such as dick head after all is said and done. But none of this really matters! This is not about me. It is about the call. It is about the guy on the other end of the line.

You don't know me, and I doubt we will ever meet. I'm not even sure why I am writing this down. When I awoke this morning and realized that the bits and pieces of what I was remembering were not a dream but an actual event, I felt compelled to put pen to paper and relate what I could remember to the best of my ability.

As I have said, I am uncertain why I need to record the event, for I did not know the man. The fact is we had never met, and I spoke to him only one time, quite by chance or fate, about whether I would believe in such things. Since that night, I have come to understand events occur for a reason: building blocks in the plan of some greater power or higher intelligence, steps on a path to the end of a journey. But I am not so sure. Perhaps there is nothing more than fate, blind luck, and happenstance. That is what this feels like. As I have said, I am uncertain.

Yesterday, when I awoke, I felt I knew who I was and where I fit. This morning, the parameters were not as clear, and I wondered if perhaps I had been living outside the lines. I don't know whom I am writing this for or if anyone will ever read it but me.

Perhaps I am not writing it for him, as he asked, but instead for me, so I can understand, at least in part, what happened to him. I spoke to him less than an hour on the phone. I did not know where he was or even if he was in the same city as me. I only knew I was to be the last call. He was 52 years old, and he told me the story of his life. Fifty-two years summed up in less than an hour. How could that be? How could one man, given the same opportunities as another, end up so alone and, in less than an hour, equate his life to fifty cents in a pay phone? It has left me cold; it has left me frightened, and it has left me uncertain.

And so I write. For you, for me, for him, for anyone whose life adds up to more than fifty cents. He wanted to cleanse himself, and in so doing, he has stained me. Colored me with doubt and uncertainty, made me question myself and my way of life, and helped me to understand there is so much more to everything.

I do not know if I was able to help him. I doubt it because I never really tried, but I know that he has helped me, and for that reason, I will tell the story.

POWERLESS

Tommy Boy woke with a groan and a foul taste in his mouth that was not unknown to him. As his head cleared, he focused on the red digits of the clock radio on the bedside table of the Main Street rooming house. His brain recognized the dim glow of digits: 6.45. Another groan and a quick shake of the head allowed the hour to register, but was it morning or night? There was really no way to tell here, in this hovel he called home. There was no newspaper from which to take the date, there was not a television to tune in to the morning or evening news, and there was not much of anything. Nothing was abundant. He threw his legs over the bed and prepared for the dizziness he fully expected as his feet landed on the filthy carpet. His head swam, and his stomach heaved as he struggled up and over to the tiny bathroom.

In what had become a daily ritual, he crossed the tiny room from the door to the toilet with a fluidity of motion that seemed somehow out of place for the events that were about to occur. He inserted a finger down his throat, lifted the seat, and vomited into the bowl. For a moment, he simply stayed in place; his head slumped over the toilet, his eyes clamped tight, as though this would close out the reality of his world. Slowly, he spitted, then coughed, then waited; waited for the second heave, which would come surely as the first had. For a moment, he marveled at the beauty of the floaters and sparks of light that lived behind his eyelids. It was as though there was a world of constant celebration behind his eyes, fireworks and laughter just a blink away but always out of reach, forever fleeting, forever floating.

Then it came. Violently, convulsively, he emptied the liquid remains of his gut in a final stream of bile and mucus. He spits, he coughed, he gagged, and then he looked. It was part of the ritual, as though he were a soothsayer or an ancient Egyptian High Priest prodding the intestines of a sacrificed chicken. Each day for the past many months, he would, upon waking, lie with his head hung over the bowl and study the spilled remnants of his gut. He really did not know what he was looking for, perhaps some meaning, some answer to the riddle that had been his life, some prediction of better days ahead. But there was none; not yesterday, not today, not ever.

He tried to read what looked like wet coffee grounds floating atop the greasy film in the bowl, and it was then he realized he had vomited up some blood. This was new, an added attraction in the ritual of the waking, and in it, he read the future. He was dying slowly and from the inside out. He closed his eyes, sighed deeply, and flushed.

That is how easy it was for him to deny the reality of what he had become and where he was going to end up. It had always been that easy, just another drink away from happiness. Just another drug away from peace of mind and just another shattered relationship away from blessed isolation. Just another flush, and it was all gone.

In a single movement that was more desperate than graceful, he pushed himself to his feet while reaching for the dirty mirrored door of the medicine cabinet. Pulling open the door with his left hand, he instinctively reached for the three fingers of vodka remaining in the final fifth of the last binge. In a single motion, he spun the top off the plastic bottle and gulped the vodka. Gagging it out of his rolling stomach into his waiting mouth and swallowed hard again. It would stay down this time. It always did. He breathed blessed relief as he watched the tremor subside in his hand more than he felt it and then finished the bottle; ritual complete.

He leaned over the basin now as the throbbing in his head slowly dissipated and splashed cold water on his face and tried to control his breathing. Cautiously, he stood erect; more steady now but never certain of his equilibrium, he leaned heavily on the basin. He closed the door of the cabinet and stood staring at the reflection in the soiled mirror. He examined every feature of the face he owned, comparing it to the face he had once owned, the one he remembered that was the face of his childhood, the face of his adolescence, the face of the young man starting out in life full of hope and ambition with dreams still intact. That face was gone, gone forever.

The face in the mirror, the one he did not recognize, was one of defeat. The man who owned this face had been used up. The eyes were vacant. The nose had been broken too many times; there was a scar on the lip and another on the forehead, both of unknown origin. Some teeth appeared loose and too large for the jaws in which they resided, teeth that would no longer be able to chew even the most tender of steaks. His skin was turning the color of the nicotine stains on his fingers. The skin on his face seemed to hang like a mask, hiding the visage that once had been. This face filled his heart with fear, for this face, he did not know. This was the face of a man who would steal and cheat and lie with no regret. This was the face of a man who had loved and lost and had nothing left to give. This was the face of a man who carried such shame that life now seemed intolerable. This was the face of the dammed and the doomed, the dying and the dead.

Tommy Boy pushed away from the mirror and the truth he could no longer bear. Walking back into the other room of this self-imposed hell, he scanned the contents, the remains of a lost life. There was little left. The majority of his stuff, such as it was, now resided at Louis's East End Pawn. His Grandfather's watch and ring, a television from his Brother, his prized record and CD collection. All had been pawned and repurchased more times than he could recall. There was the collection of books his Mother had given him. The classics she so loved, and they had shared together when he was a child, were gone as well. He could no longer recall the stories themselves, though he was certain he had read them. There was so much of him gone, so many memories which were gray and faded. His thoughts seemed wet and slippery. So much had been lost forever. Indeed, there was little left.

As he pulled on his cleanest dirty shirt, he smiled wryly, thinking of his Johnny Cash Classic 'Sunday Morning Coming Down' sitting on a shelf down at Louis's East End Pawn. Who could have known he would live the song? Who would have guessed he would be standing in this hovel? I'm not sure which day of the week was "Coming Down," not knowing if it was morning or night, and I'm not caring. He scooped up the busted clock radio, pulled on his tattered jacket, and left the room. On the landing at the top of the stairs, he stopped and turned back to the door. There, under the number 12, written in magic marker, someone had scrawled his name, Tommy Boy. For a moment far too brief, he stared at the black scrawl, and it was at that moment that he knew what must be done.

He moved down the filthy stairway with caution. The bulbs were out, and the possibility of sleeping vagrants was always present. In the pecking order of the declining world in which he lived, Tommy Boy had not yet descended to vagrant status, but it was, without a doubt, the next swirl in his downward spiral.

He smelled the man before he saw him on the step and instinctively raised a hand to cover his mouth and nose. The man's face carried a growth of several years. It was gray and stained with spit and food and vomit and tobacco. It was a tapestry, a testimony to the tragedy of this man's life. His clothing was tattered, and a dark stain seeped out beneath the filthy fold of his trench coat.

Tommy Boy stepped over the man lying in his own shit and felt a deep sense of disgust. It passed through him like a shiver and left him with a feeling of cold arrogance. He felt it deep in his gut like a stone, and as he maneuvered past this waste of human skin, he could feel his jaw set tight, and his loose teeth begin to grind together. There was no pity within him for this unknown vagrant. There was no compassion. What he felt was a relief. Relief that even in the declining state of his body and soul, there was someone who was worse than he, someone to whom he could feel superior. A sense of relief and hope, hope for his future, hope that maybe he was not all that bad, hope that maybe he could turn it all around, and maybe it was just a run of bad luck that ran through his mind. Slipping back into that lying zone, Tommy wrapped himself in that familiar quilt of denial as he spit on the vagrant, "Fucking Bum," he muttered to no one and pushed his way out the door and into the waiting Street.

The sounds and smells he walked into assaulted his senses and filled him with an irresistible excitement, just as it had done so many times before. He closed his eyes and tilted back his head and let it fill him, let it wash away his pain. He smelled hotdogs and urine and humidity and a million other things that he could not categorize. He heard sirens and garbage trucks, brakes squealing and horns honking. The Street quaked as the overhead A train raced by. He heard the whore on the corner calling out to the johns in their cars at the stop light, "Wanna party, honey"? "Let me show you a good time." "I can take you around the world. That's a sweet thing." He heard the light change to green and wondered if that was even possible. A dog barked, a baby cried, a panhandler sang Amazing Grace, and he just stood. His head back, a smile emerging on his tired face. He felt the compulsion begin to grow in his body. He felt the obsession in his mind. He drank up the sounds and smells of his addiction, and he knew it was evening. He knew he had to get 'right.' He left the stoop, turned west, and headed toward Louis' East End Pawn.

Tommy Boy moved with new conviction as he headed down Lexington toward Baker Side Road. He passed by the whore without a second look, paying no heed to her salutation. There had been a time not so long ago when she was another aspect of his addictions, but his desire for her and the special gifts she offered had faded with his increasing need for booze and drugs. He told himself that this was a simple matter of practicality, that there was not enough ready cash for her and his true love, vodka, and crack, but the reality was that his ability to perform even the most basic sexual acts had long since left him. In fact, the thought of being physically in contact with another person had become revolting to him. Intimacy had become collateral damage in the war he had been waging against his body and soul.

He told himself it was his choice and that he was better than the rest of the johns she blew for forty bucks. He told himself she was just a crack whore and he could do better, maybe meet a nice girl and try a new relationship. He felt he was on the cusp of change, big change. It was all going to turn around. All he needed was a break. All this he told himself, and all this he believed.

Her name was Rhonda, and she was a crack whore, but that never used to matter to Tommy Boy. They did their crack together most of the time, she paid all of the time, they fucked some of the time, but that had not happened for a long time. As he walked by tonight, she called out to him, and he looked the other way, like she didn't exist, like she was not even there. She wanted nothing from him. In fact, she had come to understand there was nothing left within him to give. She only needed for him to acknowledge her, to see her, to let her know that she was still there and that once they had been friends. "Go fuck yourself," she screamed at his back as he melted into the crowd. "At least I got a fucking job." A car pulled up to the curb, a window went down, and her next bag of crack sat behind the wheel. She looked west as she got into the car and watched Tommy Boy turn onto Baker Side Road. "Goodbye, Tommy," she said quietly to herself, and for just a moment, she thought she would be able to cry.

Tommy Boy weaved his way through the supper crowd on Baker Side Road, keeping an eye open for Trip. Trip was his boozing friend, and Trip owed him money. That made Trip harder to find. He would be around in one of the shitty bars on this shitty Street or hustling a buck in the pool room, snatching a purse, or doing whatever he needed to do to get the cash for a night of drinking.

Trip was a true blue Alkie, and made no apologies for it. That was what Tommy Boy liked about him. Like himself, Trip could philosophize his way through a 40-ouncer of cheap vodka in a few short hours, making more sense with each passing drink." There's nothing wrong with being a drunk if you accept it as the truth," he would say. "The only alkies that are truly unhappy are those who try not to be alkies, the ones who go to AA and shit like that. They are not being true to their nature." He waxed on, "I know a hell of a lot more old drunks than I do Old Doctors." The Trip would slur, and Tommy Boy would laugh.

Tommy Boy would laugh hard like he did long ago. He would laugh long like he did when he was a kid. He would laugh like there was still something in this world worth laughing about. He would laugh until he broke into a bout of coughing and choking and nearly passed out. Trip made Tommy Boy laugh, and that's why he loaned Trip money.

It was the single most intimate act he had partaken of with another human in a long time. The act of lending out his drug and booze money to another Alkie was akin to a Brother giving a dying Sister the kidney she so desperately needed. There was every reason to believe the Brother would get on fine with the remaining kidney he possessed, but there was also the possibility that the Brother would find himself in a hopeless situation years down the road with no backup kidney to see him through his dark time.

It requires a great deal of trust, and trust is the first lost quality of the practicing addict. Trust is a luxury ill-afforded in the world in which Tommy Boy lived, and many died. Many died because they trusted the wrong person for the wrong reasons. Tommy Boy had felt his world growing ever smaller, and on the night when Trip asked for the twenty bucks, it seemed as though that simple act of trust could save some portion of his life and somehow make it normal.

With great trepidation, he reached into his dirty jeans and pulled out the twenty. He held it tightly and looked long and hard at Trip. Tommy Boy stared at the shit-eating grin of rotting teeth, green on the top, yellow on the bottom. "Great," thought Tommy Boy, "The Grinch who stole my fucking twenty." "Come on, hand it over, crackhead," says Trip. "You know I'm good at it. A week on Wednesday is my welfare check." A week Wednesday had come and gone. Tommy Boy had found himself in his own hopeless situation, entered his dark time, and had no backup. He was no longer laughing.

He had made his way to the bottom end of Baker Side Road with no sign of the last person on this earth he would ever trust. Trip would have to wait. There was business to be done. He looked up at the flashing neon that read "Louis' East End Pawn," and the excitement he had felt growing in his gut as he had left his front step was quickly turning to anxiety. The certainty he had felt in his mind was turning to obsession, and the tremors he had quieted with vodka were beginning to stir.

He pushed open the door to Louis' East End Pawn with all the bravado he could muster. The bell above the door rang as he pushed his way through. All eyes turned towards Tommy Boy as he made his entrance into the little shop, not because his appearance commanded attention but because his mustered bravado had leaned too heavily into the door, pushing it into the stopper and flinging it noisily back into his face. Muffled laughter ran through the patrons of Louis' East End Pawn, but rage ran through Tommy. "Fucking door," he muttered to no one as he weaved through the shelves of busted power tools and old computers. He passed by the smirking onlookers without a glance and found his way to the counter.

"Hey, Louis…how's it going?" The big man behind the counter looked at Tommy Boy and did not reply. "Louis…what's up man, come to do some business."

"I ain't Louis." He said and began to turn away. "Whatever, man, how bout you give me some attention here? I come in to hawk this fine Digital Alarm Clock." The big man turned back to Tommy Boy with a puzzled look and extended his hand to take the clock. He rolled the clock over in his hand once, then once again, examining the faux wood finish on the Admiral Time and Tunes Digital Classic Clock. "Where'd you get this?" he asked.

"It's mine, man. It was a gift from my Mother."

"Bullshit, you steal this."

"No, no… I'm telling you, man, it's not hot. I paid sixty-five bucks for that just a few weeks ago."

"You paid sixty-five bucks; it was a gift from your Mother. Lying fucking junkie. I need to see a receipt. Without a receipt, I can give you ten bucks."

"Ten bucks! What did you call me? You call me a fucking junkie? What the hell kinda way is that to do business, man? You don't even know me, man, and you're calling me a fucking junkie! What kinda shit hole are you running here? I tell ya, Louis, I got a good mind to haul all my shit outta here and take my business across town."

"You got no shit here, and I told you, my name ain't Louis."

"Whatever, man, whatever. What do you mean I got no shit here? I got all kinds of shit here, ring watch, albums, appliances. What do you mean I got no shit here? I'm your best fucking customer."

"Look at your stubs, asshole. The time on your shit has run out. It is on the shelves in the back, sold or about to be. Your shit is now my shit because you've been too busy getting high and drinking your alcoholic ass into oblivion to come pick it up…I'll give you ten bucks. Take it or leave it."

"No way, man! Come on, there is obviously a mistake. It has only been a month since the last time I pawned when I got my last disability check."

"Don't know about your check, don't care, your shit has been here 121 days, and that makes it my shit, now you want the ten bucks or not?"

Tommy Boy stood motionless and stared past the pawnbroker and to the shelves in the back. He was confused. He was suddenly disoriented and uncertain of what was transpiring.

The other patrons in Louis' East End Pawn had stopped smirking and were now trying to get further away from what was happening at the counter. It was as though they sensed the danger that could erupt from this situation. They knew that Tommy Boy might snap. They knew that his things were gone, and more than that, they knew he would not be getting what he needed to get right since there would be no cash. Some made their way to the door and quickly exited to the Street. Others stood watching at a distance, unable to look away.

Tommy Boy was playing out the scenarios in his head as quickly as his damaged brain could. Had it been four months? Is that possible? He knew he occasionally lost track of time, usually when he was with Trip, and they were grooving, but four months, in no way, was not possible. This fucking Louis was pulling a fast one, trying to steal his shit. He had to do something, but the best course of action was not clear. A fog of uncertainty was enveloping him and holding him. His senses were dull, and his fear was at a fever pitch. He was filled with conflicting emotions, and the panic was growing out of his gut and spreading to his limbs, about to spill over into this room.

Tommy Boy was sick. He was sick, and he was in need, but the man behind the counter was neither. Louis was a big man, bigger than he had noticed before, and he was getting angry. The physical altercation was not going to work. Even if he got his shit back, he would be picked up in a couple of hours by the Police, and he knew he could not spend a night in the bucket, not in the shape he was in, not without getting right.

But he was smarter than Louis. He knew he was. He had been in jams before, and he always got out. He could figure things out, and people liked him. He got off on the wrong foot here, that's all. He had to start over. No need for brawn when you have a brain. Hit and run, smash and grab shit, that was for the street punks, not for him, not for Tommy Boyle,

"Look, Louis," he began contritely, "I'm not sure what I did to piss you off, man, but I know we can sort out this mix-up about the shit in the back. We're adults right, but how about a show of good faith to an old customer? Man, you know the clock is good for at least thirty. What do ya say, Louis?"

He had been standing behind the counter with his arms crossed, his chin resting on his chest just above his forearms. His arms uncrossed in a blur, and his hands slapped so hard down on the countertop that Tommy Boy swore he saw the glass bend and spring back, and he wondered if that was even possible. Some of the patrons jumped in surprise, and a woman let loose a short scream, and two more men left the shop. When he spoke, his voice was low and hissing, and there was spit accentuating every syllable." I have told you," he said, "my name is not Louis."

"Well, where the fuck is Louis, man…I want to talk to Louis…maybe he can sort this shit out, why am I even dealing with you?"

"Louis is DEAD!" he screamed so violently it pushed Tommy Boy a step back. "He has been DEAD for a MONTH. I bought this place from his widow. She told me he went home one night, locked himself in his garage, slipped a 38 into his mouth, and decorated her lawn furniture with his fucking brains. She said it was something about depression and anxiety and that his medication was off, but you want to know what I THINK. I THINK he just couldn't stand the thought of coming back down to this shit hole end of town and dealing EVERY FUCKING DAY with drunken, low life, wet brain, fucking losers like you."

There was drool running down his chin and hate brewing in his eyes, and Tommy Boy had enough street smarts left to know he was very close to a situation that would not go his way at all. How did this terrible misunderstanding get so far out of hand? It was not his fault, but the situation was not lost; he could pull it off and walk out of there to get 'right.'

"Shit, man, relax, what did you say your name was? Doesn't matter. Look, the clocks gotta be worth at least twenty, right? So let's just call it twenty. Now I know! You are the big boss; I can tell there's no way to dicker you down, man, so let's just make it twenty and really…sorry to hear about Louis, but I've been out of town working for a while, man, there was no way I could have known, just no way man, I mean you haven't even changed the sign right? What a horrible thing, I'll have to send some flowers to his wife. What was her name? Doesn't matter. I have it written down back at my place anyway, so what about it, man? Are we good on the twenty for the clock?"

The big man just stood and looked at Tommy Boy and said nothing. His head slowly sagged, and his stubble-covered chin came to rest once again on the barrel that was his chest. His jagged breathing slowed and became rhythmic, and he began to regain his composure. The few seconds the big man took to let go of his anger seemed an eternity to Tommy Boy, who looked on with uncertainty. The big man raised his head and leveled his gaze on Tommy Boy, and Tommy could see that something in the man had changed. There was no anger left in the eyes of the pawnbroker, no animosity, no contempt. What Tommy Boy saw was pity, nothing more, just pity, cold and empty.

It was a look he had seen once before, a look which left him cold. A look that took him home, back to his Mother's kitchen and the last time he had seen her. Tommy Boy had to look away, to divert his eyes from that look of cold pity, from that look of finality he had seen in his Mother's eyes, and from the knowledge that she had come to a place of emptiness in her feelings for him. He had crossed a line and could never go back. He had seen that look before, and like it had then, it now left him cold.

"Jack," the big man said. "My name is Jack."

"Ya right, Jack." Tommy hesitated, "So what about it, Jack? Twenty, Right?" Jack looked on in silence for a moment, then leaned himself over the countertop and motioned Tommy Boy to come in closer. The other patrons of the late Louis' East End Pawn shop had had their little show. They had seen Jack lose his cool with this pathetic little man; they had their cheap thrill, and now it was over. Jack would not allow it to go on. Tommy leaned in with extreme caution as Jack began slowly,

"What's wrong with you, man? You need to get a grip; you need to get some help. You've crossed a line or something. I don't know, but you need to call somebody or something."

Tommy looked at Jack in confusion. "What the fuck you on about Jack? I told you I was sorry, man, about the confusion over Louis. I was out of town, you know, working."

"You were in here two days ago, Tommy! We had this whole conversation then. Don't you remember any of that? I mean shit; you don't remember my name, that Louis is dead, none of that. Are you putting me on or what? Here are twelve bucks, Tommy. It is really the best I can do; take it and get some food for a change. You look like death, and please…. you need to get some help! Now go on, get out of here; we are done!"

Tommy Boy found himself in the Street in front of Louis' East End Pawn and knew he must have walked out but had no memory of doing so. Was he in shock, or were the blackouts becoming constant? Were the snatches of memory now the anomaly and the blackouts the norm? He didn't know, and he didn't care. All he knew was that Louis was right; something was wrong. Something was changing, and he didn't like it. He was scared, and he was confused.

He stood there feeling empty and full at the same time. He was full of despair and full of fear and shame, and still, in that hopeless state, the voice in his mind, the voice of his addiction, cried out. "This is not your fault. If Trip would have paid you the money you never would have been here in this place today. You never would have been in the situation you were in. That guy, Louis, never would have been able to steal your shit. If only that fucking Trip would have held up his end, if only he would have paid you back, you're twenty.

At that moment, Tommy Boy came back to himself. He became aware of his surroundings, of the fact he was standing on Baker Side Road, looking lost, holding twelve bucks in one hand and a pawn ticket in the other. He felt the stares of the people as they passed and knew he had to move on. He had been here in this spot too long, and people were noticing. It would only be a matter of time before there were Police and questions. Questions he had been asked before. The usual questions that came from the cops, the ones riddled with sarcasm and contempt. The ones they used on people like him.

In the past, he had been able to field these questions and deal back the appropriate amount of sarcasm and contempt, just enough to feel superior but not so much as to get run in. After all, how hard was it to get one over on a bunch of dumb ass cops walking a beat and acting like they were something special? They all knew Tommy Boy was smarter than they were, and that was why he was harassed. But today, he had no time for such encounters. There was business to deal with, time was short and Trip was slippery. He had to be found, he had to be dealt with, and he had to know he fucked around with the wrong guy when he ripped off Tommy Boy.

It was getting harder to focus as time moved further away from his last drink of vodka. The tremor in Tommy Boy's hand was taking on a new rhythm and slowly spreading throughout his body. He was soaked from head to toe, hot and cold simultaneously, and it felt as though a low-level vibration was in every organ. He had to get a drink and he had to get it soon. His addiction was in pain, and when his addiction suffered, it made Tommy Boy suffer right along. He had twelve bucks in his ass pocket that would get him a fifth. That would dull the pain and slow down the assault the disease was launching against his body. That would get him what he needed to stop the tremor and the vibration, to help him think in a straight line.

But if he could just hold on, hold on until he can find Trip and get the rest of his cash. Then he would have thirty-two. With thirty-two bucks, he had more options. If he could just hold on, he knew his luck would change. If he could just find Trip. He turned and headed back East on Baker Side Road, away from Louis' East End Pawn Shop, away from the man called Jack, who seemed to know him, who had stolen his Grandfather's ring and watch and everything else he had left in this shitty world. Somewhere in the recesses of his mind, he knew he would never be back this way again.

His stride took on a new purpose as he made his way up Baker Side Rd. He was now a man on a mission, full of focus and determination; he scanned the faces in the crowd as he moved further along the Street. There were no residual thoughts or feelings from his encounter at Louis'. There were no more feelings of fear and shame over his pathetic appearance and performance in front of the man named Jack or the strangers in the Pawn Shop. Fuck them, they were history, he would never see any of them again. Who were they to judge him anyway? They would be far worse than he had ever gone through the shit he had! There were no more concerns over the apparent loss of time and the blackouts; they were all but forgotten like they never happened. No, those thoughts and feelings were for lesser persons, losers, and whiners, not guys like him, not Tommy Boy. He held his head high, and his eyes darted from face to face, shoulder to shoulder, back to back, looking for a familiar gesture or garment, looking for a tilt of the head or a tuft of dirty grey hair, looking for Trip with an intensity he could not have mustered on his own. An intensity provided by his need, his pain, his addiction, his silent lover.

He had walked and searched for 35 minutes when he saw Trip coming out of the alley across from Baker Side Road and the corner of 12th Avenue. Tommy Boy knew by the grand gestures and ear-to-ear grin that Trip was drunk on Tommy's money and instantly became infuriated. He watched from behind a post as Trip, with an entourage in tow, made his way across 12th Ave. and headed directly towards Tommy Boy. It took all the remaining control Tommy possessed to stand in wait for Trip. Every fiber in his body, all the strength of his addiction, was willing him to bolt out and attack, to cross this ground and take back what was rightfully his. He had been pushed around for too long, and now the time for him to fight was at hand. Trip had crossed a line. Trip had taken him for a fool as so many others had for so many years, and judgment day was nigh. There would be no charm, no con, only aggression, and if the cash was not forthcoming, there would be violence, swift and brutal.

Tommy Boy watched as they drew closer, and he could see the altercation in his mind's eye. He would confront Trip. Trip would see he was deadly serious. The young punk on his left would begin to move forward, and Tommy Boy would drop him with one punch to the throat. Trip would plead for calm and claim friendship while holding out Tommy Boy's twenty. Tommy would take the money, turn to go, then wheel around and lay one square into Trip's gut. Trip would gasp and puke up his rum, and as he hit the ground, he would know without question that he would never again screw with Tommy Boy. Then the nice-looking blonde flitting alongside would look down at Trip, slowly turn, and take up with Tommy Boy as he headed for his connection. Ya… that's how he saw it happening; that's the way it would be. His luck was turning. It was all going to come together.

But that's not the way it went down.

Trip approached just as Tommy had seen it happen in the hallucination. Trip was laughing and happy and did not seem to care about the world. The punk beside him looked eerily like Trip and seemed to hang on every word that slid from the drunk's lips. The blonde looked up at him with an expression in her eyes that Tommy's mind could not identify. It was a faraway look that was vacant and focused at the same time, and Tommy remembered wondering if that was even possible. Later, much later, he would know. It would come to him. She was looking up to him with love in her eyes. Tommy would remember that look, but the memory would come too late.

Just as it had been in his mind's eye, Tommy Boy jumped from behind the post, impeding their forward progress. Trip and company stopped up short but did not look frightened or alarmed. On the contrary, Trip's smile widened even further, and Tommy remembered wondering how that was possible.

"Where's my money, you Mother Fucker?" Tommy spat the words out with such violence that it caused him physical pain, and he realized that while in hiding, he had been grinding his loose teeth so vigorously that one had come dislodged from his jaw and had been spat out with his words. All four of them looked down at the tooth for what seemed like minutes but were really seconds. Trip slowly looked up from the tooth to Tommy, who was standing with spit and blood streaming down his chin in a reddish froth.

"What the fuck, Tommy Boy!"

"What has happened to you? You look like shit, man." Trip had genuine concern in his voice, and for a moment, Tommy was confused. But the addiction spoke to him and told Tommy to be wary. Trip was slippery; Tommy Boy knew that. Trip was only as genuine as any lying fuck alkie could be. Trip was not his friend.

"Never mind me, Trip, and don't think you can bullshit your way out of this, I want my money, and I want it now!"

The young man took a step forward just as he had in the hallucination, but he was not stopped by Tommy Boy's quick punch to the throat as Tommy had imagined it to happen. Instead, Trip slowly raised an arm in front of the young man's chest and stopped his approach.

"Easy, son," Trip said. "There's no need for any trouble like that here today. This is my friend. His name is Tommy, and he looks like he is in a world of hurt. We have some kind of misunderstanding here, but I know we can straighten it all out. Isn't that right, Tommy? These here are my kids, Tommy; remember I spoke of em? Haven't seen 'em in 10 years or so and never thought to ever see 'em again, but here they are. Come and find the old man they did. We've been catching up here for a couple of days. I guess that's why I haven't seen you for a few days."

"Bull shit," Tommy screamed, and the young girl shrunk in fear." I want my fucking money, Trip. I need it now. I need to get right, I need what's mine, and I intend to get it no matter what you say; I'm done with your lies and your bullshit, man; I want my fucking money!"

Trip raised his arms in the air, palms forward, in an "I surrender" gesture, and for a moment, Tommy Boy had thought he had won. But as Trip began to speak, his hopes faded rapidly.

"Just hold on, Tommy, take a breath and take it easy. You got it all wrong, partner. You gotta trust me on this. You are making a big mistake, having some kinda psychotic episode or some shit like that, man. Take it easy. I told you, how many times I told you to stay off the shit, the booze is hard enough on guys like us, man, but no, you gotta go mix it with that crack shit now you're all fucked up, you don't know what's happening."

"I know what's happening, man, and you are not going to get away with it." Tommy was trying to be loud, but his voice was losing authority. It cracked and broke as he spoke. His lips were dry, and he tasted blood in his mouth and did not understand why. "I trusted you, man, I lent you my twenty, and you said you would give it back, man, and now I need it, and you are trying to fuck with me. People have been fucking me over my whole life, and it is stopping here today. I WANT MY MONEY!"

"Is that what this is about, man?" said Trip with that familiar lilt in his voice that Tommy hated. "The twenty you lent me two weeks ago. What the frig man; are you shitting me? Are you that screwed up? I gave that back to you last Wednesday when I got my cheque. I gave it to you at Hank's over on Lexington, and then we drank it up together at happy hour."

Tommy Boy stood frozen in time. All the mayhem around him stopped, and for moments, he was surrounded by stillness. Suddenly, he was watching this comedy of errors unfold before him, and none of it was funny. He was confused and frightened and did not have the ability to know what was true. His capacity to understand what was real and what was hallucination had evaporated. He was flying through turbulent airspace without navigation, and his crash was imminent. He was seconds from collapsing when he heard the voice, the voice of his lover, the voice of his addiction. It came to him soft and soothing, and it whispered to him the words he needed to hear. The words that would dislodge him from the cement in which he stood trapped and propel him into action. "He's lying she said," so soft, so seductive, "he's laughing at you. They are all laughing at you. You need to show them who you are; they need to understand."

Tommy Boy heard the words and Tommy Boy understood. As quickly as he had gone under, he climbed back into the reality of what was happening. There stood Trip, arms in the air, palms forward, slowly shaking his head from side to side. To his left was the punk holding his ground but looking ready to step forward if needed. To his right and slightly back was the young girl, the look of fear intensely on her face. Tommy Boy's glazed-over eyes again fell upon Trip, and he tried to focus. Trip was speaking, but the words could not drown out the bidding of the lover. Trip's face carried no fear, anger, or hostility as Tommy Boy had expected, but there was pity over the face of this lying alkie. "Is that even possible?" Tommy Boy thought as he looked into Trip's eyes. "Is it possible for this low-life alkie to pity me? I am twice the man he ever was and will never be as bad as he is. He's just a damn dirty alcoholic."

At that moment, Tommy Boy lunged forward. Palms up, elbows locked, arms straight out in front of his cleanest dirty shirt. Tommy Boy crossed the three feet between them with remarkable speed. The young man barely had time to move; the young woman barely had a chance to scream. Tommy Boy made contact with incredible force, delivering a staggering blow into the chest of Trip.

The pity left Trip's eyes as he fell back into 12th Avenue and into the path of the Up Town Bus. At that moment, Tommy Boy's life was changed forever, and Trip was set free.

CAME TO

Some hours later, Tommy Boy came back to himself. He immediately realized he was sitting in the alley behind Lucky's Last Stand. Lucky's was a dive on the north end of town where a guy like Tommy could get a cheap drink and a quick fix. The only rule at Lucky's was that the fixing was done in the alley out back where Tommy Boy now sat, where he had sat many nights before. In his left hand was the bottom half of a fifth of vodka. On his right was the familiar charred glass tube which had been his lover. At his feet was a shining black woman's handbag with a broken strap, its contents spilled out on the ground. His eyes floated over the spilled contents, not focusing on any one thing but registering it all: lip balm, glasses, house keys, change purse, used Kleenex, pennies, mints, one peanut, and one piece of ID.

He focused on the ID and saw his hand reach out and pick up the driver's license with the picture of the nice-looking girl. She had long dark hair and piercing hazel eyes. Tommy Boy thought she was perhaps the prettiest woman he had ever seen, and he found familiarity in the photo. As he looked on, he found himself remembering this woman. Her name was Petra, and she resided at Madonna Mission over on Queen and Lexington, a long way from here. Tommy knew Madonna House. There was a mission there, and he had found himself in line waiting for a bowl of soup in the past. Not because he was in need but just because it was free. Who would not go in for a free bowl of soup? He had been there, and he had seen this woman before, and he knew her to be a Nun, and he knew her to be kind. She was

Sister Petra, and she was kind to all the low life. And Tommy Boy remembered wondering if that was even possible. They were bums. They were drunks. They did not care about her or her religion. They just wanted soup, just as he just wanted soup. It was free, and she was kind.

Tommy Boy felt the confusion growing in his mind and the top half of a fifth of vodka warm and soothing in his belly. He thought hard about this woman and this purse. In his heart, he knew how these objects, these belongings of Sister Petra, had come into his possession. In his heart, he knew because he had come upon other people's property before. This was not the first time he had done the bidding of the lover and, through violence, had attained the resources he required to feed the love. This was, however, the first time he had no recollection of the act. No remorse, no feeling of guilt for the theft, nothing. He felt nothing because he remembered nothing. She had been kind, and deep in his heart, perhaps his soul, perhaps the only human part of him left, he had hoped he had not hurt this woman. This Nun was kind. This Nun had treated Tommy with respect. This Nun had asked for nothing in return. This Nun had been a victim of his crime.

He looked down at the possessions spilled on the ground and began to gather them up to place back in the purse. Regardless of how he felt about what he may have done, he understood there would be consequences were he to be found here, in this alley behind Lucky's, holding on to a Nun's purse and ID. As he picked the bundle of Kleenex off the ground, he saw beneath the Kleenex a small circle of wooden beads attached to a crudely carved wooden crucifix.

He had seen this Rosary before, and as he rolled it over in his hand, he recalled the times he had watched Sister Petra walk her slender fingers over the beads, her lips mouthing unspoken words to her God. She wishes health, happiness, and freedom from despair to those to whom she served up soup. He remembered listening in as she told the story of how she came to possess the small Rosary. He remembered the serene glow of her hazel eyes as she told the disheveled old bum about being in France after she had left the Convent and going to Assisi to pray at the shrine of St. Francis, to pray for direction to understand her calling.

As she kneeled there, deep in prayer, a man approached who had fallen on his luck. He was wearing tattered clothes and speaking a French dialect that Sister Petra could not understand. And though she was able to discern only a few words from the rapidly speaking man, she gained a sense that this man was in desperate need. Something awful had befallen this man, and he wore his despair like a cloak. It covered him from head to foot.

Tourists and locals alike had come here to worship at the Shrine of St. Francis, each with their own burdens, each with their own pain, and each seeking the miracle of relief. Some huddled in small circles of prayer while others stood off by themselves, seeking solace in silence, and all, all of these good people turned away from the approaching man. They diverted their eyes, turned their backs, and filled the courtyard of St. Francis with shame.

Lord, make me an instrument of Your peace!

Where there is hatred, let me sow love.

Where there is injury, pardon.

Where there is doubt, faith.

Where there is despair, hope.

Where there is darkness, light.

Where there is sadness, joy.

O Divine Master, grant that I should not so much seek

To be consoled as to console.

To be understood as to understand.

To be loved, as to love.

For it is in the giving that we receive.

It is in the pardoning that we are pardoned.

It is in the dying that we are born to eternal life.

These were the words of the Saint. These were the words of Francis of Assisi. This was the courtyard in which the Tourists and the locals had come to ask for the intervention of the Saint, and this is the place where they turned away from the man, the man with tears flowing across his stubbled cheeks, the man speaking gibberish and stumbling from one turned back to another, hoping to be noticed, seeking to be acknowledged and needing to be consoled.

The moment was electrified! There was no other means to describe it!

The air was filled with a filament of panic and foreboding as the man careened off an obese woman from Arkansas wearing a flowered hat and a billowing sun dress that floated about like a sail. Her very girth made it impossible for her to move in time to avoid the collision, and the already stumbling man bounced off this huge woman and came to rest mere inches from the kneeling Sister Petra.

The man lay in a heap and sobbed. He sobbed as though his tears would cleanse the world of all its sins. He sobbed as though it were the only thing he had ever done in his entire life. He sobbed as only the dying, the weary, and the hopeless can sob, with an intensity that cannot be outdone. This man was beyond speaking. The garbled French dialect he had previously been spouting was nothing more now than sobs and moans.

Sister Petra looked down upon this man from her knees and knew not what he had suffered or what he had done. She knew not where he had come from or where he would end up. She knew only that he was here, with her, at this moment. The very moment when she was seeking direction, the very moment she was looking for a purpose in her life and in her vocation.

Slowly, she extended a hand and let it rest upon the sweating, filthy brow of this man. The moment her hand lighted upon the head of this anguished soul, Sister Petra understood the sorrow within this man. She understood the loss he suffered and the void in which he had lived, for this man had lost himself. He had given over his being, his soul, to addiction.

For ten minutes, they stayed in this position. Not a word was exchanged between these two unlikely companions. They remained where they were, she on her knees, he in a fetal position by her side. Slowly, the sobs faded into silence. Those looking on looked away, uncomfortable with the power in the meeting of these two souls, ashamed of the lack of compassion they had shown.

She began to pray, her lips moving in unspoken words of worship to God, extolling gratitude for the epiphany. The man at her side began to stir, and slowly, they both rose to their feet. In silence, he reached into the pocket of his tattered, dirty pants and withdrew a small circle of wooden beads attached to a crudely carved wooden cross. He extended his hand to Sister Petra and nodded for her to take the Rosary. As she took the Rosary in hand, she began to walk her slender fingers over the beads, which would become her habit. She watched the lost man as he turned and walked straight and erect through the crowd of those who had turned their backs on him. She knew then that her God had spoken. She knew then she would give her life in service of those who needed to find their way back to themselves. She had found what she had come to find.

Tommy Boy stuffed the last of the possessions back into the black purse with the broken strap. He studied the Rosary for a moment longer and then reluctantly stuffed it into his pocket. He really had no idea why he was keeping this Rosary. It was evidence that could link him to the Nun, but he felt compelled to hold on to this artifact of St. Francis. He scanned the area behind Lucky's Last Stand and spied a stack of wooden liquor cases in the corner beside the locked dumpster. Over the top and behind, he tossed the purse.

Looking around to ensure he was still alone, Tommy Boy tried to slide the cases into the gap between the wall and the dumpster to conceal the purse. The cases proved heavier than Tommy Boy could have imagined, and he prepared to give a little extra shove. Palms up, elbows locked, arms straight out in front of his cleanest dirty shirt. Tommy Boy crossed the three feet between himself and the stacked crates with remarkable speed. As his locked arms made contact with the wooden crates, his mind made contact with the memory of what he had done. Trip's startled eyes filled his vision, and Tommy Boy fell to his knees and gasped.

"Dear God," he cried out. "Oh my sweet Lord, What have I done?"

There is nothing to describe the hell which descended upon him at that moment. He saw it all in his mind's eye, and he knew it to be true. He saw Trip fall back in surprise; he saw the uptown bus carry him away in a flurry of ripping cloth and flesh. He heard the brakes and the daughter screaming in desperation, and he saw the blood drain from the face of the young man who looked eerily like Trip.

It had all happened so quickly. It had all been so final. One moment, Trip was in front of him, concerned for Tommy Boy but happy about the reunion he was enjoying with the lost children. These children had looked at the situation with worry but looked at Trip with love and forgiveness in their eyes. Tommy Boy had seen this, and Tommy had been confused. After all, he had done to them in their lives. After he had abandoned them in their youth and chosen the bottle over them and their Mother, they had forgiveness in their eyes! Was that even possible? Then, in an instant, it was all gone. In a moment of madness and insanity, he, Tommy Boy, had stolen their past, their present, and their future.

There was a silence that fell over the entire block as the screaming of the brakes and the daughter came to a halt. For a moment, no one moved. The passersby looked on, frozen in terror. The bus driver looked white and shocked, and the young man, who looked eerily like Trip, began to turn and look at Tommy Boy.

The love and forgiveness Tommy had seen earlier in the eyes of this young man was gone. It had been snuffed out with the man Tommy knew as Trip and the man this boy knew as Dad. It occurred to Tommy at that moment, and out of the blue, he realized that he had never really known Trip's real name. How was that possible? After sharing every intimate detail of their lives over uncountable cocktails, how could he not know this man's name? This man who had been a friend to Tommy and a mentor, this man who had held him when he was sick and consoled him when he was in depression, this man whom he had trusted enough to lend his last twenty bucks. This man who had paid him back the twenty over at Hank's on Lexington at happy hour. This man he had just murdered.

The young man, who looked eerily like Trip, slowly began to turn, and in those eyes, Tommy Boy now saw a hate he had never before witnessed in a human. He saw the wild hate that lives in the eyes of fighting dogs and caged or cornered animals. He saw the need and felt the desire to hurt, destroy, and kill. He saw what Trip must have seen in the eyes of Tommy Boy as he was thrust into the path of the last bus Trip would ever catch. Tommy could clearly see his imminent death at the hands of the man who looked eerily like Trip, and he knew he had to run.

And he did run. Tommy Boy had run plenty in his life, from responsibility, from relationships, from truth and honesty, and from himself. But he had never run for his life. He had never run as though his life depended upon it. He had never run so hard to get away from something so horrible. At first, he ran out of sheer panic and desperation. He had to get away. He had crossed an unseen line into an unknown world and inflicted violence he had never before imagined possible. The consequences of his actions flooded him with simultaneous visions of courtrooms and jails, lawyers and judges, lethal injections, and a shame that only death could be revoked.

His flight became the focus of the gathering crowd, who were only too happy to turn away from the vision of blood and mayhem in the gutters of 12th Avenue. Two good Samaritans began to remove Trip from beneath the undercarriage of the Up Town Bus, and many in the crowd turned away as Trip was removed in pieces.

Voices were raised in alarm, arms were raised, and fingers were pointing as Tommy Boy bounded through the crowd. Those agile enough stepped aside to avoid a collision, and those unable to move were bowled over by the fleeing madman. An old woman lay slumped in a heap over her walker, a bone protruding from her forearm, and her just purchased bag of oranges spilled onto the ground. Fresh oranges rolled into the gutter and mixed with the freshly spilled blood of Trip.

A young mother veered her carriage into the street, and a speeding taxi squealed to a stop inches from the screaming mother and wailing child. The world around him was exploding in madness, the world within him filling with fear and confusion. He had to run! He had to stop! He had to hide! He had to go back! He had to explain! But there was no explanation.

All these thoughts swirled through his mind, and his head began to ache with the insanity. He was operating at a fever pitch and about to succumb to the madness when she spoke to him. She spoke with a calmness that was inappropriate to the situation and a certainty that was not of his mind, and he remembered thinking that was even possible.

"Tommy, you need to slow down now. Tommy, you need to think. What is it you need? Where do we have to go right now? You need to get it together and fix us, and then, then, we can figure this thing out. It was not your fault. It was them. They were attacking you, they were laughing at you, they treated you like a nobody. It was self-defense. You had no choice. You need to slow down and think about us. WE NEED TO GET RIGHT."

Tommy Boy could hear his jagged, gasping breath begin to slow and take on a steady rhythm. The events around him went instantly from fast forward to slow motion, and he could see them all unfolding. He could see his path to freedom and the road to the lover. A burly man in an Oakland A's ball cap stood his ground twenty feet ahead of Tommy. The man's feet and jaw had been set as if in stone. He was ready to catch the fleeing murderer. He was stooped forward at the waist; his arms held out in front and arched to the sides as if he were ready to pick up a whiskey barrel. Tommy Boy could see the sweat glistening on his cheeks and the muscles rippling in his big arms. In the eyes, he could see hate. Hate and determination. This man was about to be a hero and was enjoying the thought of catching and crushing some street scum. This was his moment! This was his chance to set the record straight. He was about to chalk one up for every hard-working Joe in this country who paid the welfare checks to these bums and addicts only to have them laugh at society and push a man in front of a bus. Well, enough was enough! It was going to end here and now. Or so he thought.

Tommy moved with a speed that was hard to imagine and a grace not of his own. Without hesitation, he charged toward the stooped, angry man. Without a second thought, he leveled his maniacal gaze into the hate-filled eyes. With no thought of the outcome, he raced on towards a collision which would be inevitable. And then he moved. One quick feint to the right and a step left, and he was by the behemoth, leaving the burly arms grasping nothing more than air and the dying sent of street scum. Ten more yards down 12th Avenue, Tommy Boy ducked into an alley adjacent to Hin's Chinese American Diner and was gone.

He ran at breakneck speed for blocks. When he was certain no one followed, he slowed to a fast walk, his breath tearing out his lungs as he laboured on. He stayed close to the walls and away from the illumination of the street lights. He knew he would look tattered and suspicious. He knew they would be looking for him hard, and they would know who he was. It was only a matter of time till they found his place. He could not go there. His body ached and was slick with the sweat of a sprinter, and yet he shivered in the night air, cold and clammy in withdrawal from the stinking lover, the scent of her exuding from every pore.

Her soothing words had pushed him on, but she was now silent. Searching for her with darting eyes and hungry veins, he moved forward, panic replaced with caution. She had told him what to do, and he must obey. Later, he would work it all out. There would be a way.

He moved along from block to block, alley to alley, ever moving farther away from the judgment he had leveled upon Trip. He entered an alley of Pine St., which emptied out over on Park, and stopped to catch his breath. His body was quivering with the craving, and he felt as though his sweat contained millions of ants streaming down his body. The panic was growing once again within his tortured mind, and it took all that was left of his will to hold on. Just a while longer, just till he was sure he was clear. Just till he knew he had eluded his pursuers.

Tommy Boy breathed deeply and began to jog towards the light at the end of the Alley. Once he was on Pine Street, he would head to the north end of town, a place called Lucky's, where he knew he could get some action. The thought of getting that far revitalized him, and his weary legs began to pump harder over the littered pavement. Once there, once he could think clearly, once he had communed with his 'love,' he would go on the lamb, try to get out of town and disappear.

This was the plan formulating in his sick mind as he approached the end of the Alley and the glow of lights from Pine St. He came onto Pine faster than he had expected and cut quickly into the Street. Turning right and hugging close to the wall, he collided with all of his forward motion into someone walking South on Pine. The impact was staggering, and both Tommy and the person he had collided with were knocked backward with a resounding thud.

Tommy smelled fresh strawberries on the breath of the person he ran into as their wind was thrust out of their lungs in a whupping sound, and he remembered thinking, is that even possible? He stumbled back several steps before catching his balance and steadying his feet. The person with whom he had collided was not as lucky and was quickly backpedaling, arms waving in great circles as if in some vaudevillian stage show. Completely out of control now, this person crossed feet at the ankle and solidly crumpled in a heap on the cement sidewalk of Pine St. Tommy looked down upon the person and then quickly surveyed the scene. For the first time since the point of impact, Tommy Boy realized he had run into a young woman. She lay splayed out on the sidewalk, one sensible show lying beside her, her long dark hair concealing her face. Scattered about her on the dirty sidewalk were a number of books she had been carrying as well as a small supply of just purchased groceries. Bread, cheese, some apples, a small container of milk, and a modest but substantial supply of food were revealed. Among the books were some travel magazines, a Captain America comic book, and a copy of the King James version of the New Testament. Tommy remembered thinking in passing that it was an odd collection of reading material, a collection of books he himself may have found within another life, at another time when his life held some purpose and meaning.

Tommy's brain registered all that was strewn about him in seconds with a clarity he had not been accustomed to in many months. He looked again at the foodstuffs and then the books as his eyes rested momentarily on the sensible shoes, which somehow did not fit with the shapely legs of this young woman. The dark skirt was hiked high from the awkward fall to the ground but was of a modest material and a conservative cut. She wore a navy blazer, and there on the ground at her side was a veil of sorts that had been dislodged in the collision. The hair that had been tied back and concealed by the discarded veil was a deep chestnut brown and hung like a mask over the face of the young woman. The hair was healthy and cared for. The colour reminded Tommy of the Otters who were in the ponds on the farm where he had grown up. It was a place he had not let his mind go to in many years, a place full of good memories too painful to recall.

Snapping back into the reality of his situation, he quickly swiveled his head left to right, north and south up and down Pine St., No one was in sight, no one watching or running to help the woman. Maybe his luck had changed! Maybe it was time for Tommy Boy to catch a break.

Tommy's eyes came to rest upon the shinny black purse still amazingly hooked over the arm of the woman. She lay very still as though unconscious, her back rising and falling almost imperceptibly as she drew in breath. The purse lay half under her twisted body. At that moment, there was no doubt in Tommy's mind that he would rob this woman, she would wake, he would be gone, and it would all work out.

He stooped slowly to her side, all the while surveying the surrounding neighborhood, ever watchful for evidence of interlopers. Slowly, he began to straighten her arm and ease the shiny black purse out from under her crumpled body. With a steadiness of hand any surgeon would envy, a steadiness not in keeping with the ravaged state of his nervous system, he eased the black strap off the shoulder of the young woman, slowly down her forearm and over her wrist. He was inches away from retrieving what he now considered his property, seconds from continuing his escape to Lucky's and the rendezvous with his "lover," moments away from the next event in his crime spree when the woman began to stir.

She moaned almost imperceptibly. She raised her head slightly and groaned. Tommy Boy saw his moment escaping and quickly pulled on the strap of his shiny black purse. Her reflexes were remarkable for a woman who had only just regained consciousness, and just as the strap was about to clear her hand and become firmly entrenched in Tommy Boy's, her slender fingers closed around the smooth leather with a grip that was deceiving for this tiny woman. It was a grip that was firm and used to hard work. It was a grip that would shake any hand with confidence and surety. It was a grip of the righteous and God-fearing, and as she turned to face her adversary, Tommy Boy realized it was the grip of Sister Petra of The Madonna Mission.

"No." She said groggily. "What is happening? This is my purse; no, you can not take it." And she held on.

Tommy pulled harder, and she held more firmly, and once again, Tommy felt it all going wrong. Why did this keep happening to him? Why did it always go wrong? Why was she going to make him hurt her? Tommy waited for the scream, but the scream did not come.

Tommy pulled again with all the effort he could muster, but to no avail. He pulled to free himself and his shiny black purse, but all that resulted from his efforts was that he eased the way for Sister Petra to rise to her feet. In an effort to gain her balance and settle her spinning head, she leaned forward, slumping into Tommy's chest and gazing into his troubled and desperate eyes.

For the briefest moment, the type of moment only God can provide, she saw there, in Tommy's tortured eyes, a man she had met some years before. The man who had started her on her vocation, the man who was in desperate need, the man who wore his despair like a cloak that covered him from head to foot. In the eyes of Tommy Boyle, Petra recognized the man from the Cathedral of Assisi.

"I know you," she said as her head began to clear," We have met before, at the mission." There was no fear or panic in her voice. She had regained her sense of where she was and was aware of what was happening, but she exuded peace and calm. She had not screamed out for help. She was not looking for a passerby to lend a hand. She leveled her gaze on Tommy Boy, and in her eyes, there was compassion and love, kindness and understanding.

"You're Tommy, aren't you? My Lord Tommy, you look very ill. What has happened, Tommy? What can I do to help you?"

"Help me? Help me? Do you want to fucking help me? Let go of the fucking purse!"

"I can't do that, Tommy, and you don't really want me to. I know where you ARE, Tommy. I have seen others where you are, and there is a way out. There is hope for you, Tommy. Let me help you. Whatever has happened, I can help you fix it. Just calm down and talk to me."

"Talk! You want to talk! There is no talking anymore. I need to get it right. I need to get out of this town, and I need your fucking purse, so let go, don't make me hurt you."

"You don't want to hurt me, Tommy. You won't hurt me. You are not that kind of person. I can see that in your eyes. You just need some food and some rest. Come with me to the mission, Tommy. There are people there whom we can talk to and figure it all out.

"Not that kind of person! You don't know me! Don't act like you know me! You are all the same. Come on, Tommy, you can trust me. Come on, Tommy, we won't hurt you. We can fix things; it's all bullshit! Don't act like you know me. You don't even want to know me. I don't want to know me or be me anymore. I just want to get out of here. I didn't mean to do it! I didn't mean to hurt anyone!"

"It's ok, Tommy. You never hurt me. It's not too late to fix things, so let me help you. It's only a couple of scrapes and a bump on my head, that's all. If you stop now, it will be okay, I promise."

She didn't know. She did not know about Trip. How could she? No one knew, not yet. Only those who were looking for him knew. Only those who were there to witness what he had done and were trying to catch him knew. Only those who wanted to see him pay for the heinous crime he had committed knew. He looked down into her hazel eyes as she firmly held onto the strap of the shiny black purse. He looked down into her hazel eyes, and for a moment, he saw there the compassion and love, the kindness and understanding that was Sister Petra of The Madonna Mission, but only for a moment. Then he heard her. The "lover" spoke, and the "lover" spoke the truth.

"Look at her," she whispered. "She does not even respect you enough to be frightened." Her voice was calm, and her voice had always spoken the truth. She was the only one who saw him as he was, the only one who cared. "How can this woman help you? This Nun! How can this woman be truthful to you? They have always lied to you in the past. Nothing is different now, Tommy. She is trying to deceive you as is their way! You need to listen to me now, Tommy; I have told you what you must do!"

"I don't know," Tommy muttered, half weeping, half slobbering, his words coming out in unfamiliar tones. Sister Petra did not understand. She had no way of knowing that Tommy no longer spoke to her, no longer heard her soothing, loving words. She had no way to know Tommy had lost himself to the lover, and his return was unlikely.

"I know, Tommy, I know you are confused. You are not alone. There are so many who are like you, so many who have found a way out of life, and so many who are waiting to help you. Come with me now; let me take you home to those who will love you till you can love yourself again."

But the lover was relentless.

"Do you hear Tommy, do you hear her words? Tell me, Tommy, what is it you think you hear? Do you think you hear compassion? Love! Perhaps understanding! Is that it, Tommy? Is that what you think you hear? Shall I tell you what I hear Tommy, what I see? What do I see for you because you are so weak? I hear her pity! I see her pity! I feel the pity of all those who would keep you down! All those who think they are better and smarter! I hear her lies, Tommy, and I hear her plotting to capture you and take you away from me forever!

"No, No, You Can't!' Tommy sobbed. "You can't take me away." Yes, yes, I can," replied Petra with love but without understanding—without realizing to whom she was speaking and without grasping the inner voice to which Tommy was responding.

It was quick, it was violent, and it was final. With strength not his own, Tommy pulled on the strap of the shiny black purse. Sister Petra held her grip but not her ground. The sudden, unexpected move of Tommy flung her with incredible speed in an arc from the edge of the sidewalk to the side of the building. Flesh met brick in the sickening sound of smashing bone and cartilage. First, Petra's nose splayed across her cheek in a spray of blood. In less than a second, her orbital socket was shattered, her hazel eyeball being squashed like an over-ripened grape. Her cheekbone on the right was next to go, then the lower jaw. And still, she held on to the purse. Was that even possible? Tommy Boy reached into her long dark chestnut hair with a fist guided by fear, hate, and addiction. He grabbed up a fistful of the hair and pulled her broken face away from the bloodied brick wall. With all the force of evil, Tommy slammed Sister Petra's face once more into the brick wall.

Her last thoughts in the conscious world were of her teeth. She had taken such care to keep them in good condition all her life, and now they were gone. As she slid down the wall and from consciousness, she felt the strap of her shiny black purse break, the small leather strap slipping easily through her slender fingers. The last sound she heard was Tommy's escaping footsteps. Her last thought was that she had remained true to her vocation, her calling, her lifelong work. There was no fear. There was no anger. There was no uncertainty. There was only peace. There was only love for life, for God, and for Tommy.

Tommy remained on his knees, sobbing in the alley behind Lucky's Last Stand. With the taste of crack cocaine still in his throat and the warmth of the bottom half of a fifth of Vodka still in his guts, it had all come back to him with incredible clarity. It had come back to him with the full weight of reality. There was no justification for what he had done. In five hours, his life had gone from bad to worse to irresolvable. He had never imagined this would have happened to him. He had not seen himself losing ground as he had. He was not a violent man. He sobbed as he reflected, and he called out for help.

The "lover" was first to respond to him. She came to him from the deepest part of his tortured mind, and she told him the truth. The truth he had come to wait for. The truth as he wanted to believe. She told him it was not his fault. "All the Nun had to do was give you the purse. All the Nun had to do was let go of the strap. You never wanted her to be hurt. That was her choice, not yours! And Trip! Well, Trip had it coming; had it coming for a long time. You probably did a lot of folks a favour in the matter of Trip. Now, now you just need to concentrate on getting away. Tommy? Tommy? Do you hear me, Tommy?"

Tommy heard, but for the first time in many months, Tommy did not believe. For the first time in longer than he could recall, Tommy knew what he had done was wrong. Horribly wrong. For the first time in many years, he knew he was lost. He knew he was no longer Thomas, Tom, Tommy. He was no longer his Mother's son or his Father's pride and joy. He was no longer a brother, a friend, a lover, or a person of any value to society. He was Tommy Boy; grifter, thief, druggy, drunk, murderer. He was lost.

He sobbed, and he cried out for God to help him, and for the first time in many years, the voice of the "lover" fell silent. She had gone from him, leaving in her wake a shattered life, leaving in her wake only death and destruction. She had used him until there was nothing left of him to use, and then she was gone, blessedly gone. He lay there weeping, his sorrow unimaginable. The reality of his living hell was more than he could bear. There was no going back for him. There was only going forward. What had to be done was clearer to him than anything had been in longer than he could recall. There was only one way for him to repay society. Only one punishment that would count for the lives he had taken and damaged. Only one thing he had left to offer that might square the deal. An eye for an eye, a life for a life, his life for their lives.

It had occurred to him many times before and many times before he had been dissuaded by the "lover" by the need to feed his craving. He had a plan; he'd had a plan for a while now. It had occurred to him again this very night as he left his shitty apartment. One step off the bridge by his place and into the A train would mean that everyone's suffering would be over; all problems would be solved by public transportation.

He pushed himself to his feet, and for the first time in longer than he could recall, he felt steady there, on his own two feet. He knew at that moment the "lover" was gone forever, inexplicably gone. He dropped the bottom half of a fifth of Vodka and heard it smash on the filthy pavement in the alley behind Lucky's Last Stand, a fifth purchased with money from the purse of a beaten and left-for-dead Nun. The last fifth of Vodka he would ever purchase, and he remembered thinking, "Is that even possible?" and for the first time ever, there came a reply, "Yes, yes, it is."

UNDERSTANDING

Tommy walked out of the alley behind Lucky's Last Stand and into the beginning of the end of his life. He headed south in a slow and measured walk towards his neighborhood. There was no panic in him or fear. There was, instead, a sense of calm that he had never experienced. Tommy felt no regret for the life he was about to take, for it was not really a life at all. The life he once owned, the person he had once been, had died years before. What was walking around in Tommy Boy's body was unrecognizable to him. This thing he had become was capable of an evil that Tommy could not comprehend, an evil he could not live with. An evil wrought with consequences he could not endure.

A light rain began to fall on Independence Avenue and brought with it a surreal glistening to this shabby end of town. Years before, this part of the city had lived in splendor, and Tommy wondered as he walked what had happened to bring these streets down. A little at a time, the neighborhoods and burrows had slipped into decline. The Mom and Pop stores had been replaced with big box stores. The Dry Cleaner and Garden Grocer turned into a Money Lender or Cheque Casher. Pawn Shops and Liquor Stores popped up on every corner like billboards to drunks and thieves, and slowly, these unsavory businesses began their conquest of the intercity communities.

Slowly, the element of those drawn to these unsavory businesses drove out the nice families. The butcher and baker shops sold out only to become pool halls and neighborhood bars. The stately five and six-bedroom homes that once housed the families of the community had been bought up by developers and holding companies and turned into cheap apartments and rooming houses. Without notice by or to anyone, the conquest had been completed. The neighborhoods crossed an unseen line of decline and became the haven for prostitutes, street people, and drug addicts. These quaint little neighborhoods, where people had once lived as a community, families helping each other prosper and grow, had now become the wrong side of the tracks. The city had moved on and left these neighborhoods behind to fend for themselves.

By comparison, Tommy's personal decline had been much quicker but equally devastating. He had fallen into ruin physically, mentally, and spiritually. He had become part of the virus living within the community and was beyond any type of urban renewal or spiritual redemption. "The solution lies in the path of Public Transportation," he thought, "a means to an end."

His body ached all over as he slowly made his way south on Independence. He had been running for hours on adrenalin and addiction, and he was crashing hard. The combination of the physical activity he had not endured for years and the realization of the havoc he had wrought was leaving him weary. But he moved on with a certainty he felt throughout his ravished body. As he turned off of Independence and into the Alley, which would take him to Pine, he was at peace with his decision, and the voice of his addiction remained silent.

He was nearly through the dark alley when he saw movement coming from Park St. Illuminated by the street lights of Park, a pair of elongated shadows were filling the small entrance to the alley and getting larger as the owners of these shadows came nearer. The shadows moved in, jerking distorted movements that merged in and out of each other. Tommy assumed there was a couple walking arm in arm and heading in his direction. He had no way of knowing who had heard of his crime spree, but he imagined the gravity of his crimes would have warranted some television coverage and that his face and name may have gone out on the local news wire. There was no place in his plans for being identified by some passing stranger, and there was no adrenalin left in his body to provide another rapid escape. Tommy found a nearby darkened doorway and pressed himself into the cold steel of the fire door. He stood very still and inhaled deeply.

To confirm his suspicion, a couple wandered into the dimly lit alley. As they approached arm in arm, it was impossible to tell which was leaning more heavily on the other for support, but Tommy suspected that the man in the couple was in a worse state of drunkenness than the woman. He giggled and groped the woman, and she, in turn, protested, though half-heartedly, like an actress reciting lines in a play in which she was disinterested.

"Ooo now honey, you stop that!" she said. "You are so bad," she continued. "You make me so hot, honey baby!"

The phrases seemed rehearsed but unpolished, as though from a B movie at the drive-in theater.

The closer they came to the place where he was hidden, the clearer they appeared to Tommy, and the more of their banter reached his straining ears. There was something oddly familiar about this woman to Tommy. Perhaps it was the timber of her voice or the vacancy he heard in the way she spoke to the man. Or was it the absence of emotion he sensed in her? He could not be sure.

For a moment, he was certain they would pass by without noticing him, as so many had done throughout his life. He was about to breathe out when the couple suddenly and awkwardly came to a stop.

"Ok, lover, this is far enough," she said, and Tommy knew it was Rhonda. Tommy knew because Tommy had heard this before. He had heard the silky voice, which was all for show. He had heard beyond the words and understood the need.

Tommy had watched Rhonda work before, and he enjoyed it. Rhonda had two lovers, and she would do anything for them. She would stop at nothing to please them, so she worked. She worked for the drug, and she worked for the man who needed the drug. More than anything, she wanted the man to love her as well because she knew in her heart the drug never would. She believed in her heart that maybe, someday, the man could love her. She hoped in her heart that he could, and the love would save her. But she was wrong. The man, Tommy, had lost his ability to love. He could not even love himself, so he stood and watched as Rhonda went to work once again.

His heart sank, and for the first time in many months, he felt genuine emotion. He felt compassion for this woman who, like him, had lost her way. She had crossed a line into a world with no boundaries. She had become enslaved, and in so doing, she was willing to do things she had sworn she would never do. She was not always a crack whore. Tommy knew that for sure, but he could not tell you what she had been like before. He didn't care. He never took the time to ask. She was just another means to an end for Tommy. From the beginning, she had been nothing more than a shortcut to his true love. She had been nothing more than access to funds that were previously unavailable to him.

When they met, she was a young girl with a young habit who had been mistreated for so long she was looking for anyone who would treat her right, and Tommy did. He did just that. It was easy. He said all the right words and did all the right things, and when she fell in love with him, he introduced her to his true love. The two became quickly acquainted. Soon, it was the three of them, all the time. Every night, they found the escape they were seeking in the drug and in each other, and all the while, Tommy had the plan. The plan he had heard from Trip, his mentor, his murdered friend. All the while, he knew there would come a time when her need for the drug and their need for money would be met by the need for Rhonda to turn a trick. Just as Trip had predicted, that time had come, and Rhonda went to work.

At first, she was outraged at the suggestion. Angry at the thought Tommy would ask her to do such a thing. How could he ask this if he really loved her, she wondered, and Tommy was quick to explain. It was because he really did love her that he could let her do what they needed to do for the drug. He said he would always be there for her, and she believed it because she wanted to. She believed it because she loved him even though she had no way of knowing what love really was. She believed it because the voice in the darkening part of her mind told her it was OK. It was no big deal. Do it for Tommy. Do it for me. Just try it, just one time.

That was over a year ago now and Rhonda had become quite accomplished at the trade. She had become a crack whore. Rhonda could not recall the last time she felt shame or guilt for what she had done or what she had become. She could not remember the last time she was shocked by the bizarre requests she often received from her clients. She did what she had to do. At first, it was for Tommy, then for Tommy and her, now just for her.

Now on this night in this alley, Tommy Boy looked on from the shadows and felt the tears well up in his eyes. He felt the knot grow in his gut and fought to contain the sobs in his throat. He had done this to this girl. He had done this and had been proud of what he had accomplished. What kind of a monster could do such a thing to another person? He was asking himself, but there were no answers within his tortured mind. There was only remorse and pain and withdrawal and an urgency to end it all, to make the pain subside forever.

"You know the drill, Honey," Rhonda was chiding. "Forty for a blow job, eighty for a fuck, one twenty for the whole package, anything fucked up or weird is two hundred, and the cash is the first thing that's going to come in this alley."

The man was laughing as he fished out of his wallet and handed it over to Rhonda. The man's sweat was glistening in the dim lights of the alley and Tommy could hear his rasping breath as he began to work his belt and fly. He went to lean back on a dumpster and, misjudging the distance, he fell back landing heavily against the bin. His head flopped back into the dumpster, and from the dark of the alley came a sound as though someone had struck a Buddhist gong.

From deep in Tommy's mind came a line from a book he had read with his Mother. "Ask not for whom the bell tolls. It tolls for thee." He had no recollection of the book or the story it told, but the line resonated in his mind and acted as a catalyst for him. Without his awareness, his feet began to move forward, and in that moment, Tommy Boy emerged from the shadows into the dim light of a filthy alley. For the first time in longer than he could recall, maybe for the first time ever, he knew what the right thing to do was, and he knew he would do it.

He approached Rhonda from her back and walked very slowly into the dim light. The man saw him immediately and was instantly taken with fear. Rhonda was unaware of his presence and continued to prepare for the task at hand. As she deposited the hundred and twenty into her handbag and began to search for the condoms supplied to her by the local health unit, the man spoke. The lilt had gone from his voice and was replaced with a cautious and suspicious tone, which Rhonda did not understand.

"What the hell is going on here?" he began. "Is this some kinda shake down or what?"

Rhonda looked at the man in confusion as his hands began to fasten what had been undone, and his belt was quickly buckled up. He was pulling clumsily at his fly when Rhonda sensed movement behind her. As she began to turn, the man encircled her neck with his free arm and roughly pulled her into his chest as though she were a human shield. Rhonda felt the panic begin to rise, and her mind instantly filled with the dozens of stories she had heard from the girls on the street. Stories of those beaten and raped, stories of young men and women found dead in alleys just like this, and stories of the ones never found at all. They were stories of near misses and narrow escapes, and Rhonda wondered which of these stories would be used tomorrow to describe what was about to happen to her.

The fear and panic were quickly building and about to overcome her, as a figure emerged from the shadows, moving slowly and deliberately. As if in a trance, the person came into the dim light of the alley, and in amazement, Rhonda found herself looking into the eyes of Tommy Boy, into the eyes of the man she had loved and hated, into the eyes of the man she was willing to die for and into the eyes of the man who had brought her to this lowly place in her life. The eyes of the man who had created a crack whore and then walked away from her in disgust.

She looked deep into Tommy Boy, but what she saw there was different from what she had seen there before. What she saw was not the Tommy Boy she had come to know. That Tommy Boy was predictable and unpredictable at once, filled with anger and angst, paranoia and mistrust. The eyes she was looking into now, here in this alley, were the eyes of the real Tommy. Deep in those dark eyes, Rhonda saw sadness and an emptiness that left her cold. There, she saw all the hurt and fear that had consumed so much of his life, and there, behind the hurt and fear, she saw that which was most telling. She saw surrender. The Tommy Boy who had schemed and stolen and put her to work on the streets in order to keep his addictions fed was gone. The Tommy Boy who cared only for himself and would stop at nothing to "get right" had vanished. In the place of that Tommy Boy stood the real Tommy, frightened, scared, alone, beaten, finished.

Rhonda was filled with fear. But the fear was no longer fed by the situation in the alley in which she had found herself. It was as if there was no man standing against a dumpster in disheveled clothing with an arm tightening around her neck. The fear that now filled her was the unspoken message she was seeing in the eyes of Tommy. Tommy was going to die.

"Get the fuck back!" The man spit out the words quickly in a slur which in another place may have been comical. His voice was breaking and high-pitched, which was an indication of the trepidation which was filling this man. The situation could make the man dangerous. The instinct to survive would make him rash and unpredictable. He was a big man and he had an ever-tightening grip around the neck of Rhonda. She was not unfamiliar with the dangers of street living, and she trained her voice to be calm and cautious. She could get out of this alive, but she needed to be very careful.

"Calm yourself, Honey," Rhonda began. "This ain't no shakedown, you ain't about to be rolled or nothing like that. This here is my friend Tommy. He is not going to hurt you. Isn't that right, Tommy?"

Tommy took a step closer, and the big man tried to back deeper into the cold, hard steel of the dumpster, instinctively tightening the grip on the neck of Rhonda.

"Back the fuck off," cried the man with unconvincing bravado, but Tommy calmly walked forward.

"Let her go," said Tommy. "Let her go and go home. Go home to your wife and kids." Tommy stopped three feet from the man and waited. He said nothing more. He just stood.

The alley was filled with a quiet tension. It felt like a bad Clint Eastwood movie where the camera pans from eye to eye to eye of the actors in a three-way standoff. All while the audience waits for someone to flinch, for someone to make their move that will allow the showdown to begin. But there was no one who could make a move. The man was pressed so hard into the dumpster that he would be able to see the BFI logo in his ass for a week. Rhonda was firmly held in the ever-tightening grip of the terrified man and Tommy just stood, calm and oddly distracted.

He stood and looked at the situation but he observed the unfolding events as if he stood beside himself. He watched it all as a spectator, disembodied like his spirit looked on, and waited for the chaos to begin.

He watched his hand rise up and push the hair away from his bleary eyes. He watched the man bite down hard on his lower lip as the sweat rolled, burning into his widened eyes. He watched Rhonda as she watched Tommy, looking dismayed at this man she loved. He saw no fear in her face for her own safety. He only saw the concern she felt for

Tommy. The worry displayed on her face showed Tommy, for the first time, the depth of love this woman had for him. For the first time ever, he actually considered this woman, Rhonda. He wondered if he had ever loved her or ever could. He really did not know. There was a great hole within him. A crater existed where there once had been a heart and soul. A cavernous space he had tried to fill with booze and dope and had succeeded only in filling it with despair. No, he did not love her; he could not love her, but he would not see her hurt. Not like this, not tonight. There had been enough pain already.

Slowly and without thought, his hand slid into the pocket of his tattered jeans. As he withdrew the hand his fingers began to slowly walk their way around the small wooden beads attached to a crudely carved Crucifix. Tommy began to speak.

"Please, let her go. She has not done anything to hurt you, and neither have I nor will I. I just need you to leave now, and I need you to let go of Rhonda."

The man mistook the calmness in Tommy's voice for a reluctance to engage in a physical altercation, and the misconception served to give him renewed courage. After all, he was a big man, he told himself, and after looking closely at the man in the dim light, it was evident to him that this stranger was used up.

"She's got my money, man, and I will want my money or my action before I go anywhere. You got that junkie! You think I'm some kinda up uptown mug that can be suckered into an alley and rolled by a couple crack heads? Well, you got another thing coming. Why don't you just fuck off, man, and let me and the little lovely here conduct our business? Then later, when I have had my one hundred and twenty bucks worth, you and she can have your little meeting."

"Let her go, do it now. I am not going to ask you again."

"OR WHAT? What are you going to do, you dirty used-up little piece of shit. Maybe I will just take my hundred and twenty out on you. That might be a little more fun than this stinking whore." The man quickly shoved Rhonda aside, and she stumbled to her knees amongst the garbage and discarded bottles in the alley. The man stepped forward and glared into Tommy's eyes.

Tommy remained calm, perhaps calmer than he had ever been in his life. It was amazing to him that his ravished body and tortured mind remained so clear and so still. The influence of the lover had left him. His edge, or what he had for so long considered his edge, had fled, and still, he was not feeling panicked or obsessed. He looked deep into the eyes of his erstwhile opponent, and he spoke from his heart. As he spoke, his fingers moved rapidly over the small circle of wooden beads attached to the crudely carved Crucifix and his words came quickly and with an ease that was unaccustomed to him.

"I have killed two people tonight, and I have done so brutally. Neither of them had done anything to provoke me. Neither of them had ever done anything to hurt me. I think they were both my friends. They wanted to help me, and I killed them. I am not even sure if I am really sorry about it, do you know what I mean? It has been so long since I gave a shit about anything that I don't even know if I care. I didn't want to kill them, and I don't want to kill you, and not so long ago, I don't know if I could ever have done such a thing, but now, I could kill you in a heartbeat and not even bat an eye. Look at me man; you think this is dirt on me? This is the dried and stinking blood of two people who tried to help me and died. I think on the TV show they call it splatter. You are standing six inches from me and you think you can scare me? Are you so blind you can't see a man who has nothing to lose when he is only six inches from your nose, six inches from killing you? Now go. Go away from here and go home while you can. There's been enough killing tonight."

The man stood for a moment in silence. He looked deep into the eyes of this fifty-two-year-old used-up junkie and tried to see if there was a lie in what he had just been told. He looked hard, and he understood. He understood that the lie did not exist. He understood he was standing six inches away from the man who would kill him quickly and brutally without regret. For the first time in many hours, the man thought of his wife and children, his nice house in the suburbs, and his car, three blocks from here. Slowly, he raised his arms, holding his palms out in front of him in an 'I surrender' gesture, and he began to back away from Tommy and towards the mouth of the alley. When he was five feet from the calm murderer, the man turned and began to run. He would continue to run till he reached his car or his abused heart gave out, all the while swearing he would never return to these haunts or habits of his, all the while knowing it was a lie. He would get to his car, and he would go home. There would be no calls to the Police; there would be no explaining how he came to be in the presence of this killer.

Tommy's whereabouts would remain unreported, and the secret life of the man would remain unrevealed.

Tommy slipped the small circle of wooden beads back into his tattered jeans and turned to where Rhonda had been thrown to the ground. He looked at her in silence for a moment and slowly began to smile. It was an unnatural, forced smile and absolutely inappropriate in the wake of what had just transpired. His skin hung on his face like an ill-fitting Tommy mask, and there, caked in the lines of his loose flesh, was the dried blood of innocent people. He was missing a tooth in front, and this added to the hardened look of this fifty-two-year-old man who could easily pass for 70.

Rhonda looked on in horror and amazement. Uncertain of what had just transpired and not trusting what she believed she had heard, she could only stare. It had been a month since she had been with Tommy. A month since she had been close enough to stroke his hair or kiss his cheek. Only a month, and she barely recognized this man. Oh, she had seen him from a distance, as she had tonight. Him off on the hunt her standing on the corner, always from a distance, always ending with her saluting his back with a single digit. She had been so angry, so hurt by his dismissal of her, she had never considered the possibility that Tommy Boy could have fallen so completely so quickly. She knew him, she loved him, and now she had no idea who he had become.

"Hello, Rhonda," he said, and his voice was empty and full of echoes.

"What did you say?"

"I said hello."

"NOT TO ME! What did you say to him, to Clayton?"

"Was that his name, Clayton? It is a nice name, but I don't think he was such a nice guy, you know."

"You were joking, right, about killing those people? You were just trying to scare him, right? Trying to protect me. Well, you don't need to protect me Tommy, no sir; I can take care of myself. After all, I haven't got much choice anymore, do I? There ain't no one else, is there?"

She was shifting now and trying to gain her feet and balance on top of the rubble where she had landed. Tears were beginning to escape the barricades of her eyelids and streak their way through her dark mascara and down her sunken cheeks. She breathed in deeply and tried to gain control of her mounting fear and confusion, her anger, and her tears. She could not allow herself to cry. She had not cried in so long. She had kept all those tears locked within the chambers of her damaged heart to let them loose; now would be the beginning of her end. Her defenses would be down, and she would once more be vulnerable. She had given it all to Tommy. Her heart, her love, her dignity, and her self-respect had been cast aside. All that was once her was now gone, and she would be damned if she would now give this little man the satisfaction of her tears.

Tommy looked down at the pavement where he stood, the false smile now gone. "No," he said.

"No, NO! That's it, that's all you got to say to me after all this time. NO! Well, you're damn right there ain't no one else, and there never will be again. I am through with..."

"NO! Rhonda, no, I wasn't kidding. What I said was true. I killed some people, and I am on the run. I did it, I know now, but when it happened, it was like I wasn't even there. I just don't know. I am so scared and confused and sorry… I told Clayton I wasn't sorry to scare him, but I am. I am so sorry I can't live with it, and I won't, not for much longer."

And Tommy broke into a quiet sob. Unlike Rhonda, he did not try to hold back his tears. The sobs came from his gut and up through his throat in a guttural, primal tone, but the tears would not come. He wanted to cry. He tried to cry, convinced that this one act of shedding a tear would confirm there was some humanity left in him, but his sadness was empty. His sorrow long ago had run dry.

"Oh, Tommy, no. Please tell me, no. It can't be true, Tommy. I know you. I know you could not have done this." And then she let the tears come. She crossed the littered space between them, and she took Tommy in her arms, and she cried into the blood-splattered sleeve of his cleanest, dirty shirt.

"Tell me what happened," she said, and Tommy did. He told her all that he recalled. He spoke of the swiftness and brutality of his actions, the extended periods of blackness and unaccounted-for time, and the realization of what he had become. Finally, he told her of the strange calm that arrived with the acceptance of that truth and his knowledge of what he would do.

She listened to it all in silence, holding tightly onto this man she could not stop loving. She listened, and she cried, and she thought, 'If only I had stayed with him. It would have all been alright. None of this would have happened if only I had stayed.'

In her denial, she changed the scenario completely, ignoring all that Tommy had done to her and the fact that he had left her in disgust. In her need to love and be loved, she had assumed responsibility for the heinous act of murder. As in all things throughout her life, this was her fault, more guilt to stoke the fire of shame, more justification for a life of hiding from reality in the blue haze of the smoke from the crack pipe. But at least, she was not as bad, as her Tommy.

For a long while, they simply stood there in each other's arms, saying nothing, wanting nothing more than the simple comfort of human contact, wanting nothing less than the safety of familiarity.

A passing stranger observing the scene in the alley may have walked on with a smile, having believed he had witnessed a moment of new love between a couple who had just discovered each other. Feeling a renewed faith in mankind and going on with his evening plans, he may have been just a little kinder to the waitress at the restaurant or perhaps thanked the bus driver as he left at his stop. Life is built on perceptions, and kindness often stems from our inability to see the awful truth. We are unprepared to witness the grim reality of two lost people holding to two lost dreams in a filthy alley, unknowing or unmindful of their tragedy.

As Rhonda stood immersed in her fantasy of the way things could have been, Tommy's last words echoed in her mind, something about a 'strange calm, coming with the knowledge of what he must do.' Rhonda suddenly felt it all melting away and reality once again taking control.

"What do you mean you know what you must do, Tommy? What are you thinking?"

"I can't live with it, Rhonda. It is all too horrible. There is nothing left, nothing I want to go on for. I just want to be quiet. I want the voices in my head to never come back and there is only one way I can be sure of that."

"You can't be serious! You can't mean that. You want to kill yourself, is that it? Tommy, think for a while, you are sick. People will understand. We have to go to the Police now. I know a cop over on the Lexington beat. His name is Bob Gideon, and he has always been good to me, Tommy. We could go to him. He would help us."

"It's just too late for that, Rhonda. Don't you get it? I killed those people, for a couple of bucks to get high and drunk with. No one is going to help me. I am dirt, worse than dirt. I don't know if I would even want help if it was there."

"Don't you say that, Tommy! You don't know. Not all people are bad. Maybe there are some who could help you and me maybe they could help us! After all, Trip was a dirtbag anyway. Everyone knew that, and the Nun, well, that was an accident, and she knew the chances she was taking living down here anyway. People will understand."

"No, Rhonda. They won't. I don't understand myself. How can I ask forgiveness of others if I can't forgive myself? There is no death penalty here, Rhonda. Did you know that? Can you see me living out the rest of my days in prison, always looking over my shoulder, trying to stay alive and clean? I can't do that, Rhonda. I won't do it."

"Tommy, please, what about us? We can have a life together. We can run away! I can help you, Tommy, I can earn more, just let me try to take care of us! We can get away and start over, just you and me."

"Rhonda, no! Listen to me now. It is time you heard. There is no you and me. There is no us. There never was. I don't love you now and I never loved you ever. That is not because of you, Rhonda. It is because of me. I am an addict and alcoholic, and I spent most of my life only loving myself, and then, then I stopped that as well. I don't know love. I only know using people and stealing and lying and I can't go on. I can't change and it is too late for me to start over. This life I have could have been a good one, but I ruined it. I wasted it. I destroyed it and everyone I came in contact with. Look at what I have done to you, Rhonda. Look and for once, see! I turned you into a whore, a prostitute! I let you fuck pigs like Clayton and blow them so I could get crack. Who does that, Rhonda? Would someone who loved you do that? I am sorry, Rhonda, that is what I want you to know. That is all I have to give you: an apology for taking your life. Please, Rhonda, listen to me and believe. There is another guy just like me out there on the street, and he will find you just like I did. And you will spend the rest of your life bending over for bastards in alleys, and then you will die! You need to hear me, Rhonda, for tonight, I have seen both of our futures. Mine is very short, but yours doesn't have to be. Go to the Mission. There are good people there, and they will get you the help you need. You are a nice kid, and you deserve something out of this shitty world." And with that, Tommy turned and walked out of the alley. He heard her cries, and he heard her sobs, and he hoped he had hurt her for the last time.

He walked slowly and in the shadows for another twenty minutes. He moved south on Pine and, with each step, moved closer to the place where he had savagely beaten the nun. When he was a block away from the alley that would take him back to 12th Avenue, Tommy slid into a bus shelter and leaned against the glass in the corner as though he were waiting for the bus.

Trying to appear casual, he scanned the Street further down for any signs of Police activity. Though he could not be certain, he felt as though the Police would be looking for him further afield. Had he been assigned to investigate the savage robbery and murder of a local Nun by a local low life, he would naturally assume that said low life would have fled the scene posthaste with no intention of returning. Were he to encounter the Police at this point in the night, he doubted greatly that he would have the initiative to escape, and the idea of capture was impossible for Tommy to accept. And so he moved forward with extreme care and heightened awareness of the street ahead.

As he walked down Pine toward the mouth of the alley, his hand slid into the pocket of his jeans, and slowly, his fingers began the run over the small wooden beads. With each step, he counted a bead, and each time he reached the 12th, he began again, ever drawing closer to the place where he had lost all that he had ever been. Without knowing, his lips began to move in unspoken words, and for the first time in many years, Tommy was praying. At first, the words came to him in short spurts and broken sentences, but quickly, as though he had never stopped this form of worship, the memory of the prayer returned, and Tommy continued on.

When he was twenty feet away, the first sign that there had been trouble here at this intersection of the Street and the alley came into view. There, left hanging off a signpost, was three feet of broken and left-over Police tape. The scene had been cordoned off while evidence had been collected. To the right, there were signs of discarded medical packaging where Tommy assumed the Paramedics had done their best to repair the broken Nun. In his mind's eye, he took in the mayhem of the scene. When he was ten feet away, he could see that, in spite of the light rain, there were still large stains of blood on the sidewalk. The falling rain made the blood appear wet and fresh, and it looked to Tommy as though the streaking blood on the brick wall was running red in tiny waterfalls. Tommy felt his stomach roll but continued on at a measured pace. When he was two feet from the entrance to the alley, his eyes dropped to the corner where the sidewalk met the brick wall. There, wet with rain, reflecting the soft light of the street lamps, was a perfectly formed and glistening white tooth. Tommy stopped abruptly in his tracks, looked over his shoulder, and on ahead from where he stood. When he was satisfied he was alone and unobserved, Tommy bent down and picked up the tooth. As he turned into the alley, he slid this relic of Sister Petra into his jeans pocket.

He passed slowly through the alley he had raced through earlier. It was nearing midnight when Tommy turned onto

12th Avenue, and the pedestrian traffic was heavy with nighttime clubbers. Tommy was pleased to see the crowds and quickly made his way into the middle of the streaming traffic. It would be easy for him to go unnoticed here in these crowds, but as he got closer and closer to his own turf the odds of him being seen by a drinking buddy or one of his dealers would increase. He would have to be careful.

He passed by an open fronted Donair shop with a long lineup of patrons waiting for their order of mystery meat. As the young girl behind the counter turned to call in another order Tommy slipped in through the queue and made his way down the hall to the dirty little washroom in the back. He was relieved to find the door standing open and quickly entered and turned on the light. As the incandescent bare bulb threw a harsh light through the little room, Tommy squinted and leaned into the mirror. What he saw frightened him. His hair was wet and slicked down to his head, but despite his walk through the light rain, there were obvious areas of dried blood in his hair. His face was filthy, and the lines on his neck and cheeks all carried the evidence of his violent acts. He turned on the cold water and leaned over the basin throwing water up onto his face. As he dropped his hand, he could see the skinned knuckles of his right hand, and he remembered how he had driven the face of the Nun into the brick, breaking his own knuckle on the back of her head. He closed his eyes, and he breathed deeply.

Tommy prayed to God then. He asked God, whoever God was, to help him make it all right. He knew what he had to do but he needed God to get him to where he had to go to make it right. Just five hours ago, all his world depended on 'getting right,' and now, just five hours later, he only wanted the help to make it right. For the first time since he came to himself, he felt safe. Locked here in this dingy room, he would be safe, at least for a moment.

He opened his eyes and saw the blood splatter on his shirt and jacket. Quickly and without thought, he removed the jacket and put it in the garbage can. He then pulled off his cleanest, dirtiest shirt and flipped it inside out. Washed the rest of the blood off his face and hands and headed out of the washroom and back out onto 12th Avenue.

He passed quickly through the crowd and back out onto the street. Just as he gained the curbside of 12th Avenue, the uptown bus came screaming to a stop at the shelter. Tommy looked at the people getting on and off the bus and wondered if any of them knew about Trip. If any of them cared, just a few short hours before, a bus that looked just like this one had carried a man to his death. Life goes on, for everyone that is except for Trip and Petra and soon Tommy.

He moved quickly down 12th now without incident and glanced only briefly toward his shitty little apartment as he crossed over Lexington. He would head to his neighborhood, where he would be recognized at the end, but he would do it from the alleyways and backstreets where he had lived for so long and where he would soon die. As he walked, he could not shut off his brain to the last words he had heard thrown at him as he fled the alley, away from Rhonda. "What about me?" she had cried out, "You were not even going to say goodbye!" And she was right. Had he not happened upon Rhonda, with her latest effort at self-employment, in a dirty alley, quite by chance, he would not have sought her out for a fond farewell. He had felt a need to apologize to her for his part in her decline, but the notion of doing so in a 'making my peace' kind of goodbye had not occurred to him,

As he moved on, ever aware of those he passed on the street, careful to avert his eyes or study his shoes as they passed, his mind began a self-diagnostic program, which he could not shut down. He thought of all the people whom he had been close to throughout his life: his parents and siblings, his friends, and his lovers. He thought of those whose lives had affected him and those whose lives had been affected or infected by him. Incidents and events he had not thought of or considered for years began to flood his racing mind and he found himself one moment smiling and the very next full of sadness.

He wanted this process to stop, but it went on. It went on with a will of its own and, in so doing, revealed to Tommy some truths he had long ago discarded. It was all his fault. He was the only one responsible for the station in life to which he had descended. For so long now, he had placed blame on bad luck or shitty fate, more often than not squarely on the backs of his parents or siblings. He looked to the authority figures in his life, the teachers and the clergy, especially the clergy, and he had found fault in them all. It was no wonder his life was ruined after how he had been treated! No wonder he was unable to cope, to deal with all the situations in life which had left him baffled and full of fear. It was no wonder.

But it was all bullshit! All of it, all of it was delusional. All of it was fantasy, and suddenly, all of it was clear to him. A moment of clarity which years earlier may have changed the path of his life now fell upon him like a weight he could not bear. Suddenly, he yearned for a kiss on his brow from his Mother. He could feel her lips there and the caress of her fingers as she pushed a lock of hair from his eyes. He could hear the solid and assuring timber of his Father's voice as he said, "That hair will need cutting soon, son." He could feel his firm handshake as he wished Tommy 'good luck' at the ball game.

His life had not been bad. His parents had not been monsters. His authority figures had not been sadistic. He was the problem. If only he had been open to that thought so many years before, how his life could have been different. Sadness enveloped him as he walked this unhappy road to his end, but there was no anger. Even in the realization of his active role in the ruination of his world, there was no anger. There was peace. The peace that came with responsibility. Peace that came with accountability and peace that would come with finality.

Tommy's end was in sight, but this new realization came with the knowledge that he must say goodbye. He must tell them all that they were not at fault. They were so old now, his parents, and they had lost hope that the Tommy they knew would ever return to them. He had to tell them that he was back, even though it was only going to be for a short time. He needed to let someone in his world know that he was leaving this world in an effort to make right all he had made wrong. He needed to let someone know he carried no animosity or anger in his heart at the end, only remorse that he could not live with.

Tommy's hand went to the pocket of his tattered jeans as he entered the Alley off Baker Side Road, which ran behind Louis East End Pawnshop. He removed the small circle of wooden beads attached to a crudely carved Crucifix and slowly began to run his fingers around the circle. The repetitive motion slowed his mind, and his thoughts began to shift from the losses of the past to the reality of the present. In his breast pocket, he discovered the remaining cash that once belonged to Sister Petra. Six bucks! It would be enough, enough for the calls he had to make. There was a phone booth by his house, close to the place where he was intending to catch a train. There, he would make his last goodbyes. His plan was now complete.

INSIGHT

Jack Corbett sat behind the disorganized oak desk in the back office of Louis's East End Pawn and stared down an entire bottle of Johnny Walker Red. He had been shaken by the events of the day, and the foundation of his short-lived sobriety was crumbling. Tommy Boy had been in his shop today. He had been many times in the previous weeks, but today, he had been clearly delusional. The state he was in was distressing to Jack and a frightening remembrance of a life that was not so far in his past. He had told Tommy he had crossed a line and that he needed some help. He knew this to be true for Jack himself had been where Tommy was. He had stood in those same shoes, and he had lived the same wretched life in which Tommy was now imprisoned.

It had only been five years since Jack had put the plug in the jug and got himself sober. There had been no treatment centers or programs for old Jack Corbett; just some good, old-fashioned willpower had done the job. He had been sick, and he had nearly lost everything when his moment of clarity arrived in the form of a six-month sentence for disturbing the peace, public intoxication and assaulting a police officer. Jack dried out in County Jail and it had been the first break that had come his way in a long time. While he was inside, he listened to the Chaplain, attended some of the meetings of the inside AA group, and learned how to get sober.

He learned to live in the moment and to let go of his anger and that all those AA alkies were spineless whiners who needed to be led. Seemingly, they were led by what they called a Big Book and a set of principles they called steps, plus a belief in a power greater than themselves. But Jack Corbett was never one to be led anywhere. He knew the booze had got the best of him once, and he knew that it would likely get the best of him again. It was this realization that carried Jack to his "Spiritual awakening." The booze was the higher power, and all he needed to do was to respect it at arm's length, and he would attain sobriety.

The day Jack had repaid his debt to society, he walked out of the County Jail and into the first liquor store he came across, where he purchased a bottle of Johnny Walker Red - a bottle that would become his daily companion tucked away in his desk drawer through the day and sitting in a place of prominence on his dresser at night. Johnny Walker Red had become Jack's higher power. With the seal unbroken and the cap spun tight, the evil liquor could not get out and destroy Jack's world. Every morning, he talked to Johnny Walker, telling the bottle his willpower would keep the bottle unopened, and every night, he told Johnny Walker that he, Jack Corbett, was in control and had survived another day.

He took his meals with Johnny Walker, watched his television shows with Johnny Walker, and often late at night, as he sat by himself Jack told all his problems to Johnny Walker. As it had been in the past, Johnny Walker was always nearby when Jack lost his temper and screamed at the newscaster every evening at six. He was there, too, when Jack would fly into a rage after being cut off in traffic, disrespected as he drove by some white-haired old lady who treated Jack as if he were not even there. As it had been in the past, Johnny was always there, and Johnny was always beckoning, but because Jack had gained control, Johnny was never allowed out into his world. Jack had gained control over Johnny Walker by keeping him locked away in his bottle like an evil genie in a lamp. Because of that, the television was never smashed, and the white-haired old lady arrived home alive, unencumbered by a rage and a hitherto whiskey-filled Jack. Johnny Walker was under Jack's control, and as a result, the world never had to deal with an out-of-control and delusional Jack, insane with alcohol and consumed with hatred.

He and Johnny Walker had become inseparable, and after a time, Jack simply referred to the bottle as his friend, "Red." He took Red everywhere he went. When he drove to and from the pawn shop, Red took his place on the front seat of the car, tucked safely out of sight in his briefcase but near enough that Jack could confer, should he need to vent. When he was at the shop, Red was always just under the counter where Jack could keep an eye on him. Often, as a customer would leave the store, Jack and Red would have a laugh over the state the loser had been in or make inappropriate remarks about the young women who were selling whatever they could to make their living on the streets. Red was always there under Jack's watchful and obsessive eye and just an arm's reach away.

Though he remained aware of the slow and gradual transition, Red soon assumed the power once more over Jack. The control Jack thought he asserted over this unopened bottle of Johnny Walker Red, was simply another delusion provided by the amber liquid. All the while, Jack was rebuilding his newfound life of sobriety and quasi-legitimacy. His nemesis, Johnny Walker Red, lay patiently and deadly beneath the sealed, red tin cap of the bottle.

Jack bounced back onto his feet quickly in his newfound life as a sober, slightly shady character. He had discovered he could end up on the upper end of most of his crooked deals with the drunks and druggies, and he was always ready to capitalize on their weakness and only too happy to share a laugh about his good fortune with Red. As he was the sober one in all the schemes he had undertaken over a space of a few years, he had earned enough ready cash to go legit. When Louis Barbour of Louis' East End Pawn decorated his wife's lawn furniture with his brains, Jack immediately saw the opportunity in the tragedy and purchased the establishment from the grieving widow; some would say for a song.

But legitimacy was a hard go for Jack, and slowly, he began to work as a fence for some of the small time petty thieves in the area. He seldom asked for the required proof of ownership, always paid below current value and often sold pawned items before chits expired. That's what he had done to Tommy Boyle. That's what he had done to this little shit addict who was delusional and had left his store and thrown Trip beneath a bus. He had sold most of his stuff before its due time.

The rumors of Tommy's rampage were running rampant and were most likely highly exaggerated, but the fact remained that Tommy had been here in Jack's shop just before he attacked Trip. The cops would put it all together, and they would come, and Jack would be exposed. He had to get rid of the rest of Tommy's gear, and he had to do it tonight.

Jack sat at the desk with sweat beading on his heavy brow and slowly running into the corners of his deep-set eyes, where it burned his vision into a blur. He stared at Red with hate, and in his mind, he could see Red staring back at him with contempt. He reached across the desk, and with his left hand, he grabbed hold of Red by the neck and he recalled all the other relationships which had ended in just this manner with Jack a hold of someone's neck. As his right hand moved to the cap, there was such familiarity that Jack began to salivate at the thought of the sweet, tasty burn of victory he would have over this adversary, this higher power.

Slowly, with his right hand, he applied pressure to the cap, and as he felt the very slightest turn of the cap in his hand, he was flooded with such ecstasy that, for a moment, he believed he would achieve an erection. And then he stopped. Jack knew deep within his gut that were he to open this iconic bottle, here and now there would be no fixing the problem of Tommy Boyle's property, not tonight. He had to get out of here, and he had to do it now! Jack quickly stood from the desk, tossed Johnny Walker Red into the box that contained Tommy's stuff and headed out the back door of Louis East Side Pawn, certain that he could hear laughter coming from beneath the lid of the box.

There was movement in the alley ahead of Tommy, and he slowed his pace. He tried to duck into the shadows but the man ahead had seen him and had come to a stop in his tracks. "Who's there?" the man in the alley barked, and Tommy recognized the voice of Jack, the new proprietor of Louis'

East End Pawn. He stood close to the wall and tried not to speak.

"Who's there?" he demanded. "I can see you there! You oughta know I am armed, and I am in a pissy mood, so if you plan on rolling me, count on getting hurt. Now come into the light where I can see you, and don't try to fuck with me!"

Tommy moved very slowly into the light and stopped ten feet from the back door of Louis and 10 feet from Jack. Jack was bending over and placing a box on the hood of his car, squinting hard to see who or what was coming at him from the shadows. This was turning out to be the worst day Jack could recall. He could not imagine how it could get any worse when here, out of the dark, walked Tommy Boy.

"You," he said. "It's you. That's far enough. You keep away from me, man. I have no money on me, the store is locked up, and the alarm is on. What the hell are you doing around here, man? Do you know that half the fucking city is looking for you? I can't believe you are here!"

"It's OK, Jack. I'm not looking for you, and I don't want any trouble. I was just passing by."

"Ok! It's ok? Are you shitting me? You don't want any trouble! It's a little late for that, Tommy. I just saw the eleven o'clock news, and they said you pushed a fucking guy in front of a bus and later attacked a Nun. They said it was Trip. Is that true, Tommy? I thought you and him were fucking tight. You say you're just passing through, like you're going for a soda or something. Are you for real or what?"

"Jack! Look, I just want to get past here and be on my way. I don't want any trouble with you. Think about it, I never expected to see you down here this time of night. I just got something I need to do, and then it will be all right Jack. I promise you, man, I just want to keep going by. I just need you to forget you saw me, just for a while, till I get down the road a piece."

"Forget I saw you! I want to forget I ever met you! What do you think I am doing down here at this time of night? I am getting your shit out of my place before the cops show up. They said on the news that they were at your apartment and they were canvassing the area. That means it is just a matter of time till they turn up here and start asking questions about you and me and my business. Maybe start looking to close at some of the shit I got in there. I always tried to help you out, Tommy. I always tried to treat you fair. Lots of times, I gave you cash for stuff I knew was hot, and that loses me my license man. Ya, I'll forget I saw you, and as soon as I throw this box of shit that belongs to you in the river, I will be out of this shit hole end of town, and when they catch you, they will, you just forget you ever knew me. How's that sound sport?"

"That's my shit? You said you sold it all."

"No, I said I sold some of it, and the rest of it was in the back, but your tickets were due, man, and that's how I make a living. The rest of it is here in this box, and I am getting rid of it tonight!"

Tommy moved forward slowly in an effort not to startle Jack into violence. He did not want to hurt this man. What

Jack had said had been true. He had always treated Tommy fairly. Even today, as Tommy's mind broke under the strain of the lover, even as he ranted in his madness, Jack had done his best to be kind to Tommy. He looked into Jack's eyes, and there he saw fear, but under the fear, Tommy thought he saw compassion. Compassion, an emotion which could not thrive here in these alleys, an emotion that until this very evening Tommy would have taken for pity.

Here, in this alley, Jack stood looking into the eyes of a violent offender, and under his fear, what Tommy had mistaken for compassion burned a deep obsession and a strong desire to survive. Jack didn't belong here, in this neighborhood, in this jam, and he needed to get out. He was not cut out for this level of crime. He was just a petty crook trying to get through life without hurting anyone. He told himself he was a good man, who found himself in a bad spot.

Tommy stopped four feet from the front of Jack's car and, for a moment, just stared at the man. Jack was shifting uneasily from foot to foot. Holding his hand in his jacket pocket, Jack's fist gripped the revolver that Tommy was certain was a comb or a pack of gum. The sweat was beading on Jack's forehead and about to roll down his heavily creased brow and into his eyes when Tommy spoke.

"I'm sorry, Jack. I am sorry that I have put you in this situation. I think you are a nice guy and I don't even really know what happened tonight. That's the God-honest truth. I know what I did, but I don't know what happened. I don't expect you to understand. I know I don't, but whatever happened, it has changed me. I ain't the guy you've been seeing around here for months. I don't even know who that guy is, but I do know I gotta do something. I gotta get something done because I am afraid that the other thing might come back here inside my head, and I don't know if I can fight her off. I am tired and sick. And I am sorry; I mean it. You don't need to be afraid of me, Jack. I have no right to ask anything of you, but I am going to. I'm going to ask you, Jack, if I can have a look at the box. I'm asking, please."

Jack stood solid on his feet, and his breathing slowed to a steady rhythm. He looked at Tommy Boy, and he knew what Tommy had said was the truth. It was in Tommy's eyes. There, under the exhaustion, there was something Jack had not seen before: acceptance. Jack withdrew his hand from his jacket pocket, wiped the sweat from his brow and shot a couple of Tic Tacs into his dry mouth. He had liked Tommy; he wanted to believe that Tommy could not have committed these crimes, but he had seen this man tonight. He had seen him, and he understood that the person he had seen was capable of anything. He did not know what had caused this change in Tommy, but on some level, Jack felt responsible for the events of the night. He had tried to live his life by an 'Always cover your ass' motto, and he knew that when he let Tommy Boy walk out of his shitty little pawn shop that evening at supper time, he had missed the mark. Slowly, Jack slid the file box across the hood of the car towards Tommy.

Tommy moved to the hood and popped the lid off the file box. He rummaged through some books that had been given to him by his mother, pushed aside a bottle of Johnny Walker Red and his busted clock radio, picked up the Johnny

Cash 'I Walk the Line' album and there, under it all, was the small green velvet-covered box he had hoped he would find.

Tommy picked up the box and held it to his nose, inhaling deeply. Instantly, he was sitting on the front porch of the family farm, slowly swinging back and forth on the swing his Father had made as the evening sun stretched long and golden fingers over the rolling meadow. His Mother sat knitting a sweater he would take with him to College while his Father was reading the Saturday Evening Post, mumbling to himself about the state of the world. Tommy would be leaving soon to start the next phase of his life, a life that would be wonderful and full of good fortune. A life too good to be true! A life that would prove it was too good to be true. He was taking in this vista one last time. He would never see another sunset like this one in all his life. Somehow, he was certain of that, and he was saddened and thrilled all at once.

He hadn't noticed his Father slip away until he had returned and took a seat once again beside his Mother. As he settled himself in the swing, his Father rolled a Green Velvet covered box in his hands. After a moment Tommy heard his Father clear his throat as was his way before he began to speak on issues of importance.

"Tommy, Tom, I need to tell you a few things, Son," he began slowly. "Your Mother and I are very proud of you, Tom, and we love you a great deal. It is a big deal for her and me that you are going off to College. You know, neither of us had the opportunity and we always hoped one day our kids would be able to go. Well, you're the first Son. There were times over the years when I wasn't too sure that would happen, but here we are, just a couple of days away from you setting off on your new life. It is a great opportunity, Son, and we know you will do well." Tommy's Dad sat quietly for a moment as though he were struggling with the words. He was a man of few words, and putting his thoughts together properly was of great importance to him.

"There is something I want you to have, Tommy. This here was given to me by my Pop after I came back from the war when your Mom and I got married. He said he got it from his father, my Granddad and that he wanted to give it to me before I went to Europe for the war, but his Dad, my Granddad, told him no. He said it was not the right time and he was to wait till I came home from over there to stay. My Pop said to me on the day we got married, he said: "You're a man now, Son, and I want you to take this pocket watch and ring." Then he explained to me how he got it from his own Father, my Granddad, and how his Father told him it would be our family legacy to hand that ring and watch down from son to son. Well, Tom, you are a man now and I would like for you to take it." Tommy's Father opened up the faded green velvet-covered box and there inside was a silver watch on a short chain. "This here is a simple watch, Son, but it has never missed a beat." To tell you true, I never had much use for a pocket watch, but I kept it wound full, and I looked at it there in my dresser every morning when I got up and every night when I lay down. There is something to be said for the comfort I found there knowing my Dad and Granddad were always that close to me."

He leaned forward and set the green velvet-covered box on the table, and as I looked up from the box, I saw a tear rolling down my Mother's cheek, and I don't know of another time when I saw more love and pride in her eyes and in her face. She put her hand on my Dad's knee as he continued to speak.

"No, I never had much use for a pocket watch, but this ring, this ring here, hasn't left my finger since the day my Pop took it off his and put it in this box. Now it's time for me to give it to you. I want you to take it, and I want you to know that in so doing, you are taking the pride of three generations, Son. And that's something that'll get a man through anything."

With some effort, he removed the ring from his finger. In the fading light of summer, Tommy could see the line on his father's finger where the ring had been, the callous on his palm where the ring had left a testimony to the hard work this man had seen in his life. Slowly and with some regret, his Father slipped the ring into the green velvet-covered box and handed it over to Tommy.

Tommy opened his eyes and looked at Jack. He had never thought he would see this watch and ring again. This legacy, which had been entrusted to him and which had been lost to drugs and alcohol, had somehow found its way back to him. As he held the green velvet-covered box in his hand, he felt the closeness of the three that had gone before him, and in that knowledge, he found the strength to move on. The pride of three generations is something that'll get a man through anything. He snapped the box shut, turned from Jack and walked away from Louis East End Pawn.

As Jack Corbett watched Tommy Boyle slip into the darkness of the alley, he reached into the box, went past

Johnny Cash and found Johnny Walker. He broke the seal, spun the top and began the journey that would end his life.

91

CAME TO BELIEVE

As Tommy left the alley behind Louis' East End Pawn, he was overcome by a horrible sadness. His mind began to drift uncontrollably back over the events of his life since he had left that farmhouse so long ago. He was fifty-two now, and he had left when he was sixteen, and in all those lost years, he could find no happy memories. All that he ever was and all that he could have been had been lost, given up in the chase for a quick high or that one drink. That one drink he had sought from the time he had taken the first. That one drink he was never able to find again. The drink made him feel whole.

Tommy's life had always been fragmented, from the times of his earliest memories. He had left bits and pieces of himself behind in every corner of his life, never quite able to pull it all together or to carry on as others had. And then, he had that first drink, and he became whole. All that was uncertain to him in his world had become abundantly clear. All that he had feared seemed insignificant. That one drink had pulled him together, only to begin tearing him apart. The first drink led him to the last drink, and the road from beginning to end was littered with those he had come into contact with. Some were innocent bystanders, others were willing participants, but all were equally devastated.

The panic began to build in Tommy's head, and a knot grew deep in the pit of his stomach. He knew what would come next. He had been here so many times before and had hoped against hope that it had all ended with Trip and the Nun. But the tremor was beginning to rattle his hand, and if he listened closely, he could almost hear the seductive whisper of the "lover." If he listened to her now, he would be lost forever. He tried to focus on the plan, but his mind was drifting. One moment, he was on the beach with his folks, the next at the drive-in with his first love, and then in the alley with Rhonda. It all came to him at once and out of sequence, and soon the hallucinations put him in the alley, smoking crack with his mother, and looking into the surprised eyes of his father as Trip thrust him in front of a bus. He felt himself losing the small grip he had on reality, and the fear of going back to the hell from which he had come descended upon him like the weight of the world.

"No," he screamed. "I can't! I can't go back there!" Tommy was overcome by a deep loneliness now, which seemed to emanate from his very core. The loneliness he had experienced before in his life paled in comparison to the pain he suddenly felt. Oh, he had been alone, even been lonely, mostly by choice or design, but this feeling he now endured cut him like a knife. It was a physical pain, induced by a mental realization of the state of his life. He was alone, truly alone. It was then, at that moment, that he understood the pain that must fill his mother's heart each day as she wondered if her Tommy still lived and breathed, the torment that must fill his father's mind, wondering if Tommy lay broken in a hospital or dead in a morgue. It was then that he understood that the pain his parents felt did not come from the knowing but rather from the not knowing. Tommy suddenly understood that the stark reality of any given situation was much easier to bear than the fear of the unknown. The anxiety that came with waiting for bad news had taken the spirit of his parents and left them old and unhappy.

He had stolen their lives. And he had stolen any opportunity his brother, sister, and her children might have had to enjoy a normal relationship with their parents and grandparents. Tommy had lingered on the edges of all their lives over all the years. He was in every conversation, though his name was seldom mentioned. He was remembered in prayer at every family dinner, and all recollection of childhood events ended with, "Do you remember when Tommy did this?" or, "Do you recall when Tommy did that?" He was always there, just under the surface, just under their skin.

In his selfish act of self-destruction, he had insinuated himself into all their lives, and in doing so, he had sentenced them all to a life of addiction, pain, and loss. His brother and sister, who had once loved him deeply, now held an equal amount of contempt for him. He had not only destroyed himself, but he had also destroyed their family.

This all came to him in an unwanted epiphany, and Tommy was overwhelmed by the reality of his situation. All that he had eluded throughout his life with the aid of alcohol and drugs had come home to roost. All he had run from had overtaken him, and Tommy slowly sank to his knees and sobbed. The tears came now. The tears came in great sobbing and wet sighs and would not stop. He saw them all again in his mind's eye. He saw all of his family, and they were framed in love, framed in the love he had been unable to express, the love that had filled him with a fear he no longer understood.

He sobbed and sobbed, and between sobs, he tried desperately to catch his breath. He began to speak—first a word, then another, then another, and then the sentence. Quietly, clearly, without hesitation, and for the first time in thirty-five years, "God, please help me find the way to the end. Oh God, please help me."

His hand found its way into the pocket of his soiled jeans, and his fingers walked swiftly over the small wooden beads attached to the crudely carved cross. He knelt, head bowed, and calm came over him. Once again, the lover fell silent, and the tremor grew still. In his other hand, he felt the smooth, green velvet box. The power within it seeped into his heart, and he understood that the love and pride of three generations could carry a man through anything.

Tommy rose to his feet, wiped the tears away with a soiled sleeve, and crossed Baker Side Road into the alley that would take him to Lexington Avenue and the "A" Train. He choked down his pain, pushed back the attacking memories, and walked toward his destiny.

His father had once told him he was bound for great things in his life. He had told Tommy that he would witness wondrous sights and go on great adventures. Well, what Tommy had seen fell well short of wondrous, his adventures something less than great. But tonight, at this very moment, he had determination. The closer he came to the end of his journey, the greater the panic became, but he had determination, and that was something new. That was something different, and the lover had not yet found a way to battle this newfound quality in Tommy. But time was his enemy, and given time, he knew he would succumb to her.

That simple fact pushed him on, and Tommy went forth with purpose in his stride.

As he crossed over Baker Side Road, Tommy glanced quickly east in the direction of Louis'. There, on the north side of the street, walking away from Tommy, was a cop on the beat. Tommy crossed Baker Side Road quickly, then paused in the shadows of the alley, looking toward the officer to see if his crossing had been observed. Tommy knew by the silhouette of the patrolling officer that his movement across the street had remained unseen. He could also tell by the stature of the man that this was Constable Bob Gideon on the job. He was the cop that Rhonda had mentioned, and he had a reputation for being fair.

Officer Friendly, as he was known among the crack whores who worked his beat, "Bad Bob" among the gang bangers, and "Buddy Bob" among the in-betweens. The in-betweens were the ones too young to be whores; the ones not yet recruited by the gangs as strikers or drug runners. The ones living, for the most part, on the streets. These were the ones that could still be saved, given the right opportunity, and shown there was another road. It was an idealistic attitude, but the only one that gave Bob Gideon the inspiration to get up for every shift and walk these sad streets. It was a cruel twist of fate that found him here working these particular streets. Perhaps it was meant to be; perhaps there was one kid who needed saving, some good to be done. This is what he told himself every shift as he readied his mind and body to go do battle against crime and society on the same streets where he grew up.

This neighborhood, his beat, had not always been this way. Bob Gideon remembered these same streets in the inner city as a child: vibrant, working neighborhoods with thriving businesses. Everything a person needed to live in those days could be found within a five-square-block area. And everyone in that area was a neighbor. Not necessarily a friend, but a neighbor. Even back then, there were areas carved out of the neighborhood for certain gangs of kids, and from time to time, there were scuffles among them. But not like now, not like today. Back then, the worst you walked away with was a black eye or bloody nose. Today, if you walked away at all, you could count yourself among the winners. No, back then, there was really no hate or animosity; it was more like a game—a bunch of clubs with posturing kids acting tough while being scared. There was no turf, really, no drug trafficking areas to protect. No, it was just kids finding themselves and each other, like a rite of passage.

As he walked along, checking doors and chatting to the whores and punks hanging out on the corners, he couldn't help but reflect on the passage of time and the decline of the area. It all seemed so simple to him to fix, and yet the Bosses, the ones with the bigger brains, kept screwing it up. The City Council and the Federal Ministers, with their entourage of Social Workers and Psychologists, kept coming up with new policies and improved programs to "integrate" the youth into "polite society." They had no clue. Everything they did just made it worse down here. Everything they did was counterproductive and viewed with suspicion and cynicism by the people in the area.

The old ones, the ones left trying to hang on to their businesses or homes because it was all they had, had no voice in the destiny of their neighborhood. Their influence politically had been severed by the box stores. The tax base they represented did not contribute enough to city coffers to enable them to effect change of any substance, and so they were left to their own devices. The walk-in shelters and the harm reduction policies of the city did nothing to curb the crime among the small businesses that tried to survive. Needle exchange programs did not stop the mugging of old ladies trying to get from the bus stop to the security of their triple-dead-bolted homes. It just wasn't working. All the money being spent to save these inner-city neighborhoods was being wasted on justifying the existence of a bunch of bleeding-heart liberal assholes. They may as well have built a fence around the five square blocks and said, "Job done."

And that is why he stayed. Maybe it was ego, maybe a fear of success, maybe it was fate, but in his heart, he felt he was all there was to serve and protect the good people that remained. The lives of the ones that were left behind, and the lives of the ones that may be saved, rested in the hands of Officer Bob Gideon. They were on his beat; they were his responsibility, and he would not let them down.

He could have moved up in his career long ago. In fact, he had become a standing joke among the other officers on the force. His colleagues viewed his long-standing beat as a punishment meted out by the bosses. They assumed he had been left behind in the pursuit of advancement because of incompetence or insubordination, and so they joked and jibed. Slowly, over the years, he had become a loner. He had no partner or close friends on the force. There were a couple of sergeants over the years who tried to move him up in rank, but he always resisted. There was the cop shrink who was concerned that Gideon's long-term "exposure to the criminal element" would have a "lasting and devastating effect on his personal life and judgment." He had been right, but Bob was still here, on his beat, doing his job.

For the most part, he loved it. Even when the shit got bad, and the gangs were killing each other, he had always been able to see beyond the trouble and focus on the goal of bringing something back to these fine old streets. He had developed a network of people down here who trusted him. They were among his only friends, and it was often the only place he felt connected to the world—his network, his friends. Tonight, he would call on them all. Tonight, he would test the working relationship he had developed with the street. There was a man that needed to be found. His name was Tommy, and he knew he was in the area.

The bosses were looking further afield. The bosses were convinced this Tommy was in the wind and on the run. But Bob had a feeling, a hunch, a burning in his gut. He didn't know this Tommy well, but he knew of him. He was small-time, a druggie and a drunk. For a while, he ran a whore named Rhonda, but Bob was pretty sure that was in the past. This guy wouldn't run because this guy had nowhere to run to. He would turn up here, on Gideon's beat, sooner rather than later. He would be hurting, and he would need a fix, and Gideon would find him. Slowly, and with a smile on his face and a picture of Tommy in his breast pocket, he approached a group of working girls on the corner. The hunt was on.

Tommy turned away from Officer Bob Gideon, thinking, just another dumbass flatfoot, and continued his journey through the last alley en route to his destination. When he emerged from the other end of this alley, he would be on Lexington. The point of his final departure from this earth was to be an open-air subway where the A train passed thrice daily. The train was almost always on schedule, and Tommy used to joke about how he could set his need to get a fix by the train. He was either just starting to "Jones" for a drug or drifting through that first cloud of beautiful blue smoke from the pipe as the train went by and shook his shitty little room, creating a ripple effect in his tall glass of cheap vodka—no ice. It had, in an odd way, become the only source of stability that had remained in his shattered life, and Tommy took great comfort in knowing it would always be there, three times a day, like clockwork. It seemed somehow fitting to him that this train would carry him to the great beyond and free him from the life of bondage to which he had succumbed.

As he neared the end of his last alley, Tommy saw feet sticking out from under a sheet of cardboard and looked down upon one beaten and tattered blue Adidas and one nearly new-looking red Nike. He knew immediately that he was looking upon the feet of Armist. There could be no mistake; there was no other rummy in this end of town with this same mismatched footwear. Armist was a drunk. Tommy thought this with no malice or judgment; it was just a matter of fact.

Armist was an old man with the misfortune of having an overly grateful and patriotic mother at the end of the Second

World War. He was conceived ten minutes before his father boarded a ship for Europe, and he was born nine months later as the clock struck midnight on what would turn out to be Armistice Day. His father never knew the war was over when the German tank annihilated the farmhouse in which he was pinned down. His father never knew that, almost at the precise moment of his death, the son he would never know had entered this world. His father could not have known that in his zeal to make the world safe from tyranny, he would leave a mourning young girl whose mind would never be the same, and an orphaned baby boy destined to go through life named Armist.

Armist was a professional drunk and anti-establishmentarian. There was no shelter he would go to in the dead of winter, and when he begged for money, it was always for booze, never coffee. He would never steal from another who lived on the street, for he lived by a code, and never, in all his years, was he ever ashamed of who he was or what he needed to do to survive. He was the son of a war hero he never knew.

His mother's mind had been lost forever as she waited for the return of a lover who would never arrive. The very day his mother was taken to the asylum, Armist was declared a ward of the courts, and the two of them were thrust into a system of care that was horrific in the late forties. The mother never survived, but the son did. With each whipping he received, with each instance of sexual abuse he endured, he had become hardened and cynical, and when the opportunity arose, he ran. Armist escaped to the "safety" of the streets and the anonymity of the people who resided there. They had welcomed him as one of their own. He had found a family, and no one would ever put him in a building again as long as he drew breath.

And now here he was. The son of a war hero and a madwoman, sleeping in the alley he had called home for over fifty years. He was sixty-four years old, his brain was wet, his body was deteriorating, but he was free, and he was proud.

Tommy knew Armist had something he needed. Tommy knew that there, under the cardboard, Armist slept in a Second World War parka with a funnel hood. There were five blocks of open street Tommy needed to cross in his neighborhood. He had to walk past the Mission as well as the front door of his shitty little apartment to get to where he needed to go, and he was fairly certain he would be seen and identified. Tommy felt sure he could cover the distance between here and the phone booth (which was his next stop) unobserved if the people on the street thought it was just Armist on the prowl.

He knew he could just take the parka from this sick old drunk without much of a fight, but he also knew the code and would not violate it. Tommy had no stomach left for fighting or violence. He had wreaked havoc on the world that night and would have no more of it. He would not steal from Armist, but he knew if he asked for help, Armist would not refuse. And so, with caution, he gently pulled the cardboard aside and kicked the red-and-blue-clad feet of the sleeping Armist.

With a swiftness that took Tommy by surprise and one which seemed unlikely from this tattered and decrepit old man, Armist was on his feet, a small blade extended in front of him, crouched and ready to pounce. There was a look of confused readiness on his face and a mixture of fear and anger as Armist surveyed the area. He was the son of a war hero and had survived over fifty years on the mean streets. He always awoke ready to face any challenge and was more than willing to fight to the death for the meager belongings he called his own. How he came to be in possession of the articles around him was irrelevant. Through thievery or trickery, they had all been acquired, but once in his possession, they belonged to Armist, and if you were of a mind to take them, you had better be ready for a fight. You had best be prepared to die.

Tommy fell back a step or two to ensure he was well out of the range of the blade, which sparkled in the flickering light of the alley. He had been amazed and frightened by the graceful and deadly stance of the older man, and was angry at himself for the lapse in judgment in the manner in which he woke Armist. It could have been a fatal error, and though Tommy was in preparation for death, the actual event was not meant to take place here in this alley at the hands of a drunkard. Tommy had lost so much control in all aspects of his life that the thought of controlling the event of his death had given him some perverse sense of freedom. Knowing he would end it on his terms, in his own way, made Tommy feel as though he had regained some power in what was otherwise a powerless existence. He was so close to the end now, so close to the calls he had to make and so willing to overcome the fear and pain that was brewing in his mind, that to be knifed here in this alley would be a cruel injustice. He had asked for nothing and expected nothing for so many years, but now, near the hour of his demise, he reached out for help from a power he did not understand, and one upon which he had never relied.

"Dear God," thought Tommy, "don't let me die at the hands of this old man. Help me to calm him."

"Whoa, WHOA! Armist! Take it easy, old boy, it's me, Tommy. Look at me now. Wake up and look. You know who I am; you know I would not hurt you."

"Fucking right, I know who you are. Trip knew who you were, too, when you shoved him in front of that bus. You stay the fuck back, man. I ain't one to go so easy, you hear me? I am sick, and I am old, but I got some fight left in me, and I won't be done in by some piss-ant druggie on some motherfucking rampage! That's what they're calling it on the news. I saw it on the TV at Louis' pawn! That TV says you went on some kinda rampage! I don't know exactly what a rampage is, but I don't like what it sounds like, and I don't intend to get anywhere near you if you're on one. And I knew that nun. She was all right for one of them kind, and what you did to her was chicken shit, man. My old man was a fucking war hero, kid, and I got some of that shit in me. So you just come ahead with your rampage and see what you get! Just come on ahead a little bit, and old Armist Hancock will do everybody a favor and be a fucking hero just like Sergeant Lester Hancock was before he was killed by that German tank."

"Armist, listen to me. I am not on anything, Armist. I am straight and sober. I sure as hell ain't on a rampage, Armist, swear to God, man. Put the knife away. I won't hurt you. I never meant for anything to happen with Trip or that nun. Something happened, like to my head. I don't know, man, I can't understand it, but it's over. I am okay for right now, and I need some help from you. There's something I got to do that will make it right. Armist, I need your help. Please, put down the knife and let me talk to you. I don't have much time, and I have stuff I got to do. Please, just hear me out."

With great reluctance, Armist began to rise out of his attack stance. Slowly, he straightened his posture, and Tommy was surprised that he had never before taken note of the great height of this man. In the dim light of the alley, Tommy let his eyes roam over Armist, from the dirty knitted hat on his head to his blue and red shoes. He was a big man, and his countenance carried the scars of a lifetime on the streets. There was a jagged scar on his right brow where, years before, a busted bottle had been the deciding factor in the disputed ownership of an eight-by-ten piece of turf in another alley. His sunken cheeks and distended nose were littered with thousands of bursts and healed-over blood vessels, creating a road map of misery, abuse, and hard living. He was weathered from head to foot, and Tommy suddenly realized that he never appreciated the extraordinary height of Armist because Armist was always hunched over. He never stood his full erect height, and that was a mechanism that allowed him to go unobserved by the police and general public and underestimated by potential adversaries.

It was a streetwise maneuver, and Tommy smiled to himself in appreciation of the years this man had survived in the war zone. He was a hero of a different sort. His right hand had been smashed in a fight years before, and without the benefit of medical attention, the bone had healed misshapen, giving the appearance of a talon rather than a hand. There he stood, and Tommy admired him.

Tommy understood that the circumstances of the life that Armist had endured created the person he had become. He was destined for a hard life from the moment of his birth. The streets, the boozing, the fighting, and the surviving were like Armist's birthright, and Tommy saw a picture of who and what Tommy would become were he to continue on in this life. The difference was that Tommy understood the person he would become would be as much a monster as Armist was a hero.

Tommy had no excuses. Tommy had been given opportunities to have a real life, and Tommy had chosen not to participate. Where there was a sort of twisted honor in the life of this old man, there was nothing but dishonor in Tommy's. Tommy never made the best out of a bad situation dealt to him by life, as Armist had. Tommy took a good life and wasted it. Tommy had been a failure. In that moment of clarity, Tommy could hear the echo of the words his father had spoken during their last phone conversation. His father had attempted to reason with Tommy. His father had attempted to inspire Tommy to find his way out of the rut of his existence. He had told Tommy that, "Failure is not forever, son, and success is fleeting at best." His father had been wrong. For Tommy, failure was forever, and success would never be realized.

Armist stood erect and out of attack posture, but not fully relaxed. He could be back in defense or offense mode in seconds, and Tommy had to proceed with caution. "Armist, will you help me? I need something from you, and I don't have much to trade. But if you help me, I can get you some stuff that will help you out."

"What will make it right?" asked Armist suspiciously. "You said you could make it right. How you gonna do that?"

"Huh? What are you talking about? Never mind all that right now, Armist, I need some help. I need your coat, man. Can I take your coat... and your shoes? Armist, I need those shoes as well."

"I want to know what will make it right after what you've done. You gonna run away or something? You gonna tell everyone you're sorry or some shit like that? I want to know how you think you can make it right."

"I don't know, Armist. I don't mean to make it right for them. I know I can't do that. I know what I did was horrible, and I can't live with it, so I know what I gotta do to make it right. I don't want to say any more about it. It is best you don't know."

"You gonna kill yourself, is that it? You gonna make it right for YOU, you mean; that's all. You think that's somehow gonna make what you did okay? You are chicken shit, man, you always were. Fucking druggie whiner, that's all you are. Now you gonna kill yourself, and you can't even admit you're just gonna do it because you're chicken shit. You make me want to puke. I oughta do you right here and right now in this alley, but I ain't no killer. Not unless I have to be. You ain't no hero, that's for damn sure."

"I know I ain't no hero, Armist. I am chicken shit, you're right. I won't make it in jail, man. I know I won't make it in there locked up for the rest of my life. I know I fucked up for a long time. I just want out, man. I just want some peace. I just want to stop fighting, and I need your help. I need your coat and your shoes."

Tommy reached into his back pocket and took out the key to the apartment door, the one with "Tommy Boy" written in black magic marker crookedly across the midsection. "This here is the key to my place, Armist. It is right around the corner from here. There ain't much left in there, Armist, but inside the closet, there is a good winter coat. It is about all that is left that I didn't hawk. Guess I always thought I may end up outdoors one winter down here with you, Armist, so I kept that good coat. And there is a quilt, too, Armist. It is a real good warm one!

My Grandma made that quilt for me a long time ago. I never could get rid of it at Louis', and I guess I kinda wanted to keep it. I sure wish you'd do me a trade, your stuff for mine. And you can have these shoes I'm wearing. They're a bit big for me and should fit you—both the same color, Armist. Those damn kids wouldn't laugh at you no more if you got both the same color shoes. What do ya say, Armist?"

Armist stood still for a moment, and slowly, with his good hand, he folded the knife shut and slid it into the waistband of his pants. His talon-like hand came up with slow deliberation and began to stroke his chin. "What else you got?" asked Armist. "It ain't enough. A coat for a coat, shoes for shoes, I ain't coming away no better off than when I come into this here negotiation. I gotta take your word for it *all* on top of that. And we both admit you is a chicken shit, so there's gotta be more. The quilt won't do it. You need my help to get killed, then you gotta show me some more." Armist stood quiet and waited.

"There is no more, Armist, I swear." As Tommy spoke, his hand found its way into the pocket of his tattered jeans, and swiftly, his fingers began to walk around the small circle of wooden beads attached to the crudely carved crucifix. He had been sure Armist would help him, and now his plan seemed to be slipping away. His mind was racing, and his thoughts were turning to the green velvet-covered box containing the ring and watch of his ancestors. It was all he had left of his past, and though Tommy had not planned to take them with him to catch the A train, neither was it in his plan to leave it in the hands of Armist.

As he worked the beads, his lips moved in unspoken words, and once again, reflexively, he was speaking in his mind to a God in whom he had no belief or faith. But still, he spoke on in silence and asked this higher power to show him the way. At that moment, a thought occurred to Tommy, and without conscious thought, he extended his arm out to Armist and opened his hand. There, in the center of his palm, lay the small circle of wooden beads attached to the crudely carved crucifix.

For a moment, both men stared down at the tiny rosary in silence. Everything in the alley had suddenly become more pronounced. The dim incandescent lights over the dirty back doors of the alley all seemed to team light into the space between them, and Tommy could count individual hairs on the back of Armist's big hands. Electricity filled the air between the two men. It was a power they both sensed and feared in unison. The silence lasted only for a moment, but the understanding that was born between these two men would last for all time. They both had been touched throughout their lives by all things physical in this world—both good and bad—but here, now, in this alley, and for the first time for either of them, they were in the presence of divinity, and their lives would never be the same.

"There's this," said Tommy. "It's..." He paused, searching for a word. "Special... it's special."

"It belonged to the nun," said Armist. "It's got to go back to her. I will do it." Armist reached out and gently picked the small circle of wooden beads attached to the crudely carved crucifix out of Tommy's palm. As Armist placed the small rosary into the pocket of his army pants, the misshapen, arthritic fingers of his talon-like hand began to walk around the circle of wooden beads, and his lips began to move in unspoken prayer.

Gideon had done the big circle and was just turning onto Lexington Avenue. He had not had much luck in his pursuit of Tommy. Along his route, he had stopped and talked to all the regulars on the streets at this hour. He had flashed the picture of Tommy the detectives had found in his apartment, and he had made it known that this man must be found. There was no question that one of them, at some point in this night, would make contact with Tommy, and when they did, they would call him—or wish they had. He had worked all the main streets, and his plan was now to start working the alleys. There was a whole other world in these alleys after dark, and the pursuit of Tommy in them could be dangerous for a man on his own, but that was how he worked, and that was how it would go down.

As Gideon began to walk down Lexington, a hunched and shadowed figure emerged from the alley that connected to Baker Side Road, turned south, and headed in the direction of the A train terminal. Bob Gideon had a trained and professional eye, and he knew the inhabitants of his beat as though his life depended upon it—and often, it did. In the dim light, he could see the funnel hood of the World War II parka, and if he squinted at just the right time, as the figure passed under the streetlights, he could see one red and one blue shoe.

"Who would be on the prowl on a hot night wearing a parka, one red and one blue shoe?" thought Gideon. "Only Armist would," he answered himself out loud with a short laugh. "Crazy old war hero bastard."

Armist watched from the shadows as Gideon watched Tommy, as Tommy strolled hunched over down the street. The funnel hood and multicolored shoes shone in the glow of the streetlights, and Armist was filled with an eerie sort of déjà vu as he watched himself walk away. The fingers of his deformed hand slid easily over the well-oiled wooden beads of the tiny rosary, and Armist was filled with a sense of purpose he had not experienced for many, many years. Not since the days forty years prior, when he was consumed with the idea of escaping the county orphanage, had he felt so certain of what he must do.

This rosary, which began changing his life the moment he laid eyes upon it, was indeed special. Many fingers had worked these beads in the hundreds of years this rosary had existed, and many through the ages had claimed ownership of the small circle of beads attached to the crudely carved wooden crucifix. But none had understood so quickly the power contained within these beads. Armist knew his life would never be the same as it had been. Armist knew that though he was not looking for redemption, redemption had found him. The thought of parting with the talisman filled Armist with dread, but it was, he understood, not to be kept by him.

Something had filled his heart and mind, and Armist understood that this small circle of beads, attached to a crudely carved wooden crucifix, must be returned to the mission and must find its way to where the nun named Petra would rest. Nothing on this earth would stop Armist from completing this mission, which had befallen him, and as the reality of that thought registered and set within his mind, Armist moved out of the alley.

Armist stood his full six-foot-three height and walked out of the alley with his head held high and his shoulders thrown back. The street looked different to him from this higher vantage. Somehow, things appeared sharper and more defined. It never occurred to Armist that he was suddenly seeing the world from a new perspective, which was not related to his height. He felt different, and in many ways, it left him uneasy. There was work to be done this night, and he would see to it. It would mean involving himself in the affairs of Tommy Boyle, a fugitive on the run. It would mean not minding his own business and breaking the code he had lived by for better than forty years. It would mean he would have to change, and change, to Armist, was neither wanted nor easy. Change meant uncertainty, and uncertainty always meant danger when you survived on the streets. He felt apprehension but not fear. He was experiencing clarity of thought, which was unfamiliar to him, but with it came confidence and an understanding that, somehow, things were going to turn out for the best.

Armist looked south down Lexington just in time to see the slouched figure of himself fade from the light of a street lamp. Tommy had done a convincing job of imitating the old street urchin, and sadness was building inside Armist as he watched what had been himself walk into the shadows. All of his life, for as long as he could recall, Armist had been retreating into the shadows. Always on the run, always fending off or searching for, had been the sad story of his life. Five square blocks in a downtown core had been his world. He never ventured beyond it. He had no notion of any other world than that which he had created for himself down here in these alleys. He had never loved anything or anyone other than the memory of a war hero he never met. There had been no time for love. Survival was a twenty-four-hour-a-day job. He had no recollection of the mother who could not be there for him. All his memories were of chaos.

As he watched himself slip into the shadows, he said goodbye to the man he had become and was filled with hope for the man he would be.

Bob Gideon watched as old Armist slipped out of the light and into the shadows on his way to wherever Armist went during his nighttime prowls. He did not know and did not want to know about the activities of the old man. Armist was a fixture down here and had been since Gideon lived on these streets as a kid. He knew the story of the war hero and the survival of a young orphan on the street and believed some of it. Street legends are a requirement for the inhabitants of these slums and alleys. It gives hope to the disenfranchised—hope that they, too, will find a way to exist and be safe in the mayhem and chaos of street life. Armist provided hope and never caused Gideon much trouble, so he let him be.

As Armist faded from view, Gideon noticed movement down the street at the mouth of the alley leading to Baker Side Road. There was a man leaving the alley. He was a big man, and Gideon did not recognize him as one of the regulars on his beat. He stood tall and confident and was walking with purpose. There was no skulking, no darting eyes and no swivel-neck viewing of the street, and from his body language, Gideon assumed he was not a person for which he needed to be concerned. It was a dangerous assumption to make on a dark night in Lexington, but there was other business that needed tending to this night, and Bob's focus could not be diverted. There was a man on the loose who needed to be located. Gideon took one last glance at the tall man. Satisfied with his gut instincts, he turned west into an alley where he hoped he would find some answers.

Tommy was close now, close to the place it would all play out. He was colder than the night should allow for, as his body was becoming painfully aware that it was long past feeding time. The tremor in his hand was returning, though it was slight. His shiver was more of a minor seizure than a reaction to the cool night, but his mind was clear. There would be no reprieve from the physical addiction on this night of his departure, but Tommy was grateful that his mind remained remarkably clear. The pain he felt throughout his ravaged body served as inspiration for him to move forward. He could no longer exist this way—a slave to a body and soul that craved the substance that would ultimately destroy him. A slow and hideous death was all that lay ahead for Tommy. It was better to be quick and clean, and on schedule, courtesy of the "A" train.

As he limped along, head looking down upon the red and blue shoes of Armist, he allowed his mind to wander to the calls he was about to make. He was filled with dread and calm simultaneously at the thought of speaking to the people on the list he was forming in his mind. It had been so long since he had spoken to his family, and there were those among them who had requested he never call again. It would be easier to go forth and complete his task without the calls or the possibility of confrontation that would result from them, but that would be wrong. He marveled at the notion that he, Tommy Boy, would have any idea whatsoever as to what would be right or wrong. He had spent the majority of his life in uncertainty, never knowing what the right thing to do was, always guessing and usually getting it wrong. The wrong action, the wrong words—this had been Tommy's experience in life. This had been the fear he had walked with for as long as he could recall. His guidance system was fueled by fear and uncertainty and, eventually, denial and avoidance. He avoided confrontation through using, and now here he was, on this dark and cool night, on Lexington Avenue, walking toward a destiny he would control and a phone booth he did not fear. Rhonda was right. He had introduced enough pain and anger into the lives of those he loved. He could not do what he had to do unless they understood that it was his choice. It was not their responsibility.

Tommy had walked in the shoes of Armist for two blocks, unaware of his progress. He stopped on the corner of Fifth and Lexington, just outside the range of the last street lamp he had passed through. Safely in the shadow of darkness, he turned his attention to the distance he had covered from the alley. He could see the form of the flatfoot Gideon turn west into an alley, and Tommy was certain he had been seen by the cop. He smiled to himself in the knowledge that his Armist ploy had worked. Across the street and several blocks closer, he watched a tall, confident man walking with a long and purposeful stride toward the front door of his little apartment. Tommy was amazed that this was Armist. Amazed that this man of the street had transformed before him, and Tommy began to believe for the first time that miracles did exist in this shitty world.

Instinctively, Tommy's hand reached into the pocket of his jeans for the small circle of wooden beads attached to the crudely carved crucifix. Just as his mind recalled that the talisman was in the hands of Armist, his fingers fell upon a small, hard object in the bottom corner of his pocket. Tommy removed his hand, and amidst the pocket lint that had gathered lay a single white, glistening tooth rimmed with dried blood. It was the tooth of Sister Petra from the Mission. The tooth he and a brick wall had savagely removed from her mouth.

Tommy was filled with remorse and shame as he gazed upon this disturbing trophy. He had no idea why he had taken this tooth from the wall. He actually had no memory of putting it in his pocket, and yet here it was, in his hand. The distraction of the tooth was immediate and incredible. Tommy's focus had shifted completely to the tooth. He was transfixed by the simple beauty of the tooth with its smooth and perfect lines. The small rim of dried blood and flesh that clung to its edges was brilliant red in the light of the street lamps. It glowed like an aura, and Tommy became convinced that this was what he was seeing. The spirit of Petra had somehow altered this simple tooth. Just as the tooth was a trophy of evil and depravity to which Tommy had succumbed, it was also a relic of the goodness that had been Petra.

Tommy began to feel uneasy under the weight of the tooth. The clarity of thought he had been experiencing was slipping from him with remarkable speed. He found himself questioning the plan. He found himself listening to the fear of the unknown, which had been lying in the back of his mind, and for the first time, he began to falter. He imagined the moment of impact as the A train swept him away in a blur of sparks and screaming brakes. There would be pain; there would be doubt at the last second when there was no option left to act upon the doubt. Tommy raised his arm and readied himself to fling the tooth into the street. Its power was overcoming his reason, and the sickness in his brain was beginning to stir. Just as he was about to launch the tooth into the center of Lexington Avenue, Tommy's eyes leveled upon the large cross perched on the pitched roof over the top of the mission, which had been home to Sister Petra, the mission where she had given food to Tommy and hundreds of others like him. Here, she had given food, love, and compassion freely, never expecting anything in return, never preaching or judging—just being there to help, as she had been called to do. Just showing the enduring love of Christ, her savior, and being present for those who did not yet know Him.

The gravity of what he had done slowly began to rise in Tommy's mind, and as it did, his arm—which had been cocked and ready to throw—fell to his side. The warmth of the tooth traveled through Tommy's palm and up his arm. It settled in his heart and removed the feelings of remorse and self-pity. The warmth of her love, the extension of His love, left his heart and traveled to his addicted brain, calming his racing thoughts. Slowly, deliberately, clarity returned to Tommy. He understood that his actions had removed this woman from this earth, where she had helped hundreds, even thousands of people. She would not be there at the mission to serve soup and love to anyone, and Tommy was responsible.

He crossed the street to the front door of the mission, and there he knelt, head bowed, hands clasped together in front of him, a single tooth nestled in the middle. "My God, please forgive me and give me strength," was the prayer Tommy spoke aloud as he reached forward and raised the welcome mat of the Fifth Street Mission. There, in a crevice in the cement, Tommy pushed the red-rimmed tooth of Sister Petra in the hope that the goodness that was within her soul would somehow remain here on this mission. He blessed himself in the way he had been schooled as a child, rose up, and turned south toward the phone booth, where he would say his goodbyes to his darkened world.

ARRIVALS AND DEPARTURES

Armist slowly climbed the three steps to the stoop in front of the apartment that belonged to Tommy. As he stood before the door, Armist could feel the panic rising in his gut. His heart was beating at an accelerated rate, and his pulse pounded in his ears like a kettle drum. Next would come the numbness and tingling in his arms and hands, and then— then would come the full-blown panic attack. The panic had been with Armist for as far back as his memory could stretch; never any worse, never any better, always the same. His panic was constant, predictable and unpredictable at once, and in it, Armist found an odd sense of comfort. The panic was the only thing that had been with him his whole life. It was his 'fight or flight' alarm system, and many times over the years, it had been all that kept him from harm. The alarm bells were ringing loudly in his ears as he reached for the doorknob, and every fiber of his being was telling him to run. This was not his business! Not his fight! Not his shit! He watched his gnarled hand clasp the knob and turn it without hesitation, and in defiance of the fear, he stepped through the threshold.

The hall inside was dark, lit only by a single bulb one landing up. Armist was scared; he was never good indoors, not since he was a child. The closed-in darkness of the hallway carried him back through time to the closets of his youth, where he was kept in punishment for days on end. The orphanage to which he had been sent was an evil place run by evil people. Those old, dark memories lived in the deepest parts of Armist's mind and had not surfaced in many years. He had trained himself to forget. Armist had chosen a life outdoors and in the alleys as a mechanism to keep his most feared memories at bay, and it had worked. He had vowed never to be constrained again by any man or institution, and he had lived by that vow. But here tonight, in this dark and filthy hallway, those memories had been lost, and Armist felt a tremble in his legs as he moved forward.

The smell in the hall was overpowering in itself, and instinctively, Armist moved his hand up over his nose. The stench was unmistakably that of human waste, and as Armist's eyes adjusted to the dimness of the hallway, a shape appeared, spread across the bottom two steps of the stairway. As he approached the sleeping figure, Armist saw the tattered, filthy overcoat and long white beard stained with spit and nicotine. Lying here in this horrible state was Gustav Kaminski, known to the younger street dwellers as "Gutter Gus." Just as Armist was a legend to the latest generation of vagrants, Gustav was a legend to Armist. He had been here when Armist arrived as a young man some fifty-odd years ago. Their first meeting had not gone well for Armist, and without thinking, his hand rubbed the jagged scar over his right eye where, years before, a busted bottle had been the deciding factor in a dispute over an eight-by-ten piece of turf. Poor old Gutter Gus. He was on his way out, and Armist doubted he would make it through the winter. Part of him hoped he wouldn't. They had started out badly all those years back but had become friends, or at least as close to friends as is allowed on the streets.

Lying on the ground at his side was an empty family-size plastic bottle of Purell hand cleaner, the top cut off, and a plastic spoon sticking out. This was the quick road to oblivion for the old ruby who no longer had the strength to beg or steal a proper drink but still had the need. The need was as strong as it had ever been. Every clinic, mission, or welfare office in this part of town had hand cleaners at every door and desk, all easy pickings for wily old street drunks. Truth be told, it wasn't just the old ones taking part these days; the young ones too, but it made them old quickly.

Armist poked the toe of his new trainers into the chest of old Gutter Gus with appropriate caution. An old sleeping dog was still a dog, and there could be one more bad bite on this man who had survived seven generations on the street.

"Gus, that you, Gus? This is old Army here. You alive, Gustav?" Armist kicked just a bit harder, and a groan came from deep within the sick old man. It was a groan so mournful and desperate that Armist took a step back in surprise and fear. Gustav was surely dying from the inside out. Lots of him was already dead, judging by the smell, and slowly, Armist raised a leg to step over Gutter Gus.

"You sleep well, old-timer," said Armist as he hoisted his bulk over two steps at once. "You sleep well and long, and soon we'll take a meal together over my way. One for old times' sake, eh, Gustav? One for the good old days." Gutter Gus gurgled and farted long and loud as Armist made his way up the stairs and toward the door that said Tommy Boy.

Lying in wait inside the darkened apartment of the felon Tommy Boyle was Sergeant First Class Jimmy McCaskey and rookie Johnny McFadden. McCaskey was five minutes from the end of his shift when Tommy was smashing the face of Sister Petra into a brick wall on Pine Street, five minutes away from the locker room and the shower he would take before meeting his wife for dinner to celebrate their tenth wedding anniversary, which he had missed two weeks ago. He was just five minutes away from an evening of trying to convince his wife of ten years and two weeks that made him choose between their lives together and his life as a cop was not fair. The conversation he had played over and over in his head all that day would never be required because tonight he was here, just as he always had been, putting the job ahead of life and wife.

He had never met Tommy, had only seen a photo of him they had found when they tossed his apartment earlier that evening, but he hated the man with all his heart. This man was the ruination of all that McCaskey had worked to achieve, and this man would pay dearly. Nobody cared about the con man named Trip; just one less grifter on the street. But the moment that this lowlife had littered Pine Street with the teeth of the nun, the Commissioner of Police went apeshit. Tommy had become high-profile, a person of interest! A druggie on the run! The media had descended like locusts on the station house, all running the same angle about the Sister of Mercy, bludgeoned by the very scum she had dedicated her life to saving. Not one mentioned the bum Trip. The bums could kill each other all day long without notice, but of one nun and the six o'clock news team were at the door.

All units had been called in, all shifts extended to overtime, an all-points bulletin was in place, and a manhunt was underway. The Commissioner had promised to have the man in custody by midnight, and that was two hours ago. And so here he was, with a nervous rookie, at two in the morning, seething with anger and praying to every God he could think of that this piece of shit Tommy decided to come home for clean underwear.

The place was a dump, and McCaskey was amazed that after all these years, he was still disgusted and surprised at the way these people lived. The no-star hotel across the street on Lexington had No Vacancy flashing in neon, and every thirty seconds, the little apartment was flooded with the green glow of neon gas. Every thirty seconds, McCaskey caught a glimpse of rookie McFadden, and every thirty seconds, the boy looked that much closer to losing it. He was new, brand new, and this was his first stakeout. This was the real thing—the big time—and the kid was cutting his teeth on some serious crime. All these facts made this kid as dangerous to McCaskey as the scumbag they were waiting for. He would need to be careful tonight.

For four hours now, they had huddled in the dark, the rookie with a litany of whispered questions, McCaskey trying to keep him calm. Now, there was movement in the hall. McCaskey had agreed with the bosses that this junkie was on the run and would not return to his hovel, but all the bases needed to be covered, so they waited in the dark. The seething pit of anger McCaskey had been building in his gut transformed into a calm, professional demeanor. It was showtime, and his years of experience rose to the surface. McCaskey was born to be a cop, and truth be told, he was willing to lose his wife for it.

The kid had his face pressed into the filthy door, looking through the peephole. He was breathing hard, short breaths, too fast and too deep. He would hyperventilate and be of no use if things went bad. McCaskey needed to slow him down. "Okay, son, this may be it. Remember the procedures. They work if we do what we're supposed to do. Now, what do you see?"

"I can't see shit, Sarge! Too dark! But there's someone moving down there and talking. I think I hear some muffled talk. Wait, yeah, he's coming up."

In the dark, between the surreal green flashes of neon, McCaskey heard the leather hammer strap unsnap on the holster of the rookie's service revolver. "McFadden!" McCaskey whispered as loudly and harshly as the circumstance would allow. "This is a junkie here, not some punk hopped up on PCP. He's been on the run for over six hours now, and there's no doubt in my mind this man has needed to get high in that time. He's scared and stupid enough to come back here if it's even him! I'm guessing this boy may even be ready to give up and take his due. We sure as hell won't be using any revolvers up here in the dark unless he starts shooting first, and nothing, I repeat NOTHING, gives us the impression this man is armed. Snap up that revolver, Constable, and get ready for your baton! No one is getting shot up here in this shithole tonight, least of all me. You got that, rookie? Take up your position behind that door, slow down your breathing, and calm your ass down. This will be over quickly, and if this is the perp, we'll be back in the house having coffee in twenty minutes. Be calm! Remember your training!"

Armist reached the top of the landing and looked for a long twenty seconds at the scrawled name Tommy Boy across the dirty door of apartment number twelve. All the hair on his body was on end, and Armist could feel the danger that existed in this mission he was beginning. They would have looked here for Tommy earlier in the day, and there was a chance they were still watching the building, though he hadn't caught sight of them as he entered. Armist had become something of an expert in spotting cops over the years. He reached into his pocket and took out the rusted key, which nestled there beside the small circle of wooden beads attached to the crudely carved crucifix. Slowly, with extreme fear and caution, Armist opened the door to the apartment of Tommy Boy.

The door swung open two feet on unoiled hinges and stopped against something that lay on the floor behind it. Constable First Class Johnny McFadden caught a breath in his throat and held it there in silence as the apartment door came to rest on his size twelve police-issue beat-walking boot. He was not fully in position. If he moved now, the door would swing again, and the suspect would know they were there.

Armist stood on the threshold of the one-room apartment and strained his eyes to look inside. In the flashes of green neon, Armist could see the disarray inside. Clothes and papers were strewn all over the floor, dirty dishes were stacked high on the small table in the far corner, and a foul smell drifted into the hall and mingled with the smell of the dying and the feces of Gutter Gus. Armist was reaching the peak of panic and tried to slow his beating heart and racing mind. Was this something he had to do? He needed a coat, and he could use the quilt, but mostly, he had to deliver the rosary. He could forgo entering this dark apartment with all the implications attached to it. His presence here, if he were discovered, would be hard to explain, but he had made a deal; the coat and anything else that was in here and usable was now his property. He had to collect it as surely as he had to breathe, so slowly, with a mixture of caution, panic, and fear, Armist moved two steps into the apartment.

The smell was worse in here, and Armist tried with all his power to gather his senses and calm the thunderous roar of the pulse in his ears. Slowly, he reached into his pocket for the rosary and the calmness it would bring. He smelled dust, mold, and dirty laundry. There was a combined scent of tobacco, pot, and the deadly blue smoke of crack cocaine hanging on the furniture and in the curtains, and Armist was sure this smell would cling to his newly bartered coat and quilt. He would have to air out these articles in his alley before they would be usable. He breathed in deeply and identified a week-old Kraft dinner caked and drying on a plate in the sink. The buzz of flies replaced the quieting thunder in his ears, and Armist was certain that when the lights were thrown on, hundreds of cockroaches would scurry to their places of safety. Armist understood the cockroaches and their need to remain unseen and protected.

He could smell cheap vodka everywhere in this small space, and he imagined drunken and stoned Tommy spilling vodka on the carpet as he wandered from wall to wall in this drywall cage, pacing in his insanity and addiction until he passed out in his own vomit and piss. The smell of piss was everywhere, and Armist, a self-admitted alcoholic and street urchin, could not understand how any man could live like this. In this filth and in this mire lay the dreams and ambitions of something that had once been human but was no longer, and Armist felt compassion for the beast that had been Tommy.

Armist stood there, unflinching, letting his nose be his eyes and sensing the layout of the apartment. He was about to walk to the street side of the building and draw the curtains so he could turn on the lights unnoticed when his well-tuned nose for danger picked up yet another scent—a scent that did not fit here in this hovel. He breathed in deeply, and his nose and feet began to work in unison. As he took his first step backwards toward the dimly lit hall, he registered the disturbing scent in his keen mind: English Leather cologne! The type worn by that smarmy, arrogant prick who worked at the welfare office. The guy Armist occasionally relied on for some food stamps in the dead of winter, the guy who had always looked upon him with contempt. That was what he smelled here amongst the smells of despair, and it did not fit. There was someone else in this shithole, someone who didn't belong, and Armist turned to flee.

Constable McFadden knew he had been made the moment Armist began to turn. With reflexive speed, his size twelve boot kicked the door toward the jamb. The forward motion of the fast-moving Armist was what actually slammed the dirty door shut as Armist barreled into it with all his weight. Armist bounced off the door just as McFadden moved forward to subdue the unknown perpetrator in the dark apartment, and the two collided with tremendous force.

The wind exited the young constable in a single gush upon the impact of these two big men, just as it escaped from the tired lungs of old Armist. But as the young constable's knees buckled on his descent to the dirty floor, the old bum's knees locked into his fighting stance. Armist swung hard with his talon-like fist and connected solidly with the chiseled chin of the rookie cop. McFadden continued his descent to the floor with no air in his lungs and stars behind his eyes. Just as consciousness was about to slip away, the room was filled with the green glow of neon, and McFadden got an eerie glimpse of the man who had just ended his first stakeout. An old man with a crippled hand holding a small rosary had bested the young constable. As darkness began to fill the eyes of Constable McFadden, the room was flooded with light. As he lay with his freshly shaved English Leathered cheek on the filthy carpet of the filthy apartment, he watched in amazement as hundreds of cockroaches passed his fading vision, running for cover.

Armist spun around to face the center of the room in time to catch the working end of Sergeant McCaskey's service-issued expandable baton in his solar plexus. Armist was still short on the wind from the collision with the other cop, and this last jab to the gut left him weak. He threw a left punch, which hit only air as the older and more experienced cop had struck quickly and then fallen back. As the Armist's fist swung through the air in a wide arc, the Sergeant brought the baton down across the upper shoulders and lower neck of the old street fighter. Armist went down. He lay crumpled over the unconscious young cop, with pain radiating down his spine, but Armist began to struggle to his knees.

Sergeant McCaskey called out a warning for the old man to stay down, but Armist was no longer functioning with any logic or reason. He was reacting to the situation just as he had his entire life. He let his panic fuel his limbs, and his fear direct his punches. There would be no surrender here; tonight, there could only be defeat. McCaskey had been around. McCaskey knew the type of man who was now in front of him, struggling to his feet. McCaskey knew there would be no surrender tonight, so he swung the baton with all his strength, connecting solidly with the forehead of the old scrapper. A nasty purple welt sprang instantly from the jagged scar above the right eye of the old man. His eyes rolled back into his head, and he gracefully fell to the floor behind the body of First Constable Johnny McFadden.

"There," said McCaskey, and as he looked down upon the situation, he could not suppress his smile. He took out his cell phone and snapped a shot of the old bum spooning with the young constable. "That one will make it to the locker room bulletin board," he laughed to himself as he cuffed the old man and began to shake the rookie back into consciousness.

Armist and Johnny McFadden reentered the waking world within moments of each other. The rookie cop awoke groggy and groaning, but the old hobo came to, alert and ready to bolt. He quickly discovered he had been handcuffed, and he rolled up onto his knees with remarkable agility, his wary eyes surveying the room and seeking escape.

"Just calm down there, old timer," said McCaskey as he made his way over to the younger cop. "Let your head clear a wee bit before you think yourself into more shit. Sorry, I had to smack you as hard as I did, but you and I both know it was the only way. That was quite the haymaker you laid on the chin of my young friend here! I bet it's not the first knockout punch you ever threw in your life, and as much as I do admire it, it is still assaulting an officer, and that, my friend, is bad news for you. We are sure as hell going to have to take you in, and you sure as hell are going to spend a night in the can before you get to see a judge. But we are going to take a few minutes here, just you and I and this young constable. We are going to let his head clear, and maybe while we wait, you may want to explain to me how you came into possession of the key to the apartment of a wanted man. Who knows, maybe you can help me, and I can help you after all. It was just a little bump on the chin. Isn't that so, Constable?"

"Right, Sarg," muttered Johnny McFadden as he slid his butt across the dirty carpet and rested his back and wounded pride against the dirty apartment door. "Just a bump on the chin, no harm done."

Armist's eyes darted quickly around the room as his mind calculated options. They seemed few at this moment, and Armist realized he was in big trouble. He had cold-cocked a cop, and that could not go unpunished unless he cooperated fully. To cooperate fully meant he would have to turn on and turn in one of his own, and though he felt more disgust than loyalty to the beast which had been Tommy, he understood that Tommy was one of us and the cops were one of them. He knew where he fit in the picture, and the picture looked grim.

Armist began slowly, "I don't know anything that will help you fellers with this guy you're looking for. I only came here for what's mine, what I got fair and square from the feller who lives here. A few days ago, it was, and I'm only just now coming to collect. I ain't done anything wrong; I just swung in the dark, is all. You boys never identified yourselves as policemen, and I just thought maybe I was about to be rolled. Man's gotta right to protect himself. That's the way I see it, anyway."

"And you are probably right," said Sergeant McCaskey. "Trouble is that no one else will ever know that's what happened. The young fella here found himself a little out of position, and you are a bit craftier than we maybe were ready for, so when you ran, we had no choice but to stop you. And if, in that time, someone forgot to holler out, 'STOP POLICE,' I do apologize, and I urge you to accept the apology here and now because you will never hear it again, and it will never get into any report on the events of this evening. It was all done by the book, procedures all in place, and you have been apprehended. We clear on that, old timer?"

"I suppose," whispered Armist as he felt the panic build and the room close in around him. He had to hang on, and truth be told, he would do all that was required to stay out of a holding cell that night. He lowered his head to avoid the gaze of the cop, and his eyes fell upon the small circle of wooden beads attached to the crudely carved crucifix. He took a cleansing breath, and the panic began to subside.

"Let's start over, shall we? I am Sergeant Jim McCaskey, and this young officer against the door and looking a mite peaked is Constable First Class Johnny McFadden. You may simply address either of us as Officer. We sure would like to know who you are, sir, and we sure hope we can help each other out. So, if you would like to start talking, this would be a good time."

Armist was running multiple lies through his brain simultaneously. It was as though his brain were a slot machine, and all the different stories were rolling by his mind's eye, out of sequence and disjointed. He waited as long as he could for the story to stop with three similar segments locking in place, but it was all happening too quickly, and the lie was just out of reach. He sensed the time to speak was now, and he began slowly.

"Look, officers, I'm just an old man trying to get by. This guy that lives here, this Tommy guy, he owed me some money, and he told me I could come here and get some stuff. Said he didn't need a winter coat and such things anymore, and I could have what I wanted. I don't know him real well, but we're brothers in the street. You know what I mean, officer. So, I was supposed to come a few days ago, but I've been kind of sick, touch of the flu, and so I'm just getting around to it. But I don't know anything about what he may have done or why y'all are here looking for this guy. The truth is, I got a bit of a bum ticker, and you boys near scared me half to death here in the dark. That's why I swung at the officer like I did. I meant no disrespect to the uniform, no siree. I got lots of respect for you boys in blue. Did you know my daddy was a war hero? Died over there in Normandy, so he did, doing his duty, just like you boys are doing yours down here in this war zone. You know, if there was anything

I could tell you, I would, and that's no crap! There's no need to run me in for no night in a cell over a simple misunderstanding. Just a bump on the chin, right? Just like the officer said. And 'sides which, I never been in trouble in the sixty-odd years I been down these parts. I'd hate to get a record now at this time in my life. It might affect my social security or something—who knows? So, seeing as I'm cooperating like I am, why not just pull these cuffs off, and I can go back to my camp and leave you boys waiting here in the dark on this Tommy fella? You can count on me to be quiet, and if I see him, maybe somehow I can get him to come on home, and then you got him! What do ya say?"

McCaskey looked on dumbfounded and let several seconds of silence stand between him and the old man before him, in handcuffs and on his knees in the dirty apartment.

"We can count on you? Are you kidding me? Cooperating! Is that what you said? You just talked for five minutes and never said a friggin' thing! You never even said your friggin' name, old timer, so let's start again. What is your name?"

Armist sat very still with his head down low. He knew there would be no talking his way out. This cop was the real deal, and he meant to take Armist in, regardless of what he said. There were no deals to be had here tonight. Slowly, he raised his head and looked McCaskey in the eye. "I truly am sorry, officer, but I don't have any information for you. I'm asking you now, son, if you will just take these cuffs off and let me be. I didn't do anything, and I ain't involved in any of this business, and I can't spend a night in no cell. I just can't."

Sergeant McCaskey looked hard and long at the old and tired man who kneeled in front of him on the floor of the dirty apartment and believed the man was telling him most of the truth. But not all of the truth, and that was what McCaskey required. "Constable McFadden, please help Mr. Old-timer to his feet and call in for a squad car. We will discuss this further at the station house over some nice hot coffee."

"Come on, old man. Let's get it up and get it moving. I personally need some fresh air. We'll call for a car from out front," said McFadden as he assisted Armist to his feet.

Sergeant McCaskey left the dirty apartment and entered the darkened hall, followed by Armist and then Constable First Class Johnny McFadden. Both men gasped at the smell drifting up the stairwell from the heap of human flesh lying on the steps beneath them. As they moved down the darkened stairway, the hands of the policemen rose instinctively to cover their noses, and Armist grimaced as his hands were cuffed behind his back.

"My God!" said McFadden. "What kind of lowlife bum could ever smell so bad? Someone ought to run him in for violation of the Clean Air Act!"

"Never mind, son, just keep walking and let's get out of here. Besides, it's not our place to judge or scorn these people down here. They have fallen hard, and that could just as easily be you or me lying there in our own shit. Lots of us on the job are just a paycheck away; don't ever kid yourself. We're just here to do a job—serve and protect, that's all, so keep moving and shut up."

"No way, Sarg! Guys like you and me would never end up like these disgusting lowlifes. They make me want to puke. Waste of skin and a drain on society, that's what I say, man. They serve no useful purpose—just a damn dirty bum."

Armist stopped in his tracks three steps down, and half turned to face the young policeman. "He ain't no waste of skin! He's just old, kid. We all get old, and someday you too. His name is Gustav Kaminski, and he did the best he could with life. Sometimes, we don't get it right; that doesn't make us bad; it just makes us down on our luck. I can tell you, he never in his life hurt anyone who didn't need hurting, and he never took what wasn't his unless he had no other way. He had a wife and a kid one time, mother and father, I expect, as well, but he ended up down here, like the rest of us, and he did the best he could. You oughta respect that."

"Yeah, whatever, old man. Just keep walking. I expect you're only a couple of years away from this one down here anyway, right?"

McCaskey turned quickly and spoke with authority. "Well, well, would you listen to Mr. Old-timer? All of a sudden, he knows all about the people down here, including the sleeping Mr. Gustav Kaminski, but he doesn't know jack about our missing Tommy. What a surprise! Constable McFadden, I have been trying all this night to show you the way we do things because I know you are fresh and new. I've been trying all night to get it through to you that not everything you need to know to make it out here on the job is in the procedure book. There are some things you just need to feel. I don't care to hear your theories on how these gentlemen ended up living the way they do, and I resent your judgments on them. I have a grandfather who lived just like they do, and I know he was not a bad person. Some may say he was sick, and even that is not up to me or you to decide. You get that? We are on this job to serve and protect everyone. That includes this gentleman we are escorting to the station and also Mr. Kaminski down there. When you learn that, you will be on your way to being the kind of cop that will make a difference. Now proceed and show these men some respect!"

The three turned and began to make their way slowly down the remaining stairs in the poorly lit hallway. In a single file, they approached the bottom steps and the still form of Gutter Gus. In the dim light, they could see the rise and fall of his filthy jacket moving in time with the low wheezing that was now audible in the hall. The closer they got, the more intolerable the smell of the sick old man became, and McCaskey quickly stepped over and steadied himself on the landing below. He turned and raised a hand to help steady Mr. Old-timer, who was cuffed and moving unsteadily on his feet. Both McCaskey and Armist had settled on the landing when Constable First Class Johnny McFadden began to step over the sleeping Gustav Kaminski, his hand raised to cover his nose as his stomach rolled, nearly losing its contents. He gagged hard twice, and his head was swirling as he began to speak.

"My God!" he exclaimed in disgust. "I don't know about all you said, Sarg. I only know that this is not the way people I need to show respect to smell. This is the way swine smells. Pigs at the stockyard lying in their own shit! This is a human pig, man. He's worse than that—this guy would gag a maggot!"

McCaskey was the first to see Gutter Gus move. In a single, fluid motion, honed from years of experience, McCaskey unclipped and released the telescopic baton with his left hand as he physically moved Armist off to the side and behind him, to the right. As the six-inch blade of Gutter Gus glinted under the single incandescent bulb in the dingy hall, McCaskey swung down hard with the baton.

The young constable was oblivious to the movement behind and beneath him, and his eyes widened in surprise as Sergeant McCaskey turned and released his baton, swinging it hard in a descending arc toward him. In the next second, his eyes slammed shut in shock and pain as the six-inch blade of Gutter Gus pierced through the cotton uniform slacks, broke the skin, and lodged firmly into the left butt cheek of Constable First Class Johnny McFadden. The young officer screamed in pain as he crumbled head-on to the landing below Gutter Gus, the downward swing of the baton skimming his right ear as it passed en route to the old man on the step.

"Run, Armist, run!" were the words falling from the lips of the sick old Gustav Kaminski as the telescopic baton of Sergeant James McCaskey fell across the bridge of his nose, shattering the bones filled with stenosis, sending shards through the thin membrane around his brain and killing him instantly.

Sergeant Jim McCaskey was an expert with the baton. He could take a man down instantly or flick the smoldering end off a cigarette as a warning. His precision with the baton was legendary, and his touch could be gentle or lethal. When Sergeant Jim McCaskey leveled and swung his baton in defense of a fellow officer, his touch was always lethal, and Gustav Kaminski (Gutter Gus, as they called him down here) was dead before either he or McCaskey realized what had happened. The swing of his baton had been instinctual rather than intentional, and in that moment when action was required, McCaskey had reacted with extreme prejudice, as he had been trained. He was at close quarters. His forward swing, with all its momentum, brought him down on his left knee as the baton found its target across the bridge of Gutter Gus's nose. His face only feet away from Kaminski's at the point of impact, their eyes locked together, and in those eyes, McCaskey saw a multitude of emotions.

In Gustav's eyes, as he cried, "Run, Armist, run," McCaskey had seen the gleam of victory. There in his eyes, as the baton fell with all its force, he saw the surprise of the seventy-year-old man. And there, in those eyes, at the moment of his death, McCaskey saw joy, peace, and relief. Whatever the circumstances of this man's life, they held no bearing on his death. The jaundiced eyes of Gutter Gus cleared to a pristine white in that last millisecond, and McCaskey would swear for the rest of his life that Gustav Kaminski had smiled as though he could see where he was going, and it was far better than where he had been.

The spirit of Gustav Kaminski had left, but the ruins of the body he had inhabited here on this earth remained and instantly let loose all the foulness and evil that had filled this old man. A black bile oozed out of his mouth, and his bowels let loose in a long and drawn-out flutter. The stench that had previously filled the small entrance had been a welcome smell in comparison to what was now filling the landing. The death rattle was still underway in the body of Gustav Kaminski. As the body shook and convulsed in death, it rolled off the step on which it had been precariously perched, sliding down the two steps below and onto the squirming body of the injured Constable First Class Johnny McFadden. McFadden had been writhing in pain, trying to pull the six-inch blade of Gutter Gus out of his ass. The blade had found bone and lodged deeply into it. McFadden was in great pain, and as Gutter Gus rolled on top of him, oozing bile, shit, vomit, and blood, McFadden puked violently and, for the second time in ten minutes, fell out of consciousness.

Jim McCaskey sat on the floor of the dirty hallway, looking down upon his young partner and the man he had just killed, and for the first time in a very long time, he wished he had gone to dinner with his wife. He looked up from the tangled men on the floor and out the front door of the building just in time to see a six-foot-three handcuffed man running into the alley of Lexington, and he thought to himself, Armist—what an odd name. His hand came up and keyed the shoulder mount radio.

"Unit twelve requesting immediate backup at the stakeout location of fugitive Thomas Boyle. I have an officer down and a civilian casualty. I am requesting paramedics and the coroner on the scene. Please issue an all-points bulletin for a material witness who has escaped custody. Six-foot-three, in his sixties, handcuffed, and goes by the name of Armist, last seen heading north of Lexington. Be advised this man is not being sought for the assault on an officer. He is wanted for questioning only in the matter of Thomas Boyle."

As McCaskey leaned back on the step and waited for backup, he looked once more upon the empty body of Gustav Kaminski. He felt an emptiness growing in his gut, and tears began to well in his eyes. McCaskey pushed himself slowly to his feet, exited the building, and drew in a lungful of outside air. He looked down his arm and saw there in his hand the bloodied baton and felt a new hate growing in him for Tommy Boy.

Armist ran as he hadn't run in twenty years. Fully erect, cuffed arms pumping, lungs sucking in huge gasps of air, and legs moving in large circles like a garden wind catcher. He felt the night air as it whipped over his forehead and through his hair, and he knew he could outrun the panic. This night was far from over for Armist, and trouble was bound to come looking for him again, but for now, he was outside. For now, there was no more threat of a night in the slammer. For now, he was free as he had been his entire life. As he rounded the corner into the alley off Lexington, he turned back to see if the tough old cop was following and to catch a quick breath. He could see McCaskey standing on the front stoop of Tommy Boy's apartment, taking in huge breaths of air but making no attempt to follow. As Armist turned away into the alley, he spoke aloud into the night:

"I guess an old sleeping dog is still a dog, eh, Gus? One more bad bite in that old dog and one that young punk copper will remember every time he wipes his ass!" Laughing, Armist Hancock slipped off into the night.

THE DREAM

Tommy huddled in a doorway, kitty-corner to the phone booth that stood two blocks from the overpass of the 5 a.m. "A" train. His entire body was coated in a film of cold sweat, and the tremor in his hand was worsening. He held his left hand with his right to try and slow the shaking, humming softly under his breath, trying not to listen to the voice of the "lover." She was back in his head now, beckoning to him, softly whispering her lies. Tommy had hoped she was gone, but the reality was that she had only hidden, as she had done so many times before, allowing him to believe he had some control. His skin crawled with the sensation of a thousand tiny insects, and Tommy knew what was happening to him. He was detoxing.

The pain had many names: DTs, shakes, withdrawal, climbing off the horse, on the wagon—it mattered not what you called it or how you described it; it was pain, plain and simple. It was the death that needed to occur so one could live again, clean and sober. It was the beginning of life for those who had the strength to go on and the end of life for those who did not. Tommy was the latter and understood he was too weak to live through this period of pain. Tommy had not gone a single day in over a year without using crack and booze, and now his body was letting him know the time for repair had come and gone. It was the wake-up call his "lover" was only too happy to deliver, and one which Tommy had never failed to heed—until this night. He was weak, and he was sick, but the knowledge that this would all be over in a few short hours gave him focus. He knew he could fight her off long enough to see her die, once and for all. She would be dead forever, dying in the body, soul, and mind of Tommy, dying with Tommy.

His hand slid into the large pocket of Armist's parka and withdrew the small, green velvet case that carried the legacy of the men in his family. He rolled it over a time or two in his shaking hand and then opened the case to look at the jewelry inside. Looking at the ring and watch brought forth memories of his father and grandfather and the stories they passed to him of his great-grandfather. All three had been good men, from good stock and hard-working their whole lives. Each of them seemed to go through life with an instinctive knowledge of what needed to be done. They always knew the next 'right thing to do,' and they always did it, regardless of the outcome to themselves. Their lives had been long and full, and the love they felt for each other was never hidden behind fear or regret. All they had, they offered up to each other, and all they had learned about living, they passed down to Tommy. It had all been there for him to embrace, and somehow, he had missed it. All of that knowledge, love, and heritage had gone up—literally—in a puff of blue smoke and a snort of cheap vodka.

As he slipped the ring onto his finger, his father's words rang in his ears as though he were there beside him in this dirty doorway, and Tommy supposed, in some ways, the man truly was there. "The love and pride of three generations can carry a man through a lot, son." The words echoed and hung in the chambers of Tommy's mind and heart, and he continued the thought aloud, "If you let it, Pop. It can only carry a man through a lot if you let it."

He took out the old pocket watch and wound it full. In the darkness of the doorway, the luminous digits of the old watch shone out to him like a beacon. It was 2:15 in the morning, and time was running out for Tommy. There were people he needed to contact, and the necessity of making that contact had become paramount to him. Making these calls had, in his mind, become a path to atonement for some of those in his life who had tried to love him and failed. The failure wasn't in the way others had loved him but in the way he had misinterpreted and received that love. It was he who had traveled through most of his life with a distorted and delusional perspective on the world, and he hoped he could let those who had loved him know they had not been at fault. They bore no responsibility for the end result of Tommy's life. He held the watch to his ear and was soothed by the steady ticking of the mechanism. The precision of the Swiss would ensure he did not miss his final appointment.

The obsession with the calls was all that kept his focus now, and he was thankful to Rhonda for helping him realize the need. Her pleading farewell to him as he left the alley echoed in his mind. "What about me?" she had asked. "You weren't even going to say goodbye." And she had been right. He hadn't planned on saying goodbye, not to anyone. What had he become?

The steady ticking of the pocket watch in Tommy's ear had been like a tonic to him, and for the first time in many years, huddled in this darkened doorway, Tommy fell asleep. Without booze or drugs, he had drifted into the deep sleep his body and brain had been craving for so many months— the healing sleep that the body knows it needs but the addiction refuses to allow. He lay unmoving, slouched against the doorway in the dark. A passerby might have thought him dead, as his breathing was barely perceptible, and the rapid eye movement associated with the dream he had fallen into was not visible in the darkness.

In his dream, Tommy was at home, on the farm, and his mother was busily canning vegetables in the kitchen of the rambling old farmhouse. Tommy sat in the seat at the end of the shining maple harvest table. From the chair that belonged to his father, Tommy watched as his mother moved through the cupboards with practiced precision, adding salts and spices into the brew bubbling upon the old wood-burning stove and filling the house with the aromas of Tommy's childhood. The smells flooded Tommy with the memories he cherished—the Christmases spent here with brother and sister, mother and father, the birthdays and anniversaries, but mostly just the regular days. Every day here, in this house, was magical and special, and Tommy was filled with a sense of completion as he sat here, in his father's chair, filled with love.

As the tears welled behind his eyes, Tommy's mother turned from the counter to face him. She started in surprise at Tommy and shrank back into the counter in fear. The Mason jar she had been preparing to fill with the string beans from the garden fell from her hand and shattered on the well-worn floors in front of the cupboards. The shards of glass found their way into the hollowed-out portions of the ash floorboards—indentations carved by his mother's feet through miles of loving journeys from sink to stove. The evening sun beamed through the big window above the sink and was drawn to the glass like metal shavings to a magnet, suddenly filling the room with an abundance of rainbows.

Tommy looked around the room in amazement and was struck by the differences he observed. He had sat at this table hundreds of times in his life and looked upon this room, but somehow, here in the late afternoon of this fall day, it all seemed unfamiliar to him. The rainbows hung on every object and lingered in every corner, and though rainbows had held Tommy in fascination throughout his life, the ones filling this room were different. Something ominous danced within the rainbows, and Tommy began to feel a growing dread. He tried desperately to hold onto the feeling of peace and completion that had filled him only seconds before, but the struggle seemed in vain, and he felt himself fragmenting. In a way beyond his comprehension, he could feel his life falling to pieces around him, broken and fragmented like the Mason jar and scattered string beans on the worn ash floor.

As his eyes traveled about the room, desperately following the dangerous rainbows, Tommy found himself gazing at the woman who, moments before, had softly hummed as she lovingly canned preserves to feed her family through the coming winter. She was stricken with fear. He had seen his mother in many situations over the years and knew her moods well. When she was angry, her brow furrowed like the rows of potatoes in the garden. Her eyes would grow narrow, and you knew then you were in trouble. When she was sad, she became very quiet, and often, her lower lip would tremble slightly. She would cast her eyes toward the ground, and her sadness would fill the room. But when she was cheerful, which was most of the time, her presence was like wildfire. Her joy was infectious, and the light in her eyes would overpower all the negativity in the room. She made you feel as though you were the most important person in the world, and there was no problem too large to overcome. Yes, Tommy knew his mother well—he knew her looks, her smells, her touch—but he did not know her abject fear.

He had never seen this look of terror on his mother's face before, and it filled him with fear. He tried to speak, but words would not come. He wanted to reassure this frightened woman, but each time he opened his mouth, a rainbow escaped into the room. But the "rainbows" coming from the inside of Tommy were not red and yellow and pink and green—these rainbows were brown and black and grey and slate. These rainbows exuded sickness and disease, and as they drifted into the colorful rainbows dancing on the ceiling and walls, their brightness and joy were transformed into darkness and sorrow. Tommy watched in awe as the light was slowly absorbed, and the room grew dark. And then his mother screamed.

The scream was otherworldly and seemed to emanate from the entire body of this small woman before him. Like a pinprick to a balloon, the scream instantly shattered the rainbows, and mingled colors of red, blue, black, and brown crashed to the ash floor; a shard sliced through the sleeve of the army jacket Tommy was wearing and cut deeply into his forearm. Tommy looked down upon the wound laid open by the deadly rainbow and was shocked to see open flesh but no blood. He could see his veins pulsing inside the arm, but rather than blood being carried in the veins, there seemed to be a dark, thick substance, the smell of which began to permeate the room, replacing the pleasant odors of his life.

The scream traveled through the board walls of the old farmhouse and was carried on the wind to the fields beyond the barn where Tommy's father was busy bringing in the hay. In the distance, Tommy could hear the engine of the tractor as it was turned off, and incredibly, in the next second, the door of the farmhouse kitchen was thrown open wide, and there stood Tommy's father. Except it wasn't really Tommy's father. The man here was too large to be the father Tommy had known. Tommy's father was of average height and in good shape—farmhand shape. But this man in the doorway was at least six foot six and two hundred and fifty pounds of chiseled flesh, and he was filled with frightening anger that engulfed him in a dark, hazy aura. The veins at the temples of this man were exaggerated and pulsing wildly, giving him an even more sinister and foreboding appearance. And then, as the man spoke, he transformed into a closer image of Tommy's father. He was and was not Tommy's father at once, and Tommy was left in a heightened state of fear and confusion, and all the while, his mother continued to scream.

Then, as quickly as it had begun, the screaming stopped. In an instant, the room was silent, and the man who was and was not Tommy's father stood in the doorway, staring directly at Tommy.

"What's going on in here, mister? What are you doing in my house, and what have you done to my wife?"

"He's not done a thing to me, John. It's just—I turned and there he was, just looking at me in a funny kind of way. I never heard him come in or anything at all. He was just there, and then something happened to the light, and I screamed."

"Wait," stated Tommy. "Mom, Dad—it's me! What is the matter with you? Can't you see it's me?"

"I can see just fine, mister," said Tommy's father, "just fine indeed. And what I see is a torn-down lowlife sitting in my chair! What I see is someone I don't know calling us Ma and Pa and scaring the life out of my wife. Now, how did you get in this house, and what is it you want?"

"I don't want anything, Pop. I just wanted to come home. That's all I ever wanted, but I never knew how. I just want to stay here, Pop, and have it like it was."

"Listen, mister, I can see you're in a bad way, and we're Christian folks here, so if I can help you, I will. But I need two things from you right away. I need you first to get up from that table and come on outside so we can talk about what's best for you, and I need you to stop calling me 'Pop.' You understand that? I have three children, and only one of 'em ever called me that, and I haven't seen that boy in better than ten years. So don't call me that again, and it's the only time I'll tell you."

Tommy looked on in horror. The form of the man in the door was once more growing, and the anger was seething inside this man, though the words he spoke were calm. *Something is wrong with them! They're afflicted with some* delusion and can't see it's me here in front of them, at long last finding my way home!

"Pop, Mom—it's me. It's your Tommy! I came home, finally. I'm so sorry I've stayed away so long, but I lost my way, Pop. I couldn't find my way back here to the farm. I've been in trouble and done some bad things, Ma, and I need you to help me now. I don't know how to get back to my life."

Tommy's mother began to weep. Her sobs started slowly and jaggedly but soon became powerful, rhythmic sobs she could not control or stop. Slowly, Tommy's father crossed the worn ashboards between them and took her in his arms. He rubbed her hair softly and whispered soothing words into her ear—words this man had whispered so many times before, on so many dark nights. This man, destined in life to be the strong one; this man, who had done his best these last many years to console his wife, trying to keep life normal when life was so far from it; this man, who had to pretend every day that his heart had not been broken by his firstborn child, his Tommy.

Tommy's father looked over the shoulder of his sobbing wife and stared sternly at the man in his kitchen. When he spoke, his words were quiet—eerily so—and they fell from his lips with hate.

"I don't know who the hell you are or what the hell you think you're playing at, but what you just did to this woman is beyond my capacity to forgive. You understand what I'm telling you? I want you out of my house this minute. I won't call the law on you, mister, but I will hurt you, just as sure as I'm standing here if you don't go NOW!"

"But, Pop! It's me! It's Tommy. What the hell is wrong with you? Look. Look here—I got the watch. The pocket watch you gave me. Three generations, Pop, you remember? I got the watch, damn it!"

Silence filled the room, and darkness filled Tommy's heart as he watched the man in front of him grow back into a frightening version of his father—the man whom he had loved. When the apparition spoke, the words were raspy and threatening, and Tommy felt the urge to run building in his chest and legs.

"Where did you get that watch? That watch was my granddad's and my dad's and mine, and now it belongs to my son, Tommy. If you've hurt him, I'll kill you. Do you understand that? If he's hurt, you'll pay!" He began to step out from behind Tommy's mother, who continued to weep with her back and turned to Tommy. As he moved toward Tommy, Tommy began to back away. He had to run, and he did understand that. As he turned to flee, the watch fell from his hand and crashed to the floor amongst the colored and broken rainbows. Tommy ran as he had run a thousand times in his life: from the law, from the dealers, from the people who owned the purses he had snatched, but mostly, as he had always run from himself. He left the kitchen and entered the living room of the house he had grown up in, but the room was no longer there. Instead, there was a vast, dark, cavernous hallway off the kitchen, with thousands of doors leading into thousands of unknown rooms. Tommy was filled with fear and panic, and though he could see no one following, he was certain evil was on his trail, and if he slowed his pace, he would be consumed and lost forever. He had to run, as he had never run before.

There seemed to be no end to the hall, which stretched out before him, and just as Tommy was about to be overcome by the hopelessness building in his soul, he heard the voice. At first, it was soft and gentle, and Tommy was not certain he had heard it at all over the rasping of his own breath. Then it came to him again—sweetly and seductively. It was a voice familiar to him. It was the Lover. She was there, just ahead in the corridor. The hallway, which moments earlier seemed to stretch on into infinity, was coming to a fork. The voice, now stronger and more pleading than it had ever been, came from the left fork in the hallway.

"Come this way, Tommy," it implored him, "come back to me, and all of this will go away. I am the one who loves you, the only one. I will take care of you and give you what you need. Come to me now, Tommy Boy. Come home to me. It is the only home there is for you now."

The words were sweet, and the words were true. So many times in these last many years, the Lover had spoken to Tommy, but never before as she had spoken tonight. Not since the first night they had met, the first night he had partaken of the Lover and knew he could never leave her, had she spoken so clearly. That feeling of contentment, which he had sought for so many years, lay just ahead and to the left of the path. As he approached the path to the left, he began to sob. Tommy was nearly there, almost taking the path to the left, when he heard another voice.

"Tommy, Tommy! Come to me now, Tommy. You have been there with her for so long. She cannot help you any longer, Tommy. She has hurt you. She has made you do the horrible things you have done, Tommy. Come to me now. Come to me where we can help you make it right. Come to Petra, Tommy, as you had planned."

At the last second, Tommy veered away from the left path and took the right road at the fork. But as he turned right, a vast void opened before him. A nothingness that fell away forever, and screaming in fear, Tommy ran into the open space. He fell, over and over, for what seemed an eternity when, suddenly, Tommy saw the bottom of the pit as he sped toward it. Fear and relief filled his body as he raced toward the bright light below, and for the first time in so long, Tommy felt rested—like he knew where he was going. And just then…

Tommy awoke in the darkened doorway with a start. The pocket watch, which had been on his knee, was lying broken on the cement step at his side. His breathing was jagged and forced, and he coughed three or four times from the depths of his chest. His lungs hurt as though he had been running, running for his life. His head flopped forward, and Tommy began to weep. The place he had been so real to Tommy and the image of what he had become was clear in his mind. He knew the truth of the dream. He was unrecognizable. He had become something other than Tommy Boyle. A beast with neither the right nor the will to live was all that was left of the young man his parents had loved.

The answer, the solution, lay with Sister Petra. He must go to the place where he had sent her. She would be there, behind the light at the end of the tunnel, and he would know peace. Tommy rose, looked up and down the darkened street, then walked across the street and entered the phone booth on the corner. With the Green Velvet box, he reached up and smashed the single bulb in the booth so as to remain unseen. He reached into the large pocket of the army jacket and took out six dollars and fifty cents in change, lined it up on the top of the phone, and prepared to make his first call.

ATONEMENT

Tommy stood shivering in the darkened phone booth. The night had turned cool, and the rain had transformed into a light mist that seemed to permeate his entire being. As he stood with his eyes closed, he could imagine all of his internal organs shivering, sending small, earthquake-like tremors out to the edges of his body. He could feel his fingers and toes vibrating, and he was certain that if he spoke at this moment, his voice would sound eerily similar to Katherine Hepburn—shaky and weak, like an old man, like someone who had been used up.

He took hold of the edges of the old army parka and pulled it tightly around his shaking body. With all the willpower he could muster, he tried to think himself warm. He thought of hot summer days filled with hard work and good fun, back on the farm, surrounded by family and neighbors, as the hay was brought in for the winter months ahead. He thought of the dusty hay maw where they had worked and played as children, and the wonderful smell of old and new hay mixed together. He remembered the thrill of falling through the air after jumping off the highest beam in the barn and quickly sinking out of sight into the depths of the old hay about to be covered over by new, fresh bales.

The happiness that came with these thoughts filled Tommy with the warmth he craved. Slowly, deliberately, he imagined his organs warming up. First his liver, then his spleen, then his stomach and kidneys, and eventually his lungs. Soon, the trembling was gone. He leaned against the glass wall of the darkened phone booth and marveled at the control he had over his own body. Maybe, thought Tommy, just maybe I am not as bad as I thought. Maybe it was just a really bad day. Maybe just a spot of bad luck. After all, I'm not as bad as Trip.

At the same moment, this thought occurred to him. He saw the image of Trip as he was thrust in front of the uptown bus. Tommy gasped aloud in the dark space where he huddled, appalled at the reality that struck him. He had forgotten what he had done! He truly was a monster! He truly was a person so self-absorbed that he had been blind to everything that transpired around him. He had lived in oblivion—oblivious to his own shortcomings and defects, oblivious to the needs of every person he had known.

He was so shaken by the disturbing dream he had had, and so equally elated by the memories of his childhood that he had invoked, that he had simply forgotten the heinous acts he had committed earlier that night. Just that quickly, and as he had done throughout his life, he moved those thoughts to that dark spot in his mind. Into one of the many frightening rooms that stood off the never-ending hallway, which had come to Tommy in his dream. The rooms into which he dared not venture, for within these rooms resided the truth of who he had become and who he had once been. These rooms were the warehouses of his grief. Here, he stored all the bad memories of his life, all the deeds that needed to remain secret.

Tommy looked up at the coins on top of the payphone and knew the time had come. There was no further delaying the action he was about to undertake. His swan song, his farewell to this shitty world and the few people in it he cared about. He would start with his sister, Beth.

Beth was the baby of the family and had been quite young when Tommy left the family farm. She was a child who had come to his mother and father late in life, the result of their passion rather than the good family planning preached to them with great vigor by Father Mike, their parish priest. The birth of this child had been difficult for Tommy's mother, and like her labor, her recovery was slow and painful. Something had changed in Muriel Boyle with the birth of this child. A darkness that had lived deep within her and had been kept at bay for so long had now risen to the surface, and for many hours of many days, she simply looked upon the worn floorboards of the kitchen and slipped deeper into depression.

From the darkened doorway leading to the family room of the rambling farmhouse, Tommy had observed his mother—her eyes cast downward in sadness—and somehow came to believe that he had caused her pain and sorrow. Tommy never understood what he had done to take the joy from her world, but he became convinced it was his fault. His father was so vexed by the state into which his dear wife had fallen that he, too, was behaving differently than he ever had before. The man whom Tommy looked to for strength and direction was moving through their home uncertainly— not knowing what to say, not knowing what to do, and for the first time in his life, unable to fix his family, unable to be the man.

His father was frightened, and Tommy had seen that fear and made it his own. Tommy was not to blame, but

Tommy needed to be blamed. For reasons he would never understand, Tommy took on all the pain of the family, taking on blame in a situation where no blame existed, and at that moment, he began to overcompensate for his behavior. He began to seek acceptance and approval from his mother, and most especially from his father, by caring almost exclusively for this new child, this new addition to their family, this child who had changed their world.

It was a defining moment in the young life of Thomas Boyle. It was one that a therapist or psychoanalyst would seize upon and declare, "This is it! This is the where, when, and why of what you've become! The origins of the alcoholic, the birth of the addict, the rising of the ugly head of co-dependency—this is it!"

But none of that mattered to 12-year-old Tommy Boyle. None of that was even considered. All that was important to young Tommy Boyle was that he had discovered a way for those he loved to see him. He had found a means by which he could earn the love he no longer felt he deserved from his mother. He could make it right with her by doing more for her. His father would see him take control and love him for the strength he was displaying. It was a false courage, however, designed to conceal the growing fear and anxiety that was descending upon his world.

All of these mistaken ideas came to Tommy in a flash and were, in truth, the beginning of the lie that would become his life. If the Tommy Boy who now stood huddled in the darkness of a phone booth on a wet and filthy inner-city street thought long and hard enough—with an honesty he did not possess—he would understand that this moment long ago was the first time he had heard the voice of the 'lover.' Quietly, lovingly, she had nudged him toward the lie and helped him to justify an ingenious act with a favorable outcome. On that day, Tommy had become a liar.

And so Tommy began to care for Beth. His dear mother had slipped so deeply into postpartum depression that she was able to do little more than feed the child, leaving Tommy to do the rest. He dressed and bathed Beth. He rocked and walked her when she had colic, and he sang her to sleep when the young baby wailed so long and loudly for the love of her mother that Tommy's heart nearly broke. Through two seasons of tilling, planting, and harvesting, Tommy's father worked the fields. There, he found an escape from a situation he could not control, and left Tommy to maintain the house to the best of his ability. There was help from neighbors during the days when Tommy was in school, and the walks to and from St. Jude's elementary with his little brother Billy, the invisible child, became a time of refuge for Tommy. He could escape the dysfunction of his once near-perfect home life on these walks to school, but he could not escape his mind or the voice that lived within it.

He had developed a deep love for Beth. He had formed a bond that typically exists between a mother and child—a bond born of nurturing and care, one that rarely develops outside the maternal relationship. He had moments when the love he felt for Beth was so overwhelming that it seemed as though it would burst from his heart and fill the entire world. But there were other moments when he was filled with resentment and hatred for the child. These were the times when he would hear the voice, and these were the moments when the voice spoke the truth: "It's not working. Your plan has failed. Your mother is not getting better, and she does not love you more for the role you've assumed." Neither was his father proud of the courage Tommy had displayed in filling the family breach. In fact, his father had become more distant than ever as the years passed. His mother's depression and his father's despair filled their small world, leaving Tommy as the caretaker, Billy the lost child, and Beth the unwanted baby—all of them victims of life.

The voice told him he deserved better, that he, Tommy, would one day show them all. He was fourteen now, and soon, he would be gone from this family. The thought of leaving became so real to Tommy that he could close his eyes and see himself walking down the road, bag in hand, heading for a better life. A thought that a couple of years earlier would never have occurred to him because, back then, he couldn't imagine a better life than the one he had. His life and mind were so constantly filled with conflict and contradiction—a battle between love and resentment, compassion and contempt—that the young man who had been Tommy Boyle slowly began to disappear, and the man who would be Tommy Boy was beginning to form. There, within the dark places of his mind, a creature was coming to the fore. This was a creature that thrived on fear and anger, fed on resentment and cruelty. A creature that would remain in the shadows, speaking softly to this confused young man while luring him into a world of pain and selfishness. Taking him from the painful reality of his world as it existed and transporting him to the world of fantasy that he craved. All the while, filling him with a false sense of entitlement—one that made it unlikely for Tommy to ever consider the possibility that the life he had once cherished could return to him.

And then it did. Just as quickly as Tommy's world had vanished, it returned. Without warning or explanation, Tommy's mother had climbed out of her depression and rejoined the family. It was a beautiful October afternoon, and Tommy had been rushing home from school with Billy in tow. Beth would be waiting, a toddler now, accustomed to their schedule. Tommy would come home, and together, he, Billy, and Beth would have a snack, then take a walk down to the river, and read a story before the evening meal. Tommy could not be late this evening; Mrs. Tilley, the neighbor woman, would be in a hurry to get home to her own children and start their family supper.

As Tommy crested the hill and began his way down the lane to the farm below, he knew there had been a change. There below, in the valley, with the waning October sun shining down, Tommy could see his mother hanging out the wash. Every few seconds, in amongst the flapping sheets on the line, Tommy would catch a glimpse of Muriel Boyle— the woman he loved with all his heart. She was hanging wash on the line, which meant she must have done the wash, and that was more than Muriel Boyle had done in one day in over two years. Tommy stopped short in his tracks, and Billy walked into the back of him with a thud and a groan. Together, the two of them looked on in silence.

A passerby, seeing the expression on their faces, might have guessed they were watching a lunar eclipse or that perhaps Barnum and Bailey were parading a herd of circus elephants down the long lane to the farm below. Such was the awe on the faces of these two boys as they watched their mother hang their father's long johns on the line, the legs flowing out toward them in the wind. There at her feet, sitting in the laundry basket and looking up with love, sat Beth, a smile on her face larger than Tommy could have imagined. Beside her, stretched out on the ground, chin propped in his hand and beaming with joy, was Tommy's father. Tommy began to cry, overcome by sadness and joy simultaneously, while Billy began to run. Billy ran, yipping and laughing as he had not done in two years. Billy ran to his family, and Tommy stood on the hill looking on. Looking on alone and full of fear—looking on from the outside, as he would from this day forward.

As quickly as it had begun, it had ended. Their lives resumed the path they had once followed, all but Tommy's. His parents were filled with love and joy, their lives once again wonderful. They simply picked up where they had left off, as though nothing had happened. They never discussed it. It was as though his father feared that acknowledging what had happened would bring it back, and his mother was filled with guilt that could only be endured through denial. Tommy was left with no place to put his fear and anger. These unresolved feelings of guilt, shame, and responsibility festered, burrowing into Tommy's mind. On that fall day, Tommy Boyle set out on a lifelong journey of denial. There was no fanfare, no fond farewells to the boy who had lived an ideal life—only a growing emptiness that would one day consume his world.

Tommy slowly walked down the hill and over to the wash line where his family had gathered. He stood silently in front of his mother, and in the fading fall light, he saw a single tear in her eye as she watched him approach. Muriel Boyle took her son in her arms—the son who had raised her daughter these past two years without complaint, the son who had filled the breach in their family without understanding how or why it had occurred. She held him close for a few moments without speaking. Then, in a moment that felt surreal to Tommy, she laid a slender hand on each cheek and looked deep into her son's eyes. The warmth from her hands flowed through him, and in that moment, Tommy felt the closeness to his mother that he had craved for so long. The October sky behind Muriel Boyle had become aglow in the dying moments of the setting sun, making it difficult to see the features on his mother's face. And as Tommy strained to see the love he hoped was there in his mother's eyes, he sensed that she was about to speak. He waited in hope and silence, waiting for the words that would make everything okay. And just as she began to speak, the child at her feet, Beth, began to cry.

She cried out first for Tommy, then for Mommy, and as they both bent to pick up the crying child, their eyes met once again. For a moment, Tommy saw something in his mother's eyes—a fleeting look of fear and panic. It was a panic difficult to explain and impossible to describe. It was as though the basic, instinctual need to mother this child, a need lost for two years, had suddenly filled Muriel Boyle. All the strength of nature that had been suppressed by this horrible depression suddenly surged forward. "No!" cried Muriel Boyle as she aggressively pushed Tommy aside and scooped Beth into her arms, holding her tightly to her chest.

The swiftness and aggression of the moment took the family by surprise, and for a moment, they all stood in silence. Tommy straightened and took a step back from his mother as his father rose to his feet. Billy, standing off to the side, slowly began to move away from the family, finding safety and comfort by putting distance between himself and them. Tommy's mother held Beth tightly, tears rolling down her cheeks, astonished by her own actions. She saw the hurt and fear on her son's face.

"Oh, Tommy," Muriel began, her voice breaking with a sob, "Tommy, please forgive me. I'm so sorry. I don't know what came over me."

But Tommy never heard her words. He had shut down upon seeing that look in his mother's eyes. At that moment, he knew he had been abandoned—by his mother, by Beth, by them all. His father came up behind Tommy and wrapped a big arm around his shoulders, resting his calloused hand gently over Tommy's heart. He spoke quiet, soothing words. They were meant to comfort but did not. They were meant to reassure but fell short. They were meant to reaffirm, but they fell upon damaged, unhearing ears.

"Tommy, it's okay, son. Your ma didn't mean anything by it. This has been a long, hard time for all of us, but now it's over. Your ma is back, and we'll all get back to normal. There's no need for you to work so hard taking care of the wee one. No need for you to give up all your time. You can go play ball with your friends, get back to studying hard for college and such. We're going to be okay now, Tommy. We're all back together. We're going to be okay."

It was a declaration from his father—a statement of fact. "We were all going to be okay," whether true or not, because dealing with the fallout of the past two years was more than any of them could bear. From that moment on, they all moved through life as if nothing had happened. From that moment on, the little girl Beth, who in a very real way had been Tommy's own child, never left their mother's side. From that moment on, Tommy Boyle allowed resentment and hatred for the little girl he had once loved to grow and grow.

Throughout her life, Beth tried to love Tommy. The bond that had been established between them had never left the heart of the young child as she grew into an adult. She reached out. She helped. She did all she could to save her big brother, Tommy, and in return, he stole from her. He had embarrassed and insulted her and her family, and he had physically abused her. Through all these years, Tommy Boyle did everything he could to drive his sister Beth away, and through all these years, she continued to love him without condition. He could not make her hate him as he hated himself. And now, tonight, in this phone booth at the end of his tether, Tommy Boy finally realized that he had never stopped loving his sister Beth. He had never stopped needing her love. He had only moved it to a place where it could never hurt him again.

She had done nothing to Tommy. She was a baby when he was damaged, but for all her life, he had made her pay. He had made her the object of his anger, and now it was time to set the record straight while there was still time. Slowly

and with great trepidation, Tommy dropped the first quarter
into the payphone.

ARMIST

Armist sat trembling in the dark on the cold cement floor in the emergency exit stairwell of the boarded-up Odeon Theatre. The tremors were not from the cold, nor were they from the fact that he had not had a drink in over two hours. He did not tremble and shake from the anger he felt toward Tommy Boy, though the anger was there. Tommy Boy had drawn him into a situation that left him in danger and on the run, and for that, Tommy would have to pay—when the time was right and if the opportunity presented itself. He did not shake and tremble from the exhaustion in his limbs, though his limbs felt rubbery and numb. It had been many years since Armist had run so far and so hard for so long. He tingled all over from the run, and his chest ached as the phlegm, which had settled comfortably in the bottom of his lungs, had been superheated and forced to move through his organs. He was trembling with such intensity that, were he not handcuffed, he believed his arms would flail away from his body, propelled by some unseen force.

He looked down in the dim light of the adjoining alley and could see the welts where the cuffs were coming close to rubbing through his leathered skin, and he considered all the reasons why he might be trembling. He considered them all and dismissed them in turn as his eyes fell upon the small circle of wooden beads attached to a crudely carved crucifix hanging on the ring finger of his left hand. There it had hung since he scooped it up from the dirty carpet of Tommy Boy's hovel. How could it still be there? After the fighting and, the running, and the hiding, how could it still be there? He looked upon it and understood the talisman to be the source of the trembling, and he was at once filled with fear and apprehension. Armist could feel his blood boiling and panic rising to the surface, and he focused all his attention on the small circle of wooden beads, trying desperately to regain some composure. There were things he needed to do, and this place would only be safe for a short time. He needed a plan, and he needed it quickly. Now was not the time for him to fall apart.

With great resolve, Armist willed his two huge hands together, removed the talisman from his gnarled, talon-like finger, clasped it firmly between his hands, and slowly began working the beads through his fingers. He felt a calmness descend upon him, and though his heart rate slowed, his mind did not. Armist was filled with conflict. There, deep in his gut, was the knot that Armist had spent a lifetime interpreting. Armist's knot was often present but always subtly different. It was there when he was frightened or panicked. It was there when he was criminal or violent, and it was there to tell him when to run or when to fight. It was often present, and it had become an accurate gauge of events and feelings for Armist. But this night, here in the cold dampness of this concrete haven, he could not discern what his knot was telling him to do, and it filled him with uncertainty.

Thoughts flooded his mind as he sat alone in the dark of the alley. He was angry and confused. This talisman was his. By right of the street, he had acquired it in a fair trade. It was all he had to show for the trade, as his encounter with the cops had screwed him out of the rest. Not keeping it as his own was contrary to everything Armist and his family had lived by for some six generations. It was his. Yet, even as these thoughts of ownership and right entered his mind, so did the thought of getting rid of this charm. This small tribute to a God he did not believe in or trust—a God who had never done him any favors in his long life—had only been in his possession for a couple of hours, and in that short time, it had brought turmoil into his world.

He was in trouble, and he was not running away from it. He was running toward it. At this very moment, he should be heading out of these five square blocks, which had become his world, and going to a place where he was not known and would not be found by the cops. The very thought of moving to a new district filled Armist with dread. He was known here, and he had his territory, which would never be disputed. In a new part of town, he would have to scratch and fight out his spot once again, and he feared he was too old a man for such a new beginning.

His thoughts turned to old Gustav, lying dead in the stairwell, and Armist was filled with sorrow. The old man had died for Armist. "Run, Armist, run!" were the last words Gutter Gus would ever speak. Gustav was too old for the life, and he knew it. He was dying the death of all street men: slow, dirty, and without dignity. Gustav knew he would not make the winter, and Armist was happy that, in the end, Gustav was able to go down fighting. The legend that Gutter Gus had faded with the life force of the old man, and he had become a joke among some of the newer residents of the back world. This act of courage, defiance, and street freedom would echo off the filthy walls of dark alleys and linger on the lips of bums huddled around open fires, drinking wine. Gutter Gus had cemented his place in their nighttime tales, and Armist was glad for it. But still, Gustav was gone, and Gustav had been a friend.

Armist tried to control his wandering thoughts, but the faster his fingers worked the small circle of wooden beads, the deeper his mind receded into his past. His life and the memories that it consisted of were not pleasant. There were no dreamy, long-ago moments of his mother tucking him into bed and reading a bedtime story. He had no memories of riding high on his father's shoulders and reaching for the clouds. None of the wispy, foggy thoughts of a normal childhood applied to Armist. His mother had gone mad, and his father had been killed almost at the moment of his birth. The chaos of those early years, before his mother had been committed, had only led to the brutality of his years in the state's care. And it was during those impressionable years as a ward of the court that Armist developed his philosophy of life. Those twisted and horrific years had misshapen the heart and mind of a young boy. He had grown into a cynical and sometimes cruel adolescent. The adolescent had become a cagey and dangerous man. The dangerous man had become a tired and failing legend, sitting handcuffed and hidden in a concrete stairwell.

Armist looked down at the talisman and was consumed with red-hot hatred. These intrusive thoughts had long ago been put to rest, and their resurrection was not welcome. He had become so proficient at burying his tragic past that he had been able to create a new reality. In his mind, his reality was the truth, and contained no pain, no loss, and no fear. He had managed to come to a comfortable place of denial in his world that allowed him to function and survive. But here tonight, in the dampness and cold of his buried thoughts, Armist realized that his present was indeed defined by his past, and that he would never be able to run far enough away to leave it behind.

Armist raised his bound hands to his brow and let the talisman dangle there in front of his eyes, and for the first time in fifty years, Armist began to cry. He wept tears of sorrow, fear, and pain. He cried for his mother and father and the life of which he had been cheated. He cried for Gus, Trip, and Tommy. He cried for the nun, and he cried for himself. The tears fell from his open eyes onto the lap of the soiled army surplus fatigues he had worn as a testimony to a fallen soldier. All the while, he gazed at the small circle of beads attached to the crudely carved wooden crucifix. Each falling tear cleansed a spot in the hardened heart of Armist, and as this river of regret flowed from within him, he began to feel a comfort that he had never before experienced and did not recognize. He did not know how or why, but he suddenly knew with certainty that he was going to be okay. There was something more in this world for him to do. He would not perish here in these five square blocks. He would not die the undignified death of the street, dirty and cast out. He lowered the talisman to his lips and held it there as he breathed out the last breaths of despair and hopelessness. Slowly, Armist raised himself to his feet and walked out of his concrete tomb.

Bob Gideon had reported in to dispatch and then went to radio silence as he entered the alley west of Lexington. He had a large area to cover, and he relied on a quiet arrival at the places he needed to go. Showing up unannounced, without alerting anyone by police radio, often yielded better results. It gave the streeters no time to concoct a tale and often forced the truth to come out quickly. The downside was that he was left alone and unaccounted for in the dark of the back alleys. It wasn't standard procedure, and the bosses wouldn't approve, but Bob was confident in his ability to get the job done in what he referred to as the "war zone."

He had completed a sweeping search of the back world in the five square blocks that were his beat. Working in concentric circles from the outermost boundaries inward, he had covered every alley and doorway he knew of. Along the way, he'd come into contact with about eighty of the local residents—most of whom he recognized, though a few were new faces. He had gone in hard on some, soft on others, called in favors, and made threats, but gathered no useful information. If any of them had seen or heard anything of Tommy Boyle, they weren't talking. For the first time that night, Gideon began to doubt whether he would find the felon.

As he approached Lexington from the east, finishing up directly across from where he'd begun his canvass, he switched on the audio of his radio. There was a lot of chatter on the line, and Bob slowly pieced together the events that had just unfolded. As he emerged on Lexington, a block north of Tommy Boy's residence, an ambulance sped past him. Lights flashing, sirens wailing, the ambulance carried rookie McFadden to County Hospital. Further down the block, in front of Tommy Boy's place, stood the coroner's van. On the stoop leading to the rundown apartment sat Sergeant James McCaskey.

McCaskey sat with arms dangling, head nodding, as two officers from the Special Investigations Unit stood on either side, questioning him. With reluctant cooperation, he recounted the events that had led to the death of Mr. Gustav Kaminski—'who had a wife and a kid; a mother and father at one time, I expect'—but now lay dead, oozing in the back of a coroner's wagon. He had been put down by the city's finest, dispatched by the book. No one liked the SIU, but everyone knew there would be questions, and now was the time to deal with the details.

As Gideon approached the stoop, the SIU detectives crossed the "T"s and dotted the "I"s, then turned to leave. Sergeant Jim McCaskey raised his head and looked into the eyes of the approaching Bob Gideon. In McCaskey's eyes, Gideon saw the sadness that filled the man. McCaskey looked old and tired. It was nights like these that drove an officer to the bottle and often to an early grave. Nights like these, when a life had been taken, left an officer alone, with no one on earth to talk to, no one on earth to offer comfort. Bob recognized the look and ignored it, because that was just the way it was.

"Evening, Bob," McCaskey said, keeping his sorrow just beneath the surface. "Hell of a thing went down here, Bob. Sure could have used you instead of that damn rookie. At least the kid isn't dead, but he'll have a good 'remember when' every time he wipes his ass. Fucking rookies will get you killed quicker than the plague if you're not careful."

"I hear you, Jim. At least it's one of them under the sheet, not one of us. What the hell happened? Did you have Boyle in custody, and who's lying in the wagon?"

"No, not Boyle. Some other guy came into the apartment, a big guy. We got the drop on him, but he'd already made us and tried to run. Cold-cocked the kid, and I took him down with the baton, and managed to get him cuffed. Tried reasoning with him, but the big old guy wasn't in a talking mood. He was plenty scared, though—not sure what of. We didn't have much on him, except he had a key to the place and had assaulted an officer. I'm sure he knew more than he was saying as for the guy under the sheet—unrelated, as far as I can tell. I don't get it, really. One minute, he's just an old dirty bum having a sleep on the steps. The next, he's coming up swinging a knife. He didn't leave me many options, you know what I mean? He'd already stuck the kid when I popped him. They knew each other, though—him and the big old guy. The big guy said the old man was called Gustav."

"Gutter, Gus! I'll be damned," Gideon said, surprised. "He's been living around these streets since I was a kid. Bit of a legend, you might say. I'm surprised to hear he came at you like that. He's been really sick. I've been expecting to find him dead in an alley any night now. Been in bad shape, really fragile."

"Well, that might explain why he checked out, you know. I didn't think I delivered a lethal blow—just quick and hard, you know, reflex. I still don't get why he came at us, though. The kid was bad-mouthing him all the way down the stairs, and the big old guy defended him a bit, but still, Gutter

Gus must've been used to being called down as a bum. He wouldn't try to stick everyone who said he stank. Maybe it was about the other guy. Maybe he was going after him. I just don't know, Bob."

"Did you get an ID on the big guy?"

"I did. I put it out on an APB. You must've been off the air. I got his name, but not from him. I got it from the dead guy as he was swinging the blade. They were his last words—a funny name, too. 'Run,' he yelled. 'Run, Armist, run.' And run he did. Last time I saw that old boy, he was rounding the corner into yonder alley at about 30 miles an hour, arms and legs pumping to beat the band."

"Armist? Are you sure about that?"

"Yup, pretty sure. Does the name mean something to you, Bob?"

Gideon looked up and down the street, slowly playing back the events of the night in his mind. "Yeah, the name means something, but I can't put it together with the description you're using. There's an Armist who's been living down here his whole life, but he's not a big man like you described. He's kinda hunched over and feeble-looking, drags his left leg a bit like Bela Lugosi. Sure as hell wouldn't be running like you said. Maybe someone's using his name, but what the hell would a fella use the name of a street bum for? I can't imagine there are two Armists living down here. That'd just be too weird."

"Well, it ain't your run-of-the-mill name, I'll give you that. But I'm pretty damn sure I got it right. I can have them check with McFadden at the hospital, and see what he heard. What I do know is that I'd really like the chance to speak to Mr. Armist one more time tonight. But for now, I'm going in for paperwork and questions—you know the drill."

"Something isn't sitting right, Jim. I'm going to check around. You say you saw this fella running north into the alley, but not an hour ago, I watched old Armist limping down the road heading south. He was wearing a red shoe and a blue shoe—that's been his calling card for the last few months. Two different colored shoes. You remember the shoes this guy was wearing?"

"Well, Bob, to tell you the truth, I don't remember the shoes. But if he was wearing one red and one blue, and I didn't notice, then the soon-to-be ex-wife is right, and I need to retire. You'll call me if you find this fella with the peculiar footwear, right? I'd like to stay in the loop on bringing Tommy Boyle in, maybe make some sense out of a dead guy named Gustav Kaminski."

"You'll hear from me first, Jim. Count on it."

McCaskey walked down the three steps to the dirty pavement, slid into the back of the unmarked cruiser with the two SIU detectives, and pulled away from the curb, heading toward the station. Officer Gideon stood atop the stoop and looked down over the small crowd that had gathered. He looked north, then south, then back over the crowd. One of them knew where Tommy Boy was, and he was more determined than ever to set things right.

Armist emerged from the depths of the emergency exit stairwell of the Odeon Theatre a different man than the one who had entered. Just as he had physically transformed from the hunched-over, unassuming figure that haunted the edges of society to the tall and powerful man he truly was, he had transformed mentally and spiritually. He was no longer the man who had walked into Tommy Boyle's apartment in search of a good quilt and a warm coat. The change in him had come quickly and miraculously, without any desire of his own. Change, to Armist, had always been the enemy— something he had managed to avoid throughout his existence. But now, here in this wet and dank alley, it had been thrust upon him, and it had not come without a price. It had come with the shedding of tears and the realization that his life, up until that point, had not been great—but his life was not over. Even at his age, there was an opportunity to find some peace. All he had to do was move away from the past.

Armist felt cold all over, oddly foreign in his own skin. He was no longer who he once was, and a this new person seemed to have taken residence in his soul. This person was calm. This person, who had taken shape inside him, had somehow banished a lifetime of anxiety, fear, and panic— emotions that Armist himself had never been able to escape. As he moved toward the end of the alley, his steps were slow and uncertain, and he wasn't sure if he was comfortable with the new calm that had descended upon him. For so long, he had found comfort in chaos. Agitation, panic, and fear had been his guiding forces. They had told him when to fight, when to run, when to hide. Now, with those feelings gone, Armist didn't know how to proceed. He wasn't uncertain, but he was cautious. The clarity of thought he was experiencing was new and unsettling. For once, he was being led by his heart rather than his mind, and it was an organ he had no experience in trusting.

But one thing was clear: he had to keep going. For the first and only time in his life, his path was obvious and unbending. He must, and would, do the right thing. The talisman had to be returned.

Armist made his way to the far end of the alley into which he had fled and now stood in the shadows beside an abandoned truck. He watched the street traffic for fifteen minutes, searching for anything irregular, anything that would signify danger. When he was satisfied that the street was clear, Armist moved out of the alley and halfway down the block, where he entered a darkened doorway that stood across from Polly Ann's Parlor.

Polly Ann was a not-so-young woman who had spent the better part of her life on the wrong side of the law and on the wrong end of a needle. She had worked every aspect of the sex trade throughout her life in order to feed her addiction and eventually ended up doing long-term time in a federal penitentiary. She had endured a hard life, but while she did her five-year stint, she got clean. She was smart enough to use the programs available to her inside, and after a time, the yearning for heroin left her. She had the help of many good people, both in and out of the prison system, and one day at a time, she built a new life for herself; she did some small business training and upgraded her education to a post-secondary level. Her newfound lease on life had reunited her with an estranged extended family that was more than ready to help Polly Ann build a new business when she reentered society.

Yes, Polly Ann had changed her direction, but she never forgot the road that brought her to this new way of life. She knew where she had come from, and she knew where her talents lay. There was money to be made in the misery of those who lived in the darkened corners of the world, and Polly Ann was intent on making it. Sex had been her trade when she was sick, and sex would be her trade now. Polly Ann's Parlor was a sex, piercing, and tattoo shop. She was located mid-block on a full block of biker bars and strip joints, and she enjoyed a thriving business. She rented porno videos, sold sex aids, and would snap a ring or punch a hole in any part of the human body without hesitation—she had even done a few piercings on dogs and, one time, punked up a parakeet. She had a wide range of tattoos and a couple of good artists working all night, taking the drunken dollars off tough-guy bikers and the women who loved them. As long as you had the cash and the request was within the law, you could get what you wanted at Polly Ann's.

Armist watched calmly from the alley as a couple of men left the store with videos in brown paper bags. The after-bar rush had not started, and Armist could see Polly Ann through the front window of the shop talking to the tattoo artist working the night shift. After a brief conversation, the man grabbed his jacket and left the store, probably going for coffee or a sandwich before the crazies came out to play. Armist let a couple more minutes pass, and when he was certain she was alone in the store, he began to cross the street.

Polly Ann was down here in these parts for her own gain, and the payoff had been good—just as she knew it would be. The financial rewards had been the reason she willingly and cleanly reentered this dirty world. It was her only driving force at first, but after a while, she came to know some of the people who still lived in this hellish region. It had never occurred to her when she rented the location that there were people living here—mostly drunks and druggies, all down on their luck—but people just the same, just as she had been, just as she was. She had become friends with some, enemies with others, and a friendly ear and voice to anyone who wanted to hear her story. Anyone who wanted to believe there was a way out of the life they lived could find a sympathetic heart and a point in the right direction at Polly Ann's. This den of iniquity had become Polly Ann's ministry to the street and her way of giving back.

Armist was one who had become a friend. Polly Ann was the only woman Armist ever spoke to and the only woman who had ever shown him any kind of compassion or respect. He could always count on a warm cup of coffee, a sweet smile, and a quick joke from Polly Ann. She had become one of the few people on earth that Armist would trust. Every time he turned up, he was greeted, and every time he left, he was told the same thing: "You ever need anything, Armist, you come to see Polly Ann." She always said it with a laugh and a wink, and Armist never quite knew if she was being serious or just having him on. He had always wondered about that, and as he pushed open the door to Polly Ann's Parlor, he figured he was about to find out.

Armist entered the store to the sound of an electronic bell and immediately heard Polly Ann call out from the back room, "Be right there." He took up a position to the left of the door, away from the big front window and behind a chest-high rack of porno movies. Armist tried to avert his eyes from the movie covers displaying all sizes of women in all stages of undress, performing all manner of unspeakable acts. He had spent a lifetime disliking and not trusting women, ignoring and avoiding them at all costs, Polly Ann being the only exception. But try as he might, Armist could never completely ignore or avoid the stirrings he felt when looking through the window at these raunchy displays of raw sex. Having never been with a woman or in a healthy and loving relationship, Armist mistakenly took what he saw on the shelves as the truth of lovemaking and intimacy—a truth which left him uncomfortable. Armist closed his eyes tightly, held the talisman between his big, cuffed hands, and quietly waited for Polly Ann.

Polly Ann walked out of the back office with a box of double-A batteries in one hand and a two-headed electronic dildo in the other. As she looked up from the device, her eyes registered surprise, then glee, then concern as she saw the looming form of Armist. She stopped dead in her tracks.

"Armist! Oh my God, what is wrong?"

"Wrong? Why should there be anything wrong?"

"Well, jeez, let me see. Three years now, I see you every day at some point for a cup of green tea. Rain or shine, cold or hotter than the hubs of hell, it is always out there on the sidewalk. You have never come through the door of this shop, and now here you are, halfway through the night, standing there pretending not to look at the porno movies.

Inside! You don't do inside, Armist, remember? So it makes me think there is something not quite right."

"Well, I suppose, when you put it that way. And I am not looking at these here pornos."

"Armist, why are you so big? You standing on something back there behind that rack? You look different all over—what is going on?"

"Well, I suppose this is how I really look, when I am being me, which ain't often, I guess. I need some help, Polly Ann, and you always told me I could come here for it. So here I am, and I'm hoping you are true to your word." Armist slowly raised his cuffed hands and rested them on the top of the video rack.

"Oh my God, what're you into? There's been a lot of sirens and activity going by here tonight. Is that about you? Armist, I know I said to come here, and I will help if I can, but you need to be straight with me, man. Is me helping you somehow going to get me in the shit? You know that flatfoot Gideon has been in here a couple of times tonight already looking for that loser, Tommy Boy. Please don't tell me you're somehow hooked up with all that. And there was an ambulance that went screaming by here not half an hour ago. Have you hurt someone? You need to start talking, Armist— what is going on?"

"Polly Ann, let me talk. I wouldn't be here except I need something quick, and then I'll go. The ambulance was for old Gus. He's dead. Not me—the cops did it. Yes, the cops are looking for me, and it's about Tommy Boy, but I ain't involved! Not like they think. I only did a trade with him for some clothes, and now they're trying to run me in for questioning. Old Gustav helped me make a run for it, and they kilt him for his effort. I don't want any trouble for you or for me. And there is something happening to me that I can't really figure out yet. It's to do with this cross I got from Tommy. It's making me feel different and think different, and I know there is something I'm supposed to do. It belonged to that nun—the one Tommy attacked. I think I gotta give it to the people at that mission. I want to get rid of it, and I want to keep it all at the same time. It makes me scared. But I gotta get these cuffs off, and that's why I came to see you. I know you sell these things here, and I was hoping you had a key."

"Well, good Lord Almighty, Armist. That's more words than I've heard you speak at one time in all the while I've known you. You surely do seem different. You better come on into the back, away from the street, and we'll see about getting those police-issue cuffs off you. Lucky for you I only sell the best, and I got a master key."

Armist followed Polly Ann through the store and into the crowded office. He looked around uncomfortably at all the surfaces, which were covered in various types of sexual devices, none of which Armist could imagine a use for. As they reached the desk, Polly Ann turned quickly and thrust the two-headed dildo into the cuffed hands of Armist.

"Hold this," she said, and Armist let out a shriek any schoolgirl would have been proud of, dropping the two flopping rubber dicks to the floor. Both Armist and Polly Ann stood in their tracks, looking at the dildo that lay abandoned on the floor between them. Then Polly Ann started to laugh. As she laughed, her eyes lit up with the glee Armist had noticed when she first saw him in the store. It was a look the old girl wore well, and the goodness and beauty deep within her escaped through those eyes and entered into him.

He began to laugh. It was a labored laugh at first, but it was real and honest laughter, and as it spilled out of the bottom of his belly, Armist could not recall the last time he had laughed. Tears welled in his eyes, and there was a snort or two as it continued. It rolled out of his stomach unobstructed and filled the room. Armist was a big man, and he had a bellowing laugh that the world had not had the opportunity to enjoy for a long time. His laughter came unobstructed by his knot, and suddenly, Armist realized the knot he had lived with—the knot he had often relied upon—was no longer there in his stomach where it was meant to be. He could laugh again at last.

Polly Ann's head had leaned forward into Armist's chest as her laughter subsided, and through her childlike giggles, she said, "Oh my, Armist! How I do love you!" And he stopped laughing. It took a moment for Polly Ann to sense the change that had come over Armist, and slowly, she lifted her head from his chest and looked up into his eyes. Set deep in the creviced and scarred face of Armist Hancock was a set of indescribably blue eyes. They were the blue you could find deep inside an iceberg, and they seemed timeless. Polly Ann saw in those eyes the sadness deep within this man who had fended for himself for more than fifty years, and she saw in those eyes the child Armist had never been allowed to be. And there was something else—something different, something new—and Polly Ann could not define this change that she was witnessing in him.

"Armist, I am sorry. I didn't mean to laugh. I didn't want to upset you. I know you're worried—it's just that it was funny the way you screamed, is all."

"It's okay, Polly Ann. It felt good to laugh. It's not that. It's just that no one has ever said that to me before."

"Said what, Armist?"

"No one ever said they loved me before. Not even kidding like. No one, ever."

"Oh, Armist, I am so sorry. That is terrible. Everyone should have someone to love them. And who says I was kidding? I've been watching you a long time, Armist, and I don't talk to every fella living on the street in these parts either. But I always had a soft spot for you, Armist, and the truth is, there's something going on with you. I can see it! For one thing, you seem to be a foot taller than when I saw you this afternoon. But it is more than that, Armist. I can see it in your eyes. You've changed! I want to know all that has happened to you, and I want to help. But first, let me get those things off your hands. They really don't suit you." Polly Ann turned to the desk and opened the top drawer. She rooted around for a second and turned back to Armist with a single silver key in her hand.

"Stretch 'em out, big boy. Old Polly Ann is about to set you free."

They sat and talked for a short time in the office of Polly Ann's Parlor. Armist retold the events of the evening to the best of his recollection, and Polly Ann listened in silence, all the while watching as Armist's big hands worked the small circle of wooden beads. She watched him tell the tale in complete calm while sitting in the small confines of the cluttered office, and she knew she was witnessing the steady transformation of Armist Hancock. She knew beyond any doubt that she would help this man, regardless of the possible repercussions to her, because she understood it was not every day a six-foot-five miracle walked into your life. She had entered into hell in her time and walked out the other side, on the path to a clean and sober life by the grace of God. She had witnessed the miracle of rebirth in many people, but none as quickly and dramatically as what was unfolding here in front of her that night.

"Armist, let me see if I understand what you are saying," began Polly Ann, picking her words carefully. "This talisman, the one you are holding now, the one you say is making you feel funny—it belonged to the nun from the mission, is that right?"

"That's what Tommy said to me. I know he was telling the truth because it changed him, too. He wasn't a punk so much anymore, and he seemed like he knew what he had to do. Then I did, too. I knew I had to give this thing back. I know it sounds crazy, but I can't find the right words to explain what it is."

"It's okay, Armist, it doesn't sound crazy, and you are not crazy. I can see that. And I can see you are different. But if Tommy told you he killed the nun, how are you supposed to give it back, or who are you supposed to give it to?"

"I don't know, Polly. I'm getting so confused and scared. I ain't smart at figuring things out like you are, and I was hoping you could help me, sort of tell me what's best or if I should run away or what!"

"Armist, I don't think you can run away from what's happening to you. I think we have to see it through and just trust it's going to be okay. You haven't really done anything that wrong yet—maybe withholding evidence, hitting a police officer, fleeing a scene. It sounds bad, but I know cops. What they really want is Tommy Boy, and you are incidental to that. I think I know a man who can help us if you will trust me. At this mission—the one the nun worked at—in the basement, there's a group. They meet there every night after hours, after the bars close at two a.m. They are friends of Bill, and I sometimes go there. The man who opens and closes the basement also lives and works at the mission. He's a good egg, and I trust him. He will know what we do, and he should help us."

"I don't know, Polly Ann. I only have two friends. One was Gustav, and the other is you. I don't know this Bill you're talking about, but I know he isn't a friend of mine, so why would he want to help old Armist? And how would I get over there anyway? I'd have to go right back past the place where they killed Gus. They'll be looking for me there for sure."

Polly Ann began to chuckle but quickly cut it off as she saw the look of despair drawing over Armist's face like a curtain. "Oh, Armist, I am sorry. I am not laughing at you. It's just Bill ain't that kind of friend. He's a friend to all of the folks like us—people who are down on their luck, whose lives are out of control. There ain't really a Bill there—it's just the name of the guy who started these groups to help us. The fella at the mission, his name is Hank, and he will help. I will go with you. The cops are looking for a big old boy wearing handcuffs, not a tall, handsome gentleman out walking his lady! We'll go together, and together, we'll figure this thing out."

Armist raised his big hand to the scar above his right eye. The scar was hurting him. The scar always hurt Armist when he couldn't figure out what he should do. He could think quickly when he was fighting over his turf or facing down some new adversary, but at times like these—times when he needed a good plan—all he ever got was a headache. He used to listen to his gut, but his gut wasn't talking. As he looked up at Polly Ann, he knew in his heart that she would help him. For the first time in his long life, Armist turned his fate over to another, and suddenly, he was no longer alone.

It was two in the morning when the people from the After Hours Friends of Bill meeting emerged from the basement at the mission for cigarettes and fellowship. There were five or six regular members and two newcomers. The two newcomers were so new they could barely stand, and as some of the old-timers tried to make headway with the younger of the two, Hank, the nighttime pastor of the mission, was trying to convince the older drunk to come in, sleep it off, maybe stay a couple of days and get some warm food into him. Armist and Polly Ann watched from the shadows as, two by two, the crowd walked off into the night, heading toward their homes. As they passed by, Armist heard the young one telling one of the sober members, "I'll be back tomorrow night. Gonna get clean, you'll see." His voice was slurred, but there was a glimmer of hope buried in it. Armist watched as the group slowly dispersed into the darkness. The older drunk stumbled along, cursing under his breath, and a moment later, Armist heard a trash can rattle as it was knocked over, followed by a slurred, "Go fuck yourself."

They had crossed over to this end of the neighborhood unseen, just as Polly Ann had predicted. She had brushed Armist's hair, put a ball cap on him, and dressed him in a leather jacket that belonged to her nighttime tattoo man. She hooked her arm through his, and away they went. "Just like an old married couple," Polly Ann had said, and for the twenty minutes it took them to cross over, that's just how Armist imagined it to be. Being part of something had been an exercise in imagination for Armist all of his younger years, but as he grew older, Armist had trained himself not to dream or wish for something he could never have. But for twenty minutes tonight, Armist pulled down the wall and allowed himself to dream. The fantasy of being 'an old married couple' felt real and good to Armist, and as he huddled in the shadows with Polly Ann, he may have been happier than he had ever been in his sixty years of life.

Slowly, they emerged from their shadowy lair as Hank was picking up the cans with smoldering cigarette butts in them. Hank was bending to pick up the next can as they broke through the darkness. He paused cautiously and directed his attention to the pair coming into the light. After a moment, he recognized the woman in the alley, and a smile came to his tired face.

"Polly, is that you there? Hey, it's great to see you! You are a little late though—we've finished up the meeting. Who's your friend?"

"Listen, Hank, I have brought this fellow here because he is in a bit of a bind. He needs some help, and he does not trust too many folks around here. I told him you were a good guy and that you might be able to give some help or advice or something. I know it is late, but can we talk to you, Hank?"

Hank squinted in the dim light and looked hard up and down at Armist. "Do I know you, friend? There is something familiar about you, but it's kind of hard to say out here in this alley. Why don't we all go in for a while? It's warm inside, and there's still some hot coffee in the pot. We can talk for a while, and then the pair of you can help me clean up for the night; does that sound okay?"

"Sounds fine," said Armist, and they followed Hank into the Mission.

For the next half an hour, Hank quietly sipped on a bad cup of coffee while Armist recounted his tale. He told of his encounter with Tommy in the alley where Armist lived, and he told of his struggle with the police and of the valiant death of his friend, Gustav Kaminski. The words came from Armist in the form of a confession rather than an accounting of events. Each word Armist spoke was clear and earnest. It was as though each and every word was of sacred importance, and each and every sentence carried him closer to freedom and redemption. There had been many testimonies given in this basement over the years, but none had ever been so spellbinding. None had ever been delivered so quickly and honestly. This weathered and street-beaten old man was childlike in his countenance, and though he had sinned in his life, he had not lived a sinful life.

Armist was not comfortable in this low-ceilinged basement haven, nor was he comfortable in the presence of this man, Hank, but he continued. When the panic was building in his chest, he tightly squeezed the small circle of wooden beads attached to a crudely carved crucifix, and when he could not find the right words, Polly Ann squeezed a little tighter on the big left hand she held onto, never letting go. When he was done, there was silence in the room. Armist looked uncomfortably from Hank to Polly Ann, both of whom had bowed their heads and closed their eyes, and Armist realized that they had been praying.

Hank was indeed in prayer. He had been ten years at this mission, seeking his own redemption. He had been an ordained priest who had fallen from grace and had been removed from his order. Such was his addiction to alcohol and sex that even his church, which had become proficient at covering up and hiding away errant priests, would no longer tolerate Father Hank Quinn. He had been called to the church in grace and had been asked to leave in disgrace. The God that Father Hank had been taught to know, the God his studies revealed to him at the seminary, was said to be a God of wrath and punishment. But the God that Hank was led to know through the addiction that had brought him to this mission was a God of love and understanding, patience, and forgiveness. It was this God that protected drunkards and fools, who made Himself known to addicts through other addicts, to whom Hank now prayed. Hank had witnessed many life-changing events in his ten years of work and recovery at this mission, but he had witnessed many more lost and failed lives. There were people who would die for fear of reaching out to embrace the Spirit of something they could not trust or understand. But here tonight, in the childlike innocence of an old man, Hank was witnessing the Spirit at work. Hank was witness to the transformation of a soul. He was overcome with love and hope as he spoke his silent prayer of thanks to God for bringing him humbly to this place and allowing him to be of service. 'For God so loved the world....'

Hank looked up at Armist and smiled. He set down his cup and stretched across the table, taking both Armist's and Polly Ann's hands in his own. "Bless you," he said. "Bless you both."

"Well, thanks, Hank, but I was hoping for a little more than that. I was hoping you would tell me what the hell I should do!"

Hank laughed softly and looked deep into his eyes. "The blessing is really all you need, Armist, but I do get what you are saying. What exactly do you want from me? How can I help?"

Armist uncurled his talon-like hand and let the talisman fall to the table between them. "This here cross—it ain't mine. It belonged to her, your friend the Nun. I want it, and I don't want it, if you know what I mean. It has some power or something, and it makes me feel different. I knew from the moment I took it from Tommy in the trade that I had to give it back, but I don't know who to give it back to. Polly Ann said you could take it because you knew her, the Nun. That's where I gotta start, and then I don't know. I need to get away from the cops because they want to lock me up. I ain't so sure I can handle that, Hank, not even now, after all that's happened."

"Her name is Petra, the Nun you are referring to, and she has been a friend to me and this mission for a long time now." Hank reached down and picked up the small circle of wooden beads attached to the crudely carved crucifix. "These beads, they do not really belong to her, Armist. They do not belong to anyone, really—they just belong. She told me the story of how she came upon these beads and how it affected her life. God alone knows how they affected the life of the one who owned them before her, and God alone knows how many fingers have worked these beads or for how many years. Armist, these beads are symbolic of something deep and mysterious and beautiful, but they are not magic. They are just beads. They are very old, and they hold within them the essence of all those who have offered up prayer with them, but the power you describe, Armist, is not from the beads.

The power you feel, the power of the Spirit which you say makes you feel different—that power comes from God, Armist. It is within you just as it is within me and Polly Ann. It is the power of love from God. It is a gift we all have, but a gift that not all of us can find. Sometimes, we find this gift when we are not looking for it, just as you have, Armist.

Sometimes, the gift finds us, and for those who are blessed enough to be found when not seeking, the gift is powerful. Your life will not be the same as it has been, Armist. That much you must accept. There are many things from this day you do not know or understand. Many things that Tommy also does not know or understand, but you and he must find strength now to change the thoughts and ideas you have lived by. These beads are yours now, Armist. They are yours until they will be another's. These beads can give you comfort. They are a real thing you can touch and see, but make no mistake—the power is not in the beads; it is within you, as I have said. Trust in your heart, and you will know what you need to do. Do you understand, Armist?"

There was a pause and a short sarcastic laugh as Armist began to speak. "No, I don't understand! All that stuff you said—I ain't smart like you and Polly. I am just a bum who lives in an alley, not someone with some gift. Everything I got fits in a box. That's all I am, and that's all I got, and it's all I want. I just want to be left alone. I don't know what I'm supposed to do! You are supposed to tell me!"

"Listen to me, Armist. What you have and where you live mean nothing. We are all the same inside, in here," said Hank, clutching his chest. "You need to believe, Armist. You spent fifty years out there on your own, living a hard life, fighting and drinking. How many men have survived that kind of life as long as you have? Not many, I know, Armist. I see it here every day. You think you were lucky all these years, but the truth, Armist, is that we all have a purpose. There is something we are all given in this life to do. You have been given the gift of survival all these years.

You say you are not smart, Armist, but you are! Look at how you have lived! You are wily. That's what you are. If what you have told me is true, then Tommy Boyle is about to make the biggest and last mistake of his life. I don't think God wants Tommy to die at his own hand, Armist. I think He wants Tommy to live."

"I told Tommy his dying would not fix things, but to tell you the truth, I kinda feel like it maybe would not hurt things either. You think I got some gift, but it doesn't feel like a gift to me. You got me wrong. I spent my whole life running away from things, and I ain't fixing to change the plan now. No offense, Hank, but you are not giving me the help I was looking for. Big fancy words are just getting me more confused, and now I'm feeling kinda mad, even." Armist looked to Polly Ann in frustration. "Polly, what do I do? I am scared."

She looked into his blue eyes and saw that he was scared and that he did not know which way to turn. She got it. She understood what Armist was saying. She understood what Armist was feeling. She, too, had spent a lifetime running and avoiding the next right thing because it was usually the next hard thing to do, and she had not been good at the hard stuff. Armist was a simple man who had lived a life of simple needs, and suddenly, it had all changed. He had not asked for the change, and he did not welcome it. Just as she and Hank had not willingly embraced a new lifestyle, neither would Armist. He was older now, but he was still in good shape, and there could still be a different life for him, just as there had been for her. Polly Ann had been mentored by another person, just as she suspected Hank had been. She had been walked through the first days of her new life just as she suspected Armist would need to be. As rough as it had been for her, she knew the road ahead for Armist would be rougher. She had always been told her time would come to give back what she had been given, and tonight, the time had arrived. She took both of Armist's hands in hers, and she looked deep into those piercing blue eyes.

"Armist, you trust me. I know that. You have told me that before, and I believe it. I would not do anything to hurt you, and I have done all I can to help you. But now you are going to have to do some things that maybe won't sit well with you. You don't understand what is happening to you or how you fit in all this. Neither do I, really, but I believe Hank when he says we just have to believe it is all happening as it is supposed to, for a reason. This man, Hank—he has never lied to me. He has helped me lots, just like I am trying to help you. Do you believe that, Armist?"

"I trust you, Polly, and I believe you. And I know something in me is different. I can feel that, but that doesn't take away the scared. I am still scared, but not so much when you are with me. Will you stay with me and help me?"

"I will, Armist, all the way to the end. I promise you. Now, let's get out of here. I think we need to go find Gideon. He will help us, Armist. With his help, we can figure it all out and finish this thing. Then maybe you can come on home with me and have a night indoors."

BETHANY

It seemed as though an eternity had passed in the space between the drop of the last quarter and the first ring of the phone at Bethany's house. By the time the second ring had finished, Tommy felt a new sweat forming under the old sweat that encompassed his body. As the third ring began to chime, Tommy felt a weight in his stomach that he was certain would sink him deep into the ground beneath the phone booth. The beginning of the fourth ring was the signal for him to lose his nerve completely and to begin questioning his plan. With the fifth ring came the hope of the answering machine.

Tommy had partaken in many a frank and honest discussion with answering machines throughout his career as an alcoholic and addict. He had difficulty accessing thoughts, words, and feelings with actual people, but the relationships he had developed with answering machines in the last several years would have been the envy of any psychoanalyst. He had lived life as an emotional cripple, never able to find the courage to express love, anger, or any other emotion in a rational manner. When talking one-on-one with another human, or when speaking through a telephone to another actual person, Tommy inevitably turned mute. The firewall he had built as his protection from the world had also managed to keep Tommy hidden. He had layered himself with years of buried emotion. Repressed fear and anger—the origins of which Tommy no longer even recognized—had conspired against him and had left him unable to express himself in an acceptable manner. In the beginning, the booze and dope had served him well in lubricating his heart, mind, and tongue. While they were present, he could speak on issues more than superficial. But as the years went on, the effects of the drugs and booze also turned against him until he was eventually unable to carry on any type of conversation that held any depth or meaning.

It had become a bit of a game for Tommy. There had been many years before he was completely altered, when he would try to keep loose contact with his family. Occasional visits turned to occasional phone calls, and then to calls when he knew no one would be home—calls to the machines. Initially, his relationship with the machines was quite nice. He knew when his folks would be at church, his sister at work or school, and his brother Billy was almost always away with work. He would call and leave regrets: "Sorry I missed you both. Things here are going good. See you soon, Dad. Love you, Mom," and the call would be over. His feelings of guilt could be sated without emotional injury to himself.

At the outset of Tommy's decline, he did not want his family to know the extent to which he had deteriorated as a human being. In his messages, he tried to maintain the façade of a guy who was just a bit down on his luck, looking for a bit of a break. But with the broken promises and the self-imposed isolation, Tommy's family began to understand the depths to which he had fallen. Soon, the requests for a short loan or help with rent fell upon deaf ears, and the money stopped flowing. It was his sister's husband, Carl, who cut off the cash first, soon to be followed by his little brother, and finally, his father and mother, close behind. Carl had years before witnessed a close friend who had been financially bled by a using brother and was wise to the ways of manipulation. Billy had more money than he could spend but was easily convinced by Carl—who had filled the gap of Big Brother—to stop enabling Tommy. Unfortunately, his dear parents, who refused to acknowledge the very worst about their beloved Tommy, were the last to accept the horrible truth, but not before they had put themselves into serious financial woe.

When the cash stopped, so did the calls—for a while. But Tommy was in steady decline, and it was not long before he resorted to more criminal means to attain the money he required. With each petty theft, his resentment toward the family grew deeper and the chasm between them wider. It was their fault people were being robbed, and it was their fault Tommy was directed to live in the shadows and on the wrong side of the law. And then the calls began again. Driven by booze and anger, he would call the machines, which now represented to him all the difference between him and his family. They were living high, and he was living low, and none of them cared. He would spew out his hate, sending litanies of curses and vulgarity over the landlines at his parents, who had never done anything but love him. Bethany would be called a whore and blamed for ruining the family, and he would always end with a threat of physical violence to her husband, Carl. For Billy, he saved the worst. Poor, quiet Billy, who only ever wanted everyone to be happy and to notice him, was an easy target for the vile and twisted mind of an addict.

Eventually, the calls to the machines stopped forever. As Tommy sank deeper into the depths of his addiction, there was no energy left for the calls. The hate he felt for his family paled in comparison to the hate he had developed for himself. As the weeks and days became months and years, he had all but forgotten them. They had become a distant and distorted memory of a life of which he had once been a part—a life he could never be a part of again. The texture of the memory was directly related to his state of mind and the stage of inebriation in which he found himself. At times, he thought fondly of Sunday afternoons in the kitchen with them all, and he would shed tears of remorse for a family he had lost. Other times, he focused on the perceived wrongdoings that had befallen him at the whims of his family members, and he would rant and rave in insane fits of anger. Finally, almost magically, he had reached a state of complete dependence on his 'lover,' and in so doing, he had become completely numb to all the feelings he associated with his former life. They had all become truly dead to him, and he had found in the deep blue smoke of the crack pipe a feeling he would mistakenly identify as peace and serenity. The feeling, in fact, was one of unconditional dependence and absolute defeat. It was here, in this state of denial, that Tommy had existed, until the events of this very day.

Midway through the fifth ring, the connection was broken on the other end of the line. Tommy recognized the groggy, just-woken voice of his brother-in-law.

"Ya, hello." Carl coughed and cleared his voice, and Tommy stood frozen in silence.

"Hello! Is there anyone there? If this is a crank call, you can fuck off. It's three in the morning. Goodbye!"

In his mind's eye, Tommy could see the anger on Carl's face as he readied to slam down the receiver. All that Tommy had become flooded into his mind, and he understood, with no further doubt, that the calls had to be made. Regardless of how hard it would be, he needed to close out his life in some order.

"Wait! Hello," he shouted into the phone. Tommy waited for a reply, but none came. The silence seemed to stretch on forever, and just as he was about to hang up, just as he was about to curse himself for the coward he was and had been, he heard Carl.

"Is that you? Is that you, you piece of shit! Tommy Boyle! Have you called to threaten me or call down Beth? Are you brave enough tonight to talk to me rather than the machine? Or just drunk enough! Or is it just about money or getting out of jail? What the hell reason could a bum like you come up with for calling here at three in the morning?"

Tommy could hear the jagged breath of Carl through the phone and could imagine the seething anger that would be covering his face like an ugly mask. Tommy was glad he was miles away in a phone booth and not standing on the front porch of Carl and Beth's home.

"Carl, it is me, Tommy. You are right, but I don't want anything. Please don't hang up. I just want to talk for a few minutes with Beth. I just want to say hi to her and hear her voice once more. That's all. I don't want any trouble."

"Well, Tommy, you don't have to want trouble to bring it. It is just your nature. Every time you just want to say hi to Beth, every time you take it upon yourself to call up and leave one of your two-minute little Hallmark messages on the machine, we spend two months watching her walk around in misery. Did you ever even stop to consider what it does to her each time you call? Did you ever consider what it does to me? Watching her mope around and cry, reading the obituaries and hearing about dead John Does on the street! Why can't you leave us alone? It has been three good years not hearing from you. Three good years, and I will be damned if I am going to let you change that."

"Carl, listen, please. I know you are angry, and I know all that you have said is true. I have been lost for so long, and I blamed all of you for all my problems. I know what I am, Carl, and I know what I have done, and I just want a chance to make it a bit better. I just want to come clean with you and Beth, Mom and Dad, and Billy. That's all I want, Carl—just a chance."

"Are you kidding me? Just a chance! You have been given more chances than anyone on earth, and you just keep fucking them up. You are like a virus to this family, a bad smell. Everything you do trickles down to the rest of us and stains us. You could never live long enough to know what you have done to this family, so don't even bother trying to pretend. And don't you dare call your folks? Your mom has been sick, real sick. Some days, she barely remembers who she is, let alone the rest of us! Those are the good days, according to your old man. Those are the days she ain't asking about you or crying over you. So no, I don't think I will let you speak to Beth, Tommy. I think I will just tell her it was a wrong number; after all, it really is like that, isn't it, Tommy? You're just like a wrong number!"

"Carl. I am not coming back into any of your lives to cause trouble. There has been enough trouble, and I can't do it anymore. You're wrong, Carl, in what you said. You see, I am hoping to live just long enough to know exactly how I have hurt this family, and just long enough to try and convince them I am sorry, and to let them know it was all me, not them. I know you are mad, and as I said, you've got every right, but I need to talk to my sister one time. Five minutes is all I want, and you will never hear from me again, Carl, I swear it. Listen to me. I am as clean and sober as I have been in over ten years. I know you are a good man, and I know you have spent your life trying to protect my little sister, protect her from me. I know I have hated you, and I know I have done you all wrong. I am sorry, this time it is real, Carl, so please, just let me talk to Beth."

A silence grew between them as Carl considered the words he had heard from Tommy. He had heard so many words, so many times, from this man over the years. He had watched Tommy manipulate and steal from his family. Tommy had stolen their money, stolen their hope, and quashed their dreams. Carl had always been the one to pull them all back together, to get them past the latest disappointment and prepare them for the next. He had been immune to Tommy's cons and lies from the beginning. He could always see the angles Tommy was playing, and he always knew that Tommy's motives were self-centered and driven by addiction. But tonight, he had listened to Tommy as Tommy had pleaded, and tonight, he heard something different in the voice of this brother-in-law he had come to despise. Tonight, standing in his boxer shorts at the bottom of the stairs, he could understand what his wife and in-laws had held onto for so many years—the hope that one day their Tommy would emerge and come back to them. Carl sensed the emergence of Tommy but doubted that he was coming back.

"Tommy, what's going on really? Why are you calling here this late? I don't want Beth upset, so just tell me what you need. Are you in trouble?"

"I just need to talk to her, to tell her the truth about something, that's all. Please, I will never ask for anything again. Just let me talk to Bethany."

"Okay, Tommy, hang on. I will go get her."

Tommy heard the clunk of the receiver as Carl set it down on the table in the hall and went to get Beth. He leaned his feverish forehead against the cool glass wall of the booth in which he stood and slowly began to take deep breaths. He was terrified. He had not spoken a word to this girl in three years, not a civil word in five, and now he was about to ask her to understand and forgive. He had no right. His legs had begun to tremble so violently that Tommy thought he would collapse in the small booth. His weight, slight as it was, seemed too great for the fragile bones in his legs to support, and slowly, he slid down the glass wall and came to rest on his haunches.

He waited in silence and breathed, somehow keeping the panic at bay. As Tommy squatted in the darkness on the floor of his glass confessional, he cast his eyes to the sky and looked upon the stars with wonder. At first, he was convinced he was hallucinating, but the harder he gazed into the night sky, the more he was certain that the brilliance of the stars was a reality. How many times in his fifty-two years had Tommy looked into these same heavens and not seen the beauty that existed there? His thoughts drifted back to the nights of his childhood on the farm he once loved and the wonder he held for the night sky. Not since those dark nights had the stars shone so brightly for Tommy. He had lived in a world without color or beauty for so long that he had forgotten that color and beauty existed. All about him had been grey and ugly; his days spent in darkness. The shadow of his addictions had covered him like a heavy woolen cloak. At some point during this night, Tommy had cast off this cloak of dependence without being aware he had done so, and now, while he looked into the beauty of the night sky, he understood his 'lover' was gone. There were no voices in his head; there was only quiet. A quiet he knew would last forever, just as he knew 'forever' would not be far away. Tommy wiped a single tear from his cheek and took in a long, steadying breath as he heard the receiver being picked up from the table in the hall.

"Tommy. Is it really you? Carl said it was you. Are you there, Tommy? Hello?"

"Hey, Bethy, it is me. It's Tommy. You will never know how happy it makes me to hear your voice."

"Oh, Tommy, we thought maybe you were dead this time. It has been so long now with no word. Mommy never would say so, but Daddy thinks you are dead. He is being strong for Mom because she has been sick, but I know he sits up at night looking down the road, wondering where you could be. He is so hurt, Tommy, and he is so mad. I am sorry, Tommy, for whatever it is that has caused you to leave us all. Please tell me it is over. Please tell me you are coming home."

Tommy choked back a sob and feared his heart would explode through his chest cavity right here and now in this booth, but he breathed deep and tried to begin.

"Beth, listen to me now. You need to hear and know some things about me. You need to understand some stuff that I have come to know in my heart—come to know only this very night. But it is important that you hear. It is important to me and also to you, Carl, and those babies of yours."

"They aren't so much babies anymore, Tommy. They are big kids now, both in school and doing well. But there is another on the way. He will be here soon, Tommy. I wish you could come here, Tommy, to be with me when I have him. We could talk here, Tommy; we can talk all you like here. I can speak to Carl, and I will convince him it will be okay. Just tell me you will come."

"Maybe, Beth, maybe, but not tonight. Maybe I'll think about it tomorrow, but there's something I need to do tonight. Some things I need to set straight. I haven't been much good at setting things straight for a long time now, kiddo, and I thought I should start with you, Bill, Mom, and Dad." Tommy paused briefly to consider his words. The things he wanted to tell his little sister had been deeply buried in him for more years than he could recall. He feared that the unearthing of these old wounds and hidden resentments might appear as a condemnation of Bethany and his mother rather than what was intended—a purging of his soul and a plea for forgiveness for the wrongs he had done.

"You're going to have a baby, and you know it's a boy! That's great, Beth. Two boys and a girl! Just like Mom. You're a good mom, Beth, you know that, right? And you were a good kid and a good baby, Beth. I never told you that, did I? It was a long time ago, Beth, but here, where I am tonight, I can look up at the stars, and it feels just like yesterday when I would rock you to sleep in my arms. Mom was sick, remember? I took care of you, Beth, and I loved you. I loved you more than I could ever express. Sometimes, it felt to me like you were my baby, Beth. I swore I would never let any harm befall you back then when I was just a kid. I loved you more than I knew."

Tommy fell silent and lost himself in his memories so completely that, as he breathed in deeply, he could smell the fresh baby smell of the newborn in his arms. The musty smell of the phone booth was suddenly filled with the aroma of baby—baby powder, baby oil, and just pure baby, soft and smooth and without fault.

"I remember some, Tommy. And Mom told me the rest, and Tommy, I'm so sorry. I'm so sorry for how you were hurt. No one knew, Tommy. Back then, things were different. No one knew about depression and postpartum stuff, but we don't have to let that ruin things today, Tommy. Why can't we just let it go?"

"I think I can let it go, Beth. I think, in my way, that's what I'm doing. But I wanted to tell you I'm sorry. I'm sorry for how I treated you all these years. You only ever wanted me to love you, and I did. I really did. I just forgot how to show you and everyone else. Please don't ever tell me you're sorry, Bethany, and please don't feel that way. You never did anything wrong. You were just born a beautiful little girl. I swore back then I would never let anyone hurt you, and here I am, the only one who ever did. There are so many things about me, Beth, that you don't know. So many things I've kept hidden from you, so many bad things I've done. I wasted my life and made a mess of things, and I tried so hard to blame everyone else for it. I knew how you felt. I knew how much you wanted to help and save me from myself, and I took advantage of it—for money, spite, or just to be plain mean. I did it on purpose, Beth. I did it to make my sick world seem a bit better, I guess. I hope you can forgive me, Beth. I hope you don't hate me."

"I could never hate you, Tommy. I love you. I always have. It doesn't matter what you've done or where you've ended up—not to me, Tommy. I'm not stupid! I know you were using me for money, and if not for Carl, I would've never stopped giving it to you. He convinced me, Tommy, that giving you money was no different than giving you the drugs or booze—that I was helping to hurt you! I just couldn't do that, Tommy, not then and not now. So, if you're calling for money, know that I won't give in. I'll help you any way I can, and I'll get Carl to back off if you want to come here with me, and together, we can try to get back on track. Tommy, I want you back in my life! Mom needs you back in her life. Dad says she's like she was when I was born, but worse. You could help her too, Tommy. Please just come and let us help you."

"Please, Beth. Yell or scream or tell me you hate me for what I've done. I can handle that! Tell me you'll never forgive me; that's what I expect to hear. That's what I'm prepared for. Don't be nice to me because it'll make it harder for me to do what must be done. You say you don't care what I've done or where I've ended up! You have no idea, Beth. I'm beyond redemption on this earth. You're going to hear some things about what I've done, Bethany, maybe tomorrow on the news. It's really bad, and I can't run from it. I just wanted you—all of you—to know that I'm not the person who committed these crimes, not anymore, not tonight. I've had some kind of transformation, Bethany. Something's happened to me that's allowed me to see things clearly. I don't know; maybe it's God. I only know that I have to try to make you understand that I'm sorry for what I've done and how I've treated you and Carl. It's important to me that you understand that."

"Tommy, I do understand. I've always understood, and I know you're sick. I always knew you never meant the words you left on the machine. I always knew you were lost and just waiting to be found! It sounds to me like you've been found, Tommy. It's not too late! We can all have another chance at trying to get it right, Tommy—together. Please say you'll try. You're scaring me the way you're talking. Please come here to my house. Please tell me you're not going to do anything stupid. If you're in trouble, go to the police. Tell me where you are, and I'll come and take you to the police, and we can fix it. I don't need to forgive you, Tommy, because I never felt it was you doing the hurting. You're here tonight. Right now, on the phone, I hear the words of my big brother—the brother who took care of me and loved me. The brother I haven't spoken to in ten years. I want you back, Tommy. I need you back."

"You will get me back, Beth. Focus on those nice years when we had so much love, and remember me like that. I'm full of shame and remorse, but I'm physically ill as well, Beth. Right now, I'm so tired I just want to sleep for a long time, you know? You don't need to worry about me anymore. I'm done with the booze and the dope, and I know I need to set things right. I love you, Beth—I never stopped loving you. I just stopped loving myself, and I needed to blame someone for that. I don't get why I couldn't understand that for so long. It seemed different to me, like it was everyone else's fault. I was just down on my luck, waiting for a break. Things will be better next week. That's really what I thought, and then suddenly, I knew it was all just me—weak and sick and full of self-loathing and self-pity. I couldn't stand to look at myself, so I focused my hate on all of you. But I'm done with all of that, Beth. I sank to a place I never would have believed I could've gone, and now I'm done. I surrender. I give up fighting me. I just want some peace, but I know the peace will come at a cost. I believe you would come here and help me with the police and everything else, but you need to understand that I need to take care of things on my own. I've taken so much from so many people—mostly you, Billy, Mom, and Dad—but there are others as well. All I ask from you, Billy, and the folks, is forgiveness. All I ask is that you know I loved you all always, in spite of who I've become and what I've done. I always knew better. I just never knew that I knew."

Tommy stopped speaking and felt his anxiety growing as a deafening silence filled the line. He waited for Beth to reply, but no reply came. As Tommy stood in the dark and damp phone booth, he began to doubt his plan. His old thinking lurked just beneath the surface. Tommy Boy had lived out in the open for better than twenty years, being the dominant figure for the past ten, and it had only been hours since Tommy Boyle had re-emerged. Perhaps it was wishful thinking or just naivety to assume that these people, who had been conditioned to deal with him from a place of guilt and shame, would simply hear his plea for forgiveness. That without thought or question, they would let him off the hook. Tommy felt his resolve diminishing, and as had been his pattern in life, the instinct to run washed over him. He was about to give in to his flight impulse when Beth cleared her throat and began to speak.

"So that's it? You want to kiss and make up, and we'll just forget the past twenty years! I don't need to forgive you, Tommy. And I never gave up on you. All that we've all had for all this time is hope—hope that one day this call would come and hope that you would live till the miracle happened for you. I prayed it would come before Mom and Dad died, and from the tone of your voice, I think it has—at least in part. You sound like you! Maybe that doesn't make sense, but I can tell there's been a change. But I hear something else, Tommy, and it scares me to death. I hear you giving up. All those years you've been lost, there must have been something more than the need for drugs that kept you going. In the depths of the squalor you lived in, you never ended it all. That's what always kept the hope alive for me. I was ready to hear you were killed by a druggie or that you OD'd, but I never expected to hear you killed yourself. That's what I'm hearing, Tommy. I hear you saying stuff like 'you gotta set things straight' and 'you can't find redemption on this earth,' and it scares me. Tommy, whatever happened to you tonight can be set right without you dying. Don't you get that? Whatever has caused this change in you, allowed you to see what you've become—that is a gift! Regardless of how horrible the act was that has given you this awareness, the awareness itself is a gift. To lose that now would be just wrong. Wrong for us all, Tommy."

"But Beth, you don't know. You just don't know what it's been like. The shame I feel is just too great for me to live with. What I've done, I cannot face. The consequences are too hard for me to accept. Please, Beth, I just need you to know I'm sorry. Please."

"You're right, Tommy. I don't know. And I don't care. If you do this thing, Tommy, it'll be hundreds of times worse than all you've done. I can forgive and forget the life you've imposed on this family, but if you do this thing tonight, right now, I could never forgive that. It's just more running away, Tommy Boyle. It's just more not standing up and taking responsibility for your life. It's just more of what you've always done. If you want me to believe you've changed, then prove it. Tell me where you are, and I'll come and help you."

Tommy sat on his heels in the dark of the booth and looked up at the stars. He began to cry softly, and his mind filled with thoughts of Beth. In an instant, he recalled all the times in his life when he could have turned it all around. All the wrong choices he made stood glaringly at the forefront of his mind, and Tommy wished he could take it all back. He wished he had made the choices in his life that wouldn't have led him to a darkened phone booth in the wee hours of the morning with the blood of others on his hands. But wishing doesn't make it so, and in spite of the words she had spoken, Tommy knew he could not endure the punishment that would fit the crime. Tommy was alone with his shame, and death was the only way for him to find peace.

"I'm sorry you feel that way, Beth. I'll think about what you said. I know you're right. For now, I just need some sleep, and tomorrow, I'll call the mission here. They can help me get some treatment, and I can contact you then. I do love you, Beth. At least know that much."

"I do, Tommy. I do know that. I've always known that. I can't give you permission, Tommy, to hurt yourself, though, and that's what it sounded like you wanted me to do. You have a good plan now, Tommy. Go to the mission and get some sleep. I'll come and find you there tomorrow, and together, we'll make a plan. I'll tell Mom and Dad that you're going to be okay and getting the help you need. Will you do that, Tommy? Will you promise me, Tommy?"

And Tommy did. He told her all the things she wanted to hear. He told her what she needed to hear, and he did it with the conviction and sincerity you can find in the words of all alcoholics and drug addicts. He had spent a lifetime telling people what they wanted to hear and fabricating lies. A change had come over Tommy Boyle, and a new awareness was growing within, but the part of him that lived by the lying and stealing code of the street was still functioning. The part of Tommy that steered him toward an easier and softer route was still in control of his guidance system. So he told the lies, and he believed the lies, though Bethany did not.

Slowly, Tommy stretched himself out in the phone booth, and as he stared up at the constellation Orion, he said goodbye for the last time to his little sister, Bethany. He told her he would call from the mission, and he told her he would love her forever because he knew forever would not be that long. And then, with a feeling of selfish relief, he severed the connection. For a moment, he stood and listened to the slow beating of his heart in his chest; for a moment, he allowed himself to believe the lie. Then he began to weep.

Forty miles away, in the comfortable home of Carl and Bethany Magellan, the simple breaking of a telephone connection took on the same significance as the changing of the millennium. An era had ended. Bethany drew deep, wet sobs from the lowest parts of her stomach and the deepest parts of her soul. Gripping the receiver in one hand and her pregnant stomach in the other, she slid slowly down the wall to the floor beneath her. Carl was there in an instant, and as she wept, he held her tightly. His hand fell upon hers as it cradled her stomach, and the boy growing in her womb kicked. He kicked, and he rolled, and Bethany knew at that moment she would name this child Tommy. He would be Tommy Boyle Magellan, and he would be loved. He would be loved as she had loved her brother Tommy, but this child would know he was loved. He would know this love would last forever, and that would be a long time indeed.

CHOICES

Sergeant First Class Jim McCaskey sat and stared into the half-empty cup of station house coffee, which stood on the desk between him and the final report that needed to be filed regarding the matter of Gustav Kaminski. He had sat with the SIU and answered all the usual questions, briefed his command, and completed the paperwork. The official consensus would be that Sergeant James McCaskey had participated in a good kill. The perpetrator in question had been dispatched by the book, and this stamp of procedural approval should have made McCaskey feel better, but it had not.

A man was dead at his hand, and regardless of the state or condition of the man at the time of his death, the simple fact remained that McCaskey had killed him. McCaskey had taken a human life—a job that should be reserved for God.

He sat quietly now, staring at the coffee, trying to will his mind to stop obsessing over the moment he had shattered Gustav's skull. He could hear the sound of crushed cartilage in Gustav's nose as it traveled into his brain. He could see the look of surprise in Gustav's eyes as he realized his life was ending, and then the odd look of peace and triumph as his light faded and was forever extinguished.

There was chaos in the station house as all those around him went on with their assigned duties, but McCaskey was oblivious to it all, trying to control his thoughts. He was breathing slowly and steadily, focusing all of his willpower on staying out of the "what if" scenarios. *What if* he had let the kid, McFadden, lead instead of follow? *What if* he had rousted the old bum? *What if* he had held back on the ferocity of the baton? *What if* he had not used the baton at all? *What if* he had finished his shift and gone to meet his wife for dinner? He could have done that. He could have left, but he chose not to. And now, a man was dead, and so was a relationship. Once again, McCaskey found himself staring into a half-empty cup of station house coffee, wondering about the choices he had made in his life.

He knew about choices. He often ranted to the scum in the back of his cruiser about choices. He understood people made good choices and bad choices, and he was always quick to counsel or criticize the choices others made. But with all his knowledge about choices, he consistently made bad ones for himself and his family. Somewhere along the trail of his life, there had been a distortion between the rules of humanity and the rules of responsibility. He had lost the sense of what was truly important in this world and had replaced that instinctual knowledge with a book of rules. Standard Operating Procedures, Criminal Codes, Codes of Conduct, and a plethora of manuals dictating how he should behave as a police officer had become the focus of his life. Jim McCaskey had changed.

He had once been a guy who wanted to keep the streets safe for his wife and kids, a guy who always tried to do the next right thing, a guy who wanted to serve and protect. Now, he understood he had evolved into a man who lived by the book, a man with an exaggerated sense of justice. He had become a legal technician. Just this very night, he had been telling a young officer that there was more to being a cop than knowing the rules, yet he himself had become driven by the rules. A young officer who, at this very moment, was getting his ass stitched up at County General. He wondered if either of them would learn anything from the death of Gustav Kaminski.

e allowed his gaze to wander to the personalized coffee cup in front of him, reading the words that had been painted on it: "Happy 10th to the man I love." His thoughts drifted to his wife. In his mind's eye, he could see her thanking the waiter, saying she was waiting for her husband. He could see her checking her watch as she ordered the first glass of wine, then checking again as she looked at her cell phone for missed messages. He could see her biting her lower lip in worry as she ran through all the scenarios of what could have made "the man she loved" late without calling. He could see her worry turn to anger, and her anger to resignation as she finished her second glass of wine and asked for the check.

McCaskey let his chin drop to his chest and sighed deeply as he picked up the phone and began to dial home. He had no reason to expect her to understand, no right to ask her to forgive him, and no one else on the face of the earth with whom he could share his feelings about the death of Gustav Kaminski. His focus was lost to the tears fighting to escape from behind his eyes. Just as he was dialing the last digit, he heard his name being called from across the room.

"Hey Jim, I got a lady on the line here you may want to talk to. She's calling about your man Boyle, line two."

With the thumb and ring finger of his left hand, McCaskey cleared the nearly spilled tears from his eyes. With his right hand, he replaced the receiver in the cradle of the phone, and once again, Jim McCaskey chose to put his job ahead of his life. He knew how to do police work, but he was uncertain how to do life. So, he picked up the phone again and pressed line two. "Sergeant Jim McCaskey here, how can I be of assistance?"

Forty miles away, Bethany Magellan sat on the chair in the downstairs hall. Her husband Carl was at her side, holding her hand. As had been his way for twelve years now, Carl soothed Beth and held her until her tears subsided. Carl had been a mountain of strength for Beth throughout these years and through her struggles with the guilt and shame she had inherited from her family. He had decided at the outset of their relationship that his legacy to the children he and Bethany would bring into this world was a broken cycle of dysfunction. He had been kind and patient with Beth, and over the years, he had helped her understand that the shame she carried was a false shame.

The undeserved guilt she had taken upon herself for people and situations beyond her control had threatened to destroy her life with Carl. Slowly, with the help of this patient and insightful man, Bethany began to believe she had been nothing more than a bystander in the events that had shaped her family, particularly in the life of her brother, Tommy. She was not to blame, and she no longer carried any guilt or shame for the circumstances of Tommy's life. But it still hurt. It hurt so deeply that she was overcome with sorrow as she allowed all the horrible thoughts of what might happen to Tommy tonight to overtake her mind. Carl was there, as he had always been, and Carl knew what needed to be done. He found the number for the police station in the borough where they had last heard Tommy was living. He dialed the phone, handed it to Beth, and told her it would be okay. And Bethany believed him.

"I'm sorry, did you say Sergeant McCaskey?"

"McCaskey, ma'am. Sergeant Jim McCaskey. Am I to understand you're calling in relation to a Thomas Boyle?"

"Yes, that's correct. Tommy is my brother, and I am very worried about him."

"And what is your name, ma'am?"

"Bethany Magellan. You can call me Beth."

"Okay, Beth. What is it that's making you worried about your brother?"

"Well, he called here, and he sounded very odd. I am very worried he will hurt himself."

"Do you know where he is right now, Beth?"

"No, I'm sorry. We've been out of contact with him for some time, and I don't know where Tommy lives. He's been very down on his luck, heavily involved with drugs."

"Beth, I know he's not at his address. Did he give you any idea where he was calling from?"

"Excuse me, Sergeant McCaskey. How is it you know he's not where he lives? Is there something going on here that I'm not aware of? I was calling because I'm worried my brother may be suicidal. Frankly, I was quite stunned when I was put straight through to you and not given the usual runaround about waiting 24 hours. I would appreciate it if you told me what's going on."

"Beth, the truth is, we've been looking for Tommy Boyle for several hours now in connection with incidents that occurred earlier this evening."

"What kind of incidents? Tommy said he had done something, but he didn't say what it was."

"I'm sorry, Beth. I'm not at liberty to discuss the details of an ongoing investigation. The fact is that Tommy is at large, and a lot of cops are looking for him right now. If you could help me find him, it would be best for all concerned."

"Officer, please understand, I have no misconceptions about the state in which my brother lives, and I'm quite certain he has resorted to crime to feed the addictions that have taken him. But there was something different in Tommy tonight when I spoke to him. He said he had changed, and for the first time since I was very young, I believed him. All I know is that he spoke of going to a mission in the morning. He said he wanted to sleep, and in the morning, he would go to the mission and get some help. I hope that helps you. Now, I'm asking you to help me. Whatever Tommy is accused of, can you promise me you'll try to get him safely into custody, get him someplace where he can get the help he needs? Can you tell me you'll find him before he hurts himself?"

"I can tell you, Beth, that I will do everything I can. This has been a long day, and a lot of people are on edge. We need to locate Tommy—the quicker, the better. If you give me your number, I'll make sure you're kept informed. That's the best I can do, Beth. I hope you understand."

And she did. Tommy was in trouble—big trouble. She had given her number as requested and had been given Sergeant McCaskey's extension in return. She hung up the phone, took Carl's hand, and went to bed to wait and pray that she would see her brother Tommy again.

McCaskey hung up the phone and dialed the PA at the front desk. "Janis, I need you to find me street locations and indoor locations for every payphone and outdoor phone booth within a square mile of Thomas Boyle's apartment address, and I need that information ASAP. I also need to know how many missions there are down in the district, as well as their addresses and phone numbers. Lastly, I need you to find Gideon for me, or at least his last point of contact. He may be off radio."

"Is that it?" Janis asked the question with an extra dose of her usual sarcasm, which did not go unnoticed by McCaskey.

"That's it for now, Janis, and thanks." McCaskey picked up his half-empty, half-cold cup of station house coffee and drank it down, not noticing the words "Happy 10th to the man I love."

Bethany sat quietly in the dim light of the bedside lamp and waited. She looked down at Carl, who had drifted off to sleep despite his best efforts to sit and wait with her. He snored softly, as was his way, and though his snoring was never loud enough to wake her, there were many nights when she sat deep in thought, breathing to the rhythm of his snorts and sighs. Many nights, she lay awake, unable to drift off, just waiting.

It seemed to Bethany, on this quiet early morning, that she had spent her whole life waiting for one thing or another. She had waited for her father to show her love, waited for her mother to slip completely away from this world, waited for Billy to somehow engage with anyone in the family, and waited for Tommy to forgive her for all the pain in his life, which he had attributed to her. But mostly, she had waited for the entire world to find out who she really was. She had waited for everyone who thought Bethany had it all together to find out she was a fraud, to finally know she was unstable and had been her whole life. Everyone looked to her to be the strong one, the one with the answers. She was the one who had it all together and needed nothing to help her cope. *If only they knew!* If only they understood. If only they could listen to her and hear her pain, they would know the depths of her dysfunction, as Carl had. They would understand that the strength she so openly exhibited on the outside was simply a mask for the fear with which she lived inside.

And so, once again, she waited. This time, she was waiting to hear that Tommy had been killed. As she sat and waited, accompanied by her snoring husband, she was filled with a sense of calm. So many nights had been spent in fear and anxiety, wondering all the while where she had gone wrong. She had wondered why they all hated her so much and how her family could be so different from her—so different from the family she really needed. So much time had been lost to worry and fear, and so much energy had been expended in trying to keep everyone from knowing her pain. She had believed that if she could keep it hidden away from the world, the world couldn't hurt her. So, she built her walls, and they were well fortified. But her walls held no windows, so there was no chance for anyone to see inside. The walls she had built to protect herself had become the walls that imprisoned her, the walls that kept her concealed and unavailable to real, pure love. So much time had been wasted, and so much of life had been missed, because her family could not walk in love with themselves or with each other.

Tonight, after she had made her calls, after Carl had calmed and consoled her and taken her to bed where he knew she would not sleep, after Carl himself had drifted off to the wonderful places his dreams took him, Bethany had lain with her thoughts. And tonight, as she endured the early hours within the confines of her mind, she was at peace. Bethany Muriel Boyle-Magellan was at last without torment. She was free of guilt, and she was without shame. She was not to blame for what had happened to her family. She was not to blame for what was happening to her brother Tommy. She, too, had been stained by the effects of the life she had lived but had not succumbed to alcohol and drug abuse. While she held great love and empathy for Tommy and Billy, she no longer held a sense of responsibility.

Her experience of their childhood had manifested differently in her life than in Tommy's or Billy's, but they were all part and parcel of the same illness that permeated their family. She carried her mother's chemical imbalances and bipolar tendencies. Billy had become as aloof as the generations of men in their family before him, and

Tommy—Tommy, who felt too much—had been overcome by his denial and inability to cope. He had inherited the best and the worst of both their parents and had been consumed by the conflicts that raged within. For so long, Bethany had known all of these things in her mind. But here, now, tonight, for the first time in her life, she felt it in her heart, and she was at peace.

As she carefully slid out of bed, she looked down at the sleeping Carl and smiled. *Thank God for Carl,* she thought. *Thank God for this man who was able to see beyond her wall to the shattered and frightened little girl who lived behind it. Thank God for Carl, who was filled with goodness and patience, who did not exploit the frightened and easily manipulated Beth, but instead encouraged her and helped her find the path back to reality.* Her reality had been forged from years of work and patience, years of therapy and medications, and most of all, from years of love. *Thank God for Carl,* who had encouraged Bethany to feel the pain, allowed her the time she needed to walk through it, and waited for her on the other side as she found her way to love. *Thank God for Carl,* who had helped her understand that she was worthy of love. She smiled down at her sleeping, snoring, receding hairlined prince, as she turned and walked out into the hall. She was at peace.

Bethany walked slowly down the hall, passing the photo gallery of their lives. Her mother had always said they took a good picture, and the evidence of that hung here on the walls of the dimly lit upstairs hall. She stopped in front of a favorite picture of her father, perched on the steel seat of his red Farmall tractor. His straw hat was tipped rakishly to one side, and his long cherry-wood pipe hung easily from the side of his smiling mouth. On his lap sat Billy, only two years old, and over his shoulder, you could see the smiling face of young Tommy standing on the far side runner of the tractor. God only knows what Muriel must have said or done to get them all smiling like that, and God only knows how many times Bethany had looked at this picture throughout the long years of her self-imposed exile, filled with guilt and sorrow. How many times had she told herself that they were all so happy until she had come along? That her birth had stolen their joy? How many times had Tommy told her the same thing?

She continued down the hall, feeling joy tonight in the knowledge that, at least for that frozen moment in time, they had been happy. She stopped and looked for a long time at the photo of herself as a baby in the arms of Tommy, getting ready to receive the warm formula from the bottle. Fed from Tommy's hand rather than her mother's breast, but still eager, baby Beth's eyes were bulging, her mouth open, and her gums wet as she reached for the hand of her big brother. Beth recalled the many times she had wished her life could have ended at that moment—filled with trust and unwavering love.

The next frame held a picture of Muriel Boyle. She sat alone in her kitchen, in the chair that had been there for Beth's entire life and still sat there today. There were fresh-cut flowers in a vase beside the chair, so it must have been spring, and in the window hung the prisms her mother so loved. The sun was beaming through the window, and the photo, quite by accident, had captured the beam of light in such a way that you could easily imagine the rainbows dancing on the ceilings and walls of the kitchen. This beam of light, which only the camera would have seen, fell over Muriel and gave her the look of an angel at the window. The photo was quite beautiful and very artistic, but for Bethany, it had always held so much mystery. The mystery was seen in the eyes of Muriel Boyle. She was looking toward the camera but not at it. She appeared to be looking at nothing. Her eyes were vacant, and Bethany always believed that these early photos had shown the sadness that existed in the soul of her mother, and the illness that was growing in her mind. There were people over the years who had assumed Muriel had posed for this photo, that she had been positioned by a photographer at the perfect time in the perfect spot to capture the light and the mystery. Sadly, this was not true. It was not a pose; it was a snapshot of a deteriorating mind. Bethany found herself wondering how often today her mother sat and stared at the same spot in space, and what it was she saw there, what it was she had been looking for.

Bethany walked away from the sadness of the picture of her mother and stopped in front of her wedding picture. Both her and Carl's families had gathered around them for the photo, and there in the picture was the evidence of the difference between the families. Carl's family stood arm in arm with genuine smiles and open love, happy to be united and easy in each other's company. Bethany's parents and brothers wore the same artificial photo smiles that they wore in pictures in every other album—rehearsed and phony, uncomfortable with the closeness of each other and the required display of love and affection. They stood as if by court order for the photos, and when the picture had been taken, she recalled how quickly they had dispersed. And there in the center of the photo stood Bethany, and in her eyes was the same vacant look that existed in the photo of Muriel. The eyes of each were searching for something that was not there to find.

Bethany moved on down the hall, feeling blessed once again that she had been able to join in a real life with her husband and children, and feeling a deep sadness for her family of origin. She walked to the open door of her oldest son John's room and looked across the hall to that of her daughter Muriel. She let her hands drop to her stomach, where her new son, Tommy, kicked and turned in his sleep. She watched them as they slept, and she let her love spill over them. Through her eyes flowed a love that she had never known as a child, and she swore once again that these children would always be loved and always be aware of love. She stood in the wee hours of the morning and wondered how many times her father had stood in the dark night and looked down upon his children with a love he could not express. How many times had he smiled down as he pulled the covers up and slipped dolls or action figures in beside the sleeping children, knowing they would never know he was there?

She turned and started back down the hall of memories toward her sleeping prince, and she was filled with thoughts of her father. She imagined him sitting alone by the fire, as was his way these last couple of years. Alone in his sadness, alone in his guilt, alone in his shame. And she determined to call him in the morning, to continue trying to unlock his heart, which she knew to be good and kind. Love deferred is love lost, but love unleashed can fill the world. She crawled back into bed with her Carl and she waited.

Bob Gideon had just emerged from the darkness of an alley off Wall St., where he had conducted another lengthy interrogation with a gathering of bums. Another conversation that had started with inquiry, ended in threat, and bore no information. As hard as it was for him not to trust his gut instinct—an instinct that had served him well for more than twenty years—he was beginning to believe that the felon Tommy Boyle had left the district. He was tired, frustrated, and filled with mixed emotions as the realization that he might not find Tommy sank into his head and heart. These crimes had been a personal affront to Bob Gideon, not only committed on his beat but carried out mere blocks from his actual home. As he began to walk south on Wall Street, he decided it was time for him to back off for a while. It was time for him to call in to the station for a black-and-white to come and get him and take him to the house for some coffee and an update on the dragnet for Tommy Boyle. Maybe he could discover a fresh perspective if he stepped back for a while.

In his mind, he ran over the events of the evening, reviewing all the interviews he had conducted on the street and considering all the people he had spoken to. He had called in favors, chatted to some, leaned on others, and had come to the conclusion that they were all being square with him. If Tommy Boy was still in the area, no one knew about it—at least no one he had spoken to.

Still, something was nagging at his mind, something he was overlooking. It was then that he realized he hadn't spoken to Armist Hancock. He had seen Armist a couple of hours earlier, but he had opted not to actually speak to him. Armist was one of the irregular regulars down here, and as such, he had a way of blending into the background. He almost always kept to himself and never drew attention. But there was something else as well—it was what McCaskey had said about his runaway perp. He had said the guy's name was Armist, a big man, and Bob remembered questioning that because it didn't add up. The Armist on his beat was bent over and arthritic. Officer Bob Gideon was no Sherlock Holmes, but he was smart enough to realize that in twenty years on the beat, he had never met another man named Armist. This could not be a coincidence. Somehow, Armist Hancock had become involved with Tommy Boyle, and somehow, he had failed to make that connection. That now made Armist Hancock the only thing close to a lead for him.

Gideon stopped in his tracks and turned south. With a renewed sense of purpose, he began walking toward the alley that was the home of Armist Hancock. Just as he reached for his right shoulder to key the radio and check in with his precinct, the cell phone in his breast pocket began to ring. The cell was his pipeline to the street. He handed out his card and number regularly to anyone he thought would be of use or in need, and the practice had often borne fruit. There had been many times when a person on the street wouldn't talk in the open but would share over the cell rather than end up in a cell.

"Bob Gideon here, how can I help you?"

"I'm not sure, sweetie; maybe it's me that can help you!"

He immediately recognized the raspy smoker's voice on the other end of the line and smiled as he responded.

"Why Polly Ann, whatever could you mean? How on earth could you help out an old flatfoot on a cool, wet night?"

"Well, Officer Friendly, you might be well surprised, you surely might."

The banter between Bob and Polly Ann was one of those things in life that evolved naturally, was completely consensual, and something that both parties looked forward to on a daily basis. It was an interaction that was always extremely witty, full of sexual innuendo, often sarcastic, but never mean-spirited. For him, Polly Ann Polanski represented everything he had become a cop for. She was the perk at the end of each day that kept him suiting up for the next shift.

He had first met Polly Ann when she was on the wrong side of the law and on the dying side of heroin addiction. She was a hard girl in a hard spot, and in those days, she was not one to ignore. She had come from a good Polish family with whom she had long since lost all contact or support, and she would undertake any means to facilitate her drug use. Many a middle-aged businessman had taken a walk down a dark alley with Polly Ann expecting sexual rewards, only to end up robbed, their heads split open, wondering how they would explain it to their wives. The calls always came into the station house as muggings. The johns could never adequately explain what exactly they were doing off the beaten trail in darkened alleys, and Gideon always knew it had been Polly Ann. He knew. She knew he knew, but he had never been able to bust her.

In the end, when Polly Ann was near death and in more trouble than she could talk or fight her way out of, she had come to him. He had helped her live through her legal problems and stood by her as she took the sentence she was due. When she started her bit on the inside, it was Bob who facilitated the contact she needed to get clean and sober, but it was Polly Ann who did the work to reclaim her life and reconnect with her family. They had become friends, but that was not his goal or intention at the outset. The help he offered Polly Ann Polanski was, in his mind, part of his job—to protect and serve. The fact that Polly decided, upon her release, to come back to the neighborhood and make Officer Bob Gideon her friend was the perk—the perk that brought him the daily assurance he needed, knowing he was in the right business, knowing he could make a difference.

She began slowly, measuring her words with caution and awaiting his responses in anticipation.

"Bob, I am in a bit of a spot, and I may need to call on a friend for some help."

"This friend anyone I know, Polly?"

In spite of the situation at hand, Polly Ann found herself chuckling into the phone. He had a gift, where Polly was concerned. Regardless of the situation, he could always make her laugh, and she loved him for it.

"As a matter of fact, Bob, this friend is someone who has helped me before and someone I know I can trust, even if he is a bit of a dick!"

"Okay, okay, what's up? Is someone bothering you over at the Parlor? I hate that you stay open all night, but I know you're too stubborn to talk out of it."

"No, no, nothing like that. I'm okay, but I have a friend who needs your help. He's in a bit of a spot, and I told him if he trusted you, like I do, maybe you could walk him out the other end."

"This fellow, did he commit a crime?"

"Yes and no, he's kind of caught up in a misunderstanding situation. He's not sure what to do! He's close to high-tailing it, you know, but I told him there ain't no running away. He needs some help, and he doesn't trust too many people, especially cops."

"Jeez, Polly, this is about the worst night ever. I'm right in the middle of the shit here in the District. We've got a bit of a manhunt underway. I've been pounding the beat all night looking for a suspect. Can it wait till tomorrow?"

"Well, Bob, that's the thing. I think maybe this friend of mine is kind of involved in the same thing you are."

"Are you friends with Tommy Boyle? Tell me you're not friends with Tommy Boyle! Polly Ann, you listen to me! If you're somewhere with Tommy Boyle, you need to tell me right now, and then you need to get away from him. He is a dangerous felon!"

"No, Bob, no! I'm not with Tommy Boyle, but I know he's the man you're looking for. I know that and a whole lot more. I want to help, and my friend wants to help, but he's scared. I need to assure him that he can trust you—and me, for that matter!"

"You know me, Polly, and therefore you know the answer to that question. If I can help, and if this friend—and you, Polly—aren't involved in criminality in the case involving Tommy Boyle, I'll do the best I can. But if you or your friend have crossed a line, you know I'll have to do the right thing. I'm a cop first, a friend second. Always."

"I know that, Bob, that's why I'm calling. There's been no big lines crossed, but my friend sort of hit one of you guys and then he took off. He's just scared, you know, and a little fragile. I think he'd come in or cooperate if he knew you guys would look away from the assault charge."

"Well, well. I was just wondering, not two minutes ago, where I might find old Armist Hancock, and here it turns out he's with my good friend Polly Ann Polanski! Where is he, Polly? I need to talk to him. He may be the only lead I've got to find Tommy Boy. You tell old Armist if he's done no more tonight than leave a rookie cop with a sore jaw and a bump on his head, then I'll keep him out of the slammer. But if it turns out there's more to it, no promises from me. That's the best I can do."

"That's the most I would ask you for, Bob. Just to listen and give the fellow a chance. He's good people inside, you know what I mean. I can be back at my shop in fifteen minutes. How about you meet us there?"

"Fifteen minutes, I'll be there, Polly."

As Gideon hung up the phone, he considered calling in for backup and dismissed the idea just as quickly. Polly Ann had a good head on her shoulders, good street sense, and she knew people. She was still on parole and wouldn't do anything to jeopardize that. If she was willing to vouch for Armist Hancock in the matter of Tommy Boyle, that was good enough for him.

Fifteen minutes later, Bob Gideon walked through the door of Polly Ann's Parlor and Pleasure Emporium. His entrance was heralded by the digitized door chime, which spewed forth a few electronic bars of the theme song from *Love Boat*. Mike, the tattoo man, looked up from a half-finished Japanese character he was imprinting on the half-bare ass of a fully drunk young girl. In the corner sat the snickering, dirty-looking boyfriend of the half-assed young girl. He was covered in ink and piercings on all the visible parts of his body, and Bob did not even want to think about what lay beneath the dirty leather and denim he wore. Both seemed oblivious to the fact that a police officer had just entered the establishment. They exchanged mindless chatter and seemed capable of focusing on only one thing at a time. Gideon wondered, as he often did, how much these kids must hate the lives they lived. It was so sad that they believed another existence could be created, a better set of circumstances attained, or the attention they so earnestly craved, realized through the application of ink and stainless steel. Mike nodded his head toward the office in back, and Gideon walked through the Parlor with a feeling of deep sadness for a generation lost.

He often wondered about this world he had taken an oath to serve and protect. Perhaps the time had come for Bob to think about ending his lackluster career. Days like this one played harder on his mind than they had in the past. It was his job to do police work, not to run a commentary in his mind on the decline of the world, as was more often than not the case these days. His eyes darted over the racks of pornographic material and the shelves of sexual devices, and he felt the anger rise up from his gut and settle. Polly Ann was a dear friend. Polly Ann was a woman who had turned around a lost life, and for that, Bob held her in esteem. But this business she had chosen filled him with dread. It was a sign of decline for Bob. It was part of all that he deemed to be bad in this world, and it kept Polly Ann on the edges of a world to which she had nearly succumbed. He had done his best to dissuade her, but she had made up her mind, and she was a stubborn woman.

She was Polly Ann Polanski of Polly Ann's Parlor and Pleasure Emporium, and she was in no way ashamed of it. On the outside, Gideon displayed moral dislike for Polly's stock and trade, but inside, in the places cops kept hidden from the world, he was only concerned and worried for Polly Ann's safety and well-being. She was in a tough business in a tough part of town, and if Gideon were to put an end to his career, who would be there to look in on her? He sighed deeply, cleared his thoughts, and walked into the small office of his friend Polly Ann Polanski.

She looked up from her desk and smiled, and the room took on a different feel. He could sense some of the tension leave his jaw as he looked down upon her in the ten-by-ten, clutter-filled office, and Bob smiled back at Polly.

"Well, Officer, after all this time and all this effort, at last I have you in the back office."

"I suppose that is true, Polly. You have me here, but only for police work, I fear. Where might our mutual friend be?"

Polly motioned toward the door leading to the washroom off the back of the small office. She smiled and bantered as always, but Bob could feel the tension in her. He could sense her concern, and something more. He had known her in the past to make projects out of people she had come to know in the neighborhood. He had seen her get involved and invest the time it took to get a young man or woman off the street. But something in her aura was different tonight, and he suddenly realized it was possible that a deeper connection existed between Polly and Armist than he had known. He looked past the overflowing ashtray to a discarded pair of police-issue handcuffs lying on the desk. He reached past Polly Ann and picked up the cuffs.

"I take it these belong to a friend and colleague of mine?"

Polly Ann nodded in silence.

"You'll understand if I return them, right? And you do understand that this is aiding and abetting, Polly, right? And that aiding and abetting is a violation of your parole, which could ultimately threaten everything you have and hold dear? You get all that, right, Polly Ann? It seems to me that you've put yourself in a very bad situation."

"Yes, Officer, I get all that. Can we get past all the cop stuff now and get to the helping-a-friend stuff?"

No, Polly. I'm not sure we can. It's not easy for me to look the other way, and I can assure you that in twenty-five years, it's only happened once. And that one time made me feel sick to my stomach for ten years. I don't think I'll put myself through that again. Armist Hancock is not my friend. He's a guy that has lived around the corner in one alley or another for as long as I can recall. I've never known him to be a man looking for trouble, but I do know he has always lived on the edge of the law, and I have no doubt he's crossed over from time to time. You are my friend. That's the only reason I haven't shown up here with a couple of black-and-whites, and with one cop in particular who would like to have another go-around with Armist at the station house. I promised McCaskey I would call him if I heard anything about the guy he lost tonight—the guy who actually does turn out to be our Armist. So, until you convince me otherwise, until I see who comes out of that bathroom and what kind of mood he's in, I will proceed as an officer of the law. You got that, Polly?"

"Wow! Big speech! I've got it. I had no one else to call, Bob, and I only want the help you're willing to give. No special favors, okay?"

"Fair enough," replied Gideon, not diverting his attention from the bathroom door.

PERDITION

John Boyle sat in the dark parlor of the farmhouse where he had spent his entire life. The two years he had spent fighting in the Great War were the only time he had ever been away from this farm. He had buried his parents on this property, watched his kids grow and move on, and spent a lifetime with the only woman he had ever loved, all within these four walls. These two hundred acres had been the only world John Boyle required, and all he needed to bring him joy. But on this night, sitting by the light of the open fire and gazing into the glowing embers, he was overwhelmed with sadness.

It was three in the morning, and once again, there would be no sleep. His wife, Muriel, was at rest in the room they had shared for over sixty years, and for that, he was grateful. The week had been hard, and her condition was deteriorating. Muriel Boyle had spent her life battling depression. At times, she had succumbed to the darkness that lurked on the edges of her mind, and during those times, she had been taken from John. Those periods of depression had been hard, but nothing during those times of illness could have prepared John for the devastation that her dementia and Alzheimer's would bring into his life.

The disease had gone unnoticed by him, likely concealed by Muriel for a couple of years. Lost keys and missed appointments were laughed off as signs of old age. But eventually, the changes in her behavior became so pronounced that John knew something was wrong.

Muriel was no longer herself. John knew this, but as was his way in life, he chose to ignore it. Then came the day when he came in from the fields for supper to find the stove cold and the table empty. He searched the house for Muriel and found her sitting in the corner of their oldest son Tommy's room. She must have been rocking back and forth for hours when John arrived. Slowly, he crouched down beside her and asked if she was all right, and when she looked at him, her eyes were empty.

"Where is Tommy?" she asked, and John looked upon her but had no words. He bent to lift her to her feet, and Muriel cringed back in fear. For the first time, John understood that she did not know him. He remembered that day, how he had stood there in silence, never feeling more alone in his entire life. John Boyle knew pain, and he knew loss. He had been in the Great War, had seen men die, taken lives, and been wounded. He had lived through the pain of losing his oldest son, Tommy, to addiction, and his other children, Billy and Bethany, to neglect. He knew pain, and he knew loss, and he survived it all because he always had his Muriel. With her, there was nothing he could not endure. Without her, there was just nothing.

He turned in silence and left the room. That evening, John found himself sitting in his big chair in the corner of the kitchen as the light of the day faded. The rainbows of light were slowly fading from the ceiling as the last of the day's light drained from the prisms Muriel had placed in the windows. He wept into his pitted and calloused hands as darkness filled the room and color drained from his life. He wept in his big chair as he had never wept in all his days. He wept tears that had no end and sobbed with a pain that knew no bounds. As he sat in the depths of his despair, he heard her voice.

"John, oh John, what is the matter?" Muriel had spoken from the darkened doorway. Then she came to him, cupped his head in her arms, drew him into her breast, and kissed him as she had done so many times before. Muriel was back, and she had no idea she had been gone.

That night was when John Boyle's life changed forever. Up until that point, John had proceeded on a need-to-know basis. He never really needed to know why his wife was angry or depressed, why one of his kids was acting out, or why a milking cow had stopped producing. All he needed to know was how to fix things. Like his father before him, John was a fixer. He was uncomfortable with the knowledge that came from digging deeper into the feelings and emotions of himself or others. He never had a big need to be right; his only goal in life was to get along, avoid confrontation, and make things okay for folks. When he could fix things, he was happy, and when he couldn't, he was at a loss.

This distorted philosophy, which he had inherited from his own father, had served him well in the Great War and helped him establish good relationships in his business life, but it had created a chasm between Muriel and the kids. Just as he had respected his father, his children respected him. His mother had learned to live with and love a man who could never become more for her than a loving and practical provider, and so Muriel had learned to live with and love John. It was a good life for John, as he was never forced to challenge the limits of his emotional prison. But what he never understood was that it was not okay for Muriel or the kids.

It wasn't that John withheld the love he felt for his wife and kids. He loved them truly and deeply. The simple truth was that he had no idea how to express that love. It was something he had never learned from his father. The times when he allowed himself to be emotional, early on in their life together, had left him feeling awkward, uncomfortable, almost dirty. When times were hard, as they had been after the birth of their daughter, Bethany, John simply disengaged. If he couldn't fix it, he couldn't deal with it, and that was the sad and simple truth.

So, although they appeared to be a happy, balanced family on the surface, the fact was that John Boyle provided food and shelter, while Muriel provided everything else. The love and understanding that John was incapable of providing were given twofold by Muriel to the children, when she was able. When she wasn't, the children relied upon themselves, and more often than not, on Tommy. The feelings that John could never express in times of joy or sorrow remained unspoken as Muriel rocked him back and forth. She held his head to her breast as she wondered where the man she fell in love with had gone and tried to understand the man who had returned from the Great War in her John's body. The emotions that were alive in his heart would die in his throat before they could emerge as words of love or encouragement.

Muriel had always said their family "took a good picture," and John never understood what those words really meant until that night. They had always been a one-dimensional family.

That night, two years before, was the first of many nights that John would sit by the fire and examine the events of their lives together. He could no longer pretend everything was okay, because Muriel was no longer there to take his share of the pain. She was no longer there to deflect the truth, and John began to see his part in what their family had become. From the beginning, their oldest son Tommy was a sensitive and loving boy. John remembered Muriel often saying, "He feels things deeply, that one," and John remembered thinking he needed to "fix" the boy.

Back then, John's father still worked the farm with him, and when the two worked side by side, they were prone to hollering. It was just their way, as it had always been, and both John and his dad understood that, but young Tommy did not. Tommy would be alongside them in the barn, and as the hollering grew louder, Tommy would begin to cry. The harder John tried to get Tommy to stop, the harder Tommy cried. John's father would become angry, telling Tommy he would need to "toughen up some if he expected to amount to anything in this world." He also told John that he, too, had been like that as a child—emotionally disturbed—and had "needed fixing."

As a result, John set about trying to "fix" Tommy. He tried to find ways to deaden the depth of emotion in the boy, and to some degree, he succeeded—at least on the surface. However, John was never able to toughen Tommy up enough to satisfy his father, and Muriel was no help. When John sent Tommy to his room for crying, Muriel would go sit with him. She would hold him in her arms, read him her books, and fill his head with poetry and dreams of faraway places, telling Tommy it was okay to feel. She assured him that it was okay to be who he was, and that his father loved him in the best way he knew how.

The bond that developed between Tommy and Muriel was deep but incredibly complicated. Both desperately needed the emotional love of a man who was not capable of giving it to them, and in an effort to ease each other's sense of loss, they created a world in which John could never be a part. The conundrum of their existence had been created by John's emotional dysfunction, but the bricks and mortar of the wall this family would live behind were inadvertently laid by Muriel and Tommy.

As time passed and the family grew, Muriel became resigned to the relationship she and John would have. She understood that John loved her, just as she understood that he would never be able to express that love adequately. Muriel had settled. She had settled for a life that left her wanting because it was the easy and practical thing to do. John was a good man, and in his way, he had always been gentle with her. She could have done worse. She had reached a place of acceptance, but Tommy never could.

Throughout his young life and into his teen years, Tommy never stopped seeking his father's love and acceptance. John Boyle had become a hero to Tommy. Tommy placed him high atop a pedestal where John neither deserved nor wanted to be. John was just a simple man, unable to connect with the emotions that coursed through him like the wildfires of summer. To Tommy, a young man in emotional turmoil, the quiet calm and steady strength of his father were traits to which he aspired. He wanted to be like his father—solid, in control of his feelings, never showing fear or anger, every bit the hero. Tommy did not know the burden his father had hidden behind his exterior. He did not know that John himself longed for the courage to sit with Muriel and Tommy, to be able to give them his love, to share in their secret world, and to be accepted. Tommy never understood that the love he craved had always been there, just beneath the surface, just out of reach.

So life went on. Muriel did her best to maintain her inner light, which illuminated the grey that hovered at the edges of their world. Meanwhile, Tommy learned not to feel. He learned to be the man he thought his father would be proud of, rather than the boy that he was, and John pretended not to notice the problems in his life. Then, in the winter of 1955, William Boyle, the second son of John and Muriel, was born. He was a beautiful Christmas baby, and for a time, it seemed his arrival would herald a new beginning for the troubled family.

John embraced this new son with a gentleness of heart Muriel had not seen in him since before the war. She was filled with hope at the expectation that John might rise above the obstacles of his emotional trauma and become the man she had always hoped he would be. In her fanciful way, Muriel imagined a world where they all lived, loved, and grew old in quiet contentment. This world had become so real in her mind that when it was shattered, she lost a part of her spirit that she would never regain.

Tommy also saw the changes in his father and was immediately filled with confusion. What had this new baby done to gain the affection and attention that Tommy himself had been unable to earn? He was confused by the mixed feelings of love and hate he felt for this innocent new baby. The more Tommy craved attention, the more he seemed to fade into the background of everyday life. John was never mean to Tommy. He never punished him unfairly. As with his relationship with Muriel, whom he also loved, John merely existed alongside Tommy. John was always fair and generally patient, but never loving, and that was what Tommy needed. When John began showering the new child, Billy, with affection and physical contact, Tommy became jealous, then resentful, and finally angry. These feelings, incubated in neglect and sorrow, were not the fault of the new baby but would stay with Tommy for the rest of his life.

John was now seeing the truth of what he had done to his family. Throughout the long hours of his sleepless nights, memories assaulted him, leading him to the horrible realization of what he had become: a man unable to express a single emotion for fear of unleashing a lifetime of suppressed feelings. He remembered the children when they were young and recalled how he would cling to them when they were small and helpless. He remembered how Muriel would be filled with hope because of his attentions, and how, slowly, as the children grew, he would withdraw. As these sweet and innocent babies began to turn into actual people with personalities, John would close off his heart. When he felt they could expect his love rather than simply accept it, John knew that there would come a day when he would disappoint them—a day when they would see him for what he truly was: a man who was shattered and full of fear. That was a day John could never live through, so he pushed them away.

Just as he had turned his relationship with Tommy into a practical arrangement, he did the same with Billy. As a result, just as Tommy spent his youth—and much of his adult life—seeking his father's love, so would Billy. Muriel, whose hope had blossomed with the birth of their second child, began to experience long episodes of depression as she realized the fantasy life she had created would never come to be. And so they all moved forward, all hurting, all seeking, yet never finding the balance between love and life. The patterns of their lives were set on an unstoppable journey of denial and a never-ending cycle of dysfunction. They all began to endeavor to survive in a one-dimensional world.

For a few years, things went along not too badly. The boys played, studied, and worked the farm alongside their father, while Muriel kept a fine home and provided the boys with the love and dimension to life that John was unable to give. Tommy was bright and never stopped trying to please, while Billy followed along, never causing trouble and never expecting anything too good. John, a man who could plan his crop rotations and livestock requirements years ahead, never lived beyond each day in his personal life. His "one day at a time" philosophy was not based on serenity or acceptance but was born of an inability to cope and a fear of change. Had John possessed the courage to look inward, he might have changed the path his family had taken. On those long nights as he sat by the fire, he wished he had summoned the courage such change required. But wishing doesn't make it so, and hoping won't change what's been done. For folks like John Boyle, hope only led to sadness—or so he thought.

Then came Bethany. To say she was unexpected would be an understatement for John. To say she had been unplanned by Muriel would be naive. Muriel had been slipping further into flights of fancy and deeper into depression more regularly by the summer of 1960. John had grown worried about her pronounced highs and lows. Unable to fix or understand her erratic behavior, he decided to seek counsel from a source beyond himself. The very act of opening up to another about a problem within his family—a family that outwardly appeared perfect—was of great difficulty for John. It was the only time in his life that he reached out to another, and that act of reaching was a testament to the deep, unspoken love within him. It was a love that gave him the courage to ask for help, the same love he would later rely on when Muriel began to disappear from his world.

John was not a spiritual man in the commonly understood sense, though when alone with the soil, he found a peace and serenity he couldn't attain anywhere else. He was not a religious man in the traditional sense, but he understood and appreciated religion. It wasn't the dogma or rituals of any denomination that attracted John; it was the regimentation of religious organizations that aligned with how he conducted his own life.

The only time John truly felt he fit in was during his military service. Even in the midst of war, living each moment as though it might be his last, he felt a kind of security and well-being. In the Army, he knew exactly what was expected of him. Never in his life did he experience a clearer understanding of his role. If he screwed up, he was told immediately, and more often than not, he was given the tools and inspiration to fix it. When he excelled, as he often did in this controlled environment, he was rewarded briefly and directly, with no fanfare and no ongoing attention. John enjoyed the Army because it suited his controlled emotional life. The military gave him a place where being unemotional was not only accepted but encouraged. He could bury his emotions beneath piles of regimental procedure, and that suited him just fine. He was able to fit in; he was able to get along.

This same attention to ritual and need for control drew John to the church when he returned to the farm. He had attended church as a young man at the insistence of his parents and had been involved as an altar boy and later as an usher. The old priest who presided over the flock in this part of the diocese was later understood to be one of the lesser clergy, but as a young man, John saw him as all-powerful, full of the knowledge of God. John was fascinated by the control this priest, Father Mike, had over his parishioners. He instructed them in his sermons on how, what, and when to feel. He read them the Word, explained its meaning, and told them how to apply it to their lives—and they all listened. They listened because they believed this man of the cloth knew something they did not. He was a man of God, and they were his sheep, all willing to be led.

When John returned to the real world after the war, he married Muriel and instantly, gratefully, gave up control of his life to her. She was strong, and John was damaged far more than he had been when he went away. He was indeed deeply damaged, but in ways unseen by the eyes of the world. He was damaged in ways that, in those days, society dictated should remain hidden. However, he was willing to be led, and the concealment of the extent of his damage was managed through the well-ordered life Muriel put together for him.

They began to build their one-dimensional family with the birth of their first son, Tommy, and carried on with the birth of their second, Billy, some four years later. They were the perfect family—two kids and a good, working farm. Their neighbors were close, but not so close as to get a good look inside their lives. Fellowship took place in a church that knew them well, but only on Sunday mornings. Everything had been going along so well—until Muriel began to get ill.

Her depression became more frequent and lasted longer, only to be displaced at a moment's notice by a whirlwind of manic behavior, where she might repaint the house or reupholster a couch. She joined volunteer activities, at one time even joining a civil rights march. It was during one of these high points in her illness that Muriel began to talk of another baby. She told John her depressions were caused by her longing for a little girl, that the happiest times for her were when she had babies, and that was when she and John were closest to being a real family. She became convinced of the necessity for a new child, but John was convinced that a new child would bring disaster. He felt his world dissolving and sought counsel from the only man he felt he could speak to—Father Mike.

John entered the church through the large front doors and stepped into the dim light of salvation. He felt comfortable here in the soft glow beneath the high, painted ceilings, and slowly, he began to walk down the center aisle. It had been many years since he had been alone in the church, and he stopped to take in the scents of incense and the lingering smell of extinguished candles. His eyes followed the stations of the cross, and John searched deeply in his memories, trying to connect the images before him and the smells surrounding him with a happy memory from his childhood. He searched, willing for one of the few times in his life to be introspective, hoping to connect to a feeling. But no happy memories rose to the surface.

The brief comfort he had been experiencing left him, and he stood with the grim reality of who he was—a man who would never be at ease, a man unable to reconcile who he was with his perception of what the world expected him to be.

John sighed deeply and continued to walk over the plush carpet down the long aisle, wondering how many brides had passed this way, how many coffins had been rolled to their final resting place, and how many husbands had come seeking solutions to problems with their wives. As he approached the altar and the door behind it, which led to the priest's inner sanctum, he felt a sense of foreboding course through his body. He stopped in his tracks and, for a moment, felt certain he should not be here seeking advice from a man of the cloth who knew nothing of his world, except for what John had allowed him to know.

But John had a problem that needed fixing, and the ability to fix it did not lie within his grasp. So, with renewed determination, John crossed over the altar to the heavy oak door that stood between him and a man who would give direction and take control.

The door swung open on silent hinges, and John found himself standing in the vestry behind the altar. His eyes roamed from cabinet to cabinet, taking in the multicolored vestments waiting to adorn the priest during Mass. He looked upon the neatly stacked boxes of altar candles and the cases of hosts waiting to be blessed and transformed into the body of Christ. He saw the closet where the altar wine was stored, and felt an unfamiliar twinge of guilt as he recalled the day he and Greg Kuntz had sipped from the leftover wine after an Easter Mass service—wine that had been consecrated and turned into the blood of Christ. Father Mike had felt certain the sacrilege would cement their place in hell.

John saw the large candleholders, the incense burners hanging from large chains, the brass and copper crucifix, and all the colorful hats on Styrofoam heads—hats that made little Father Mike appear larger than life. John was filled with an odd sense of order and control, which calmed him and lulled him into a blessed state of denial.

There was another door at the back of the vestry, slightly ajar, and from within that room, John could hear Father Mike moving inside the church office. He knocked lightly and walked in as Father Mike finished pouring three fingers of Johnny Walker Red into a tumbler on his desk. Father Mike looked over his shoulder and motioned for John to enter, spinning the cap back onto the bottle and sliding it into the desk drawer with a fluidity of motion that could only come from years of practice. Father Mike lowered himself into his chair in a way that suggested it wasn't the first time that day—or perhaps even that hour—that he had renewed his acquaintance with Johnny Walker.

"John! John, please, come in, have a seat. It's been a long time since you've been in this room, hasn't it? You remember, John—I caught you drinking the wine with that Kuntz boy. What was his name? Greg, I think. Yes, Greg. He's dead, John. Did you know that? Drank himself to death when he was still young—not twenty years old! Tragic, really. I remember wondering, as I presided over his funeral, if it had anything to do with the wine that day, John. What do you think? No, of course not—just the musings of an old man, I suppose, eh, John? After all, you're still with us, even after a couple wars, eh? But I digress. Come sit, John, and tell me what's brought you back here after all these years. How can old Father Mike help?"

"Well, Father, I'm not really sure where to begin. You know I've never been much good at talking, not really. Muriel's the one who can get across to the kids and other folks what it is I'm trying to say. I'm only good at plain talk about work and such."

"John, you can speak to me about anything. Nothing can be so hard that we can't take a look at it. You don't need to sit there looking all fearful, John. 'He that knows no guilt can know no fear.' Did you know that? Philip Massinger said that. Is there something you're feeling guilty about, John?"

"Guilty? Well, I suppose so, yes, in a way. I'm having some trouble at home with Muriel, Father, and I'm not sure what to do. I don't do well with problems, you know."

"Have you been unfaithful to Muriel, John? Is that where your guilt lies? In your infidelity?"

"What? No, nothing like that, Father, I assure you! Muriel is sick. She's been getting these bad bouts of depression. That's what she calls it. Then other times, she's like a house on fire, ready to save the world and paint it all at once. I can't figure it, Father, and I don't know what to do, or what kind of mood she'll be in at any given time. I'm at my wit's end, and I need some help. I feel guilty because I can't fix her, and I don't know how to be with my kids when she's not okay. She does most of the thinking and all the caring for us. I'm just a farmer."

"You, John, are a farmer, a husband, and a father! You're also a member of this congregation and make a weekly offering that we appreciate. Maybe you're overreacting. Though I don't see you here every week, your pretty wife is, with your boys. She seems fine to me, son. What you're describing sounds like women's issues. Now, Muriel is far too young for 'the change,' so maybe what you're dealing with is just regular women's problems that come each month. Those kinds of problems can work on a man, John—that's a fact! 'In this life, we want nothing but facts, sir; nothing but facts.' Charles Dickens said that." Father Mike chuckled at his own wit.

John watched as Father Mike threw back his hand and drained the scotch from his tumbler, all while opening the desk drawer and spinning the top off Johnny Walker again. He poured another three fingers and replaced the bottle in the desk while John was still trying to make sense of what the priest had just said.

"Father, I don't think you understand. This is worse than that regular stuff. I've been married to Muriel for nearly eleven years, and I knew her a good many years before that. I'm used to her regular ways, but this is something different. I'm worried sick about what to do. Now she seems to think having another baby will fix things, but I don't think she can handle another one right now. That's what I came to talk to you about, Father. I think we need to take some precautions, if you know what I mean, because she's sick and all. I think I'd like to talk to a doctor about her getting some of those new birth control pills."

"Worried, John? Or just fearful? So fearful, in fact, that you would put your own selfish needs for sex above the needs of your dear wife—above the needs of the child you carry in your seed? 'Fear is stronger than love,' did you know that, John? Thomas Fuller said that, and it's so true. Do you think you know better than a woman when she needs to be with child, John? Perhaps your Muriel isn't the problem at all. It seems to me she's acting responsibly, in keeping with the wishes of our Pope, who speaks directly to our Lord. Do you presume to know better than the Pope? Better than God himself? I'm filled with disappointment in your attitude toward Muriel. Are you suggesting she might be insane because she wishes to have another child? Did you really think you could come here and get my permission to kill an unborn child with pills sent to this earth by the Devil himself?"

"Father, please stop! You don't hear what I'm saying. I'm really scared! You're right, but not because I want sex and no babies. I love babies—maybe better than I can ever love anyone. But she's sick, Father, and I don't know what to do! I only know how to work. I don't know how to take care of kids and a sick wife. I need help. I don't need you yelling at me. I need you to tell me what to do. Muriel always tells me what to do, and now she can't. I don't know how to act differently, Father; I really don't."

Father Mike finished his second glass of scotch and filled his third as he sat glaring at John. His face had become a glowing red, and John could see beads of perspiration on his upper lip and forehead. He wondered if this was from anger or the effects of ten ounces of Johnny Walker Red, neat. Father Mike was wheezing in wet breaths, trying to control his breathing, and John could see the good priest was searching for calm before he spoke.

"'Men acquire a particular quality by constantly acting in a particular way.' Did you know that, John? Aristotle said that. Do you know what that means? It means you need to act differently. It means you need to summon up whatever courage you can and help Muriel through this hard time. It means you don't need doctors or birth control pills, but must work from a position of faith. Trust your priest, your church, and care for your wife and the child she will bear. Do you understand that, John? 'Frailty, thy name is woman.' Shakespeare said that. Do you understand what I'm saying?"

John began to sob. His mind was running in a thousand different directions at once. The information he was trying to absorb was melting together with Father Mike's ridiculous quotes, and John felt himself getting angry. The words he was trying to articulate were lost in the confusion of his mind, and he did not understand what this priest was saying to him.

"No, Father, I don't understand! I just can't, Father. I can't have another child in our house."

Father Mike sipped his scotch, sitting in arrogant judgment of this man who had come to him for help—this man of his flock, all so needy, all so sinful, all so annoying, all so small.

"Do you know the story of Solomon and the baby, John? Do you know that Solomon ordered the baby cut in two? Obviously, in these enlightened times, we would never suggest cutting a child in two. However, it strikes me, John, that there is a similarity in your situation. It also strikes me that, in this case, there are too many babies in a house rather than too few. Mmmm. 'These are the times that try men's souls.' Thomas Paine said that. What do you think he meant?"

"Huh? I don't know what he meant, Father. I don't know what you're talking about with anything. It's like you're not even hearing what I'm saying!"

"Indeed, John, indeed it is. Which of your boys would you like to get rid of, John, so Muriel could have another child?"

"What?"

"Which of your boys, John? Tommy or Billy? There's a family over in Odacre that can't conceive. They'd truly feel blessed with the child you would abandon."

John rose in a fury, his chair flying out from under him and crashing onto the hardwood floor. His temper surged, and for a moment, he feared for the life of this pathetic, drunken man of God. He stepped forward, then stopped. At that moment, he understood that the man locked deep within him for so many years must stay hidden. John let his clenched fists open, and his arms fell to his sides. Father Mike sat staring in his drunken arrogance, unaware he had been moments from meeting his Maker—moments from having to atone for a life wasted and the lives he had violated.

"You rot in hell and go fuck yourself on the way, Father. John Boyle said that. I think you know what it means."

John turned and left the church for the last time. He would never enter it—or any other—again, nor would he allow any of his family to do so while they lived in his home. John drove back to the farm and sat alone in the barn for a long time. He had gone to the priest for direction, and he had returned with none. He had no action plan, so he planned no action. That night, he found Muriel in a good mood. He took her in his arms, kissed her on the lips, and they all continued on as though everything was okay—as was their way. Ten months later, a beautiful little girl named Bethany was born. She arrived, and Muriel left, and none of their lives were ever the same again.

As much as John had tried throughout his life to pretend none of it had happened, it had all returned to him on those nights when he sat alone in his penance. They had moved on, he and his Muriel. They had all gotten past it—or at least, that's what they believed and hoped for. But hope for men like John Boyle only led to sadness, and his sadness led to bitterness. His bitterness turned to anger, and his anger to hate. He hated that his wife was mostly gone to him. He hated that she called out for a son who was lost to him and that he couldn't find it within himself to reach out to the son and daughter he still had. He hated the priest who had set them all on this road to perdition, and above all, he hated himself—for all he had done and, more so, for all he had not done.

Their long journey into uncertainty had begun nearly two years ago. The spells of confusion were short and regular at first, and the moments of complete memory loss were few, but John never knew when they would come or how long they would last. The doctors had prepared him for the worst, assuring him that in the end, his Muriel would be gone forever. John had accepted his responsibility as the caregiver to the woman he had loved inadequately for most of his life—the woman who had always cared for him the best she could. For a short time, he had managed to keep the severity of her decline from Beth, and Bill had long since stopped calling. But Muriel never stopped calling for Tommy. The days when she was completely lost were sometimes better than the days she spent crying out for her lost son.

So John Boyle sat by the fire, wearing his sadness and hate in silence as a testimony to a love that had never faltered, a love he was never able to return. He looked down at the Stephen King novel *Insomnia* he had just finished reading, and smiled to himself, feeling a kinship with the main character, Ralph Roberts, sitting alone in his room and missing his wife, Carolyn. So too was John, unable to sleep, unable to move on, waiting for the little bald doctors to come and take his wife.

His oldest grandson had seen him reading Stephen King and had been excited. "Here, Grandpa," he had said. "You gotta read this one, it's really good." So John Boyle, at three in the morning, opened the cover of the thin novel and read the first line: *The man in black fled across the desert, and the Gunslinger followed.* And John Boyle allowed himself to flee reality.

BILLY

It was six-thirty in the morning when Bill Boyle checked into a day room in Amsterdam International Airport. Billy had made a night crossing of the Atlantic and was facing an eight-hour layover before boarding his twelve-hour flight to Johannesburg, South Africa. He had not slept much on the plane—he seldom did—and rather than spending the time in the airport lounge with his two colleagues, he decided to sleep the day away. Amsterdam was one of the few airports left that offered day rooms inside the terminal, and Billy always felt more comfortable keeping to himself.

After the usual prodding and jeering from his traveling companions and the usual excuses from Billy, he separated himself from their adolescent boozing and sought out solitude in an eight-by-ten airport day room. Billy was not against an occasional drink, but drinking in excess or drinking solely to pass the time seemed a foolish waste to Billy, and time was a commodity he did not like to waste. For as long as Billy could remember, he was aware of the minutes and seconds ticking by, and for the majority of his life, he lived in an agitated state. He could never quite say he was constantly anxious—he never experienced panic attacks, as he understood them—but Billy always felt as though he was just a little late. Regardless of where he was or what he was doing, he always felt as though he was supposed to be somewhere else, doing something else. Billy was a timekeeper and a clock-watcher, and though he saw this as a character defect, in reality, it made him a highly organized and efficient thinker. The traits that made him feel a little apart from the rest of the world had turned out to be very useful in his business life.

Bill Boyle was a civil engineer and an accomplished one at that. He had walked off the farm his father had hoped he would work for the rest of his life and had worked his way through university with honors. He finished in the top three of his graduating class and had a dozen options for employment upon graduation. The day of his graduation should have been a big deal, but it was not. He was proud of what he had accomplished and excited about the prospects ahead, but as he stood on the platform erected on the university football field with fifty-four classmates he had known for five years, he felt completely alone.

He scanned the crowd for signs of his mother and father, but he did not see them there. In the back, though, arms waving wildly and standing alongside Mr. Perkins, he could see his little sister Bethany with her boyfriend, Carl. She was always there—Bethany had always tried to make their family something it was not. Billy's dad had called the night before to tell him that his mother had taken a bad turn and had been secluded for the past several weeks. John Boyle told Billy they would do their best to be there, but he could not say for sure. By the end of the conversation, Billy knew they would not attend. Still, he looked for them and hoped, and even though he knew they would not be there, he was disappointed. So Billy sat alone in the crowd as he always did, smiling and pretending he was happy on his graduation day.

He had known his mother would not be able to attend because it was supposed to be Tommy. Tommy was the favorite; Tommy was the first in the family who would get a degree, the one they saved for and sent all the money to, and Tommy was the one who had let them down. Oh, Tommy went off to school, and Billy was certain he had started with good intentions and had given it his best in the beginning. But Tommy had problems, and Tommy had issues, and Tommy began to drink. Not much at first, probably no more than anyone else in his dorm, but something changed in Tommy with the onset of drinking.

Billy looked up to Tommy as though he were the first and only big brother in the world, and when Tommy first left, Billy wrote to him every week. And Tommy replied. He told Billy everything about university and made it sound exciting. Tommy joined the debate club and student union and met more people in one year than he had on the farm in a lifetime. He was funny, popular, ambitious—but he was not a good student.

It was the little things, unnoticed at first, that eventually ended Tommy's career as a student: late papers, missed classes, ridiculous excuses. The kind of things every professor knows to watch for and eventually addresses. But Tommy somehow stayed under everyone's radar, slipping through the cracks, and by the time he was discovered, it was too late, and his first year was lost. The loss of the year in itself was no great consequence; many first-year students go the same route. Overwhelmed by the pace of university life and the freedom it offers, they fail. Usually, such students face the music, swallow their pride, and move forward. But that was not the path Tommy Boyle chose.

Tommy was filled with fear and insecurity from the moment he left the two hundred acres that had been his world. He had worked so hard, for so long, to earn the love his father was incapable of expressing that he viewed higher education as the mechanism by which that love would be delivered. His father had told him many times, even on the night he gave Tommy the family heirlooms, that Tommy would be the first to go to university. Tommy was to be the best and brightest of the Boyle men, and because of that, his father was proud and reluctantly said so. It was the closest his father ever came to expressing the love Tommy craved, but he stopped short. His father's pride was not his father's love, but it was something Tommy could settle for—something that gave him hope and made everything seem worthwhile.

John Boyle had scrimped and saved for years, amassing enough money to put the boy through university. It was his goal for all his children, but there would never be enough for more than one to attend, and Tommy knew it. So, he never told them about that first year. He continued to write letters, letting them believe he was doing well. That was when the lying started, the cheating began, and Tommy Boyle started his journey away from the family, never to return.

Billy was the first to suspect something was wrong. Over Tommy's first year, the letters he wrote to Billy dwindled, and by the middle of his second year, they stopped completely. Tommy did not come home that first summer, claiming he found work in the city and could not get away. He missed Christmas, too, having met a girl with whose family he spent the holidays. He did not come home for

March break, giving no explanation. Muriel Boyle entered a depression, her way of signaling that she sensed something amiss with Tommy, while John Boyle spent long hours in the fields, both refusing to confront the issue.

So, it was Billy who decided to visit Tommy. It was Billy—cared for throughout his young life by his older brother, who admired Tommy and tried so hard to emulate him—who was certain Tommy had fallen into misfortune. Billy imagined all sorts of explanations for Tommy's silence, but none were unfavorable to him. Tommy was such a source of strength and responsibility for Billy and Bethany that Billy could not conceive a scenario where Tommy was at fault. Sixteen-year-old Bill Boyle could not imagine his brother, his hero, as anything other than a hero.

Billy took his savings and purchased a bus ticket to the city, where he took a taxi to the address where all his letters had been sent. As he stood in front of the stone block house on the campus edge, he was in awe. Students were moving in every direction: some with purpose, some confused, others scared. Some were skateboarding, biking, or on scooters. Many were in groups, chatting; others walked alone, reading or listening to music. Couples walked hand in hand, laughing and oblivious to the chaos around them.

Billy stood in place, spinning in slow circles, taking it all in. He understood then why Tommy had stopped writing. Why would he take time from all this excitement to check in with a bunch of hicks on the farm, even if they were family?

Billy understood, and once again, he found himself envying Tommy, wanting all that Tommy had. For the first time, Billy had a dream. He had a dream and a plan, one he would pursue whether or not his parents supported it. Until that moment, his father's plan for Billy had also been his own: stay on the farm, work alongside his father, and maybe earn the recognition he longed for. It seemed a good life before, but now that Billy had glimpsed the larger world, he wanted more. He wanted to be a part of it, to contribute, and he could not wait to tell Tommy.

Billy was uncertain how long he had stood at the end of the sidewalk leading to the stone house that served as Tommy's dormitory, but he suddenly sensed he was no longer alone. As he completed one of the many 360-degree turns he had been making, he found himself toe to toe with a very amused young man with shoulder-length hair and a large, drooping mustache. Billy took a step back in surprise, and the young man began to laugh.

"Hey man, are you out of it or what? I've been watching you from my window for over twenty minutes now, just spinning in circles. I thought for sure you'd fall over from dizziness! I even bet my buddy Tom five bucks you would! Guess I'm out five bucks, huh? Anyway, I couldn't wait any longer; I've got to get to class. See you around!"

"Wait, did you say your buddy Tom?"

"Yup, my buddy and my roommate Tom. He's skipping class this morning because he didn't get the assignment done that was due—freaking geometry, man, what a drag! So, he's suddenly 'sick,' you know—bagging off class."

"Not really. I'm not sure what you mean. What's your name anyway?"

"I'm Neville, man, but everyone around here calls me Devil. You know, man? You know what I mean?"

"No, not really. Is he in there now? That's great! Tommy is who I came to see!"

"Tommy, huh? Far out! That's hilarious—I always thought he was too cool to go with the 'Tommy' thing. He's just plain old Tom around here, or 'Tom Cat' if you get my drift. Most kids just call him 'Cat' or 'Cool Cat' because he's the man!"

"Really, wow, that's neat. Back home on the farm, he was always just Tommy."

"On the farm? Whatever, man, he's in there." Neville (also known as Devil) pointed over his shoulder without turning away from Billy. "Room 212, second floor. Gotta fly, man; see you on the flip side."

Billy watched in amazement as Neville—also known as Devil—in a single motion dropped and mounted the skateboard he carried and pushed off down the sidewalk, en route to his geometry class. As Billy watched Neville glide across the paved beauty of the university campus, he tried to understand why anyone would want to be called Devil.

Billy turned again, taking in the image of the dormitory in front of him. It was a large, stone-block building with a gleaming white wrap-around porch and dozens of large, multi-paned windows. The building rose a full four stories high and appeared to be almost entirely surrounded by sprawling flower beds, filled with perennials, annuals, and shrubbery of various kinds and colors. The east wall was covered by a climbing vine, fluorescent green with deep red berries interspersed among the leaves. It had crept from the foundation to the eaves, gripping the porous mortar and strategically avoiding the large windows where it could lay no root. Billy felt the age of the vine and the tradition of the entire university, somehow sensing that the vine symbolized everything good about the place. The vine climbed steadily, always upward, like a student working toward success—a pursuit of excellence, like Tommy's. His eyes traveled high above the roof of the dormitory to the flag whipping in the wind, and Billy was filled with hope and pride as he entered the building.

Inside, it was quieter than he expected; in fact, it was nearly deserted. The grandeur and heritage visible from the outside seemed lost as he crossed the threshold, entering a large foyer with chairs and couches on both sides. Tables were covered with newspapers and editorial magazines, and in the corner, a small television was tuned to a documentary on pollution in the Love Canal. At the far end of the foyer sat an older man with wispy white hair, wearing a button-down shirt with a school tie and jacket, bifocals perched on his nose as he absorbed himself in the *New York Times*. On the walls were hundreds of photos of former students who had lived in this residence over the years. Billy looked on in awe, wondering about the fates of those pictured. How many had become lawyers or judges, doctors or scientists, presidents or philosophers? It was almost overwhelming, and Billy was unaware of how long he had been staring until he heard the man clear his throat.

"Excuse me, young man, is there something I can assist you with? I would love to know where your mind was just now; it's been a long time since I've seen that look on a young man's face."

"I'm sorry, sir. I'm not sure what you mean."

"That look—the one on your face at this very moment. The look that comes with knowing the world lies before you and that your future will be exciting and full of hope. That look, my boy, is what I mean and what I see in your eyes. I recognize it because I once had that look myself, though many years ago. That's why I returned to my alma mater in what some mistakenly call the 'golden years,' so I could be around young men with such a look, hoping to draw on their energy and perhaps gain a few more years of life."

"Well, sir, I'm not sure if I have any 'look' at all. I can tell you I never thought much about what lies ahead for me. Mostly, I thought I'd work the farm like Pa—until today, that is. Being here at this place has made me think maybe there's something more I could do. I've always been good at fixing things, like my Pa, but it doesn't seem to have left him too happy. So maybe I need to do something more—something more important than just being a farmer. I think maybe I could build things, too. I think I'd like that."

"An engineer, perhaps, or an architect. All things are possible here if one applies oneself. The possibilities really are endless. I myself am an architect—I specialized in bridge design, civil architecture, and I've enjoyed a wonderful and rewarding career that's taken me to all corners of the earth.

As I said, I've traveled far and wide, yet here I am, back at this institution, still learning."

"Learning? What are you learning now?"

"Well, today, my young friend, I'm learning about you! Who do I have the pleasure of speaking with, and how may I assist you? You seem a bit young to be here as a student, so I assume you're on some sort of mission."

"Well, my name is Billy, sir, and I am on a mission, of sorts. I came to visit my brother, who lives here. I've been mailing letters for some time now, but he stopped replying, so I thought I'd find out if he's okay. Now that I'm here, I can see there's so much going on that I'm sure he just hasn't had the time to write. I don't know if I would either, in a place as exciting as this one. It sure beats farm life, I can tell you that."

"Well, young William, it may beat all out of the farm, but I can tell you a man should be proud of what he does in life, regardless of what it is. I would never be so presumptuous as to assume I was in any way better than the man who provides the food I eat. Farming is a skill few excel at and even fewer understand. It is really quite an organized science—when to plant, where to plant, how to till, harvest, and so on. I can design and build a one-thousand-meter-long bridge over a ravine a thousand meters deep, but ask me to grow one turnip, and I wouldn't have a clue where to begin. All things, Billy, are relative, one never being greater than another. So, what is the name of this young and inconsiderate student you seek?"

"His name is Tommy, but I met a kid outside named Neville, who says around here they call him Tom Cat or Cool Cat. He said he was on the second floor."

"And so he is, Room 212. Though I must express my surprise—I consider myself a good judge of character, and I see much of it in you, young man. All things being equal on the farm where you were raised, I honestly have no idea how you and Mr. Tom Cat are brothers. You are a well-spoken and polite young man, and Cool Cat is an arrogant and self-absorbed goldbricker. I have great difficulty understanding how this young man also grew up in the farming culture where hard work is the norm. Please accept my apology, young man, but I hope you can find and hold a focus should you enter these halls of higher learning in a way that your brother has not."

"Excuse me, Sir, but you're wrong. My brother is the one who showed me the way to be polite. He has never been rude in his life, and I would appreciate it if you wouldn't say so. Now, if you'll excuse me and if it's okay, I would like to go up to room 212 to see my brother Tommy."

Billy brushed past the old man and headed straight to the long, curved stairway that led to the upper floors of the dormitory. He moved up the stairs and down the hall with great trepidation. Something was wrong. Both Neville, also known as Devil, and the elderly scholar standing watch in the dormitory lobby had described his older brother, his lifelong hero, as something less than what Tommy was. Tommy had always been there for him, and though Billy was unfamiliar with the culture of this institution and city life, he could not imagine Tommy would be held in such low esteem by an academic and raised on a pedestal by the likes of Neville, also known as Devil.

He made his way down the long hallway that led to the back of the building, taking in all he could of the halls. Each space between dorm room doors held a bulletin board. The boards were covered with announcements of social events on campus, class schedules, notices from the college administration, want ads, and items for sale. There was artwork, photos, petitions, jokes, and poetry, and Billy's eyes locked on each item with fascination. Each step down the well-lit hall brought Billy closer to the realization that this world of knowledge he'd never known was the world he would embrace. This was where his future lay, and Billy, for the first time, felt he had found a place where he could belong—a place where he would be seen and accepted, a place where he would never have to live in the shadow of another. In these halls, he would be able to carve out an identity for himself, controlling the outcome of his life. His end would be determined by his means. Hard work would be the key, and Billy was a hard worker. Here, he would never be invisible again.

He suddenly found himself standing in front of room 212, frozen in his tracks as he looked upon the door. He had come here with little thought or planning, and now, as he found himself at the door to his brother's world, he felt as though he were intruding. Tommy's life was here now, in this place, and it seemed he had turned his back on his family and roots. Perhaps being here with these people had caused his brother to be ashamed of his origins, and Billy's presence would be an unwelcome reminder of a life Tommy had abandoned. Thoughts of leaving filled Billy's mind as he looked at the door, covered in magazine clippings of bikini-clad women and arm-flailing rock stars—all of which seemed so out of character for Tommy. His confusion was growing, but his uncertainty quickly disappeared as the door to 212 suddenly opened.

Stopping abruptly as he exited the room was a long-haired man with a short-trimmed beard. He wore only boxer shorts covered in Playboy bunnies and a pair of sandals. Several beaded bracelets encircled his wrist, a peace symbol hung around his neck, and he was clearly shocked to find a young man standing inches from his face.

"Whoa! What the fuck, man? You scared the shit out of me! What the hell are you doing, standing here staring at my door? Admiring my collage art, or just getting off on the bevy of beauties I've collected here?"

"Excuse me! No, neither. I'm sorry to have startled you; I was just deciding whether or not to knock."

"Really? That seems like an odd thing to be deciding. Like, just knock or don't—what could possibly make that a big decision, man? You some kind of weirdo or what?"

"No, I'm not any kind of weirdo. I'm looking for Tommy."

"And you've found him, though no one other than Mommy Dearest has called me that in some time. I'm generally known as Tom Cat, though I certainly prefer Cool Cat, and my close friends just call me Cat. You, my little unknown weirdo, are none of the above, so you may call me Tom—never Tommy. What can I do for you, kid?"

"Well, I'm sorry, sir. There must be some mistake. I was directed here by the man downstairs to see my brother. This is his dorm room, 212—I know because I send him letters here, though he hasn't written back for some time now. I came to see if he was okay. Is there another Tom that lives here? Do you have another roommate named Tommy— Tommy Boyle?"

Cool Cat looked on in silence for a moment, and then began to snicker, which soon turned into a laugh. But it was not a kind laugh. It was not a laugh of mutual jest, good humor, nervousness, or joy. It was a laugh filled with meanness and scorn, and Billy suddenly felt naked and exposed in front of this stranger. The tone of his laugh amplified in Billy's mind as Cat slowly raised his bracelet-adorned hand and pointed at him, speaking through snorts and chuckles.

"Oh, man," he said, "you must be Billy. Wow, wait till I tell Devil! I never thought you'd leave the farm, man. What the fuck! This is too hilarious."

Billy looked at this grinning moron, feeling anger rise from his gut. The knot in his stomach had evolved from concern over Tommy to anxiety about his journey, to outright fear as he looked at the door of room 212. The knot was quickly becoming anger, and the anger would turn to rage. Billy had only reached that point twice in his life, and when he gave over to it, he lost control completely. When all the frustration and fear Billy held in his mind reached the point of boiling, it generally came spilling out through his fists.

"How do you know my name is Billy, and where is my brother Tommy? I don't like you laughing at me as you are. It's quite rude. Please stop it now."

"Oh, please forgive me, Billy—I know being rude is frowned upon back in the holler, right? I know Ma and Pa would probably give you a whooping, right?" Cool Cat laughed sarcastically as he backed into the room he had just been leaving.

Billy followed Tom Cat into the room and took in the chaos there, but the only thing that registered in his mind was the fact that there were only two beds, one for Neville, also known as Devil, and one for Tom, also known as Cat. There was no evidence of his big brother here, and though Billy remained confused, his anger grew stronger, and he spoke more quickly and assuredly.

"Where is my brother? What is going on here? How do you know my name and about my Ma and Pa? You had better stop laughing and start talking, you jerk, or you'll be sorry!"

"Oh, I'll be sorry? Relax, kid. Your brother's not here. Your brother Tommy, also known as The Boyle, is not here. He hasn't been here since Neville arrived two semesters ago. Sorry, Billy, but I ain't the Tommy you're looking for; I'm the Cat, he's The Boyle."

Cat's voice was growing meaner, and Billy wondered how such arrogance and spite could grow in the heart of a person who had the opportunity to be in a place like this. Cat reached out to a shelf by his bed, dramatically sweeping aside a stack of magazines, their pages full of cutouts in the shapes of women. From beneath the magazines, he picked up a tattered shoebox, and with a grin more evil than Billy had ever seen, he flung it on the floor. The box landed heavily at Billy's feet, the lid flying to one corner of the cramped dorm room, and its contents spilled out in front of Billy.

Billy stared down in disbelief as he recognized what he was seeing. He looked at the scattered thoughts and feelings of his entire family lying there: letters, birthday cards, Christmas cards, Easter cards, and pictures his little sister Bethany had drawn in red, green, and blue crayon. He saw his own neat penmanship, carrying all the secrets and dreams he had shared with his brother. He saw his mother's handwriting and the little hearts she drew as periods, and to his dismay, even a letter in his father's hand—a man Billy had never known to write a letter.

Looking down at the scattered mail, Billy began to understand why Tommy hadn't responded. Billy's eyes slowly moved from the scattered mail to the sneering man before him, and he felt a sense of violation. He had identified the unknown feeling overcoming him; he had been violated, as had his entire family, by this sneering fool. That feeling of violation, coupled with his rage, created an emotion he had never experienced. He felt the hair on the back of his neck stand up, and he knew that the option of self-control was slipping away. Even though he hated this man, a part of Billy prayed he would speak no more. If Cat would just stop now, perhaps Billy could turn and walk away. Perhaps he could leave this dreaded feeling behind. For the first time, Billy longed to be invisible. But he was not, and Cat could not hold his tongue, for evil knows no bounds.

"And that, little Billy, is how I know your name," Cat continued. "It's how I know about your little sister, your Ma and Pa, and your pathetic family. And not just me, either! There's a whole bunch of the gang who know about you and your family. Every time a new letter arrives, we all gather 'round for a couple of drinks and a few laughs. It's really a blast, man. In fact, some here never even knew your loser brother before he took a powder—literally. You know, it's one thing for guys like me and Devil to waste Mommy and Daddy's money because, well, Mommy and Daddy have money. But your loser brother got into all kinds of shit with drinking and drugging and spent all the cash. He just couldn't fess up to the poor family—again, literally poor— so he started trying to be some big-time pusher to get the cash, and that's when he got caught, and they kicked his ass out. Don't really know where he is or what he's doing, and I don't give a shit. There, now you know the whole deal, so get the fuck out of my room."

The moments that followed felt like an eternity to Billy but must have only lasted a few seconds. He thought of a novel he had read the year before. It was a story about a pirate and the woman he had kidnapped and then fallen in love with. There was a hero in the novel who would have traveled to the ends of the earth to find and free this woman because he too had loved her. There was a passage where the pirate and the hero met face to face on opposite sides of a wide canal. They each spoke of their love for the maiden, vowing to destroy the other. But the pirate possessed the woman, and the hero did not. The sentence that rang in Billy's ears was: *The nobleman looked across the mist hanging over the canal at the adversary who stood there in his arrogance and sneered. In that moment, the nobleman knew he had been beaten, and in his defeat, he seethed.*

Billy remembered asking Tommy what it meant to seethe, and Tommy had laughed and told him, "Someday you may know." In that moment, Billy understood the feeling he had never before experienced or identified. Billy understood what came after rage, and he looked upon his adversary and he seethed.

Cool Cat was shocked by the sheer speed with which Billy launched himself into the air and landed upon him. Locked together, they fell back against the bookshelf, sliding to the floor in a rolling heap of arms and legs. Cool Cat was two years Billy's senior and twenty pounds heavier, but Billy seethed. His rage boiled over, and his blows fell in a flurry onto the face and chest of the once-sneering, arrogant college student. Cool Cat soon realized he was unable to defend himself against the madness that had taken hold of this young man, and in an effort to minimize his injuries, he began to curl up beneath Billy to protect his most vulnerable areas. Cool Cat whimpered and cried and screamed out for help, but Billy heard none of it. Billy had gone to a dark place in his mind. He had blanked out, and his body no longer responded to reasonable thought. His only purpose was to destroy Cool Cat, and were it not for the ensuing intervention, Billy might have killed him.

The first realization Billy had as he came back to himself was that he was being grabbed from behind. Arms encircled his chest, pulling him away from Cool Cat. As his vision returned, he saw the beaten and bloodied body of Tom Cat beneath him, and in that moment, he assumed the arms around him belonged to Neville, also known as Devil. Billy began to panic. He was not an aggressive boy, nor was he a fighter. As his senses returned, his rage faded, and along with the rage went the adrenaline-fueled strength. Billy feared he would now be vulnerable to attack by Neville and ultimately Tom Cat. He began to struggle against the arms that bound him, and with the struggle came the tears. Soon, Billy was sobbing uncontrollably. His body went limp, and he collapsed in a heap on top of the beaten student, waiting for the blows he was certain were coming.

"William. William! Whatever have you done, my boy? What has happened here? Please, let me help you up, my boy. Do not be frightened; I will not allow anyone to hurt you, though it seems I should be making that assurance to Master Tom Cat here."

Billy opened his eyes, and gazing down upon him was the kindly old gent who had been sitting in the foyer of McMillan Hall when he arrived. He was confused and disoriented, and as Billy tried to catch his breath between sobs, Tom Cat began to struggle to his feet. He was bleeding badly from his nose, both eyes were beginning to blacken, and as he pushed himself to one knee, he gasped and clutched his ribs tightly with his right hand.

"I'll tell you what the fuck happened. This psycho prick just attacked me! Look what he has done to me, Mr. Perkins!

Just look what he has done, and you let him in. You sent him to my dorm room, you useless old sack of shit. I want the police called immediately, and I will have your ass, you old fool. When my father hears what has happened here, you will be dismissed. Do you hear me?"

Mr. Perkins slowly bent from the waist and extended a hand to Billy as he cowered amid the spilled letters on the floor.

"Please, William, get up now, Son, and clean yourself up a bit. Tuck your shirt in and look smart, lad." He smiled at the boy kindly, but when he turned to Tom Cat, his expression grew stern. "Now, Master Tom, I'm not certain what exactly has transpired here, but let me assure you I very much doubt you are innocent in the proceedings. I take it young William here is not, in fact, your dear brother, and you and he have had a disagreement of sorts. And it would appear he felt quite a bit more passionately about his point of view than perhaps you did. As for the police, I am sure that if you think really hard about it, you will not want them snooping around in this room. Regardless of what you may have done to this young boy, I am quite certain there are materials in this room that the police and college administration would frown upon, which would likely leave you expelled. What would your father think of that, I wonder? And as for having my job, well, you see, I volunteer here, and I also make a sizable donation to the institution annually, so I doubt you'll have much influence there. Not to mention the irreparable damage to your well-honed reputation when word gets out that you had your ass kicked by a boy much younger than you. So, why not just skulk off and get cleaned up while I escort young William to the front door.”

Tom, holding his ribs and muttering under his breath, pushed his way past Mr. Perkins and Billy Boyle, cursing as he walked down the hall and into the washroom. Billy watched him in fear as he tucked in his shirt and straightened his jacket. Mr. Perkins stood silently for a moment before beginning to speak.

“William, this is not a good situation. Do you understand that this boy Tom could get you in a lot of trouble? If he were any brighter, he would understand he has some rights and choices and wouldn’t be frightened by the words of an old man. You must leave here, Son, and do so quickly. I don’t know what has transpired between you and him, but what I do know is that regardless of how annoying Tom Cat may be, there is no place in this world for the kind of violence you have just displayed. I told you not so long ago that I am a good judge of character, and I believe that to be true. I judged you a smart, polite, hardworking boy, not a hoodlum. I believe I was correct in my assessment, but you have anger in you that is greater than the sum of yourself. When I entered this room, you were as if in a trance, and I believe you may have killed that young man. You must find the source of this anger and remove it from your soul. It must be banished from your world if you wish to succeed in this life. Do you understand, William?”

Billy wiped the tears from his eyes and looked up at Mr. Perkins. “I don’t think I understand much anymore, Sir. I don’t know what has happened to my brother or what is happening to me, but I want to learn. I want to be better.”

Billy pointed to the shoebox on the floor and stooped to gather the fallen letters. "I will go, Sir, but these letters don't belong here. They are from my family, and I will not leave them here for this bunch to make sport of. I will go, but I'll tell you this: I will be back if it is the last thing I do. I will find my anger, and I will turn it into ambition, and I will get out of this life I am in, and there is nothing, or anyone, who will stop me."

Mr. Perkins led Billy out of the room and down the stairs to the foyer below. They stood there for a moment, and as Billy was about to exit the building, Mr. Perkins took him by the arm and extended his right hand for a handshake. As they shook hands, Mr. Perkins pressed a card into Billy's palm.

"I believe you, young William. I believe you will find your way, and you will return here. I would offer you my assistance in any way I can, when you are sure and when you are ready. Please call me. There is much of me that I see in you, and I feel you have a lot to offer this world. Goodbye, young William, until we meet again."

William left the building, and he walked for hours. He walked as though he were trying to walk out of his life, and in many ways that day, he did. He walked until it was time to catch his bus back to the farm, returning to a home that would never again hold any meaning for him. He never told anyone about where he had gone that day or what he had learned. He never told anyone about the letters he had found or that he had lost one hero and found another that day. Mr. Perkins had been there for Billy from that day on, and with his kindness and gentle way, he had mentored Billy and brought him through those hard years into the life he enjoyed today. It took Billy a long time to find the anger in his soul and banish it from his world, but he had, though not without a cost. Little by little over the years, he had removed himself from the dysfunction and disappointment of his family, and now here, alone in a day room in Amsterdam, he was overtaken by an emptiness he felt would never be filled. There had been several failed relationships, hours of therapy, and there had been success—and still, he could not escape the need to be something better than he was. To find some mythical acceptance and love that never existed for him and likely never would, to feel as though he belonged somewhere.

As he did every time this feeling of absolute isolation threatened to overtake him, he picked up the phone and began to dial his little sister, Bethany. She would fill him in on Mom's condition, Dad's continued isolation, and maybe even she would have some news of Tommy. Mostly, she would tell him about young John and young Muriel and the new child she carried in her womb. She would talk about Carl, and the love she lived would seep through the transatlantic line and fill a portion of the void that existed in Bill Boyle's soul. Then, perhaps, he would sleep.

REALIZATION

Armist stood and looked into the small mirror that hung over the sink in the bathroom off the office and storeroom of Polly's Pleasure Emporium. He stood and looked deeply into the ice-blue eyes that gazed back at him from the beveled mirror, and for the first time in longer than he could recall, he did not avert his gaze. He finally saw the truth of the man who looked back at him. He was Armist Hancock, the son of a war hero he had never met, the son of a woman who could not cope with a world where she found no peace. The product of a coupling that never had a chance, he was the victim of those circumstances. He was not a bad person. He was not to blame for any of it, and he wondered why it had taken him over sixty years to see that simple truth. He had made his life so needlessly complicated. He had hated everything and everyone and had allowed the circumstances of his past to define his life. He had fended for himself, been full of anger, and, through it all, he had never understood that it was not his fault. Life was just life.

He reached up and stroked his freshly shaven chin. It was a strong chin, and it had received its share of knocks over the years, but it had served him well. He wiped away a leftover dab of the strawberry-scented feminine shaving cream he had found in the bathroom and wondered briefly if Polly herself had to shave. That thought seemed strange to him. She never showed any hint of a beard. He examined the crook in his nose and remembered the big black man who had given it to him years before, but he could not recall the name. Then, with reluctance, he ran his fingers over the jagged scar above his right eye, and his thoughts went to

Gustav. Good old Gus. He was a tough one, a hard one, but, in the end, he had been a man of honor. He had died a hero's death in the act of saving a friend. Armist bowed his head and looked at the small circle of wooden beads that lay on the basin. He said a silent prayer to a God he never knew, a God he was trying to understand for the first time in his life, and a God he was beginning to believe could restore him. He prayed for the soul and redemption of Gustav Kaminski. He raised his head once again, peering into the deep-set blue eyes of Armist Hancock, and for the first time ever, Armist dreamed of a better life and dared to hope that he might achieve it.

He thought of his father and Gus and then held his own life up for scrutiny. He had always fancied himself a hero, but he was not. He had become a legend on the streets in many ways, but being the oldest of a group of people who existed only to run away from life did not make a man a hero. It just made him a runner. It had made Armist a better runner than the rest of them. Armist figured that everyone on this earth was searching for a hero, regardless of the circumstances. In a world where the bottom is all around you, Armist's long survival had, in some twisted way, made him a hero. However, in a moment of sudden clarity, he understood that he was not. He had spent a lifetime running from fear, from responsibility, from social anxiety, all the while blaming anyone and everyone else for his condition. He had achieved exactly what he had set out for in life: nothing. He had no job, no home, no family. There was nothing that had ever caused him to live up to the man his father had been. He had lived an invisible life, and in doing so, he had nothing to show for it. Those folks out there who just got by, the ones who held down a job and kept a family together—they were the heroes. The people who were willing to take a risk and meet life head-on, to do what had to be done no matter how scared they were—those were the heroes. Gus had become one of those people at the end. Somehow, he had found the person he perhaps once was and managed to get back there, even briefly, before he died. That might or might not be the truth of it, but it made Armist happy to think that it was.

He stood as straight as he had ever been in his memory and looked at his own height in amazement. He moved his fingers over the small circle of wooden beads attached to the crudely carved crucifix and vowed to himself that from this moment on, he would try to live a life of honor. He could then remember the sacrifice of an old alcoholic bum and remember, too, that he was Armist Hancock. He was the son of a war hero, and he would no longer be afraid to participate in life. Honor was the only gift a man could give to himself, and Armist was ready to do so. He smoothed an errant hair on the crown of his head with his large, talon-like hand, took a deep breath, and turned to leave the room to face the music with the cop Gideon, and he was not afraid.

Armist opened the door and gazed directly into the eyes of Constable Gideon. Though Gideon was mid-sentence, he was not looking at Polly, to whom he spoke. His focus had been on the door to the washroom, and now it fell fully on Armist. For a moment, the two stood locked in time, neither speaking, neither moving. It was as though the world had stopped, and all Armist could hear was the beating of his heart and the wheezing in his lungs. But there was no panic.

There was no pounding in his ears or churning in his gut, and there was no auto-response to run or lash out. Armist held his ground and met the officer's gaze straight on. He felt the security of the small circle of wooden beads tightly held in the palm of his twisted hand, and he felt himself stand even taller as he waited motionlessly for Gideon to speak.

Gideon had stopped speaking to Polly Ann, and all his senses became acutely aware of the giant of a man standing before him in the doorway of Polly Ann's office. In a way that was in keeping with his training, he quickly assessed what was happening in the small room and knew his back was to the door, which offered relative security. Polly was sitting at the desk, looking apprehensive, and though he never would have considered her a threat, at this moment, he was uncertain. He was uncertain because a huge, hulking man not six feet from him met his gaze with certainty and confidence. There was no fear of the police in this man. Gideon could sense it instantly, and that simple fact made this unknown man dangerous and unpredictable. The man was very large and close enough that he would not need to be quick to be on Gideon. With just a couple of normal strides for a man this size, the stranger could be all over him before he could release his baton or his service revolver, and Gideon, a twenty-year veteran of the city's finest, doubted he had the stamina to engage physically with the big man. The man was obviously older than Gideon, but he seemed to be in good condition, and Gideon was already thinking about the chewing out he would get from the station house for entering this situation without backup or even calling it in. He was on his own, with the outcome to be determined.

He chanced a quick glance toward Polly Ann and found her looking at the big man with a familiarity that Bob could not understand. The thought hurt him more deeply than he wanted to admit, and he was starting to feel as though she had set him up. He steeled himself for the possibility of an attack, slowly slid his hand to the grip of his baton, and started to speak.

"What's going on here, Polly? Why have you asked me here, and who the hell is the giant?"

"Giant?" Polly began to chuckle, and a small smile broke on the face of the big man in the doorway. "Why, this ain't no giant, Bob! This here is Armist Hancock!"

Gideon allowed his focus to fall on the man who stood before him, and rather than readying himself for imminent danger, Bob began to look at the features of the big man. His hair had been wet down and roughly combed; it was a soft auburn color graying at the temples. The army toque, moth-eaten and worn by Armist Hancock regardless of the time of year, was not present on the head of this big man. However, just above the right eye and falling toward the right ear was a jagged, cruel-looking scar—one Bob had seen before. The man before him was cleanly shaven, and from across the room, Bob caught an odd scent of strawberries. There was no three- or four-day stubble on the face of the man before him, as was the norm for Armist Hancock, but there was that chin. It was a chiseled, strong chin, the kind you could picture on a war hero or a football star or an astronaut, and Bob remembered thinking in the past that Armist Hancock would be classically handsome if he were not a bum.

His gaze shifted to the ground in search of the telltale red-right and blue-left runners, and as his eyes fell, he noticed the big man had a clenched and deformed left hand. In it, he seemed to be holding an odd-looking set of worry beads, perhaps a rosary. The hand, when unclenched, would surely resemble a large and dangerous-looking talon. There were no blue or red shoes, but rather an almost-new pair of athletic runners clad the feet of the big man. Bob's eyes came back up to his face and locked onto the deep-set blue eyes leveled upon him. He looked deep into those iceberg-blue eyes and recognized Armist Hancock. Bob could not explain away the great height, nor could he allow himself to believe that for all these years, virtually his entire professional life, he had been conned into thinking this fit old timer was a crippled and pathetic bum. But there it was—in his eyes, the unhidden truth of his identity—and Gideon was instantly more wary than he had been moments earlier. For not only was this man big, bigger than Bob could handle, but he also understood at that moment that this man was very clever. And a big, smart man would prove to be more of a threat than a big, stupid one.

"I'll be damned," Bob began. "If it isn't really old Armist Hancock! Maybe not the Armist I am used to, but damned sure the Armist I am looking for. What is your game, Mister Hancock? I'd like to know in which direction this meeting is heading. Are we talking here or going to the station to have a sit-down with McCaskey? You remember Officer McCaskey, don't you? One of the officers you assaulted earlier this night."

"Well, I ain't sure who assaulted who, but I do know the officer you are talking about never laid a hand on him. Now the other one, that punk kid, he got his due if you ask me, and he got it at the expense of an old friend of mine, but when I knocked him out, it was pure self-defense. I am hoping you will believe that, Officer, and that is what will determine how this little sit-down will go. I will talk to you and tell you all I know about Tommy Boy. It isn't much, I can tell you that right off. But I am not going down to the station, and I ain't cut out for a night in no slammer, even though this one is almost over. If that works for you, then we can talk; otherwise, I am leaving here right now."

"Leaving, are you, Armist? What about the police officer between you and the door here? Maybe he will have something to say about who leaves and when. Maybe you are not running things here. Maybe that job is mine, the police officer's. Maybe your job, as the vagrant, is to do exactly as I say."

Bob looked up at Armist from a distance of eight feet, and for the first time since his rookie year, he was scared. Not scared in the way he had been on many nights in many situations, but scared in a way that made his skin crawl— scared in a way that caused him to react differently from his normal way. Armist was a mountain. Bob was sure that should he try to leave, he would be unable to stop him. His fear rolled out in sweat and made its way down his spine, creating a cool space between his skin and the loose cotton uniform shirt he wore. Though it was almost imperceptible, there was a waver in Bob's voice and a tremor in his body.

"You going to go all tough-guy cop on me, Officer?" Armist smiled down at Bob as he continued, and there was no fear in his eyes. "Well, that don't surprise me none. You cops are all the same. You think you are different or special because you live down here with the citizens of these fine neighborhoods, but the fact is, Bob, you are just a cop like all the rest. You live down here because it makes you feel good, like somehow your job means something, but the fact is, you are nothing to those folks out there, those vagrants, as you say. They are only nice to you to your face because you can take away the little freedom they enjoy. When you ain't around, they all laugh at you, Bob. Polly here thinks the sun shines out your ass because you've been good to her, but you look at me, and all you see is a bum—a bum and a criminal. Well, let me tell you, Bob, you don't know me. You don't know where I have been, or what I have been through, and you don't know where I am going. But I do, Bob! I know where I am going for the first time in my life. I don't know what happened to everyone else on this crazy night, but I know what happened to me! I changed. I am going toward something instead of away from something, and there is not a blue uniform anywhere going to change that, Bob. I will leave here when I want, and you won't stop me unless you do it with your sidearm—and I doubt you will. I'm done running, and I'm done fighting, Bob, but if you think I am going down to the station house for a wee chat with McCaskey, you are mistaken. I am willing to make an exception one last time if fighting is the only way out. So, in answer to the question you asked, we are talking here, or we ain't talking at all. You can relay my words to McCaskey, but you will understand if I have no desire to see him or blue justice in this room or any station house tonight."

Bob was listening to Armist's words, but all the while his attention was drawn to the deformed hand of Armist and the object he was working through and around with his misshapen fingers. It was small and wooden, perhaps beads, but Armist moved it so quickly that Bob could not focus on the object. He had the feeling you sometimes get when you almost know a name or almost recall a dream. Even though he could not give full focus to the object in the big man's hand, there was something mesmerizing in its movement. There was something comforting and calming in the way Armist held the object, as though it were an extension of his broken appendage. He had seen Armist for years and knew his habits and possessions. A man on the street became known or gained renown by the things he acquired and his ability to hold onto them. Armist was legendary in this aspect of the street pecking order. He had his turf, his shipping-crate abode, his army tunic, cap, and parka, and his red and blue shoes. There was no one in the five-square-block radius of paupers and squatters who would dare try to separate Armist from what was his. There were those who had tried and those who had failed, all of whom ended up lying in their own blood or being carried into the emergency rooms of local hospitals. None of them were willing to lodge a complaint.

In the topsy-turvy world of the street, people who challenged a man like Armist and failed held nearly the same status as those who had challenged him and won. Provided you kept your mouth shut and took your lumps as per the unwritten code of street ethics, you could walk the street with pride. Your scars and lacerations were worn like medals of honor, and your name became part of the nighttime lore shared around burning fifty-gallon steel drums, as people drank their cheap wine or home brew from paper bags.

And Armist always won. He always held his possessions, protecting them with his life like an old bear with a young cub. He never lost, but as he aged, the challenges came more frequently. It was only a matter of time before someone younger and harder crossed Armist's path, and only a matter of time before the big man fell. In falling, he would become like Gustav Kaminski, surviving in stairwells and awaiting his ultimate demise. If Armist intended to remain upright as he now stood, he would lose the crucial element of surprise that had carried him through many a back-alley brawl.

Bob could see that now. He had often wondered how the stooped and feeble-looking man with the crippled hand and supposedly crippled mind had managed to be ruler of his domain for so long. Bob had assumed his edge came from never getting involved with the crack and heroin that so quickly sapped the strength of younger vagrants. But now, tonight, in this room, Bob supposed Armist was just a whole lot smarter than he had ever been given credit for. He owned his turf, and Armist kept his stuff. That was how Gideon knew the object working through the deformed fingers of the big man was something new.

While Gideon was lost in his thoughts of the object and what it might mean, Armist had moved. He was surprised to realize that, seemingly without his knowledge, Armist now stood beside Polly Ann, who was seated at the desk and watching the two men in silence. On the cluttered desk was a large bowl full of jelly beans, and Armist was picking through it with his good hand, finding the black ones and tossing two or three at a time into his mouth. "What's it going to be, Officer?" said Armist. His teeth stuck together with the pasty jelly bean, causing his words to slur, and Gideon assumed he had been drinking.

"What is that, Armist?" asked Gideon, looking at the hand held out in front of Armist.

"It's a jelly bean, Bob, a black one to be precise. I know you blue bellies are all about the details."

"In the other hand, Armist, what is it you are holding, almost concealing, in your bad hand?"

Armist held his hand out in front of him and slowly turned it over in the air between himself and Gideon. "This here ain't no bad hand, Bob. This here is the hand that has kept me alive a long time now. This here is the hand that taught me, when I was just a new boy here in these parts, that there was never anyone going to help me out. This here is the hand that never had a chance to be set right after it was broken. Just like all kinds of people down here in this place we call home—your own backyard, Bob. They just never got set right. Oh, it has done bad! There is no doubt on that subject, but it ain't bad. It is just the way it is. And this here," Armist let the small circle of wooden beads attached to the crudely carved crucifix dangle from the end joint of one of his disfigured fingers in the space between him and Bob, "this here is something I got this very night that somehow is making me see things differently. Somehow, it's making my mind quiet, and maybe my soul too, if I got such a thing, Bob."

Armist reached down and this time took a multicolored handful of jelly beans, tossed them into his mouth, and began to chew aggressively. His mind was quiet, and he had not had a drink in over three hours, but his body was feeling a craving that it had never been given the opportunity to experience before, as Armist never went long without a drink. He had a cold sweat living just above the surface of his skin. It was as though the clammy sweat never really made contact with his skin; it enveloped him with just enough space between his body and this cold force field to create a slight, imperceptible shiver that ran from head to toe. It was as though it was at once part of and apart from Armist, and he was certain that should the small circle of wooden beads fall from his possession, this imperceptible shiver would grow into a seismic tremor that could send him into a seizure and render him incapacitated. Somehow, he knew this to be the truth, but that did not fill him with fear. He chewed hard on the jelly beans and instinctively knew that the sweet syrup running down the back of his throat, along with the talisman he had been given by Tommy Boy, would keep the tremors at bay.

"It seems to me, Armist, that you are full of big speeches tonight, but very little information. Maybe you are just full of shit, and maybe we should just run you in, but something tells me there is more to the story, so I am willing to sit and talk. Just the three of us, but you need to tell me everything! You get that? Everything! Start with how the hell you got hooked up in this mess in the first place, and we will take it from there."

A big sigh escaped from the stern face of Polly Ann Polanski of Polly Ann's Pleasure Emporium, and both men instantly averted their gaze to the woman they had all but forgotten. She was sitting behind the cluttered desk in the small back-room office. "Well, hallelujah!" said Polly, raising her arms in a mock gesture of praise. "You two have finally got to the end of your pissing match and are ready to get to the heart of our situation. What a joy! I was starting to think I was going to have to measure your dicks to see who was the toughest, baddest, biggest man! Men are such assholes!"

Bob and Armist both laughed and looked to Polly Ann with a different type of love in their eyes. She would be the bridge between their two worlds, and the love they both felt for her would enable them to move forward.

Armist told it all to Bob, leaving nothing out. When it was over, Gideon sat quietly and considered what the next action would be. Armist sat quietly and finished the last of the jelly beans in the bowl. He felt a peace and freedom overcome him as he parted with the story of the night's events. He was purged.

Polly Ann brought them all fresh coffee, and as Gideon swallowed the hot coffee, he looked over to Armist and pointed to the talisman in his hand.

"Armist, I know you have become attached to that rosary, and I know you attribute some psychic change in Tommy and in yourself to the beads, but the fact is, Armist, that it is evidence in an ongoing investigation. You are going to have to turn it over at some point."

"We'll see, Officer, we'll see. This here set of beads may just seem like mumbo jumbo to you. I know the fella I spoke to earlier at the mission didn't think these things that are happening were because of the beads either, and I am starting to know there is truth to that. These here beads are just something being used by something bigger to help me through. But I know who these beads belong to, and I intend to get them back to her somehow. They aren't going to go to no evidence room!"

"We'll see, Armist, we'll see. Right now, I am more concerned with finding Tommy Boyle before he hurts anyone else."

"The only other person he plans on hurting tonight is himself, Bob. I can guarantee it. You'll have to find him to save him, or come morning you will be looking for a corpse. I know you boys think he is in the wind, but he ain't. He is right down here somewhere, and if I am still able to walk out of this room a free man, I will do my best to help you find him. He don't have no idea about what he has done to me, Bob. He has given me something to hope for, and I sure would like to thank him for it, alive if possible, dead if need be. But I will help find him if I can. You got my word, but you will have to call off McCaskey and all the others out there looking to take me as a trophy. I lived my whole life in these five square blocks, and I never had a mind to go anywhere else. I built a big fence around me, and I felt safe inside of it. But I know now that the fence never kept folks out. It only kept me in. I also know that every fence has a gate. It has taken me some time, but tonight, tonight I have come on the gate. Not only did I find it, but these here little beads gave me the will to throw it open. Kind of like a key leading me out to a better place. I know you are looking for Tommy to make him pay for what he done, but I am looking for him in hopes that he will live so I can someday thank him for what he done. Not to those other folks, but to me! Somehow the evil he brought to the neighborhood is going to give me a life. I can't explain it any clearer than that, Bob, but I also can't start looking for this new life with a bunch of you boys on my tail. Like I told you at the beginning of this, lying, hiding, and running ain't going to work for me no more."

"Leave it with me, Armist. I am willing to work it like you said, but I may not be able to get McCaskey on board. I am overdue to call in, so I will see what he has to say and get an update on the investigation."

Armist leaned back in the office chair and felt the hot coffee flow down his throat and into his belly. The shiver seemed to be abated, and the physical craving he had endured had succumbed to the power of the jelly beans. He looked over at Polly Ann, and she smiled, filling him with a new kind of warmth. He marveled at how his world had taken on new color in just a few short hours, and he said a silent prayer to a God he was beginning to understand, that Tommy Boyle would see the morning light.

DELUSIONS

Clayton Beday sat staring at the televangelist on the TV and drew deeply from the vodka and milk in the tumbler he had held all evening. He had refilled the tumbler several times since he had seen the eleven o'clock news and listened to the story about the man who had gone insane. It was a story about a man who had thrown someone in front of a bus and then smashed a nun's face into a brick wall. It was the story of the same man who had stood toe-to-toe with Clayton Beday in a dispute over a skanky crack whore and one hundred twenty dollars. His stomach burned as though a fiery pit was ablaze within his organs, but he did not blame the vast quantities of vodka he had consumed that night. Nor did he blame the scotch or the beer he had earlier in the evening and over the supper hour. No, Clayton Beday blamed the burn in his belly on the crack whore named Rhonda and the scumbag fugitive who had been identified as Tommy Boyle. Clayton Beday blamed the burn in his belly on all the people in all his life who had turned him away and caused him to retreat in fear. It was the fault of all the people who had treated him as less than and had never given him his due. It was the fault of all the people who never saw the potential he had within for greatness and of all the people who never even realized Clayton Beday existed.

He had stood toe-to-toe with a skinny, burned-out junkie and run away in fear. Clayton was bigger than Tommy and Clayton was meaner than Tommy, but Clayton had run away in fear as he had done his entire life. This self-awareness filled him with such loathing and shame that Clayton was slowly being eaten away from within. His ulcerated stomach led to his diseased intestines, which led to his inflamed bowel and colon. His liver was swollen, and his heart was hidden beneath a layer of fat. His kidneys were acting up regularly, and it hurt when he pissed. His hemorrhoids were monumental, and it hurt when he shit. He blamed his burning urinary tract on his kidney trouble and not on the fact that his only sexual satisfaction these days came at the expense of cheap whores in back alleys. They were women he could lord over, women who would do as he demanded when he demanded. They were women who saw Clayton for what he wanted to be, rather than for what he was.

His after-work excursions were getting longer each month as his addictions grew more demanding, and the need for the women had rapidly outgrown the need for the booze. Clayton's home life was about to implode. Had it not been for the abject fear in which his wife and children resided, they would have left long ago. Long ago, Clayton's wife stopped asking where he was spending his evenings. Long ago, Clayton's children stopped looking out the window late into the evening, wondering when Dad would come home from work. Long ago, his wife had stopped wondering why Clayton no longer wanted sex and began to be grateful that he did not. To the people who had loved Clayton Beday, he had become a stranger. He had become that which he had always assumed himself to be and that which those who loved him could never have imagined him to be. Clayton Beday had become the sum of all his fears and insecurities; the personification of all he had despised in men. Clayton Beday was a self-fulfilled prophecy, and Clayton Beday was evil.

He had arrived home this evening just before eleven, more disheveled than usual. His shirt was stuck to his overweight body with the cold sweat of fear, and his graying hair was plastered to his head as though he had been doused in a bucket of sweat. Clayton's breath came in short, raspy gasps even after the half-hour drive from the area he had come to cruise on a nightly basis. Whether it was a moment of lasting love and concern or hopeful anticipation of an impending and freeing massive coronary, Clayton would never know, but his wife came to his side that evening in urgency. She came and asked Clayton if he was okay. She asked Clayton if he was sick or injured and then, lost in the moment and caught up in the frenzy that had become Clayton Beday, she asked where he had been.

Clayton could only remember the first blow he had delivered to his wife, though he was aware there had been several. That first blow filled him with the same sense of power he had felt the first time he had ejaculated in the mouth of a young crack whore as her boyfriend stood watch. He looked down on the woman he had once loved as she lay weeping and bleeding on the floor and was filled with the same self-righteous indignation he had felt as he looked down on the whore wiping her mouth on her sleeve after spitting out his semen. He deserved so much better than these women who had entered his life—those he had purchased and the one he had married. She had never appreciated him for all he could be and had held him back from reaching his potential. Tonight she had questioned him, and she had paid the price. It was the first time he had lashed out at her physically, but it would not be the last, for Clayton had felt alive as his fists left the mark of his cowardice on her face.

Clayton's wife wept quietly in the upstairs bath, nursing her bruised and battered body and praying for the rapid death of her husband. Clayton's children cowered in their rooms, listening to the distant sobs of their mother and the harsh curses of their father as he spoke to the man on the television. Too frightened to go to the aid of their mother, too frightened to leave their rooms, almost too frightened to breathe, they just cowered. While the shame of their inaction began to leave its stain on their lives, Clayton finished another vodka and milk and cursed the world.

He listened to the preacher as the preacher talked about the wages of sin. "The wages of sin is death, sayeth the Lord," the televangelist spoke the words with vigor and conviction. Over and over, Clayton listened to the televangelist as he spoke of reaping what we sow, and Clayton's mind was filled with death and retribution. People would have to pay for what had taken place this evening. Just as his wife had been made to see his strength, so too would the whore, Rhonda. She had taken his money and kept his pleasure, and that was unacceptable. He would leave the punk Tommy to the cops, but he would help them in their quest to locate him. He had information that was valuable, and that made him important. He had seen the fugitive, and he had seen him close to the area of his crimes. The news had said there was an extended dragnet, but Tommy was still close, and that was big news for the cops. He would not mention Rhonda or her involvement in the story. He would say that he had been attacked by Tommy Boyle but had been able to fight the crazed junkie off. He would say he was just out of the car to get a coffee and a newspaper at the corner store. He was on his way home to his family after a long day at work and just ended up in the wrong place at the wrong time. They would want to know why he had not called right away, and they would be angry at that point, thinking they could have had Tommy Boyle hours ago. But Clayton was smarter than the cops, and he knew he could pull it off. He would tell them that he was afraid to call because he had busted the kid up pretty good. Tommy had tried to rob him at knifepoint, but Clayton had overcome him, and in his adrenaline-induced state, he had been overzealous in his retribution, beating the boy pretty badly. He was only calling now because he was a man of faith and was repentant of his acts. The thought of the sick young man perhaps still lying hurt in an alley was too much guilt for Clayton to ingest. They would buy it. After all, they were only pawns for Clayton to move around as he saw fit.

As for Rhonda, she would pay dearly for her part in it all, for her insolence. It had not been the first time Rhonda had been with him to the alley. It had not been the first time she had succumbed to his sexual desires. She knew what her role had been, and she did not perform as required. She had actually listened and obeyed the junkie rather than Clayton, and that could not go unpunished. Yes, she had been with Clayton in the alley before, but never like she would be in that alley tonight. Clayton thought about the rush of heat that had enveloped him as he laid his fists on his wife, and he began to get sexually aroused. He began to understand that the true power he desired would be found in the fear of the women, and at that moment, his arousal began to shift from sex to violence. Clayton was filled with a twisted sense of justice that needed to be served swiftly and without prejudice. Rhonda's sentence would be meted out by the hand of Clayton Beday, her penance paid in blood.

Clayton looked around him at the broken lamps and overturned tables and marveled at the hue of the room. His eyes went back to the televangelist who was speaking and moving, not quite in slow motion and not quite at normal speed. Clayton had entered the dimension he strove for every day. It was that place you could only reach through copious amounts of alcohol, where the world took on a different look and speed, and where Clayton was Lord of all things.

He saw his arm reach out and pick up the phone, watched his fingers dial the numbers for information, and heard his voice ask politely for the number of the midtown precinct, number fifty-eight. Clayton placed the call and, in that act, Clayton took up what he believed was the Lord's work.

***

Jim McCaskey had just left a twenty-minute meeting with all the bosses and was returning to his desk. There had been a lot of yelling, cursing, and finger-pointing, and some of it had landed on McCaskey's shoulders. He did not like it, but he accepted it. Shit ran downhill from the Mayor's office, and McCaskey was close to the bottom. The pursuit of Tommy Boyle had not gone well. Though the force had made every effort, followed protocol, and deployed all available personnel, their efforts had borne no fruit, and the felon had eluded them. To top it off, a civilian was dead, and a rookie cop was injured—ingredients for the perfect storm, making bosses desperate for someone to blame.

McCaskey was shaping up to be the fall guy of the hour. Not for the failure of the dragnet but for the injury to the officer and the death of Gustav Kaminski. He had gone through the debriefing with SIU and filed his report on the incident. McCaskey had shouldered the responsibility. The final determination from the investigators would likely cite negligence on his part as the senior officer, failing to ensure the area was properly cleared and secured. It didn't matter that they were on a stakeout. It didn't matter that the rookie cop had put them in the situation from the start. It didn't matter that Constable Johnny McFadden had earned getting stuck with the dirty blade of an old drunk. McCaskey was a twenty-year veteran, and a small blemish on his record wouldn't mean much, but for a rookie, it could impede his career indefinitely. Everyone knew the score. Everyone played the game. Everyone won—except Gustav Kaminski.

Kaminski was not the first man McCaskey had killed in his two decades on the force, but he hoped he would be the last. This death had been unnecessary. It was a case of poor procedure, plain and simple. McCaskey searched for some justification for taking a life but found none. Like most officers, he would have to live with it and act as though it were routine. But it wasn't. He knew Kaminski's weathered face would be etched into his memory for the rest of his life. The sound of the man's skull yielding under the force of his baton would haunt him on cold, sleepless nights. The wind would whisper the name, "Gustav Kaminski," joining the list of others dispatched by the so-called blue justice. If there was any consolation, it would come from the coroner's report indicating that Kaminski was so cancer-ridden and dehydrated that he likely would have died by morning anyway. That was something, but it wasn't enough.

The bosses had decided to call off the local search. Too much time had passed, and they assumed Boyle had escaped the area. All officers on overtime were cleared to check out, go home for a few hours of rest, and return to regular shifts in the morning. The investigation would shift focus to bus stations, trains, airports, and highway patrols on alert for hitchhikers and suspects at truck stops. This should have brought some relief to McCaskey, but it didn't. The thought of going home filled him with dread, knowing the reception would be icy. It wasn't anger that filled him but regret and remorse. His relationship was another casualty of this dark night, another shadow added to the wind.

As he approached his desk, the phone began to ring. He let it ring twice while he wiped out his coffee cup, a sad smile crossing his face as he read the words, "Happy tenth to the man I love." He knew another marriage was over. On the fourth ring, he reached for his coat, thinking, "Forget it; they told me to check out." On the fifth ring, an officer at a nearby desk hollered, "You going to get that or what?"

On the sixth ring, with a heavy sigh, McCaskey picked up the phone. "Sergeant McCaskey here, how may I be of assistance tonight?"

"Jimmy, Bob Gideon here. I'm glad to hear you're still in the house. How'd things go with SIU?"

"Well, you know the routine, Bob. They chewed me out and told me I'd be getting an official reprimand. Everyone's worked up about the Boyle case, and Kaminski is just an irritation to them."

"Rookies, eh, Jim? They always land you in the shit. That's why I try to work alone."

"Speaking of which, where the hell have you been? I heard you've been off the air for over an hour. You know that's against protocol. We can't afford another officer down tonight, Bob."

"I know, Jim, but that's how it goes down here on my turf. No one steps into the light to offer information; I need to go into the dark and dig for the truth. We're the good guys, Jimmy; we'll be okay, right?"

"I don't know who's good and who's bad anymore, to be honest. It's been a long day, and this coffee's starting to turn on me. I was just heading home, so get to the point."

"I'm sitting with someone you might want to talk to—a big guy named Armist."

"You found him?"

"He found me, Jim, with a little help. We've been talking, and I think there might be a development. I thought you should be the first to know, given everything that's happened tonight. But there's one condition: I promised Mr. Hancock there'd be no jail cell, not even a trip to the station."

"That's a tall order, Bob. The man was present during the assault of an officer and the death of a civilian. We need his testimony on record."

"He says he's innocent of the assault; it was self-defense against an unidentified assailant. And with all due respect, Jim, it was us that got Kaminski killed, not Armist."

"There have been updates on this end, too, Bob. The bosses are calling off the local search; they're sure Boyle's gone. And off the record, maybe Mr. Hancock's version holds up. Is his information worth the deal?"

"I think Tommy's still here, Jim. I believe if we work with Armist, we might find him. It could take some heat off us about Kaminski."

"I'm not worried about the heat, Bob. I did what I did, and I'd do it again. But the man is still dead, and that matters."

McCaskey paused, and Bob understood as only a fellow officer could. Regulations and training wouldn't erase the weight of taking a life. Sometimes, that weight was the only thing that kept an officer grounded.

"Alright, Bob, your call. Where are you? I'll be there in fifteen minutes."

McCaskey noted the location and started to pull on his jacket. The night had been wet and long, and the dampness seeping into his bones was wearing him down. Maybe she was right, he thought for the first time in the ten years they'd argued. Maybe it was time to retire. Let someone else protect the city. Let someone else be the good guy.

As he headed out, the admin called after him, "Sergeant McCaskey! Can you take a call?"

"I was just leaving, Cheryl. Can you take a message?"

"I can try, but the caller insists it's urgent, says it's about Thomas Boyle."

"I'll take it at my desk. Thanks, Cheryl."

McCaskey turned back, all thoughts of retirement vanishing. He took the call, proceeding by the book.

"Sergeant McCaskey here, how may I be of assistance?"

"Well, Sergeant, I believe the real question is, how may I assist you?"

In the surreal light of his broken living room, intended as a safe haven for the Beday family, Clayton leered at the television. The televangelist's arms waved wildly, his mouth delivering the muted message of retribution. Upstairs, Clayton's wife had sunk so low into the cold bathwater that only her nose remained above the surface. Just one more inch would bring relief and freedom. But the thought of leaving her children with the monster she once loved stopped her. The preacher's silent words roared in Clayton's mind, and with twisted conviction, he told Sergeant McCaskey his story. In his madness, Clayton's plot began to unfold.

ACCEPTANCE

John Boyle sat snoring in his favorite reading chair as the once-blazing fire had died down to soft, glowing embers, painting the room in an odd reddish-orange hue. The book he had been reading had fallen to the floor, but the story was living on in his dream.

He was the gunslinger Roland, and his Muriel was the woman he had loved. In his dream, he tried desperately to free her from the prison in which she was held, but he could not. His Muriel was trapped behind some sort of magical membrane, which he could see through but could not penetrate. He forced himself against the membrane, but to no avail, and in his anguish, he screamed her name over and over; his words bounced off the membrane, echoing back at him. She stood not five feet from him, her gaze falling directly upon him, but she could not see him. He was invisible to her. As he looked on in sadness, he saw a smile forming on the beautiful, full lips of the woman to whom he had given his life, and for a moment, he was certain she could see him. For a moment, he felt that, on the very edges of her vision, she could see his form through the membrane and knew he was there, ready to do whatever he could to set her free. But then the moment passed, and the smile faded. Muriel stood, staring through the membrane, through Roland, and into some unseen world to which she had been banished.

The man in the dream who had been Roland—tall, brave, and full of determination—now became John himself. The John in the dream was old and feeble, much older than he actually was and decades older than Muriel. There was a pronounced hunch in this John's back, and the jowls, where there had once been a strong jawline, flapped and swung as John lashed out against the membrane. The John in the dream railed against the barrier, but there was no chance he would be able to set his true love free. The John in the dream was slowly filled with the realization that he would fail. He was no longer the man he needed to be to set Muriel free— perhaps he never was. The John in the dream was suddenly overcome with the knowledge that his life had been a failure. The woman across the invisible membrane, the young, beautiful woman he had known as Muriel, had never understood the depth of his love. She had never known, because he had never been able to speak the words of romance she had so longed to hear. And now, it was too late. As a bell rang in the distance, John wailed in pain against the membrane, and the resonance of his words filled him with dread.

The bell rang and rang, and as it continued at perfectly spaced intervals, the image of the old man and the young woman gave way to the reddish-orange glow of the dying fire. Above the fire on the mantle stood a photograph of the woman in his dream, surrounded by children. John awoke to the ringing of the phone, tears in his eyes and an emptiness in his heart.

He sat forward quickly, suddenly filled with the anxiety that comes with calls arriving late at night. He looked at the grandmother clock on the mantle, which was about to strike three, and wondered how long the phone had been ringing.

He wondered if it had awakened Muriel, who slept in the big room off the kitchen, the one that used to be the living room.

His thoughts turned to Bethany and possible trouble with the latest baby, due soon but not yet. He then thought of Billy, away again on one of his trips to a God-forsaken country where Westerners were often kidnapped and held in horrible conditions while ransoms were arranged. This worry was great for John, though Billy would never be aware of it. With great trepidation, John Boyle reached past the lamp and clasped the telephone. As he brought the receiver to his trembling lips, the memories of the horrible dream faded from his mind forever, replaced by the sense of uselessness he felt in the reality of his life.

In the big room that had once been their living room, Muriel Boyle lay in her bed, listening to the phone ringing. She counted eight rings but made no move toward getting up to answer. She had no idea what time it was, though she knew it was late, and she wondered who would be calling. Mostly, though, she wondered why she was sleeping in the living room.

She could see a small lamp on the table beside the bed as the moonlight streamed through the stained glass window by the piano. She leaned forward and switched on the small lamp, allowing it to throw dim light into the far corners of the big room. Slowly, she took in the room. There was the piano that had belonged to her mother. On its top stood pictures of her babies—Tommy, Billy, and Bethany. A photo of John, looking so handsome in his infantry uniform, stood beside one of Muriel in her grandmother's wedding dress on the day they wed. Next to them was a picture of her father standing on the docks the day he boarded a ship to leave for the country that had nothing to offer him but freedom. And there was her mother, holding a parasol, undoubtedly the most beautiful woman Muriel had ever seen. There were other pictures: photos from the beach, children building snowmen, graduations. All the high points of Muriel Boyle's life stood still, as they always had, atop her mother's piano.

Hanging on the wall was the fish that John had caught in 1956. He had mounted and hung it, and Muriel had hated it every day since. Tonight, however, in the dimly lit room, a smile crossed her face as she recalled the joy it had brought her John the day he caught the big fish. She remembered how she had glimpsed her pre-war man that day and how it filled her with hope for the future. The windowsills and shelves were covered with the knick-knacks and figurines she had collected and loved over the years, and the cabinet in the corner was filled with a lifetime of photo albums—albums she had begun to organize long ago and never finished. She determined, as she looked at them that night, to get that project finished so she could move on to another. Projects had always been her refuge.

The rocking chair next to the now-cold fireplace had a crocheted afghan thrown over the back, a gift from a neighbor the year she had pneumonia. Behind the chair and next to the footstool stood a large walnut bookcase that held all the dreams and fantasies that had kept Muriel Boyle alive through these long, lonely years. Each time Muriel had needed a place to escape, she had found it on those shelves. A dark castle, a strong fortress, lush jungles, dry deserts, rugged mountains, or the big sky country of Montana—all waited on those shelves. Blessed escape was merely a page away. It was all there. Everything was in its place. Everything, that is, except for Muriel Boyle, who, for some reason, was lying in a bed in the living room instead of in her bedroom upstairs.

She threw her legs over the side of the bed and onto the cool floor. As she slid into slippers she did not recognize, she reached for the dressing gown she had worn for nearly twenty years. Muriel felt an odd sense of danger. She did not understand why she was in this room or why she did not recall getting into her nightie, dressing gown, and bed here. She supposed she must have been ill but had no memory of it. She sat for a moment, listening to the nighttime sounds of the house she had lived in for over sixty years. The refrigerator was running, and the wind rustled the limbs of the weeping willow, causing it to scrape against the steel roof of the summer kitchen. In the hallway near the front door, she could hear the steady ticking of the grandfather clock that had been given to John and Muriel along with the farm. When John's father moved to the small apartment he occupied until his death, he left the clock for them. "This old clock has always been in this house in that very spot," he had said. "To move it now wouldn't be right. This is where the clock lives. This house belongs to the clock as much as the clock belongs to the house." Muriel had laughed at him when he'd said it, but now, now she understood what he had meant. Muriel had become like the clock. She belonged to this house; she had never been able to see herself in any other place. Within these walls, her life had unfolded. Not always good, not always bad, but always here. She would never leave.

Muriel listened closely to the sounds of her house and realized it was as if she were listening to her own heartbeat. It occurred to her that her own heart had always influenced the other hearts in the house. When she was happy, her family was happy, and when she was not, neither were those around her. Her moods and emotions had often affected all those who loved her. Her mental state had been fragile throughout most of her life, and the guilt she carried compounded her sense of responsibility for her family's overall dysfunction. Like the house, Muriel Boyle required regular maintenance.

At the edges of her hearing, she thought she could hear a voice, and for reasons she could not understand, a cold shiver of fear ran down her spine. She listened hard but could not make out any words, only tones. They seemed gruff and angry to her. She wondered who would be on the phone at this hour and if her own fear was affecting her perception of the conversation in the study down the hall.

Slowly, Muriel slipped from the bed and made her way across the tattered colonial carpet toward the door that led to the hall and the study beyond. As she crossed the room, she stopped to gaze into her budgie cage. She stood there in the dimness, recalling the many times over the years when her budgies had been her only companions, providing the only music her heart could hear.

The large aviary had been a gift from John, crafted for their anniversary many years before. She looked upon the brightly hanging swings and hoops, the ladder that spanned the cage, and the feeders and waterers, all in their proper places. The bells and mirrors were strategically positioned, as were the bath station and the millet hanger. Everything was there, except the budgies. Muriel looked and looked again, but the birds were nowhere to be seen. She checked the door of the aviary and found it securely locked, her sense of foreboding growing with each moment. She turned away from the empty cage and walked into the long, darkened hallway.

A dim glow came from under the study door, and as Muriel approached, the voice on the other side grew louder. She scanned the familiar furnishings of the hall, letting her eyes drift over various wall hangings and pictures as she passed. She saw them and yet did not see them, her focus elsewhere. Her hand slid along the top of the walnut chair rail that ran the hall's length, holding everything from Christmas cards to serving as a measuring stick for her growing children. In the dim light, her hand came to rest on the great mirror beside the grandfather clock. The mirror had been purchased before the Great Depression and had hung proudly in the Boyle family home ever since. The first new piece of furniture purchased by family members long gone, it represented a family's steps toward security.

Muriel had loved the mirror with its contoured top adorned with acorns and oak leaves, meticulously carved to give it balance and depth. The cast hooks, shaped like oak branches, had held every type of garment over the mirror's life of service. Slowly, she turned to face the mirror and was filled with memories of standing in that spot countless times, adjusting a hat before church, straightening a scarf before parent-teacher night, placing a corsage before her daughter's wedding. Much of her life began with her facing this mirror, scrutinizing her image more critically than anyone else ever would. Being the daughter of a beautiful woman had never been easy.

Muriel turned, and in the dim light, she was transfixed by the image that looked back at her. Slowly, with surreal caution, her right hand rose to the place where her auburn curls had once fallen on her shoulders. Her hand landed with great care on the straight, gray hair. Gently, her hand brushed over her wrinkled lips and the extra skin beneath her chin. Her left hand joined the exploration, tracing her eyes, nose, and ears, mapping the face of this person who looked back from Muriel's beautiful oak mirror.

She remembered a movie about Helen Keller, marveling at how the young blind girl identified her family members by mapping their faces. Now here Muriel stood, doing the same thing. But she was not blind; she could see too well the woman in the mirror. She saw the woman looking back with liver-spotted, arthritic hands roaming her face. She could see that woman—the woman was Muriel Boyle, or some version of her.

Muriel felt confused, and fear began rising to her throat. It must be some horrible dream, she thought, some nightmare she could not awaken from. If she could scream, John would hear and shake her from her slumber. She turned toward the light under the study door and, with all her strength, called out to her husband. She called to John—the man who had never been able to love her as she needed, but who always kept her safe. The man who would always be there to save her from real or imagined fears.

In her mind, she called out with all her might, but the voice that escaped her lips was feeble and old, her words falling softly onto the dark hallway carpet. It was then that Muriel noticed the tattered carpet in the hall and the musty smell that pervaded the house. She was alone in the dark, as she had always feared she would be. In unfamiliar slippers, she walked toward the voice she could now recognize as her John's.

"Hello?" he said into the black, cold Bakelite receiver, but no answer came. "HELLO!" he shouted, and this time, he thought he heard someone breathing. "Is anyone there? Do you have any idea what time it is?"

A faint reply came from the phone, the voice so distant and weak that John Boyle could barely hear the words.

"Dad, hello? Dad, it's me."

"Billy? Is that you? You must be far away—I can barely hear you, son. Must be one of those satellite delays. What time is it where you are? Where are you? Is everything okay?"

"No, Dad, it's me—not Billy."

or a moment, John Boyle sat confused in his chair, wiping the sleep from his eyes. This had to be a wrong number. But if not Billy, who could it be? It certainly wasn't Bethany, or Carl, and that could only leave... John's breath caught in his throat. He wondered if this were some extension of his dream. It would have been impossible for

John to articulate what he felt in that moment. There is no word for the emotion that flooded him: anger and fear, sorrow and relief, all rolled into one indescribable feeling. He found his words.

"Tommy? Oh my God, Tommy, is it you?"

"It's me, Pop. It's Tommy."

"I thought you were dead this time. I was sure you were dead, and now here you are, on the phone in the middle of the night. 'It's me, Pop!' Is that all you have to say, boy? After three years of silence?"

Tommy could feel himself shrinking in the dark phone booth as his father's harsh tone filled the air around him. Tommy was filled with fear and shame, and the words he thought his father needed to hear quickly reached his lips.

"I am sorry, Pop. I know it's late, but I had to call. I had to talk to you and to Mom. There are things I need to say. Dad, I am so sorry."

There are things you need to say! You are sorry! So many things needed saying, so many things could have been said, but now it's too late for that. I am too old, and I cannot go through this again with you, Tommy. I thought you were dead this time, and though I never said it aloud to your sister, brother, or—God forbid—your mother, I was sure you were gone forever, and, Tommy, I was relieved. I was happy to think you could no longer hurt this family. Do you know what kind of guilt that gives a man, Tommy? To hope his firstborn son is dead? No. Of course, you don't. You never understood love or respect or loyalty. You just never had it in you, son. I guess that's my fault, too. More guilt for the old man. More…"

John could not hold back the tears. He began to sob thick, wet sobs that came quickly and violently, shaking out all the hurt his body had held onto for too long. He shook and sobbed, trying to form words, but all that escaped him were pathetic sounds of despair, and John Boyle hated himself for his weakness. Just as he could not save his love in the dream, he had not been able to save his boy. His son had been lost to him all those years ago when they had both been younger. When all that was required was a father's love, John had been unable to give it. He had been unable to reach through the invisible membrane enveloping his emotional self to touch this boy, and now, on this dark night, sitting by a dying fire, John had spoken the words out loud that had rattled around in his heart and mind for so long. He wished his boy was dead. Not because of anger, hate, or disappointment, but because it was easier than trying to fix what had gone so horribly wrong. It was easier than openly loving Tommy, for John was incapable.

Tommy slid down the glass in the darkened booth, listening to the harsh words of his father and then to his sobs. He had never heard his father cry like this, and it made Tommy uncertain about how to proceed. It felt like this call had been a mistake, but Tommy knew the pain he heard in his father's sobs had begun with him. Tommy had spent a lifetime blaming others for his life's predicament, blaming others for the bad choices he himself had made so frequently. The list started with John Boyle and ended with anyone who had ever slighted him in any way. The whole world had been

Tommy's nemesis, and through it all, above all, his father John was the villain. But something had changed this night. Something in his heart had softened; a feeling had been rekindled. All his senses and all his fears were at the forefront of his mind, but Tommy resisted the urge to run. For the first time in his life, there was nowhere left to run. For the first time, he resisted the urge to let his father own that pain and guilt, to let the old man take the pain and guilt with him to his grave.

ommy would walk to his own grave this night, and he would do so knowing he had set his father free. He would die knowing that no one else had been to blame and that no one else would ever have to hurt over him again. He took a deep, cleansing breath and spoke.

"Dad, Dad, please stop! Please listen. There are some things I need to say and some things you need to hear. Can you do that, Dad? Can we talk this one time on a deeper level than we ever have before?"

Tommy paused, and in his mind's eye, he saw his father sitting in his big chair by the fireplace. He saw John Boyle, weathered and fit, just in from the fields with his pipe in hand and a newspaper on the table beside him. John Boyle, with his dinner done and a day's work behind him, sat alone, wanting solitude. That was the memory Tommy had of his father. He understood there must have been times in his life when his father had been there for him, times when he had laughed and tossed him a ball. But he could not remember those times. Tommy's memory of his father had always been the same: an isolated man, sitting at a distance, happy to be alone. A man unable to hide the fact that he was more comfortable in the barn with the animals than in the house with his family.

John Boyle cleared his throat from a hundred miles away, regaining control of his emotions—it was what he did. He controlled his feelings and never broke down. Not then, not now, not ever. The person John Boyle truly was had always strained and pushed violently within his skin, trying with all his might to escape from the crippled vessel in which he had been held captive for eighty years. But escape proved impossible. The walls were too high, the skin too fortified and thickened with fear. The breach that had just occurred— the letting go of the sobs—had felt good to John, too good, in fact. Far better than any man who wished his son dead deserved. Far better than any man who had a broken-minded and neglected wife deserved. A man who could not hug his children or tell his grandchildren he loved them. Control covered him quickly, like an old sweater, and as John slipped into it, he felt safe.

"Say what you have to say, Tommy. I am listening, but I need to warn you I may not do the talking you want to hear. As I said, Tommy, there will be no repeat of times gone by when you called in the night, and I came running. I don't have the will to care about your troubles anymore, and your mother is beyond able to do so."

"What do you mean, Pop? Is Mother ill?"

"Ill? I suppose she is ill, though I never really thought of it as such. She is probably healthier than I am physically, Tommy, but her mind is gone. They say it is dementia and Alzheimer's together. Most days, she doesn't know who I am, Tommy. It's like she sees right through me, like I am invisible. Many times I wonder if that's how she felt all these years—maybe the way you all felt. Maybe this is how it's supposed to be for me. Penance of some sort for the life I have lived. I don't know; I try not to think about it too much, to be honest. Mostly, I'm just here, waiting to see what happens next, and then along comes you."

"I didn't know, Dad. I didn't know she'd gotten so ill. I mean, there were always problems with her mind, but I didn't know it had been diagnosed."

"How would you! You haven't so much as called for over three years, haven't actually seen you in ten. You know what that's been like for her? You son of a bitch! You know what that did to all of us? Don't you of all people comment on the troubles she has had with her mind. Do you even care?"

"I can't tell you how much I care, Pop. I don't have the words. I can't tell you how much I wish it had been different. I'm not calling to hurt you anymore or Mom. Something has happened, Dad, something worse than all the other times. All the times I was in jail or the hospital. All the times you came and bailed me out and took me home. Way worse than all that. But something else has happened, and I don't know what it is or why it had to happen now and not a long time ago. I have done something beyond horror, and you are going to know about it, Dad, soon. I want you to know it was not me who did these things—well, not who I am now. Not who I have been. Not who I was raised to be. I have been lost to drugs and booze, and I know now, at least a little, how that has ruined lives, taken lives. You always told me I could come home. All these years you told me there was always a home for me there, and I hated you for it. I hated you most of my life and blamed you for all the shit I went through. I don't anymore, Dad. I wanted you to know."

"Don't stop hating me, boy. Not if it makes you feel better. This is just another one of your cons. I always said there was a home here for you, and I used to mean it, but not anymore. I see you walking down this lane, and you'll be sorry. I am old but not so old I won't stop you."

"Dad, I'm not coming there—not ever again, don't worry. I only wanted you to know how sorry I am. I wanted you to know I don't blame you any longer for my life or for who you are. I know now something happened to you to make you like you are, and that you are a good man. I know you did the best you could, and I only wanted to make sure you and Mom understood that. I won't be back in your lives. I won't cause any more pain."

"You won't be back in our lives? You say that as though you have been gone. You say that as though there has been even one day in the past twenty years when you have not filled this house. One day when your mother hasn't looked down that lane, hoping to see you there. One night when she hasn't prayed or cried herself to sleep, wondering where you were or if you were alive. That woman's mind has been tortured right up till it could stand no more torture, and then it just quit. That's not all on me, boy. You get that? Some of that is on you! So don't stop hating me because I am just getting started on hating you. She talks to you most of the day. Did you know that? She asks me where you are, and I have to talk to her like you're downstairs fixing us some tea!

Sometimes she looks at me, and she thinks I am you! She thinks I am you. You are right, Tommy. You won't cause any more pain in our lives. Not because you have stopped causing it, but because it is not possible."

Tommy could not see in his mind's eye the broken old man who sat by the dying fire, filled with regret and self-loathing. He could not see the wrinkled, tired face of his father, contorted in anguish and pain, deformed through anger and confused feelings of love and hate. It had been ten years since Tommy had stood face to face with his father, and in those ten years, the lives of John and Muriel Boyle had devolved into something Tommy could never have imagined, something he never would have wished upon them. His father defeated by guilt, his mother defeated by dementia. All their lives trapped in a cycle of unresolved anger, fear, and addiction. Tommy had begun the journey into their pain, and this night, he was determined to end the sorrow. For his father, for his mother, for Trip and Sister Petra, he would have to die.

One time you told me something, Pop, when I was going off to school the first time—the first in the family. You were proud, and I knew it, but I didn't appreciate it. You told me that 'honor was the only gift a man could give himself.' You remember? I didn't know what you meant. I didn't ever know! Not until tonight. I left and wasted all the money you worked so hard to save, and I never amounted to anything. I was too ashamed to come home. Too ashamed of what you would think of me. I sure never had any honor in my life. Not even close. But I know now what I have become and what I have done, and I think I know a way I can give myself that gift, Pop. One last thing I can do that maybe can make up for all the bad stuff. Maybe I can leave with some honor."

"Leave? Where are you running to now? Running away won't bring any honor, Tommy. Standing and fighting gives you honor. Standing and doing what needs doing, even if you don't want to. Even if it hurts—that's what brings a man honor. I saw boys not old enough to buy a drink in the war, with men being blown to bits all around them, and them wanting nothing more than to turn and run! But they didn't, Tommy—they stood and did what had to be done and lived with the consequences. You think you are the only one in this world with problems? Count yourself lucky you never had to live eighty odd years in my head. You never had to spend your whole life pretending you knew what the right thing to do was and never ever being certain—being full of fear. Honor! Honor! Honor is doing the right thing. Honor is fixing things when they are broken or wrong. Honor is doing what you can for others, even when you don't think you can stand one more day. Whatever trouble you got yourself into this time is your trouble. It's for you to start fixing. I've been trying to fix this family my whole entire life, and I am too tired to do it anymore—was never much good at it as it turns out anyway."

"You remember the old McCormick?"

"What?"

"The old McCormick tractor—the one you worked on for years and years. I used to come into the barn and sit watching you work. Mostly we didn't talk, but sometimes we did. You remember?"

"I remember, Tommy. I used to like those nights when you came out. I always wanted to talk."

"I know, Pop. It doesn't matter now. I know. One night I came in the barn, and you were cussing and threw a big wrench across the barn. I was scared when I saw you. You looked so mad. I never saw you look like that before. When you saw me, you could tell I was scared, and you changed. You got all soft and came over to me, crouching down. You told me you were sorry and not to be scared. It was the only time I saw you like that, Pop. Out there in the barn, it was like you felt safe out there. I asked you what was wrong. Do you remember what you told me, Pop?"

"Yup, I said sometimes a thing just can't be fixed anymore."

"Sometimes a thing just can't be fixed anymore. I guess the trick is knowing when that time comes before you spend too much time trying to fix stuff that can't be fixed."

"What is it you're saying exactly, Tommy?"

"Guess I'm saying goodbye, Dad. Guess I'm saying sorry. Guess I'm saying I love you. Guess I'm saying all those things because I never said any of those things before, and I thought you needed to know."

"Where is it you intend to be going, Tommy?"

"Tommy laughed a short laugh into the receiver and marveled at the unfamiliarity of the sound. Something as simple as a short laugh had become foreign to his ears. His being had been so entirely transformed by his addictions that he did not recognize himself as he displayed genuine feelings. Tommy heard genuine laughter instead of biting and cruel sarcasm, instead of sneering laughter.

"Well, Pop. I guess that's the big question. Where will a guy like me end up? I can't imagine it will be anywhere too good."

Both men sat in silence. The silence that had existed between them throughout Tommy's life had been a silence filled with pain and neglect, but the silence that now stood between the two men, late this night, somehow seemed serene. Tommy had said all he needed to say, and he was okay with the quiet.

"Tommy, old tractors sometimes can't be fixed. I think men always can. You are not that old, Tommy. You can start again. Just not here, son. I am sorry, but I can't do it anymore."

"I know you are, Dad, and it is okay. I said there was nothing I wanted from you tonight, but there is one thing. Can I speak to Mom, just for a minute?"

"I'm sorry, Tommy. I don't think either of us could bear that. She is sleeping now, and I think sometimes it's the only time she has her life back, in her dreams. I won't take that from her."

"Will you tell her I love her, Dad? Will you tell her I never meant the harm and that I tried to make it right? I know you don't like lying to her, but will you tell her I'm doing okay so maybe she won't remember how I have been? I love her, Dad."

"I'll make it a grand tale, Tommy, and maybe, when you get where you're going, you can send a letter or call again. Maybe when you get yourself fixed, we can have another chance, maybe. Tommy, I love you, son. Please take care."

Tommy fought back his tears long enough to say goodbye and slowly placed the receiver back into the cradle of the filthy phone. Both men, approaching the end of their lives, sat in the dimness of light and sobbed into their hands.

Muriel Boyle had reached the end of the hall and slowly pushed open the heavy oaken door to the study, just as John had placed the receiver in the cradle of the old phone. From where she stood, she looked across the dimly lit room to the wing-back chair, nearly as old as their marriage. She could see John's shoulder and left ear, with thin wisps of gray hair gently moved by the fan blowing from behind the dying fire. "John needs a haircut," she thought as she began to enter the room.

There was a stillness in the room and in her John that filled Muriel with a curiosity not founded in fear or anxiety, but rather in a sudden interest in her husband. She was invisible to him as she entered the room, and it occurred to Muriel that John had spent many hours of their marriage alone in this room. Often, he had sat late into the night in the wing-back chair, reading or writing, or just staring into a dying fire. She never quite knew how he spent the time, and here, in the dimly lit room, she realized she had never asked. Perhaps she had never cared.

She wondered when it had happened that she stopped worrying about her husband. She wondered when her loneliness and sorrow overcame her worry and concern for John. John had been damaged long ago, and Muriel had known it. She had known him before the trauma of war and after. The man he now was was not the man he had been, and Muriel wondered this late night if she had done all she could have done to help John deal with his demons, or if she had just left him to them.

She had filled her loneliness with her children and the day-to-day activities of a growing family. She had escaped her sorrow in her novels and fantasies. And she had left her John sitting alone in a wing-back chair, never considering what torturous thoughts filled his mind on these long nights. Together they had lived life separately. Together they had denied each other's pain. Together they traveled through the years as though it would magically be better tomorrow—and it never was.

She stopped in the middle of the large oval rug, hooked years before by John's mother. She made fists with her toes through the unfamiliar slippers and was filled with a happy sense of familiarity as the thick pile of the carpet bunched between her toes and the balls of her feet. She watched her husband as though he were an exhibit in a zoo; a rare and seldom-seen animal, alone in his natural habitat—a wing-backed chair in a dimly lit den.

Muriel thought for a moment that John was asleep, for he did not move. His stillness was disturbing, and just as Muriel began to move forward, John raised his hands slowly to his face. He cupped his hands as though readying for a sneeze, then, leaning forward out of the depths of the wing-back chair, John buried his face in his hands and began to sob.

Muriel was taken aback. She had seen John Boyle throughout sixty-odd years of life. She had seen him bury his parents and walk his daughter down the aisle. She had seen him ill and she had seen him angry, but she had never seen him cry. He was—and had always been—her rock! He was the constant in Muriel's life upon which she had always relied and often taken for granted. While she was lost in fantasy or memory or depression, John had always been there to hold it together, and in the deepest recesses of her mind, she knew he always would be. She knew she could check out at any time and John would keep it all together. Yet now, here he sat, sobbing.

Muriel saw his pain. Muriel felt his sorrow, and for the first time in her life, she allowed herself to see the reality of John Boyle. He had always held it together because that was what needed to be done. Not because he was strong. Not because he was incapable of feeling, but because he had seen no other choice for himself. He buried his pain, and he buried his love for all his family for so long that he had become stone. John Boyle had been sculpted from the hardened emotions of a damaged life. He had been the rock upon which they had all smashed themselves.

She wanted to run, as had been her way, and as she slowly turned in the room, her eyes fell upon the sofa. Blankets and pillows were folded neatly on the end of the couch, a towel hung over the back of a chair, and a small dresser stood where none had stood before. On top was a picture of Muriel wearing a red suit that John had bought for her on their tenth anniversary. It was his favorite picture of her and had always stood on the dresser in their bedroom. Muriel understood that, just as she had awakened confused in the front room, John had been sleeping here in the study. She did a full circle, taking in the room, and once again, she looked upon John, weeping in his chair.

The sobs were violent, his back rising and falling with the release of each memory and locked-in emotion. Muriel noticed John's big hands as they covered his face. The hands were scarred and arthritic from a lifetime of hard work on a farm in both hot and cold weather. On his wrinkled hands rested liver spots she did not recall seeing before. They sat like small islands amidst the waving wrinkles of skin and scar. His hands were so pale, so unlike Muriel's memory of her John with his dark and weathered-looking hands, so strong and so capable. His gold wedding band shone brightly upon his long, pale finger as a tear escaped from between swollen knuckles. Muriel crossed the room and quietly kneeled at his side. She reached out and took hold of the hand that had provided for her without question or regret.

John was startled by her touch, and a sob was quelled instantly in his throat as his head sprang back from the hands in which it lay. In the dimness, his frightened eyes fell on the woman who knelt at his side. The visible fear in his eyes faded to shock, then to confusion, then to concern as he leaned forward, his brow only inches from the eyes and lips of the woman he had loved without question for over sixty years.

"John, what is the matter, John? Why are you weeping? Has something happened to one of the children? John, please say something—you are frightening me. I don't know what is going on. Why are we sleeping downstairs? Please, John, tell me what is happening. Where are my budgies, John? The cage is empty. I am confused."

But John sat silent. The evidence of his sorrow was running down his cheeks and spilling onto their locked-together hands. The fingers of John and Muriel Boyle were entwined together as they had been so many times, so many years ago. The golden wedding rings caught the reflection of the dying embers in the fireplace and seemed to shine like a beacon into the eyes of Muriel Boyle. In that instant, the fear, fright, and confusion clouding John Boyle's eyes were replaced by a joy that had not resided in this man for longer than he could recall.

"Muriel! You know me, Muriel? Do you see me, Muriel—John, your John?"

"Well, of course I see you, John. And I see you are upset. Please tell me what is going on. Why do I not remember going to sleep in the living room? Why are you in the den? And why, John, why do you seem so much older than you should be?" Her voice became a whisper. "Why am I, John? I am old. I don't remember being old."

"Muriel, you are as you should be. As beautiful as you have ever been. I love you, Muriel, did you know that? I love you more than anything I can imagine. I always have."

John paused and looked deep into the eyes of his bride of long ago. He saw that she was frightened and saw the confusion covering her brow in worry, but mostly, he saw that she knew him. He saw an opportunity he would not let pass by on this lonely night. Slowly, John untwined their hands. He raised Muriel to her feet and then sat her on his lap. Together, they settled as one into the depths of the well-worn wing-back chair, their combined weight pushing the old air out of its cushion in a sigh of familiarity. In the soft glow of a dying fire, John raised his hand and smoothed the errant, graying hair of his wife. He saw his weathered hand stroke her wrinkled cheek, and he heard himself laugh—a soft laugh, a freeing laugh, a laugh filled with love and hope.

Muriel lowered her head and nestled into the shoulder of her John. As she brought her knees and feet up under herself, she became a small ball in his lap. It had been more than forty years since Muriel Boyle had sat with her John in this position, in this room, in this chair. So much had changed in their lives, so much had happened to them, but the warmth that permeated through her was the warmth that had always been there on late nights long ago as she crawled into her John's lap. It was the warmth of familiarity and safety, and Muriel realized that there was nothing in this world that could steal this warmth from her. It was the warmth of love.

John felt her weight. It was more than it had been, and his strength was less. He felt his legs beginning to tingle as the circulation in them slowed with the weight of his Muriel, and he felt the circulation in his heart increase as it beat rapidly with the excitement and joy of this time he would have with her. John recalled the times years gone by when Muriel would find his lap, and in her comfort, she would fall asleep. John was young then, and strong, and he would sit sometimes for hours. The pain in his legs would grow as the circulation lessened, but there was nothing on earth that could make him wake her. They were his fondest memories, sitting alone with her asleep in his arms. With no reason to speak on those dark nights and no one to hear, he let his love fill his heart in silent joy. He would endure the pain this night as well. But as his old legs held the love of his life, he would not endure the silence. He could no longer lock the love he had for Muriel Boyle away in a damaged heart.

"Everything will be okay, my love. You needn't worry about all these things right now because I have you. You are here with me, and you are safe. I will never let anything or anyone hurt you. I will take care of you always and forever, and knowing that, I know now there is nothing on this earth that we cannot deal with, together. I have been such a fool, Muriel, an old fool. I thought myself unable to change who I was, but I can, Muriel. I know how I have loved you, and I need you to know. Oh, Muriel, so much time wasted. Can you ever forgive me?"

She was quiet in his arms, barely moving. The shallowness of her breath fell upon the nape of his neck, and John squeezed her as tightly as his old arms allowed. He heard her giggle, so quietly at first that he thought he had imagined it. She raised her head from his shoulder and took his cheeks in her slender, frail hands. She looked deeply into his eyes, and then she smiled. Her smile filled the dim room with light and filled John's heart with schoolboy joy.

"There's no fool like an old fool, eh, Mr. Boyle? You have always been too hard on yourself, and I have always been needy and selfish. We did the best we could, John, with each other, with the world, and we muddled through. If only we could have just been the people we were. I know there have been problems, John, and I can tell by the state of myself and this house that I have been gone again. Like when Bethany was born—only worse, I am guessing. I am frightened, and I am confused on many things but one. I know you will always care for me and that you always have. I know that is how you have loved me, John. I know."

She put her head back on his shoulder, and she was quiet for a moment. Their hearts beat as one in the old wing-back chair, and the mistakes and failures of their past were consumed by the forgiving silence of the old house. They were happy at that moment, though they both knew it would be fleeting.

"I also know what I saw, John. You were weeping. You were speaking on the phone, and I thought your tone was angry, but then you wept, John, as though you were hurt deeply. So tell me, John, what has happened? Who were you speaking to?"

"It was Tommy. Tommy was on the phone, and he wanted to speak to you. I didn't want to wake you because you were sleeping so peacefully. He is doing well. He has a new job to go to, and he will be leaving—maybe for a long while. But he said he would call when he got things right. He sounded very good, as though perhaps there have been some changes."

"Oh, John, if only it were true. You mustn't lie to me, John. And you mustn't lie for him. He does his own lying— I know that. I heard your tone, and I saw you cry, and I know what our Tommy has become. I know how it has hurt you, hoping he never comes back. I know how it hurts you to watch me wait for him. I miss him so. I miss the boy he was, but I don't miss the man he has become, John. You never understood that. So tell me, John. Tell me all that was said, all that he has done this time. Don't tell me the grand tale I heard you speak of; just tell me the truth, John. It is time I faced it."

He looked at her in silence and contemplated the truth. He wondered if he knew the way through the truth. It had been so long since he had experienced openness and truth. He had tried so hard to protect her from the inevitability of Tommy's demise. John had known for many years, deep in his heart, that there was only one end for Tommy, but his fear of death and all the havoc it would bring into their lives had kept him from ever talking honestly to Muriel about his concerns.

The irrational fear of death had gripped John when he was a young man—a boy, really—standing in a field in Europe in the midst of blood and mayhem. The fear was real, and the danger was imminent, but if it had crippled him, he would never have survived. He learned to manage this fear, to hide it deep within himself, and he learned to never let the fear be seen by the world. And it worked for him, or so he thought. But here tonight, John understood that people who are afraid of death are more afraid of life. And so he told her. He told her all Tommy had said and all that he had feared, and when he was done, she understood, as John had, that Tommy would not be back. That Tommy had said goodbye for the last time.

She cried softly into his neck for some time, and John never spoke. His own tears rolled down his wrinkled cheeks and mixed with hers on the collar of his shirt. Together, and in silence, they wept for a son they had lost so long ago. Together, and in silence, they mourned the loss of the hope they had carried for so many years that Tommy would find his way home. Together, they wept, and in silence, they both prayed that Tommy would at last have peace.

Muriel raised her head from John's shoulder and wiped the tears from her face. Slowly, she unfolded herself from his lap and took John by the hand.

"I am tired, John Boyle," she said. "Please take me up the steps to our room."

He took her arm, and together they left the dimness of the study. Slowly, they made their way together down the long hall, past the grandfather clock, past the oaken mirror, and up the creaky steps they went. His hand slid smoothly over the well-worn, varnished banister, and John could feel the tight grip of Muriel on his forearm. She never spoke as she climbed the curving staircase, and her eyes never left the stepped photos of their children, parents, and grandparents. All who had ever lived in this house adorned the walls of the staircase, and all their eyes were on John and Muriel as they walked once more to the bedroom they had shared for over sixty years.

They reached the big room at the top of the stairs, and John leaned over and kissed her cheek. "I will just get cleaned up," he said, as he turned across the hall and went into the upstairs bath. As he turned to close the door, he watched Muriel as she skipped into the room that was so familiar to her. She did a quick pirouette as she entered, her arms extended at her sides, and as John shut the door, he was laughing out loud. There is that sound again, he thought. And there is that feeling—a feeling he always sought but always feared had left him. John Boyle was happy. John Boyle was content. Just for now, just for this moment, but that was more than he had ever hoped for.

He brushed his teeth and combed his hair, and behind each sagging jowl, he dabbed some cologne—her favorite, English Leather. He stood back and looked in the mirror and was not completely displeased at what he saw. He had aged as most farmers do—weathered, slightly paunched, but overall in good shape, considering. The only difference he saw this early autumn morning was the smile he wore. He turned and crossed the hall to their room.

She sat on the loveseat by the bed, the light on over her shoulder as she looked down upon a book in her lap. He watched her in silence for a brief moment, then slowly, she looked up, perhaps alerted to his presence by the wafting scent of the cologne. She smiled at him, and he felt his heart leap. She patted the loveseat beside her and said, "Come, come sit by me." He moved slowly across the worn plank floorboards, and as he drew near, she looked up again. "Come, Tommy, sit with Mother, and we shall read. This is one of your favorites, and though we have read it many times together, I think tonight would be a good time to start it again. It is The Catcher in the Rye. I do love it so. What do you think, Tommy—should we give it a go?"

He just looked down upon her, smile frozen on his face, feet frozen in mid-stride. Like water frozen in a rock, dementia had shattered his heart.

"What is it, Tommy? You look so sad. Tell Mother what is the matter."

"Nothing is the matter," he replied. "Everything is fine." Slowly, John walked over to the loveseat and settled in beside her. She took his hand in hers, and she smiled. She smiled in a way that John had never seen. She smiled as she did when she was with Tommy.

INSANITY

It was just after two a.m. when Rhonda stumbled into the alley that ran behind Lucy's Last Stand. She let her weight fall heavily onto the brick wall at the back of Lucky's and leaned there, listening to the air slowly escaping her lungs. She ached all over, and she knew she had been hurt.

There was a large bump over her left eye, and Rhonda could feel her skin as it turned from blue to yellow, leaving the marks of her trade out in the open for everyone to see. The air escaping her lungs hurt her throat as it made its way out of an airway bruised by the big, meaty hands that had squeezed her neck from behind. She could taste dried blood in her mouth from where she had bitten down into her own flesh in order to get through the ordeal—to help her live past the shame, give her control over the pain, and get her here into this alley with crack cocaine in her purse. She had a need in her soul and a need to forget.

Her ribs ached, and her knees were scraped raw from the leather seat she had knelt on as he drove hard into her. With each hate-filled thrust, he damaged her physically. With each brutal punch to her hips and vicious slap to her backside, he bruised her flesh and left scars on her soul, scars that only the blue smoke could heal. She had been in bad spots before and had been hurt before but never like this. For a moment, she was certain he would kill her as his rage filled the car. It was as though the weight of the air inside the car itself was pressing into her, not him. It was as though she had been taken to a place of such evil and darkness that it was consuming her, and at that moment, she wanted to live and die at the same time.

There was a cut on her cheek from where the automatic window button had sliced deeply as he drove into her, the window coming down two inches and then going back up for what seemed like hours but had only been minutes. Her earlobe was torn through, one of her yin and yang earrings—the ones Tommy had given her in the beginning—caught on the door handle as he threw her out into the street. And she was badly hurt, down there, where he had finished with the bottle.

The guy in the big Cadillac Seville seemed okay when he rolled down the window and began to chat. He seemed okay when they went through the shopping list of what he wanted and what she could provide. He seemed okay—maybe a little drunk—when they agreed on the price, and he seemed okay when she climbed into the big Caddy and they drove down Forty-Second Street to the park by the river. She had access to a flop room and knew how to work the alleys, but the guy in the red Caddy wanted to take her in the car. The car was warm and dry, and in truth, much more comfortable than the alley or the flop house, so Rhonda jumped in.

She had never been in a car so grand in all her life. Instantly, she melted into the warmed leather bucket seats of the Seville. She seemed to be surrounded by warmth and comfort as the soft lights of the electronic dash lit up the inside of the Caddy. For a moment, Rhonda imagined herself and Tommy driving in such a car, maybe on the way to the theater or picking up friends on the way to a club. It could have been like that for her and Tommy. This could have been their chance to start again. But Tommy was a coward. And Tommy couldn't live with what he had done, though in truth Rhonda believed Tommy couldn't live with what she had done—what she had become. She was an addict and a worker; Tommy was just an addict and a violent felon.

"So, what's your name, or should I just call you Big Caddy Daddy?" Rhonda gave him her working smile and let her hand rest on his thigh.

"My name is Jack," he said. "But you can call me Red. Sometimes, I am Red."

"Well, which one is it tonight—Jack or Red? Not that it'll make much difference, honey. In fact, for a few dollars more, Jack and Red can get what they need from little Rhonda. Tell me, Jack or Red—is there a bar in this big old Cadillac?"

Jack laughed to himself as he turned the car down the street that led to the park.

"Jack. Let's start out with Jack. The other guy, Red, thinks he can be the boss of me, but tonight Jack is in the wheelhouse, and he's doing just fine. There's a nice little bottle of Johnny Walker in the console, baby; get us a drink. No glasses required."

"Ooooh, Jack and Red and Johnny as well! That'll be just fine with me—a little foursome," Rhonda said as she reached for the bottle of Scotch, spun off the cap, and took a drink of the amber fluid. "Mind if I play some music, Jack? I see you have a nice collection of oldies here. How about some Tony Bennett? I love Tony Bennett. I know you, don't I? Jack, Jack, you're the new guy from the pawn shop, aren't you?"

"New guy! Feels to me like I've been there a fucking lifetime already. I know you too; you used to live with that punk, that junkie Tommy. You're a junkie too, aren't you, honey?"

As Jack spoke, his tone became more aggressive, and he stared directly at Rhonda as the Caddy veered closer to the curb, bouncing the tires along it. He reached over and took the bottle of Johnny Walker roughly from her hand, lifting it to his lips and drinking deeply. Rhonda realized that Jack was much drunker than she had first suspected, and an alert went off in her head. She would have to handle this situation. She would have to do her work, get her cash, and get out of this car as soon as possible. She had already had an altercation tonight and wasn't up for another. She just wanted to get her trick in, get her cash in, and get her drug in. That was the imperative.

"Hey there, Jack, best keep those baby blues on the road. We don't want a nasty accident damaging this fine car before we can party or get pulled over by the city's finest. That would be a bummer. Why not just slow down and tell Rhonda about your night…had a little tiff with the Mrs., or just out to get yourself some selfish pleasure?"

"Red. Call me Red. And no Mrs. What brings me down here is a complicated fucking life and a fear of getting involved—or, I guess, more involved—with that fuck boyfriend of yours!"

"He isn't my boyfriend. Not anymore, anyway, Jack. I mean, Red. Why don't you calm down a bit and pull over here so I can make it all better for you?"

"Because this ain't where I want to pull over, you got a problem with that, bitch?"

"No problem here, Red! None whatsoever. Just anxious to help you lose some of that tension you're carrying in those big shoulders." Rhonda heard the second stage alert bell ringing in her head and started to think of how she'd get away from Jack, or Red, whichever one was about to get out of control. She started to rub Jack's thigh from knee to groin in an effort to distract him from his building rage.

Jack reached down and roughly removed her hand from his leg and continued speaking, but as he spoke, Rhonda realized he wasn't exactly speaking to her. He was just talking as though there were someone else in the car with them. The third alarm in her head began to ring loudly, but Rhonda feared it might be too late.

"Years, years it's been since I let you out of the bottle, fucker! Fucking red bastard genie has won again, and look at me now. You prick! You son of a bitch! Look at me now, driving around with a whore in my car, running from the cops, everyone out to get me."

Rhonda watched in fear as Jack, or Red, ranted at the windshield, realizing he was talking to his reflection as if she wasn't even there. The alarms in her head were now drowning out all other thoughts, and Rhonda knew she was in trouble.

"No one's out to get you here, Red. Just me and you now. Why not pull over and let Rhonda fix all your problems? This is a good spot, Red, and I'm not sure how much longer I can wait for it, you know what I mean, Red?"

"I am Jack, not that Red bastard. And don't try to play me, whore. I'm sick to death of people telling me where and when. I'm doing the deciding here tonight, not you. We're almost to where I want to go! Not you! Not Red! Me! You get that, whore?"

"I do, Jack. I get that, and all I want is what you want, Jack. Fuck Red, man! I just want to make Jack happy. Whatever Jack needs tonight is what Rhonda wants, man. I may not even charge you, Jack, because I can see you're hurting, and I want to help."

"Charge me…I don't give a shit about money. I want the fucking respect I am due! From you and them, the whole fucking world seems to conspire against me, and I'm sick of it. I don't need money; I need respect."

Jack reached into the pockct of his suit jackct, and as he drove, he pulled out a wad of bills. Mostly twenties, some fifties and tens, which he violently threw across the seat and into Rhonda's lap.

"Take what you need, baby. Take what you think you're worth. Take it all for all I care; you're going to earn it—on that, you can be certain."

Rhonda was full of fear, but Rhonda was also in need. Her addiction allowed her to look past the imminent danger and focus on the loose bills lying in her lap and on the floor of the Cadillac. Slowly, she began to gather the money and stuff it into her pockets. The same uncontrollable thirst that brought her to the streets, which put her in this position tonight, had taken over and convinced her she would be okay. She could handle this crazy man, and when she was done, she'd have enough cash to feed her need for several days, and that made it all worth the risk. She looked up with her best working smile as Jack continued to rant.

"You have no idea how hard I've tried. I've been off the booze, bought that fucking pawn shop. Been straight and narrow for the most part, maybe scamming the junkies a bit here and there, but no one cares about them fucks anyway. Maybe I fucked over Louis' widow a bit when I bought the place, but she wanted out anyway. I was doing her a favor. You know, I even went to an AA meeting tonight. I even went back to those fucks because I thought maybe they were right about a few things the last time I went to see them, but no way. That fuck there in the mission, Father Hank, the ex-priest diddler or something—who knows? He tells me, 'Why didn't I come there before I drank?' Fucking deviant. He thinks I'm going to listen to a fucking low-life drunken deviant, he's got another thing coming. And I told him so too. Go fuck yourself, I said, as I left that bunch of losers. I don't need 'em now, never needed 'em before either. Fucking Red will be put back in his place before this night is done, I can assure you, Rhonda. When I'm done with you, I'll be done with him as well."

Jack skidded the big red Seville to a stop beneath a huge oak tree by the side of the river. He was breathing heavily, and Rhonda prayed his heart would explode. Beads of sweat dotted his forehead, glowing in the eerie light of the electronic dashboard. The droplets were so prominent on his forehead that they resembled huge boils, giving Redjack the look of pure evil. He roughly grabbed Rhonda's hand and placed it on his crotch, and Rhonda could feel the rapidity of his pulse in the hardness. He held her hand there for several minutes, and slowly, Rhonda began to stroke him. Quietly, she cooed in his ear, "It will all be okay, Jack. Rhonda will help. Rhonda will make it better now."

Without a word, his meaty hand took her wrist. Jack threw open the driver's door and, in a single motion, left the car, dragging Rhonda over the center console and out into the cold night. She stumbled to get her footing, and before she realized it, Jack had lifted her off the ground and set her down at the back door of the car. She hadn't realized until now how big Redjack was. She hadn't realized until now the power that had been concealed beneath a suit jacket and a winning smile. She hadn't realized until now, as she looked up into his vacant eyes, that Redjack was insane.

"Get in the back and get on your knees. I'm ready to finish this thing." He opened the door and roughly pushed her in. Rhonda crawled on hands and knees to the other side of the big Caddy, reaching for the door handle as Redjack came in behind her. He pulled her roughly away from the handle and hit the auto locks as he flipped up her skirt and ripped off her panties. Rhonda felt the roll of bills in her coat pocket reassure her, and she let her mind go to the place it stayed while she worked.

Meanwhile, Clayton Beday had driven slowly and cautiously down to this deviant part of town. He was on a mission to establish order in the life of Rhonda, the woman. He would sanctify her in pain, and she would know the power of Clayton Beday. He didn't need to explain his actions or his inebriation to some low-level cop in a cruiser, so he moved with caution and patience. He would find the girl, and she would be made to suffer. With each passing second, the pleasure of his mission increased in his diseased mind. Clayton was savoring his insanity.

It was just before two in the morning when Clayton walked into Lucky's Last Stand and ordered a vodka and milk. He had been to four other bars in the past two hours and had walked calmly through six or seven alleys, finding no sign of Rhonda. The places to look for the girl were running out, but Clayton was a patient man, and he would persevere until his goals were realized. If not tonight, then tomorrow, or the next night, he would find her. There was no timetable on divine retribution.

He made some small talk with the bartender, then found his way to a darkened corner booth in the seedy bar. The shadows fell over his face and shoulders as he sat in the corner, and Clayton was only visible from the chest down. Occasionally, his scraped and swollen hand would gather up the double vodka and milk from the table, and the drink would disappear into the darkness that had enveloped Clayton's head. Moments later, the drink would return to the table, a little less full. Other than the aging waitress in the bar, no one noticed Clayton Beday. But Clayton noticed them. He noticed them all.

From the darkness of his booth and the darkness of his mind, Clayton passed judgment.

Though Rhonda was the subject of tonight's hunt, it was becoming evident to Clayton that his mission extended beyond her. Everyone he observed in this den of iniquity was in need of direction. Everyone in this pit of vipers was calling out for correction, and as Clayton sat in the shadows, his mind was filled with the voice of the televangelist: "Seek them out in the dark places. Go forth and shine the light of self-righteousness upon these sinners." It was up to him, Clayton Beday, to bring the sins of these people into the light and sanctify them with fire and pain. It would begin tonight, but it would go on for many nights to come, as all around him stood the unworthy. Clayton's insanity was such that these thoughts, born in addiction, rang true, and his certainty that he had been chosen was unshakable.

He watched the table in the far corner with interest as, one by one, the addicts came to the man sitting there. He was a small man but, unlike all the rest in this place, he was sober. He drank from a bottle of Perrier water while those around him guzzled booze, clearly drunk in their actions. He was a small man, but Clayton could see he was in control. He had an ease and arrogance about him as he slid his small packages of crystal death to the addicts. One by one, they came, one by one, they sat, and one by one, they left. Alone, these denizens would find a hole, and alone they would seek refuge from whatever demon beset them—refuge in the blue smoke.

He watched the small, tidy man who was the big and messy drug dealer, and slowly Clayton began to smile. This man would be number two for Clayton. This man would be subject to the swift and final justice that Clayton had ordained himself to deliver. This man would be cleansed by Clayton, just as Rhonda would be.

Lost in the fantasy of how he would deal with the little man, Clayton did not see Rhonda as she entered Lucky's. She made her way slowly to the bar and, once there, ordered a double Jack Daniels. She took the drink, and on shaky legs, she threw it back and ordered another. The pain she felt in her body and her soul would not easily be lifted this night, and Rhonda craved numbness. The second double Jack went down like the first, and Rhonda's physical pain lessened enough to get her moving again—toward the table on the far side of the bar and the little man known as Hotdog.

Rhonda stood at the table, as was the rule, and looked down at Hotdog in silence, waiting for the nod of permission to sit, which she knew would come. He was a small man in physical stature, yet he had risen to some height in the underworld of drugs and guns. He was not the man in the organization controlling the traffic in this part of town, but he was a man, and as such, he was filled with a false sense of his own importance—a false sense that would one day be his undoing, but not here, not tonight.

Rhonda knew him well, having stood many times at the edge of this very table, willing to do whatever was required to get what she needed. Tommy had introduced her to Hotdog, but over the months and years, she had developed her own relationship with him. It wasn't always necessary for Rhonda to have money to get what she needed; sometimes, she just needed to submit to Hotdog's unique fetish to acquire her drugs. Yes, she knew Hotdog well—perhaps too well.

The sight of him repulsed and frightened her at once. He had been born with some genetic, freakish anomaly that left him completely hairless. He had no brows or lashes, no hair on his head or anywhere on his body. His skin seemed a size too small for his little frame, and he was oddly translucent. You could almost see through him, but you couldn't see into him, and in that, there was a kind of salvation; for to look deeply into Hotdog would be to gaze upon pure evil.

He sat with a couple of young girls whom Rhonda recognized as she had once been herself. They were new to the game, new to addiction, and probably had some boundaries yet to be crossed, some principles yet to be burned in the crack pipe. They looked at Rhonda and smirked. They looked at her as though she were used up and beat up, telling themselves they would never sink to such depths. And Rhonda understood. Rhonda had occupied the same seat, and it had not been so long ago—though it seemed a lifetime.

Hotdog also looked and smirked, no doubt remembering the times he had belittled her, recalling the power he wielded in a little zip-lock bag—the power over life and death. His beady eyes held her in contempt, and he took pleasure in letting her stand in silence, knowing by her appearance that she must be in great pain. She hated him with all that was left of her heart and simultaneously knew she would do anything for him, even now, less than an hour after she had been viciously raped.

"You look like shit, little girl. You been having a bad night?" He laughed at his own wit, and the two on either side of him joined in. Rhonda stood in silence, knowing the game, knowing the rules.

"This here is Rhonda, ladies. She has been a friend to old Hotdog for a couple years now, isn't that right, Rhonda?"

"Whatever you say, Hotdog, whatever you say."

He looked at her for what seemed like an eternity but was merely seconds, and then, ever so subtly, he nodded his head. If you were not aware of Hotdog's required ritual, the nod would have gone unnoticed—as it did with Clayton Beday, who watched from the shadows, biding his time.

Hotdog leaned back and extended each of his hairless arms over the shoulders of the young girls on either side of him. Rhonda could see the slight stiffening of the two girls as the cold, clammy, hairless flesh of Hotdog came to rest on their bare shoulders, and she smiled bitterly to herself as she remembered their revulsion to his touch. They looked to him with forced smiles, their eyes glazed over from the magic of the pipe. Soon they would need more, and soon they too would be forever at the mercy of Hotdog.

"Rhonda here has been a special friend to old Hotdog, ain't that right, Rhonda?"

"Whatever you say, Hotdog."

"Mayhaps some night soon, Rhonda can join us all up at my place for a special night, and she can show you the way to old Hotdog's heart. What do you say, Rhonda?"

"Whatever you want, Hotdog."

Rhonda knew what he meant and what it meant. She had once been the girl at the table, the one under Hotdog's hairless limb, smirking at a crack whore arrogantly. Her name had been Hope, and she had shown Rhonda the special thrills that Hotdog sought; then she was gone. Now, he invited Rhonda to initiate these two new, pretty prey of Hotdog's, and then he would be done with her. She had been used up and would be cast off, lost to the world as Hope had been.

"Is there something old Hotdog can do for you this late night, Rhonda? You look like shit, like maybe you need something a little more relaxing than your normal rock. Perhaps old Hotdog can help you out. I got me some real nice H here tonight, girl. Gonna set you free and take away all those bad thoughts, all that pain you're wearing on your face. Gonna make you my pretty again, Rhonda. What you say, girl? Old Hotdog gonna fix it all for you?"

"Maybe, Hotdog. Maybe. I don't ever do the heroin, but tonight, maybe it is what I need. Maybe tonight is the night I take the big ride, eh? Forget about it all for a while."

Rhonda reached into her pocket and pulled out the large roll of cash that came from Redjack, staring at the money. The price of her dignity and the cause of her pain were all gathered at the table in this scummy bar, in this shitty neighborhood, and for the first time in years, Rhonda thought of her mama. She thought of her dad and her sister and wondered if they ever thought of her. She wondered if they were still looking for her, and she wondered if anyone would find her before it was too late. She hoped not. She hated herself, she hated Tommy Boyle, she hated Hotdog, and she hated the world. It had used her up and left her here at the mercy of this hairless beast. And she didn't want them to find her, not like this, not as she had become. She wanted to be Daddy's little girl again, but she knew she could never be. That girl was gone forever. They would not find her because she was no longer recognizable to them. She was alone in the world, and so she reached out to Hotdog with a handful of cash and purchased her only friend.

"Now you're talking, little girl! Ole Hotdog gonna fix you up for a good ride, and that wad of cash you're sporting will keep you well for a couple of days. You must have worked a little overtime tonight, eh, Rhonda?" Hotdog laughed at his own wit as he reached into the knapsack at his feet and removed the clear plastic bag Rhonda had come for.

They made their exchange—money for drugs—in full view of the patrons of Lucky's Last Stand. Hotdog operated here with impunity and arrogance, as he placed himself above the law.

Here, in this place, he was in charge. He was the man with the merchandise, and he lorded over the addicts as he pleased. He had locked their destinies in a knapsack full of celluloid bags, and he loved the power he had over them. He was the man.

Clayton watched from the corner booth as the deal was made. He watched Rhonda stuff the bags in her pocket and Hotdog stuff the cash in his, and he felt contempt for them. Rhonda stood on shaky legs and leaned into the table as she placed the bag of dreams in her pocket. She saw the two young ones laugh to each other, and she knew their day would come. Nodding to Hotdog, she turned and walked out the back door into the alley behind Lucky's Last Stand.

Clayton finished his drink, paid the waitress for another, which he drank in one gulp. He wiped the film of milk mixed with sweat from his upper lip onto the sleeve of his shirt as he rose and headed for the alley behind Lucky's.

Hank Quinn had been restless since meeting with Armist and Polly Anne. The story of the old-timer's transformation and the violence of Tommy Boyle had left him inspired to act, but he was uncertain as to how. His long, endless work at the mission was often frustrating, and though he lived in hope that some would be brought to the Lord and healed of the compulsion to drink and use drugs, he was aware that those numbers would be few. He would get some into programs and others into harm reduction therapy, but most would drink, and most would die. The story Armist had revealed to him this evening had spoken to his heart and rekindled his faith. He could see the miracle that Armist could not. He could feel the spirit working in Tommy Boyle, though he doubted Tommy would understand. There was something powerful happening tonight in these five square blocks, and Hank Quinn wanted to be a witness to it. So, in the wee hours, he began to walk.

It was not unusual to see Hank Quinn walking the streets late at night. Often, at the end of his late meeting, he would clean up and walk a few blocks looking for those who might be in harm's way, maybe get a few back to the mission. The difference tonight was that Hank was not looking for wayward souls or fallen drunkards. Tonight, Hank was looking for Tommy Boyle and, in a greater sense, searching for himself. Since he had heard the details of the violence that had befallen Trip and Sister Petra, he had become obsessed with finding Tommy.

You see, Hank Quinn had spent a lifetime teaching of miracles and telling the downtrodden to have faith. "If you believe in the miracle, the miracle will happen for you," he had said a thousand times. He had even witnessed the miracle of lives changing in recovery programs. He preached it, he saw it, but still, in the deepest part of Hank's heart, he did not believe it—at least, not for himself. Hank had lost everything when he lost his ordination. Oh, he had wrestled his demons and come to terms with his many addictions. He had experienced physical and mental transformation, which could only be attributed to God, but he still had an emptiness deep inside and a shame forged from years of Catholicism that he kept for himself. Hank had taught others to shed the sins of their past and accept forgiveness, but he did not believe, in the darkest parts of his mind, that he had earned the same favor from a kind and loving God. In his mind, he knew it was not so, but a thousand miles lay between the head and the heart.

So, on this dark, damp night, in the hardest part of the downtown core, Hank Quinn searched for souls—Tommy Boyle's and Hank Quinn's. He knew that both of their survival depended on the outcome of this night. Tommy's physical body and eternal salvation were in jeopardy, and Hank knew he could no longer go on as half a man. He needed to fill the emptiness within him to maintain a spiritual condition that would allow him the serenity and peace he craved. He needed to shed the years of shame and remorse completely in order to move forward in his own life. Hank had become convinced that the solution to his problem lay in the transformation of Tommy Boyle and Armist Hancock. God was working, and He was working overtime here in these five square blocks. As has always been His way, God was working with a purpose, a divine plan which Hank felt he was being called to. The forgiveness he sought would not come from amends or another fourth step, but from God and God's promise of propitiatory salvation alone. That redemption needed to begin with Hank, and somehow, with Tommy Boyle.

Rhonda found a spot in the alley between the dumpster and a tall stack of empty soda crates. She fell heavily into this urban cave and groaned softly as her back came to rest abruptly against the brick wall. Every part of her body ached and cried out for the cure, but her energy had been so depleted by the events of the evening that her body moved in slow motion. The dullness of her movements did not testify to the urgency in her brain or the ravaging pain that wracked her body. It was as though she watched from another world as her hand slowly and mechanically moved to her handbag and removed the small cellophane pouch containing the heroin.

In a surreal sort of haze, Rhonda looked on as her hand pulled out the lighter, the spoon, and all the fixings required to ride the red dragon. She had never done heroin, but she had watched many times as Tommy had fixed for himself. She had assisted as Tommy went under with the first assault of the dragon and stood by to make sure he never vomited and swallowed his own bile. He never did, and Rhonda was certain she would not either, though if she did, it would not be a bad way to end this night. In fascination, she observed her hands as they gently poured from the bag into the spoon, and deep in her head, she heard a voice say, "There, that is the right amount." But her hand kept pouring.

"Stop," cried the voice, but her hands did not respond, and soon there was triple the right amount. "It's too much," said the voice, but her hands didn't hear as the lighter was lit and the cooking began. "You need to stop now, or it will be too late," pleaded the voice in her head, but her hands slowly filled the syringe and wrapped the strap of her handbag tightly around her bruised arm. "Please, I don't want to," sobbed the voice, but the part of Rhonda that desired to live was no longer stronger than the part of her that wished to die, and her hands lovingly slid the needle into her vein.

The dragon raced quickly through her blood and into her heart and brain, and Rhonda stiffened at the assault before slowly sliding down the wall until she lay on her back in the damp, filthy alley. Her skirt had pulled up to her waist, exposing her bruised and bleeding nakedness to anyone passing, but Rhonda was beyond caring. She was gone. She was leaving this horrible place as she always did with the cure, but this time, tonight, would be her final departure. She would not come back to the alley. She would not return to a man who cared nothing for her or to the johns who beat and abused her. She would be shed of the burden of these five blocks forever. She wanted so desperately to see her mother once more, and suddenly there she was, standing in the alley, looking down upon her. Her mother smiled at Rhonda, and

Rhonda felt her heart soar. "Oh, Mommy," she said, "I have been such a bad girl. I am sorry, so sorry."

"Never mind," her mother called out as she bent to take her hand. "I have been looking for you."

"Really?" cried Rhonda. "Really, Mommy? I thought you were mad. I thought no one was looking for me anymore." Rhonda smiled as she began to let go of her life. She felt happy for the first time in as long as she could recall—happy because it was finally over and she could see her mother.

But suddenly, something changed. The hand that had been extended to her in love was rough, hard, and meaty. It was not the gentle touch of her mother's slender hand, and an alarm went off deep in the dying brain of Rhonda. Her eyes fluttered several times and finally opened, fighting to focus. There, squeezing hard on her small hand, stood a man—a man filled with evil and seething anger.

"I have been looking for you, my dear," screamed Clayton Beday as he dragged Rhonda out into the openness of the alley. "I have been looking all night. We have unfinished business, you and I, and by the look of you, you are ready to give me what I paid for earlier this evening. You look like you're dying, Rhonda, but you will not die with a smile on your face as I just found you. Neither will you die by your own hand, for that is sinful. You will die at the hand of righteousness, and you shall die in the manner in which you lived. You shall be strangled in fornication, and this act of intercession will set you free from the trials of this wretched life forever. You will be saved by Clayton Beday, now and forever!"

Rhonda tried to scream, but there was no breath in her. Rhonda tried to struggle, but there was only limpness in her limbs. Rhonda was dying, but not as she had wished. Rhonda was going to be murdered.

Hank Quinn had come to the end of his circuit with no success. Tommy Boyle was nowhere to be found. He had searched all the usual spots and seen no one. All the street people were underground tonight. All the street people knew there was trouble afoot, and tonight was a good night to remain unseen. He had been so certain there was a call to him this night, so sure that he was meant to be out here on this wet night and involved with whatever was about to happen, and yet there was quiet. Perhaps it was his ego leading him forward through alley after alley and not his God. There was a time when Hank knew the difference, when he knew so surely when God had touched his heart, but that certainty eluded Hank now. His faith had been fractured, and in the healing, his heart had not set correctly.

He came to the mouth of the alley that ran alongside Lucky' s Last Stand and looked into the dim light, straining his eyes against the wet darkness to see if there was movement in the alley. All seemed quiet to Hank as he turned to walk inside Lucky's for a quick look before turning back to the mission. Hank entered the bar and allowed his eyes to grow accustomed to the even darker dinge of the barroom. He scanned the crowd for signs of Tommy Boyle, but there was none to be found. His eyes fell on Hotdog— not one of Hank's favorite people, and the disdain was quite mutual. It had been months since Hank had exchanged any words with Hotdog, and those words had not been pleasant, but Hank began to move closer to the drug dealer.

"Well, lookee here," said Hotdog. "If it isn't Father Hank Quinn…messenger to the Lord and fancy man to the young angels of the parish." Hotdog laughed and pulled the two young girls closer to him, his hairless hands clasping their shoulders.

"You looking for some crack from old Hotdog tonight, Padre, or just looking for some sweet young thing? I could set you up right here, Father, with one of my new best friends. Ain't that right, girls? One of you would be happy to please old Father Hank, right? Why, maybe old Hotdog could watch on and make sure the Father is doing it right. What you say, Father? Sound good to you? Oh, wait a minute, you really ain't a Father no more, are you, Hank. Ex officio or some shit, excommunicated maybe. Now you're just some do-gooder down here fucking with my business. Some pervert out looking for a young one."

Hank looked down at Hotdog silently and took it all in. In his heart, he longed to reach out and choke the life out of Hotdog, and so in his silence, he prayed. He prayed for this depraved and arrogant drug dealer and the two young girls under each of his hairless arms. He prayed for their redemption and asked God to intercede on their behalf. He prayed so he would not lose ground to his anger, and he prayed that he would not judge this man before him but would leave that work to God. Hotdog was a resentment Hank Quinn could not allow to fester and poison his heart and mind.

"That's funny, Hotdog. I always said you were a funny guy. You'll break them up when you're in prison." Hank and Hotdog both laughed, but the girls sat in fear of what might transpire. "Thanks for the offer of the drugs and the women, Hotdog, but I think I'll have to pass on both tonight. Doesn't really fit into what I am trying to do here in the borough. And you're right. I am no longer a priest. Excommunicated, I believe, is the correct term."

"Oh, so sorry to hear that, Hank. You know I didn't mean no disrespect. I was raised Catholic myself, you know."

"I didn't know, actually, Hotdog, but to be honest, not so surprised. So can we get past all this bullshit, Hotdog, and get to the point of why I am here?"

"Please do, Padre, please do."

"I am looking for someone, and I thought you might be able to help. Maybe do something good for once, Hotdog. What do you think?"

"I think everyone is looking for someone, Padre, and you may need to be a bit more specific. I think old Hotdog always remembers better when he is paid for his talent, but maybe just for tonight, I'll give you a break. Be a nice guy. You know, Padre, one fallen Catholic to another. Who is it you are looking for, Hank?"

"Tommy Boyle. I am looking for Tommy Boyle."

"Whoee! You and every other swinging dick in these here five blocks. That crack head is a hot commodity right now! I'd give him up myself for the reward if I had that motherfucker."

Hank looked down at Hotdog and knew he did not know where Tommy was. Slowly, he turned and, without a word, started to exit Lucky' s Last Stand.

"Whoa, Padre. Hold up. Hotdog is a man of his word. Said I would help, and help I will. His whore, Rhonda, she just scored a bag of H and headed out the back way into the alley. Not fifteen minutes ago, man. The way she looked, that psycho Tommy maybe already dealt with her tonight. I don't know, but she got what she needed to get right, and she's most likely still out back, riding the red road to freedom. There you go, Padre. Don't say old Hotdog never helped you out. Maybe say a wee prayer for me and my girls here tonight—we're all going to need it, especially them. Ain't that right, girlies?" Hotdog laughed hard at his own humor as Hank Quinn crossed the floor of Lucky's Last Stand and walked out into the wet darkness of the alley.

Clayton was rushing as he held onto Rhonda's arm and fumbled with his zipper. He slapped her hard once on the cheek, and she stirred slightly in her dying. He needed her to hold on, just for a moment while he readied himself. He would take her, and it would be the last thing of this earth she would know. She would not fight him, for she had no life left in her to do so. She would not scream, for there was not breath enough to escape her lungs. She would lie there dying, and for the first time in his life, Clayton would be completely in control. The thought of control was working, and Clayton felt himself harden. He felt the blood moving in him for the first time in many months, and he smiled as the man he had always known himself to be was about to be born just as the woman he knew Rhonda to be was about to die. He breathed heavily as he completely tore away the panties that had already been torn earlier. Rhonda bled from the violation she had endured at the hands of Red Jack, but Clayton did not care. She would die, and he would live.

He did not hear the footfalls behind him as he discarded the soiled panties. He did not see the shadow fall over him like the outstretched arm of God as he began to enter. He did not see the rising arms of Hank Quinn as his excitement grew. And he did not expect the searing pain he felt as the side of his head was laid open by the swing of a discarded beer bottle from the alley.

Clayton rolled off Rhonda with a scream, his hand rising to the gushing blood at his temple. He did not turn to face his attacker. He did not rise up to fight his unseen assailant. He did not curse the man who had wounded him so deeply. Clayton's power and control left him quickly, as did his erection, and Clayton was left whimpering, scurrying away toward the mouth of the alley. For the second time in this long night, Clayton was running away in cowardice. For the second time in this long night, Clayton was filled with self-loathing and unimaginable fear. As he rose from his hands and knees to his feet, he began to run. Clayton was running for his life. In his escape, Clayton looked over his shoulder into the darkness of the alley to see his attacker.

He saw the man there, bending over the whore Rhonda, taking her in his arms and holding her to his chest. Then he kissed her, and Clayton was filled with hate for this man he did not know. This little man, half Clayton's size, had bested him—just as the junkie Tommy had earlier this same night. Just as had been the pattern of his life, Clayton always lost in all his pursuits. But it was not his fault. Just as all men of God will face persecution, so too would Clayton. In his heart, he knew he was righteous, and that Rhonda the whore, Tommy the junkie, and this unknown man in the alley would all have to pay. He was not running in fear! He was running away to fight another day.

With each labored step, the distance between Clayton and his attacker grew, as did Clayton's delusion. As his diseased mind regained control over his damaged emotions and his legs carried him to the lights of the street at the end of the alley, Clayton shed his fear and let his courage prevail. He felt strong now, fleet of foot. In a remarkable move resembling that of a pass receiver crossing the goal line, Clayton pivoted on his left foot and, in full flight, began to run backward into the street. As he backpedaled toward the lighted street, Clayton raised his arms above his head as though reaching out to summon the power of the Lord. The street light behind him picked up his form and cast a demented shadow the full length of the alley, falling over Hank Quinn as he feverishly performed resuscitation on Rhonda.

His breathing was ragged, but his voice was strong as he bellowed from deep within the raging pit of his stomach. They would hear him, and they would know! They would all know that he, Clayton Beday, was the shadow that fell over them. He, Clayton Beday, would exercise extreme judgment upon them, and soon he, Clayton Beday, would send them all to hell. Screaming in his insanity, running backward through the alley as he had run backward through his life, Clayton Beday exited into the street.

"Fly me to the moon and let me gaze upon the stars…" Jack Corbett came to from his blackout to the crooning sounds of Tony Bennett on the radio of the big red Cadillac Seville. He sat unmoving for a moment, letting the confusion wash over him. He was drunk, that he knew, and the evidence lay at his side on the leather seat—an empty bottle of Johnny Walker Red. His bottle, the bottle he had been talking to for so long now, was gone. He looked at the bottle, and a remorse poured over him that he was certain would choke the breath out of him. He had done it again. He had gone so long this time in control, but in the end, the bottle had won.

There was blood smeared on the bottle, and Jack began to feel anxiety grow in his gut. He was sitting in the back seat, and the car was running. The back door of the car was open to the night air, and Jack felt damp where the wind had carried the light night mist in to settle upon his suit jacket. He looked down over himself and saw that his pants were open, and his belt was off. The belt lay on the floor of the car beside one of his shoes. He could see blood on the buckle.

Jack took it all in, but he had no idea what it all meant. He ran his big, meaty hand through his hair and tried to rub a memory back into his brain through his eyes, but it was of no use. The memories were lost forever in the blackout. He pulled his hand away from his face to look at his watch and saw blood on the band. He knew he had to get out of there. It was nearly three in the morning, and Jack's last memory was just after midnight. He'd been in the alley behind the pawn shop, talking to Tommy Boyle. Fucking Tommy Boyle! It always came back to the shit-head junkie! Jack looked at the blood on his watch band and then at the blood smeared on the bottle of Johnny Walker Red and wondered if it was the blood of Tommy Boyle. Had he found Tommy again and in a blackout fought him? He had no idea, but Jack Corbett was not about to stick around to try and figure it out. He had to move, and he had to move now. He hoisted his bulk from the back seat of the big Cadillac and slid in behind the wheel. He looked in the rearview mirror, and for the quickest moment, he thought he saw a young girl in the back. A fleeting moment of disjointed memory shook Jack Corbett, and once again the remorse washed over him. What had he done? He may never know, or worse yet, he may.

Without hesitation, Jack slipped the big Caddie into gear and left the park, slowly at first and then with more speed. Jack weaved through the park and onto the street. As had been the pattern throughout his life, Jack tried to leave the wreckage behind him, but it was to no avail. The haunting would follow him. The uncertainty would stalk him, and eventually, the truth of what had happened would discover him, and he would be revealed. Revealed to himself and others for the hopeless alcoholic he was. He had been masquerading in the guise of a legitimate businessman, but he had been and always would remain a liar and a fraud.

Tears streamed down the big man's face and pooled in the jowls where his neck should have been. His fat stomach moved against the steering wheel of the big Caddie as he sobbed. He took a corner too fast, and his tires screamed as the big Caddie fishtailed on the wet pavement. Clumsily, he wiped the tears from his eyes and tried to focus on the road. He realized where he was and knew that in three blocks, there was an exit to the freeway. If he could just get to the freeway, perhaps he would be okay. If he could just get out of the hell hole of these five blocks and back to the safety of his little apartment, he might be able to start again. It would be different this time. Maybe he could even go to some of those meetings again.

Another snippet of memory assaulted Jack. He was in an alley, telling that little guy from the mission to fuck off. He had been to a meeting earlier tonight. Could that be where he fought? Could the blood be Hank Quinn's? The memory was there and then it was not, and as hard as Jack tried, he could not put the whole of the evening together in a single line of events. But he knew he had been in the borough. He knew he had been seen that night, and that could be a problem.

There was just one block to go now to the freeway, and Jack's foot pressed down on the gas pedal of the big Caddie. He was in full flight now, and escape was at hand. The 400-cubic-inch engine roared as Jack made the final turn too fast and too wide, his hands slipping on the leather-covered steering wheel as he tried to correct the fishtailing Cadillac. It was then that the world went into slow motion, and in this slow motion, Jack witnessed a man running backward from an alley. His arms were extended over his head, his index fingers pointing to the heavens, his mouth open in a demonic sneer as though his jaw had been disjointed.

Jack squeezed his eyes shut once and shook his head hard, as if trying to jar loose this hallucination that had appeared before him. As his eyes opened, Jack realized too late that what he was seeing was no hallucination. He could not tell what the man was screaming or who he was screaming at as the big red Cadillac took the legs out from under him. He could not tell if the man had seen the car at the last moment or not, though he looked surprised. Jack watched in horror as the man careened in slow motion into and then through the windshield of the Seville. He felt the shards of glass rip into his jowls as the man exploded through the windshield, pinning Jack to the driver's seat and forcing his right foot hard to the gas pedal. Jack was screaming now, and as the man's face smashed into his own, the pain was incredible. Jack Corbett stared straight into the eyes of Clayton Beday as the life was draining from him, and what he saw there was evil. Then, in the flashing of his mind's eye, Jack saw Rhonda bent over and screaming as if he had violated her in the most unspeakable way. He saw the outstretched hand of Hank Quinn beckoning him into the mission earlier that night. He saw a couple in love as he passed them roughly in an alley, cursing over his shoulder at Quinn and heading for the Caddie. He saw it all. He knew what he had done, and in that moment, as the Cadillac Seville sped out of control toward the concrete retaining wall of the freeway, Jack Corbett asked God to forgive him. With all his heart, he pleaded to the Lord Jesus for mercy, and as the Cadillac burst into flames, Clayton Beday took up his place in hell, and Jack Corbett found salvation.

The light from the cell phone illuminated the face of Armist Hancock as he stood in the shadows across from Lucky's Last Stand, uncertain of what he had just witnessed. He rubbed the scar on his forehead with his twisted, talon-like hand and waited for Bob Gideon to pick up the call. In his other hand, he worked the small circle of beads attached to the crudely carved wooden crucifix as he tried to understand what he had just seen. He could feel the heat from the fire, and he could hear the scream of a man as he burned to death in his car. Hank Quinn was calling out for help as he rapidly performed CPR on a girl in the alley, the light of the burning car illuminating the scene in a surreal fashion. Armist's every instinct was to melt into the darkness and disappear, but he stood, cell phone to ear, and counted the fourth ring.

"Gideon here."

"Listen, Bob, you better get yourself and McCaskey down here to Lucky's on 5th pronto—there's been some trouble."

"Armist, what kind of trouble? You find Tommy?"

"Not just yet, Bob. You'd best get over here—there are people you know who need help quickly. Bring some other cops and an ambulance. Better get a fire truck or two as well, and you may as well get the coroner. I'm pretty sure there's at least a couple of dead guys here."

"Armist! What the hell is going on?"

"No idea, Bob. But I can't help thinking it's all about Tommy Boyle somehow. Gotta go, Bob. Don't want to be around here when the boys in blue come a-running. I'll be in touch."

Armist closed the phone. He held his hands up in front of him and felt the warmth from the fire. It felt good—the first time he'd been warm all day. The man in the car stopped screaming, and Armist was glad for it. He looked down the alley to where Hank Quinn was huddled over the girl Rhonda.

"Help's coming, Hank," he yelled. "Keep that girl alive!" He turned and walked into the darkness.

THE END IS NEAR

Tommy Boyle woke with a start to the sound of a distant explosion. He was slumped with his feet folded beneath him and had slept for nearly an hour. True sleep, not an alcohol-induced pass-out, nor a drug-filled respite from the grim reality of his life. Sleep, pure and real, like he had not experienced in years.

He looked around from the place of his slumber and laughed in spite of himself. In all the places he had woken in all his years lost, in all the places he had come to, this was his first time at the bottom of a phone booth. He had a burning ache running from just behind his ear down through his neck and into his upper back. The receiver hung by his temple and had been his makeshift pillow. He could hear the sound of the fast, busy signal filling the booth and was amazed that he could have slept through it. Grabbing the receiver and using the serpentine metal cord that dangled from the phone, Tommy began to unfold himself. His legs ached, and his feet burned with pins and needles. With great effort and much distress, Tommy clawed his way to a standing position in the darkened booth.

He strained his eyes against the wet darkness of the street, and when he was certain there was no one nearby, he pulled open the door of the phone booth and clumsily, like a new foal taking its first steps, walked into the abandoned street. He stretched and bent, allowing the blood to push away the piercing pins and needles in his lower extremities. He rolled his head and listened as cartilage and vertebrae cracked, settling into their proper positions in his neck. He stretched his arms high above his head and yawned a deep, cleansing yawn. He breathed in deeply, letting his arms free-fall to his sides, and for a moment, ever so brief, Tommy forgot he was an addict, a drunkard, and a murderer.

He wondered about the explosion and was not sure if he had heard it or if he was, in fact, dreaming. He looked off in the direction he thought the blast had come from but could see no signs of smoke or fire in the darkened distance. He looked again to the left and the right, then marveled at the quiet of the street. This was nighttime in the borough! This was the peak time for the denizens that subsisted in these five blocks to be out and about their business. The business of survival! Scrounging and stealing, selling themselves or someone else, getting the drug they needed and the shelter required to survive another day here in these five square blocks of hell. Where were they?

As quickly as the question sounded in his brain, the answer followed: they were hiding. They had taken to their lairs and flops because the place had been crawling with Cops. Cops were looking for Tommy Boy! A panic began to grip Tommy, and slowly, he backed his way into the phone booth and closed the door.

Tommy waited in the darkness. Not for the panic to leave, not to be discovered, not to alter or come up with a new plan. Tommy waited for her; he waited for the lover. But she did not come, and for the first time in his life, he understood he was truly alone. She was all that he had left, and now she was gone. He had turned his back upon her, and she had fled, and in an odd way, he missed her.

The miracle of his condition did not go unnoticed by Tommy, and his thoughts went to the small circle of wooden beads attached to the crudely carved crucifix. He was not sick. Oh, he ached, and he was tired, and his heart was broken in ways he could no longer express. But there was no real pain.

Perhaps his withdrawal had not yet begun, though it had been hours since he last used. The thought of detoxification yet to come filled him with fear, though he could not imagine that physical pain could ever surpass the pain he felt in his soul. Tommy had been spiritually bankrupt for so long that he could not recall ever feeling anything but the void. Then, this evening, it all changed. He changed. Tommy was not the man he had been as he smashed Sister Petra's face into the brick wall. He could see the image of the man who threw Trip beneath the bus but no longer knew who that man was.

He thought of his call to his sister and his Dad, and he felt something move in his heart at the memory of their voices. Perhaps there was some semblance of good left in him. Perhaps those seeds of love that had been sown when he was a child were planted so deeply that they were able to survive the long drought of addiction. Perhaps he could still be human. Maybe, in the end, he would have some dignity. Maybe at the end of it all, he would remember what it meant to want to live. He hoped it would be the case. He hoped that at the moment of his death, he would want nothing more than to live. That every nerve in his body would scream for survival. If he could feel that, if he could understand that thirst for survival at the point of his death, maybe then it would atone for what he had done. Giving one's life when that life accounted for nothing was no sacrifice.

The phone booth was suddenly flooded with red and blue light as an ambulance screamed around the corner and past Tommy's booth. The panic rose in him, and he knew his time was short and his task was incomplete. He thought again of his family, and he knew there was one more call to make. He reached to the top of the phone, dropped in his last fifty cents, and began to dial the number for Billy.

The ambulance screamed through the night, careening around corners and running red lights. In the back lay Rhonda. An oxygen mask obscured her face, and saline solution dripped slowly into her arm. It was the only good thing that had entered Rhonda through a vein in a very long time, and Hank Quinn prayed with all his might that it was not too late. The Medic was on the radio, announcing their ETA to Mercy Hospital and monitoring Rhonda's vital signs. She had died there in the alley, died in Hank's arms. He had felt the life and breath run out of her at the same moment he heard the cry from Armist Hancock.

"Keep that girl alive, Hank," Armist had yelled, and Hank was sure that it was too late. Furiously, he had begun to do mouth-to-mouth on Rhonda. Short bursts of breath twenty seconds at a time, alternating with chest compressions. He remembered the CPR course he had taken. He remembered not paying much attention as he sat through mandatory training, thinking he would never be in this situation. Hank prayed for recall and clarity, and suddenly, he could see the woman as she demonstrated compressions on the dummy. He heard her words as though she sat beside him and coached him on in the alley. Hank prayed, and the Lord heard his cry as Rhonda stirred slightly, then lurched violently and threw up all the poison that was in her onto Hank's lap. Just as she had died in his arms, she had come back. Hank had been weeping and thanking the Lord, holding Rhonda tight to his chest when the ambulance had arrived.

He sat now in the back of the rig, swaying in rhythm with the ambulance and trying to sort through all that had just happened. He had left the shelter tonight with such conviction. He had felt God touch his heart and thought he was being led to Tommy Boyle, but the Lord had sent him on a path to Rhonda. In humility, Hank praised the Lord and marveled at His presence in Hank's life, the author and finisher of all things.

Hank looked up from his prayer of thanks to the Medic who loomed cautiously over Rhonda.

"Is she going to make it, son?"

The paramedic sat close to Rhonda, monitoring her condition. Hank read his concern in the deep-cut lines in his brow and looked on with dread.

"You want the truth, friend, or do you want the standard reply? Hell, you shouldn't even be in here, but the truth is, if not for you, she wouldn't be here at all, so I guess that earns you a ride and some information. She'd be in the coroner's wagon with the rest of the carnage out there had you not performed CPR. She died, Hank, plain and simple, in your arms, and then once again on the way into the bus. You brought her back, then we did. The question is, can she come back on her own? She is in a coma right now, but she is stable. I really can't say how much damage has occurred from lack of oxygen, but judging from the track marks and the condition of the rest of her, I'd say this girl suffered massive damage in every way tonight. One thing for sure, if she comes out of this, she is going to need a friend, and I'd say at the moment, you are the only one she has."

"Thanks. You may be right. I have known her for a while, but maybe now I will get to know her more. I am just happy I was there and able to help. It was God, really. He took me there."

"You mind telling me why, Padre?" Bob Gideon sat in the front seat of the ambulance and listened in silence. He had tried to question Hank Quinn in the mayhem of the street to no avail. McCaskey was cleaning up the scene, and Gideon jumped in the ambulance to question Hank Quinn.

"Bob! Sorry, I actually had forgotten you were there. What is it you want to know?"

"I want to know what the hell is going on! I want to know who is burned to death, who has been crushed and burned, and why Rhonda is lying here dying, obviously having been raped and strangled as well as overdosed. But mostly, Hank, I want to know how you happened to be there just in the nick of time. I want to know what you are doing wandering around down here at three in the morning. I really want to know how you and Armist Hancock connected tonight. Start wherever you like, Hank."

"Well, Bob, lots of questions, eh? I don't know who was in the car or who the guy was who was crushed by the car. I do know the crushed guy was the one who was choking and trying to rape this girl. I came upon him in the alley as he was accosting her. I intervened."

"You intervened? What exactly does that mean, Padre?"

"It means I hit him over the head as hard as I could with a bottle. Please do not call me Padre, Bob. It does not sit well with me these days. I don't know who he was; I did not recognize him. He ran screaming out of the alley, and as he entered the street, he turned back. He was screaming something when the car hit him. I couldn't make it out. I suspect he was insane."

Hank reached down to Rhonda and took her by the hand as they rocked gently to and fro in the speeding ambulance. She looked helpless as she lay connected to the machinery which afforded her life. Hank knew this girl from the mission, and though he had no way of knowing the depth of the despair Rhonda had descended into, he felt as though he had failed her. They did what they could at the mission, but Hank realized it often fell short. He wondered sometimes if he was there for the client or if his work there was a salve for his own guilt. He promised himself that this girl, should she survive, would not slip through the cracks. He would be her friend if she allowed him, and he would see her into a different life.

"Sorry, Hank, I meant no disrespect. What can you tell me about Rhonda? I know she was Tommy Boyle's girl for a while. You know anything about Tommy, Hank? We really need to find him."

"I don't know much about her, Bob. I really don't. I have seen her at the mission. I've seen her there with Tommy, but not lately. I think maybe their relationship, whatever that was, had come to an end. I was down here looking for Tommy. I thought I could help. I felt as though I was being led to do something, as it turns out, it had to do with her, not Tommy. I don't know where he is, Bob, that's straight. I know he needs to be found; I was just hoping he could be found alive and not be shot on sight by some Blue justice."

"It's what I want too, Hank. It really is. There has been enough death here in my neighborhood this night. I won't say you are wrong about the blue justice, but I will say there are a couple of us trying to avoid it."

"I don't know anything, Bob. If I did, I would say. As for Armist Hancock, you know what he's like. One minute, he was not there; the next he was. To tell you the truth, I never even saw him; I just heard him telling me to keep her alive, and help was on the way."

"Can you tell me anything else about the girl?"

"I can tell you how I found her. I can tell you who gave her the crank. I can tell you about a hairless devil named Hotdog. But you already know about him, don't you, Bob? You guys know where he is and what he does, but you never seem to be able to stop him."

"No one ever talks about Hotdog, Hank. You know how it works down here. It's all backed up, the bad guys get protected by the victims, and the good guys, which are supposed to be us cops, get shut out of the information loop.

You want to tell me about Hotdog, I will listen, and I will act. Count on it."

"He told me he sold her the stuff. Told me she was in bad shape and he was doing a public service by helping her out. He's the one who told me she was in the alley. He's the one who said he sold her the high test. I will happily testify to that if you think it will help get this guy gone from here."

"It will help, Hank. I promise you when this night is over, and this mess is behind us, I will get a Hotdog. His time down here is over. We need to take back our streets, and all this has made me more determined to do so. I hope Rhonda pulls through, Hank, and I hope if she does, she will accept your help."

They all sat in silence as the ambulance screamed into the emergency department of Mercy Hospital. The three of them, all drawn together in the early hours of the morning, trying in their own ways and for their own reasons to save Rhonda.

LAST CALL

The fourth ring had come and gone, and Tommy was full of dread as he waited for the answering machine to pick up. In years past, this fourth ring would have brought a sense of relief in anticipation of the machine. Talking to the machine had always been easier than talking to Billy.

Tommy could lie to the machine and not be held accountable. He could be angry or sarcastic with the machine and never have to deal with the consequences. He could even laugh with the machine. All those things he couldn't do face to face or voice to voice with his little brother, because Tommy couldn't bear the weight of Billy's disappointment. In a lifetime of regret and a world of remorse, few things cut Tommy deeper than the apathy he heard in Billy's voice whenever they spoke. It wasn't even a fear of Billy's anger; it was the realization that Billy no longer cared. Billy felt nothing for Tommy anymore—not even contempt.

The years and the secret they had kept between them created a gulf that had become impossible to cross. It had begun with the crack in Tommy's character, which Billy had discovered so many years before on his trip to the university. The ensuing years of compounding lies and empty promises of change had caused the crack to widen into a fissure. As Billy lost hope for normalcy or love in his family, the fissure became a canyon. And into that canyon, Billy had cast all his naïve notions of life and love. Billy had become aloof and cynical in an effort to survive. Throughout those many years of lies and deceit, the canyon had eroded into a gulf so vast it seemed insurmountable. Sometimes, a thing just can't be fixed.

Billy had never told their dad about the letters or the fight he had been in with Cool Cat, simply because he knew there would be no point. He never spoke of the relationship he had developed with Mr. Perkins—a relationship on which Billy had been able to rely for many years and which had never let him down. It was not a relationship that afforded Billy the love he sought from his father, but it was a relationship based on respect. It was nurturing with purpose, mentoring that would carry him through life, and it filled the void left in Billy by a distracted father, an ill mother, and a fallen brother. Mr. Perkins had replaced Tommy as Billy's hero and had shown him the path of higher education as a way to freedom. And somewhere on that journey, Billy had cast off all attachment to Tommy.

Bethany's husband Carl and Mr. Perkins had spoken the truth into Billy's life regarding his enabling relationship with Tommy. And now, here tonight, on the fourth ring, Tommy recalled the last conversation he had with his little brother— the one where Billy told him there would be no more loans, no more bailouts, no more late-night calls. "Come on, brother, just give me one more chance," Tommy had pleaded, to which Billy had replied, "I have no brother. Never call here again," and hung up the phone.

It was not what Billy had said but how he had said it that penetrated Tommy's wall and delivered a blow to his heart. There was no anger or disappointment—not even pity or disgust. There was nothing. All the emotion in Billy had withered and died, its dust blown away on a wind of regret as can only be experienced by the family of a man lost to addiction. Billy was gone forever, and Tommy took one more step down in his descent into hell.

He would not say his goodbyes to a machine. He would not do his mea culpa to the digitally enhanced voice of his little brother. Tommy was about to hang up the phone and head to the A train when the connection opened up, and an unfamiliar voice barked insultingly into the phone.

"Yeah, yeah, hello! Who is it, for frig's sake, at 2:30 in the morning? Don't you know most decent folks are in bed by now? Lucky for you, I ain't one." The unusual greeting was followed by laughter, laughter that Tommy recognized as having its origins in liquor.

Tommy took a deep breath and spoke. "Who is this?"

"Who is this? Isn't that the question I should be asking, huh, buddy? I think so. So I will: who is this?" This was followed by more laughter.

"My name is Tom. I'm calling for my brother, but maybe I dialed the wrong number. Or maybe his number's changed. His name is Billy."

"Billy boy, my buddy, my pal! Well, the number's right, but you're out of luck! The man himself is not here," the voice on the phone continued, then dissolved into nonsensical laughter.

"Well, where is he? And who the hell are you?"

"My name, sir, is Joe…and I am a friend of Billy boy. Actually, we work at the same place. Billy boy is out of the country at the moment, and I, well, I'm sort of on a forced holiday from work, if you know what I mean. Oh yeah, and also out of the house at the moment too—taking a wee break from my broken marriage, if you know what I mean." He laughed at his own humor and continued on in a ramble. "My wife and my boss—now there's a team that would work well together, eh? Both of them spend their days trying to put me down. It's no wonder I drink, eh, my friend. Wait—who did you say you were again?"

Tommy. My name is Tommy. Where is Billy? And, by the way, he doesn't like being called Billy Boy. Never has. If you were a friend, you would know that." Tommy felt sweat growing under his clothing and an anger growing toward this man he didn't know. His time was short, and he didn't wish to spend any of the moments left to him in conversation with a drunken stranger. No sooner had this thought crossed Tommy's mind than he realized these had surely been the thoughts of his mother and father, his brother and sister, and Carl, as he called late at night, drunk and out of control.

"Oh boo-hoo, Billy Boy wouldn't like that, eh?" The laughter came in a low, rolling wave through the telephone line and began to build as Joe continued. "So this is the famous Tommy, is it? Let me see, is that Tommy the loser? Tommy, the drunken junkie? Tommy, the pathetic brother? That Tommy?"

Joe's laughter was loud and out of control. It had become harsh and cruel as he spewed out the truth of Tommy's life in descriptive waves of pain that crashed down upon him like a roaring surf. The words echoed in his ears, loud and thunderous, and Tommy began to feel anger welling up inside him. Tommy was no stranger to anger. The self-righteous outrage he had felt in his life when ripped off in a drug deal or when some asshole drank the last mouthful of vodka had become part of the fabric of his existence. It was an anger that fueled his addiction and gave him the means to function in the shattered world he had created.

But something was different now, as these words from a stranger assaulted him.

Tommy believed he was feeling the sting of true emotion. The words left him raw and exposed, something Tommy had not felt in years. It wasn't the alkie, junkie anger he encountered daily and had become comfortable with. This was the anger he had felt long ago in a dormitory as he was berated by Tom Cat and Neville, also known as Devil.

It was an anger that had left him exposed and vulnerable to their bullying—an anger born of the idea that Tommy just wasn't good enough, fast enough, or smart enough; that he just was not enough. It was this repressed anger that had become the rudder in his life, directing him into and out of every situation he encountered.

And in that moment, the emotion was so real. With the absence of his drug-induced force field, the anger ate at Tommy. At that moment, locked in the grip of real emotion, Tommy realized no one in this world had ever told him he was not enough. Not his mother or father. Not his sister or brother. Tommy realized that it had only been he and the lover who whispered those demeaning words in the dark of the night, in the recesses of his mind. He had willingly walked into a prison of his own design and spent a lifetime there. And this realization, delivered to him in the slurred words of this man Joe, filled him with rage.

"Joe, is it? Listen—you want to call me a loser. Meanwhile, you're sleeping in the spare room in the house of a guy you barely know. You're pissed drunk at 3 in the morning, by yourself, full of self-pity. Sounds like you're not much different than me, asshole!"

"Ha! I am nothing like you! You are a lowlife scumbag. Me? I'm just a little down on my luck. And by the way, I do know your brother. He's a dick, man. A real rule guy, right? Sucks up to the bosses, always doing the right thing—yes sir, no sir. That's why he's over in South Africa working a job that should have been mine, and I'm here under suspension. I tell the bosses like it is, and they get threatened by me—but not Bill, no, not Billy. You know what he does? Whatever they want, man, that's what he does. He keeps the rules and never takes hard chances. You know, he even has a list of dos and don'ts for me as long as my arm. You know the only one I remember? No? Well, just let me tell you, asshole! It was: 'Above all, DO NOT let my junkie brother Tommy into my place when I am gone.' You're right, Tommy. I am in his spare room. Where are you sleeping tonight, junkie?" Joe took a breath, and Tommy could hear several gulps of a bottle being drained down Joe's throat. "Yeah, wow, that's real brotherly love, eh, Tommy Boy? That's what family is all about, right? Really warms my heart."

Both men sat in silence in the wee hours of the morning, haunted by truths that had invaded their realities late on a wet night. One was ready to face them, the other locked in a struggle to bury them beneath gallons of alcohol. After a time, Tommy began to speak.

You're right, Joe. My brother has no use for me at all anymore, nor does my father, for that matter. I've stolen the lives of many people, Joe, and the truth is I'm very tired of it. You ever get that feeling, Joe? When you're just so tired of it all? When it feels like you just can't go on another step, tell another lie, take another drink? No, you probably aren't there yet, are you? Well, I am, Joe. I crossed some lines there's just no going back from, and I want out, out of it all." Tommy paused in the phone booth and began to pick his next words with care.

"There's something I have left to do, Joe. I wanted to talk to Billy, you know, but what I got was you. I wanted to tell him I love him and I'm sorry, and that none of it was his fault. All of it has been on me. Will you tell him I called, Joe? Would you do that for me?" Tommy waited for a reply, which would not come. "You know, Joe, I wasn't always what I am today. I used to have family who loved me and wanted good things for me. It was me who screwed things up, Joe, but I spent a lifetime blaming everybody else—just like you're doing now. When I heard you talking, Joe, it was like listening to a recording of myself. It's not too late for you, Joe. You can still fix things. You have a wife and some kids out there, Joe, who want you to fix things. It's up to you. For me, it's over, but who knows, maybe this one act of saying goodbye might help you. Maybe it was you I was supposed to talk to. I don't know, Joe, but you haven't hung up on me so far, so I'm going to hope you'll listen. And I'm going to hope maybe there'll be some redemption for me when I meet my maker. And I'm going to tell you my story, because sometimes, when a man meets his end, a story is all he has."

Joe was quiet for the next 45 minutes as Tommy slowly told him the whole, sad story of his life. He was quiet and drank through it, all the while thinking, "What a loser this guy is." He wanted to laugh, he wanted to hang up, but all he did was listen and drink Billy's good vodka, the stuff he had purchased while working in Russia. He smoked Billy's good cigars, the ones he had brought back with him from Cuba—another project Billy had stolen out from under Joe. And he thought to himself, "If I ever get as bad as this guy, I'll quit drinking."

"If I ever cross the lines this bozo has crossed, I'll get my life back in control." He never heard Tommy as he tried to explain that the lines were not clearly marked, and that by the time his life had been lost, the battle was out of control.

Tommy finished. "Well," he said, "not sure if you're still there, but if you are, I hope you heard me."

"Yep, still here...still listening to your boo-hoo sad story."

"Well, Joe, like I said, sometimes when a man reaches an end, a story is all he has. Goodbye, Joe; you may be the last person to ever hear that from me. Tell them I was sorry."

Tommy hung up the phone and slid to his haunches in the bottom of the phone booth as Joe passed out, the telephone receiver lying beside him on the couch, the good vodka spilling onto the floor, and the glowing embers of a Cuban cigar moving slowly but unstoppably toward his fingers, en route to leaving another scar on a life lost.

THE A TRAIN.

For a long while, Tommy sat on his haunches in the dark, damp confines of the phone booth. He mulled over the conversations he had initiated that night—with his father, his sister, and the stranger at Billy's house—and for the first time in many years, he felt no remorse. Hearing his own story from his own lips had somehow cleansed him of his guilt. While confession was good for the soul, words could never undo the damage he had inflicted on their lives. But Tommy believed action could.

In his despair, Tommy mistakenly believed the action he had decided upon would clear the slate for him. That this offering of his life would somehow heal a lifetime of festering wounds that had descended upon them all like a pestilence. He was so tired. He was so ashamed and fearful that he could not hear the echoes of Beth's voice telling him there was another way. He could not hear the street wisdom of Armist, telling him he was taking the easy way out. He could not hear the longing beneath the stern words of his father, who just wanted his son back. He could not allow himself to believe they would forgive him—for it was not within him to forgive himself.

ith great effort, Tommy pushed himself to his feet, the cool glass wall of the phone booth pressing through his army parka and leaving a chill in his spine. Tommy was frightened. He was not a brave man, and after spending a lifetime avoiding emotional pain, he was poised on the edge of great physical pain. He was now only minutes away from launching himself in front of the A Train. His limbs felt heavy, and his motions seemed otherworldly as he saw—more than felt—his arm rise up to turn the light bulb tight into the socket in the ceiling of his glass confessional.

Light flooded the compartment, and Tommy covered his eyes with one hand while his other hand reached into his parka pocket, withdrawing the pocket watch that had belonged to three generations of better men than him. He had 15 minutes before the A Train would shake the street as it emerged from the tunnel and crossed the level crossing at Lexington. That was where he would do it. That was where he would take his last steps on this earth, walking into the path of the train. There would be no honor in it, but he hoped there would be peace.

Slowly, he closed the cover on the pocket watch and set it on top of the phone. He looked down at his bony, beaten hands and removed his father's ring, setting it beside the watch in the hope that these items would somehow find their way back to his family. Almost symbolically, the phone booth fell into darkness as Tommy opened the door and stepped into the street. It was as though the curtains were being drawn on his life. The tragedy that had been Tommy Boyle was over, and the crowds were about to exit. There was no applause, no ovation, just a lingering sense of sorrow at the waste of a life. And somewhere in the deepest part of his mind, Tommy believed he heard a familiar laugh—the laughter of the lover, that great deceiver, who knew she had won and celebrated her final victory.

Armist had just left the walking alley that cut through from Main to Lexington. As he emerged from the crosswalk, Armist turned north, thinking he would swing one more time through the neighborhood of Tommy Boyle. Armist stepped away from the safety of the storefront shadows, maneuvering past some garbage cans that had been rifled through and left like dead soldiers on the sidewalk for decent folks to step over.

He was moving east, and with each passing block, the neighborhoods fell further into decline. Armist understood that the high glass and steel towers of power, which looked accusingly down upon him from only ten city blocks away, stood in mockery of those who survived off the discarded garbage cans he had just passed. As much as he hated everyone who worked in those castles—everyone involved in making decisions that maintained this disparity between the classes—Armist was also drawn to the great rising beauty of the lighted glass monoliths. Many nights, he would sit in his alley and look up at the lighted buildings, often imagining they were alien ships coming to change the circumstances of all those the real world had left behind. In these moments, these private times, Armist allowed himself to be taken by the beauty of the notion.

Almost without thought, Armist looked over his shoulder to take in the lighted beauty of the buildings. As he turned, a light sparked to life in the phone booth at the end of the block, and Armist knew instantly he was looking at Tommy Boyle. Armist pressed himself into the wall in front of a local shop and instinctively reached for the phone Gideon had provided him. As Armist pressed *send* on the cell, the booth was plunged back into darkness, and Tommy Boyle was on the move.

Armist hung up the phone and imperceptibly moved along the glass windows of the storefronts, weaving in and out of the indented doorways, now in pursuit of Tommy Boyle. An eerie sense of foreboding shrouded Armist as he watched a phantom of himself fade in and out of the streetlights heading away from the phone booth. Tommy appeared to be almost floating in the oversized parka, wearing one red shoe and one blue shoe. Slightly hunched over but moving with purpose, Tommy pressed on. Armist shook off the shiver running down his spine, made his way to the phone booth, and immediately spied the pocket watch and ring atop the phone. He quickly scooped them into his good hand, continuing his pursuit of Tommy while hitting *send* on the cell phone in his other hand.

"Gideon here, how can I help you?"

"I got him, Bob, I got Tommy." Armist's breath came in short gasps as he fell into step behind the fleeing Tommy Boyle.

"What do you mean, Armist? Do you have hands on him? Where are you?" Gideon felt his heart rate increase, as it always did when police work began to unfold.

I'm following him, Bob. He's on the move, and it feels like he knows where he's going. He's not being careful, you know what I mean? He's just walking. I think I could catch him if I jogged, but he'd hear me coming. Maybe he'd bolt. Not sure."

"Don't approach, Armist. Leave that to us. You understand?"

"I don't know, Bob. Something feels wrong."

"Armist, where are you? I'll get McCaskey, and we'll be there."

"Well, right now, I'm on Main, passing over 5th, heading north toward Lexington. Kind of like he's going home, Bob, but that doesn't make any sense at all. He knows you'd be looking for him there for sure. Something just feels wrong."

"Armist, you stay back. I mean it. I'm on my way. I'm on the other side of the borough. McCaskey has a squad car—I've already clicked him on the radio, and he's on the way to get me. We'll head south toward you. You've got him covered from behind. We've got him, Armist—there's nowhere left for him to run. Just stay back now and let us come to you."

As Gideon closed his phone, McCaskey pulled to a stop beside him. Gideon climbed into the squad car, and they sped off toward the fugitive, Tommy Boyle.

Armist closed his phone and slid it into the pocket beside the watch and ring of Tommy Boyle. He took two more steps and stopped in his tracks. Cocking his head, Armist listened intently to the street. He pressed his weight down into the soles of his feet and felt the street beneath him. These were his streets, and he knew them with every sense of his body. He knew them in a way only a man who had lived his entire life in five square blocks could. He knew the sound of every building, the schedule of every delivery truck from every shop and vendor. He knew the habits of the night people and the places they abode.

Armist knew the way the wind sounded as it furled around and through the lighted castle office towers before what remained of it settled on the borough. He knew the sound rain made as it bounced off the dirty pavement and washed through the gutters into the storm drains. He knew the name of the dog barking a block away and could identify birds by their songs. He even knew the size of every rat by the sound of their scurrying feet.

And he knew what it was that felt wrong. Something was coming.

He wiggled the toes of his big feet in his new runners and, like no other man on earth, felt the imperceptible vibration of his street. He understood that the A train was only five minutes away from emerging at the level crossing on Lexington, and he knew what Tommy had in mind. Armist broke into a jog, hoping there was still time to get to Tommy.

ommy stepped onto the track a couple hundred feet from the mouth of the underground tunnel. He stood still for a moment, listening to the night. It was unusually quiet for this time of night on the street, and he wondered where everyone was. Grateful for the solitude, he took solace in the privacy. Though he'd been alone for most of his life, he felt as though he had never enjoyed true privacy until now.

Tommy slowly began a three-hundred-and-sixty-degree turn, taking in the street he'd called home for so long. A light breeze brushed over the neighborhood. The rain had stopped, and somehow, at this moment in time, the place seemed peaceful.

He thought of Gutter Gus sleeping on the steps as his gaze fell upon his apartment. He looked at the corner where Rhonda would be standing come noon tomorrow, hoping she'd somehow find her way out. He glanced with a mix of anger and gratitude at Louis's East End Pawn Shop, which had robbed him and kept him alive simultaneously. He wondered how the new guy, Red, would fit into the neighborhood.

He smiled as he recalled the old woman at the little coffee hut on the corner who so many times had given him a bagel. *"Just so you have something in your stomach,"* she'd say. He remembered that there was good in this world. His eyes fell on the mission where Hank Quinn had reached out to him so many times, only to be scorned and laughed at. It was also the mission where the nun had often offered him soup and a smile—a smile no one would see again.

For a moment, he wondered if they would miss him at all. Quietly, he laughed at the notion. He would just be another casualty in the borough. Within a day or two, someone else would be living out their life in Tommy's soon-to-be-vacated apartment. Life would go on without Tommy Boyle, without Trip, without Petra. That's what life does—it continues.

Tommy was jarred from his final thoughts by the familiar blue-and-red flashing of cruiser lights over the tops of the shops. They'd found him. Even in his last stand, he couldn't catch a break.

As he turned toward the A train tunnel, he saw the shape of a man moving in and out of the streetlights, advancing toward him quickly. Completing his final pirouette, he saw the distant light of the A train shining from the darkened mouth of the tunnel. Tommy began to run toward the light.

Gideon and McCaskey raced around the corner onto Lexington as the train emerged from the tunnel. Silhouetted in the bright light of the oncoming train, they saw Tommy Boyle running.

"We're not going to make it, Bob," said McCaskey. "We can't get there, get out, and grab him before the train gets him. Looks like Tommy Boyle is going to get his own justice tonight."

"I sure didn't see this coming, Jim, and I sure don't want to see what's about to happen. Look—here comes Armist, but he's too far out. He won't make it either. Boyle is running to the train."

"I wouldn't bet on it," McCaskey said. "I've seen that old boy run before. When we were after him, he had a whole other gear I never would've imagined."

"The car screamed to a halt. Gideon and McCaskey leapt out and began sprinting toward the mouth of the tunnel and the oncoming A train.

Armist looked ahead as he ran toward the scene of the impending crash. A voice in his head spoke harshly—the voice of Gutter Gus: *What are you doing, man? This is not your fight. Those are cops you're running toward—and a low-down druggie who's never lived by the code. These are not your people, and this is not your trouble! That's McCaskey running at you—he wants to lock you up! And*

Gideon? Just because Polly Anne trusts him doesn't mean you should. Veer off now and run the other way. You're home free. You won't get to him anyway, and who knows? Maybe if you do, he pulls you into the damn train with him. Suicides often take someone with them at the last moment. Listen to old Gus now... run, Armist, run!"

As he ran, Armist's hand slid into the pocket of his new sports jacket and found the small circle of wooden beads attached to a crudely carved wooden cross. It hung on his finger as his hand pumped up and down in smooth unison with his feet. The talisman came in and out of his line of vision, and with each glimpse, Gus's voice grew quieter. In its place, Armist focused on the rhythm of his feet as they slapped the pavement in his new runners.

Calm washed over him, and his pace intensified. His legs moved like pistons, his arms pumping in perfect harmony. He locked his focus on Tommy Boyle and the glaring light of the A train. Whether he could make it or not no longer mattered—Armist Hancock had committed to action. The son of a war hero, a man who lived by the code, he ran with everything he had toward Tommy Boyle and possibly death. Somewhere in the recesses of his mind, he heard the words, *"Run, Armist, run,"* spoken in the soft, reassuring voice of Sister Petra.

The train emerged from the tunnel at 45 miles per hour. Its estimated stopping distance at that speed was 300 feet. The engineer hit the emergency brakes in horror as the light from the A train fully illuminated the figure of a man sprinting down the tracks, only 200 feet ahead. The screeching brakes screamed like banshees, and somewhere behind him, the engineer heard the terrified cries of passengers being thrown forward by the abrupt deceleration. Some had been sleeping, heading home from long nights on the town; others were on their way to work. There were even a few who simply rode the trains by night, seeking solace from insomnia. All of them were now unwilling participants in the tragedy of Tommy Boyle's life.

Tommy ran toward the light with all the strength of a dying man. He hadn't run like this before—not as a child, not as a thief, not even when he had betrayed Trip. Then, he had run for his life. Now, he was running *from* his life, toward the end, seeking a reconciliation he could never find in living. Pain coursed through his body, and he welcomed it as a precursor to the ultimate release that would come on impact—a pain that would lead to peace.

ideon and McCaskey ran toward the scene, their desperation mounting. They knew they would be too late. The aftermath would be horrific, but they had to try. The light was blinding, and from his position on the far side of the tracks, Gideon could only make out Tommy running down the center. McCaskey, closer to the tracks, could see Armist Hancock—a blur of motion—running like an Olympic sprinter closing in on the finish line.

"Oh my Lord," McCaskey muttered. "He's going for it. Armist is going to try to stop him! He'll never make it, Bob—they'll both be killed!"

Gideon's mind raced, searching for a solution, but none presented itself. He was too far away. He had promised Polly Anne he would look out for Armist. He had sworn to keep

Armist safe. Now he was watching as Armist ran headlong into what seemed like certain death in an effort to save Tommy Boyle. A crushing weight of helplessness settled over him, pressing down with an unbearable force.

Gideon and McCaskey shouted in unison, their voices rising above the chaos, "Stand down, Armist! Break away, Armist! Let him go!" But their words were swallowed by the ear-splitting scream of the A train's whistle.

The engineer could do nothing but watch as the scene played out before him. He saw the two cops break off—one to the left, one to the right of the tracks—ceasing their pursuit. Their anguished faces contorted in silent screams, words drowned by the train's deafening roar. He saw the big man—Armist—running faster than anyone he'd ever seen, moving like a figure in slow motion. The engineer was certain the man wouldn't outrun the train. Unable to bear the sight any longer, the engineer turned away, sinking into his seat and sitting with his back to the horror about to unfold. This night would haunt him forever, but he didn't need to see the bloody conclusion to know it would stay with him. Later, when he finally returned home after hours of questioning, he promised himself he'd tell his son how much he was loved.

The moment was upon them.

The light blinded Tommy, but he kept running. He felt no one and nothing between himself and his fate. Pain seared through his body, accompanied by an overwhelming fear, but he welcomed it. He knew it would soon be over. The cacophony around him—the roar of the engine, the screaming brakes—was deafening. Yet in that chaos, there was an odd clarity. The train was like a wild stallion, snorting and spitting, held back by the steel bit of its brakes.

rmist was close—so close—but still uncertain if he was close enough. The noise was overwhelming. He glanced quickly to his right, seeing Gideon and McCaskey giving up the chase, turning their backs on the train. They shouted, but their voices were lost in the noise. Armist turned his gaze forward just in time to see Tommy, running full tilt. His eyes were wide with terror, his face twisted in a sudden, dawning realization—he had made a mistake. But the time for second thoughts was gone.

A sudden and profound silence enveloped Armist. He felt, rather than saw, the small circle of wooden beads and the crude wooden cross. In that instant, he understood that this was the defining moment of his life. Tommy's choices had created this chaos, but it was Armist who was now running toward it. Tommy had given up on his life, but Armist had decided to give his own to save him.

Armist Hancock was more than the son of a war hero. He was a hero in his own right. If he died here, in the next moment, he would die an honorable man—and that was a good way to go. Armist closed his bright blue eyes, saw Polly Anne's face, and leapt into the path of the A train.

Tommy Boyle was completely blinded by the light. In his mind, he saw his mother at the wash line, his father in the driving shed, Billy walking down the lane, and Beth crying on the porch. The impact was sudden, the pain was instant, and the light was extinguished.

EPILOGUE

Well, there you have it. That's what he told me, and that's what I wrote. I remember that at the end of his talking, he said something kind of strange. I never really thought about it at the time because—well, because I never really thought about anything during that time. He said, *"When a man meets his end, a story is all he has."* But he never said it like he was saying it to me, you know? He said it like he was hearing it in his ears and just repeating it.

I don't know why that has occurred to me just now, but it has. It was kind of spooky—maybe because it felt like an omen or something. For me, it kind of felt like it was the end of *my* story, though I was too sick to understand that at the time.

But it was not the end of Tommy's story, even though it had been the end of our conversation—at least as much as I can remember of it. To be honest, that could have been the end of Tommy Boyle and his story, as far as I was concerned. During that time in my life, I wouldn't have been able to muster an ounce of compassion or feel any type of empathy toward him. I didn't care about him one bit—he was just a loser. The only connection I had to the man was through his brother, Billy, and believe me, that connection was quickly lost when Billy returned to the country.

No, it was not the end of Tommy Boyle's story at all, and, in some ways, it was the beginning of mine. I guess I'll need to explain.

I have written down all that he told me. I wasn't there for any of it, and some of it made no sense to me at the time. Perhaps I remembered it differently than it actually happened. Perhaps I invented parts of it—I don't know. My mind was in bad shape back then. A lot of the holes have been filled in by other people who were around that night. They told me what happened after he had called me. How I met them is part of the beginning of my story.

So here it is. Here is the rest of the story—the truth of which I can absolutely attest to, for the people who conveyed it to me cannot lie. Their lives depend upon that simple truth. So, I'll start at the end—and the beginning.

THE END

Joe stood in the shadows of a doorway across the street from the 5th St. mission, trying to understand what had brought him to this hopeless state of mind and body. He was not drunk, but he was not sober either. He was somewhere in between—a state he seldom left these days. He was due for a top-up, but he had no money, and the feelings of fear and desperation were closing in. He knew it wouldn't be long before he crashed. He was going to have to do something, but what that something was remained unclear. Watching the tremor in his hand, he lit the last half of a cigarette and retreated further into the shadows.

Across the street, they were all there, standing in front of the mission, and he detested them, though he didn't know any of them personally. Alcoholics and drug addicts—that's what they were—the worst of the worst. Each one of them was a lowlife in their own way. Now, though, they were clean and sober, attending meetings, acting high and mighty as if they were better than him. "There's nothing worse than a reformed sinner," his Grandpa used to say, and Joe now knew it to be true.

If only they understood how hard it had been for him these last seven years. If only they had seen him when he was at the top of his game, with a good job and a loving family. They were lowlifes, but he wasn't. He was just riding a long streak of bad luck. He'd pull out of it eventually and put it all back together. He just needed a break—just needed to get through the night. A couple of drinks and a place to sleep would fix him up until tomorrow. Maybe things would turn around then. But there was no money for drinks, no place to sleep, and he was starting to doubt his ability to pull himself together. He hadn't seen the line, but he feared he'd crossed it. Perhaps there were no tomorrows left for him.

They were loud, their joy carried across the street on the tepid night air and into the alley, assaulting him. He hated them with all his heart, but somewhere deep in his tortured soul, a voice called out to him: "Go, Joe. Go over there, and they will help you. Go now before it's all lost forever."

fHe grimaced against the voice, for he had heard it before. Many times over the past months, he had stood in this alley and watched them laughing, hugging, and shaking hands. Drinking coffee, smoking cigarettes, and being happy—too happy. They were frauds and conmen. They couldn't possibly understand his life or know how badly the world had treated him. They had no idea what it felt like to carry his burdens. They were bums, and he wasn't. They had nothing to lose, but he had—and it was gone. All of it. He would never join them. He would rather die.

He spat onto the filthy street, his gaze falling on the big, dapper-looking man who leaned down to light a cigarette for the old woman who owned the tattoo shop. He remembered being surprised the first time he saw her here. She seemed to have her life together. She seemed happy. He watched her slender, bejeweled hand steady the old-timer's gnarled, street-worn hand as she drew in deeply, exhaling her first delicious, warm puff of nicotine. Even from the dim light of desperation, Joe could see they were lovers, and his heart ached with a deep sense of loss.

Generally, he guarded himself against such feelings—against all feelings, really—and seldom allowed himself to recall the years of happiness he had once known. The life he had walked away from. He felt like an interloper here in the dark, watching and waiting. Waiting. Waiting for the despair to become unbearable. Waiting for the night when he would find the courage to cross over and join them.

Waiting. His life had become an endless cycle of waiting. Waiting for the world to see his full potential. Waiting for his wife to forgive him, for his kids to miss him. Waiting for the justice he believed he deserved or for something—anything—good to happen in this shitty world to keep him going. Just waiting.

He stepped forward into the streetlight, taking three hesitant steps toward them before freezing in his tracks. Not tonight. It's not that bad yet.

A shuffling sound came from the alley behind him, and he turned too quickly, feeling his head begin to swim. He stumbled back to the wall he had been leaning against and steadied himself, waiting for his head to clear. Slowly, his vision began to focus. Standing in the ashen darkness of the alley was a man.

Joe gasped in astonishment as his eyes took in the hideous figure before him. The man was completely hairless, the whites of his eyes a blood-red hue. A thin black strip ran vertically across his bottom lip, the only splash of color on his otherwise translucent skin. Joe blinked reflexively, and in that split second, he imagined he could see every vein in the man's face and neck. He could see the rapid pulse of blood coursing to his heart and wondered if this creature even possessed one. Fear gripped him, and he opened his eyes quickly, sensing the odd figure could pose a threat.

The man looked up, his voice deep and raspy. "Hey, brother. What's happening? Think you could help a guy out tonight? Spot old Hotdog a few bucks for some coffee?"

Joe stared in disbelief, the awareness dawning on him: this was a human being—a breathing, speaking human—and not some nightmarish figment of his deteriorating mind.

"I don't have a few bucks, and you aren't my brother," Joe replied, backing away into the shadows.

otdog stepped closer, undeterred. "Just a figure of speech, man. No offense. Brothers on the street, you know? What about a smoke? Spot me a little nicotine, friend."

"I don't have a smoke for you either. I don't live on the streets." Joe turned to leave, but Hotdog veered in front of him, stepping close, his agitation palpable.

"Oh, excuse me! My mistake. Guess you're from some fancy uptown condo, huh? Down here on a sightseeing mission to see how the street folks play? Well, let me tell you, friend. Give me a fucking smoke, or old Hotdog's gonna show you he don't play too nice!"

efore Joe could react, Hotdog shoved him hard against the wall. The man leaned in, his blood-red eyes locking onto Joe's as pure rage radiated from his translucent face. Joe's blood ran cold. How had it come to this? He could smell the man's breath, a rancid blend of filth and desperation. For the first time, Joe realized despair had an odor.

Did he have that odor of desperation? Was it the smell of defeat or despair? Or was it just the way men smell as they die from the inside out?

"Look, man, I told you I don't have any money or any smokes. I wasn't trying to blow you off; I just got some place I'm supposed to be. I'm kinda in a hurry."

"Oh, you got somewhere you have to be, do you? Well, maybe it's that fancy condo. Maybe you should just take old Hotdog home for the night, huh? What about that, asshole? Maybe introduce old Hotdog to your lady, shit, man. You think I'm stupid? You think I'm some kind of low-life? I used to run this neighborhood, man. You know who I am? I am *fucking Hotdog*! Men fear me, and women can't wait to take me as their own. And you're gonna stand right in front of me, blow smoke in my fucking face, AND THEN TELL ME YOU GOT NO SMOKE FOR ME? Maybe I just smash your ugly uptown face in, take your smokes, and your money, man. Maybe that's just what I do."

Hotdog leaned into him and allowed all the rage of the past six years to bubble to the surface and fester just beneath his transparent skin. He felt as though his anger had become a living thing, with a will of its own. It rolled and squirmed beneath his flesh, a living evil. Hotdog knew, by the look of abject fear on the face of this uptown poser, that he, Vladimir Hawdawkovitch, had attained a new level of insanity. His fall from mid-gangster status had been rapid and hard. And though he'd survived a five-year sentence in a medium-security federal institution, all he had once been—everything he had aspired to be—had been lost.

While he had lived here, in these five square blocks, he had been *something*. He was connected with his brother Russians, feared and respected. There were women and money, drugs and guns, and he had his finger in it all.

Or so he had thought. Like so many other young men in baggy pants and sideways hats, Hotdog had only been a minion in a small gang of thugs and drug dealers. He had ridden high on a dream of infamy, which had existed only in his mind, in the place where his own self-worth should have been. After all the crap with Tommy Boy and the girl and the car fire, the cops needed some "tough on crime" media bullshit, and they came down hard on the entire precinct. The cop Gideon had set old Hotdog in his sights, and he was relentless in his pursuit. After six months of investigation and some trumped-up charges, Gideon, with the help of that pedophile priest Quinn, had seen to it that Hotdog went down.

Once he was inside, doing time, his Russian family had forgotten him instantly. Hotdog came to understand his situation was bleak. He was alone. Throughout a hard five years, he had learned to survive—the only real sacrifice having been his remaining sanity. He had lived inside his mind, which had essentially left him alone behind enemy lines. He lived and relived his life as a refugee from his mother Russia, as a casualty of an alcoholic father and his disappointment in a mother to weak to protect him. Working through his thoughts and emotions in the solitude of a cell and in the confines of a damaged mind Hotdog came to an understanding and believe that he was nothing. All he had aspired to be was an illusion and the truth of Vladimir Hawdawkovitch had been concealed in the creation of Hotdog. He came to know that he was despised among men and reviled among woman who had only used him as a means to an end, the end being their drug of choice.

Though he had heard it said that "the truth will set you free," Hotdog had no capacity to understand those sweetly whispered words in the confines of his cell were not the truth, but the lies of his evil past. He could not understand that recovery and freedom exist in the present and in the future, and that relapse and regret can only survive in the past and the present. No one had ever told Vladimir there was another option for his life. In his despair and insanity, Vladimir offered up his life as a sacrifice to the demon of his addiction. He sank into the mire of prison hooch and a never-ending supply of prescription drugs and jailhouse meth. Somehow, he survived his five years—or a semblance of him had, at any rate. He left that place a mere shadow of a shadow, with no past or future he could hold onto. With only the reality of his lost and addicted present, he returned to the one place his twisted mind had ever felt it had some control over his destiny.

He had returned to the borough—the five square blocks that had once been his imagined empire, and the very place where he now stood poised on the edge of another crime. He looked into the eyes of the man he held roughly against the wall and felt his grip tightening.

Hotdog knew he could kill this man here and now without a second thought, without an ounce of remorse. He knew because he had done it before. He had killed a dealer in prison, and though he could not recall the man's name, he would never forget the look in the man's eyes as he realized he was dying. He would never forget the tensing, then easing, of the man's body as Hotdog squeezed the life out of him. He would never forget the sense of power and control. It had been easy, and it had been necessary.

Tonight, it was not necessary, but it would be easy—and satisfying. Slowly, Hotdog's grip tightened around the man's neck. With increasing pressure, he could feel and hear the closing of the man's windpipe.

Joe struggled as the air in his lungs began to dissipate, and there remained almost no passage for new air to enter. He clasped the hand of this demented stranger and quickly realized it was a grip he could not break. He struggled as the oxygen left the blood going to his brain, and though the life was being violently squeezed out of him, he moved from a place of panic to a place of euphoria. He was high. He was better than drunk, and though a small part of his brain knew he was dying, the larger part was enjoying the experience.His choice was to die; to stop the struggle.

His desire to fight for the life with which he had been blessed, and the people that had cherished him, had ended years before. It had ended the night he walked away from his family and chose a bottle. Slowly and with absolute awareness, Joe let his arms drop from the vise-like grip of the creature that held him almost lovingly at the edge of his death. With happy anticipation, Joe welcomed the end to his earthly struggle. There would be no more long nights filled with remorse and recrimination. There would be no more days filled with panhandling or stealing in order to buy a drink. He would finally be free of the shakes and tremors, free of the dry retching or puking up of blood. Released from the denial and the never-ending need to escape responsibility for where he had ended up.

In that moment, he knew there was no one else to blame. There was no buck to pass. There was just him, and the booze.

He wanted to have been able to tell his wife he loved her, his children he was sorry. He wanted them to know it was not their fault, but that it had been his disease that destroyed their happy family. But he had never had the courage. Now it would be over. He would set himself and his family free in this one last act of desperation and cowardice. It would be the last time he would ever give up on anything.

In his last moments of consciousness, his disease told him he was not dying—he was killing his failure. He was destroying that which had hurt his family in an act of nobility, not being murdered by an unsightly creature over a cigarette he didn't even have. Mustering all that was left, Joe opened his eyes and looked into the face of Hotdog, into the eyes of the instrument of his death, and he smiled as the light drained out of his world.

What the fuck, Hotdog thought as he dropped the poser to the ground. The guy just gave up. He just quit. There was no struggle in this man's demise, and Hotdog was enflamed with anger at being denied that moment of power and control. That moment when he felt all the fight drain out of the man, along with all the life—like it had been for him the first time, in prison. How could a low-life drug-dealing scumbag doing a five-year bit for child molestation fight harder for his life than this man on the street?

The world no longer made sense to Hotdog. He looked down at the poser where he had fallen to the ground and spat on him in contempt. Hotdog's eyes darted up and down the street as he bent down to rifle the man's pockets. There was no money. There wasn't even a cigarette. The guy truly was a poser. Hotdog laughed quietly to himself as he turned and disappeared into the emptiness of the alley.

THE BEGINNING

The darkness exploded into a beautiful, brilliant light, and Joe felt warm all over. He could not recall the last time he had been warm—truly warm. Though he knew not where he was, he smiled because he was happy.

There was someone coming out of the light, but he could not tell who it was. Then, he realized he was not afraid. Joe tried to recall the last time he had not been afraid, but he could not. It seemed as though he had always been full of fear and shame, even when things had been good in his life. As he lay there, so still, he became aware that the shaking was gone. There were no tremors, and he was not sick. Even his insides were still, and he felt no need for anything. All his desires had been replaced by the longing to meet the man approaching him from the brilliance of the light.

Though the man was still far off, it was as though Joe could feel Him holding him. He held Joe so close and so tightly that it felt as if He had pressed into Joe, as if Joe could feel Him inside, close to his heart—close to their heart. This man was filling Joe with such love and contentment that Joe was certain he would burst. For the first time in his memory, Joe realized he had no feelings of remorse. For one fleeting moment, he understood that all the harm he had brought into his life and the lives of his family would be set aside and forgiven within the embrace of this Man. For the first time ever, Joe felt love, and it emanated from this Man who was walking toward him but was somehow already there. This Man—whom Joe could not recognize but somehow knew.

These feelings of peace and contentment were so new to Joe that he began to grow wary. He had existed for so long running from all emotion and trusting no one, but now there was this Man. This Man, in whom the insanity of Joe's life simply vanished.

Being unfamiliar with this sense of peace, Joe gave in to his panic and anxiety. He could not process the emotions he was experiencing because, deep within, Joe believed he did not deserve this. This Man was making a mistake—a big mistake. Joe had done nothing in his pathetic life to earn this feeling of absolute love. His wife had loved him, his children had loved him, but he had spurned their love. He had preempted their departure with his own because he knew that sooner or later, they would realize he was unworthy. He had no merit, no substance; he was just a damned, dirty alcoholic—just like his grandfather. Exactly what he had sworn he would never become.

Slowly and with some reluctance, Joe allowed that sense of peace and serenity to seep out of him. With an expectancy that surprised him, he fell back into the familiarity of fear. He did not think he was dead, but neither was he fully alive. He seemed trapped in this place—between a world he hated and the unknown brilliance beyond the light. At once, he felt both drawn and repelled. Suddenly, Joe realized the Man was not walking toward him; rather, Joe was being drawn to the Man. He was being led through a long tunnel at incredible speed, transported without really walking, all the while his eyes fixed on the brilliance of the light surrounding the Man.

It seemed he was looking beyond the center of the universe, where all the light in the world existed. And though he tried to stay in his comfortable place of fear and remorse, he was unable. Joe felt as though he were a speck of dust being carried on the wind into the sunlight. As he moved, bits of the light permeated his body.

The first spike of light removed his fear completely. The fear had not just moved to that place in his gut where it usually lived during the moments Joe could control it—it was gone. Another fragment of light pierced through him, and he was filled with a peace and joy he had never experienced. Suddenly, the things of the world that had baffled him became clear.

The end of the tunnel was near now, and Joe could clearly see the Man as he approached. His arms were extended, and the light emanated from His very flesh. And then, Joe was there, standing right in front of Him. Joe looked deeply into the Man's eyes, yet he could not focus on His face. In that moment, Joe witnessed his entire life.

Joe had no idea how long he had stood gazing into the beauty of this Man's eyes as his life played out before him. It may have been seconds, or it may have been hours. But in an instant, the trance was over, and Joe was filled with an understanding of how he had lived—of how he had squandered the gifts he had been given.

Then he heard the voice. It was sweet and soft, fierce and strong, rising and falling like a great symphony in an ancient theater. The words washed over him like a wind. Though they were unfamiliar to Joe, he understood each thought perfectly. The voice dripped like honey and glittered like gold. For a moment, Joe could almost see the words as they came from the mouth of this Man of light and he understood. It was direction and it was purpose and for the first time in all his life Joe felt as though he belonged. He felt as though he understood and he knew he needed to get back to his life. He needed to get back and make things right, to change everything he had previously know about life.

With great effort, Joe caught gulps of breath and began, with difficulty, to form a sentence. He had so many questions. He wanted this Man to keep him folded into His heart forever, and yet he knew he would not be able to stay. He understood this Man had a plan for him, and it required life. Just as Joe was about to spew forth all his questions, the Man smiled. The smile spread through Joe like a warm light, and he lifted his own arms to reach out and embrace the Man. It was in that moment that the Man closed His eyes, and as He did, the light left Joe. The void engulfed him, and Joe felt himself beginning to fall. Back he went, down through the passage that had drawn him up to the place where the Man had waited, and as he fell, he could feel a great rush of air fill his lungs.

With sudden impact, he landed back in the alley from which he had come. His chest ached, and his head was splitting, but there was no fear, no anxiety, and no remorse. He knew he would be okay because he knew there was a plan, and the plan was not his.

Joe's eyes flew open as great gulps of air escaped his lungs. There was a man pressing hard on Joe's chest. As Joe looked over his shoulder, he saw the man calling out to someone. As Joe's senses returned and the buzzing left his ears, he could hear the words the man was calling out.

"Rhonda, call 911, do it now I think this guy is dead."

To his left Joe saw the girl. She was young and she was pretty and as she scrambled to find her phone she began to speak.

"What the hell, Hank. Did you see him? Was that Hotdog walking away from this guy? I mean, if he is out, Hank, and back around here, we gotta go! We gotta tell somebody or do something." Rhonda felt the tremble in her hand as she frantically removed her cell phone from her bag. She felt the fear growing deep within her as all the memories of that long-ago night fell heavily upon her.

"Rhonda, it's okay. Trust me, I saw him, but now we have to deal with this guy. I really think he might be dead! I did CPR and mouth-to-mouth, but he doesn't seem to be responding. Gideon is over at the meeting. We'll tell him, and they can deal with Hotdog, but now we have to make the call."

Slowly, Joe lifted his hand and covered Hank Quinn's hands, which were forcing life-saving, though unrequired, rhythms into Joe's heart. With a shrill and startled scream—which begat an equally shrill and startled scream from Rhonda—Hank leapt from his straddled position over the stranger on the street and backed into the alley wall beside Rhonda.

"Mother of Mercy and saints preserve us!" hollered Hank as he leaned into the jagged brick wall and began to compose himself. Instinctively, he circled a protective and reassuring arm around Rhonda, who stood trembling in fear and uncertainty. She nuzzled her head deep into his shoulder, as was her way when she felt threatened.

Hank had come to know all of her ways in these past five years as he had journeyed with her. He had been her only support system throughout her long and painful ordeal. Through the days when her survival seemed unlikely, Hank had immersed himself in prayer and, in the process, began to heal his relationship with God. During his bedside vigil, deep in prayer and meditation, Hank relived his past. Leaving no stone unturned, Hank came to understand that the Lord had forgiven him, and it was now time for Hank to forgive himself. With tears of joy, he let go of the mistakes of his past and cleared the pathway. If he were to be of use to God, to Rhonda, and to all his fellows, he needed to be free from his guilt—free from a past that had kept him in bondage.

Hank had been everything for Rhonda during her physical recovery from massive trauma, her detoxification from crippling addiction, and her emotional journey back from a lifestyle that had decimated her self-respect. If there had been any family out there for Rhonda—and Hank was sure there was—she had refused to divulge their whereabouts. It would take a great deal of time before Rhonda could step beyond her shame and reach out to a family that had long ago stopped searching for their little girl. Hank related to her shame. He understood her reluctance to forgive herself, and he understood that these two lost and damaged souls had been placed together for a reason. They would recover together. His ability to reach out to and help Rhonda would, in turn, save his own life and restore him to a place of relationship with the Lord.

Hank became her guardian of sorts, and advocating for Rhonda filled a space in his life that had been vacant for too long. He tended to her physical healing, addressed her addictive behaviors, and counseled her on her spiritual relationship with the Lord. Together, they began working through 12-step programs and building fellowship in recovery. Rhonda, having no place to go, decided to stay in the five square blocks that had previously been her hell on earth but would become her sanctuary. She moved into the mission with others in recovery, and together they worked and recovered by the grace of God.

Hank's life took on new meaning, and the fire he felt for serving the city's most lost and forgotten was reignited within him. He moved through the boroughs with an ease that had previously eluded him. His association with Armist and Polly Anne gave him credentials with the street people, who had never before seen him as an ally. God began to grow his programs. The mission was full, and needs were being met.

Through it all, Rhonda was by his side. She proved adept at listening to and relating to the girls on the street, who were living the life she had survived. Together, they developed programs designed to meet the needs of these women where they lived. They were there to listen, direct, counsel, but mostly to love. Mostly to let these women know there was another way, and they were not alone.

Somewhere along this wonderful journey, Hank had fallen in love with Rhonda. There was no specific time or event. There was no special moment or epiphany when this became evident to Hank. He had just awakened one morning and knew—he loved her; he wanted to be with her forever. Together, and slowly, they embarked on a new journey of discovery. The way was, at times, marked with caution, as neither Hank nor Rhonda had ever experienced a healthy relationship. But through their ups and downs, they survived and grew. Their love became a story of survival and joy in a place where survival and joy seemed unlikely.

And so it was that they found themselves together, here in this place, on a dark night, heading to the local meeting and witnessing the violent attack on this man. God had once again placed them in a situation that would require them to face and deal with demons from their past. And once again, He gave them the privilege of being of service to one of the many lost.

"You're alive!" Hank blurted.

"I am," Joe replied as he pushed up to an elbow and then into a sitting position.

"But you weren't, man! I know! I know! I've been here before. I was working CPR on you, but you weren't responding! Rhonda, you better make that call; we need paramedics."

"No, please don't. I... I am okay. I was gone, but now I'm back, and I really am okay. I... I can't really explain it all, but I know I'll be okay. No paramedics, no cops, please."

"No cops? That guy tried to kill you, man. Do you know who that was? Are you somehow connected to him?"

"I don't know him. He said his name was Hotdog, and he wanted money. I didn't have any, and he got angry. Did she call you Hank?"

"Yeah, she did. Who are you?"

"And she is Rhonda?"

"That's right, pal. Listen, are you sure you're okay? I mean, really, man, you were unconscious. You weren't breathing." As he spoke, he moved toward the stranger on the sidewalk, extending his hand to help him to his feet.

"You're the priest," said Joe.

Hank stopped suddenly in his tracks and began a slow retreat to the wall where Rhonda stood in silence. He felt her tiny hand slide into his, and he could feel the sweat on her palms. Hank knew Rhonda was frightened, just as he knew he must proceed with caution.

"Ex-priest," Hank replied slowly. "How did you know that? Have we met? Because I have to tell you, buddy, I'm pretty good with names and faces, and yours isn't ringing any bells."

"And she is Rhonda, the girlfriend?"

Rhonda squirmed uneasily in Hank's grip, and he could tell she was becoming increasingly agitated. Quickly, Rhonda exploded from her position on the wall and crossed the three feet of sidewalk between her and Joe with great speed and intensity. She was mad, and Hank knew it. He had witnessed her in this state of anger on one other occasion, and Hank was aware of how quickly Rhonda could revert to her street self. He kept pace behind her and reassuringly laid his hand on her shoulder. She glanced at Hank and then began to speak, the edge in her voice somewhat diminished.

"Yeah, I'm the girlfriend, Hank's girlfriend. What of it?"

"Hank's girlfriend? Oh, that's different," Joe replied, somewhat perplexed and aloof.

"Different? Why is that different? Look, man, if you have something to say to me, just say it! I don't much like that you seem to know us, but we have no idea who you are. As it happens, I have an old friend across the street right now. He's a cop, and I'm feeling like he needs to be in on the conversation. What do you think, Hank? Should we get Gideon over here?"

"By all means, Rhonda. No point in us taking any chances. I'll give him a call right now."

As Hank began to dial his cell phone, Joe clambered to his feet, and Rhonda quickly retreated to the wall.

"Wait, wait, please. I'm sorry. I didn't mean to frighten you or freak you out. It's just that I… I thought Rhonda was Tommy's girlfriend."

"Tommy? Tommy Boyle? You know about Tommy Boyle?"

"Well, no, not really. I mean, he and I never met. I sort of knew his brother, Bill. I was kind of crashing at his place five or six, maybe even seven, years ago now. I kind of lost track of time—well, and everything else in these last bunch of years. You see, I drink some—a lot, actually—and I need to get some help. I never thought I'd end up in this part of town. In fact, I never even knew about this part of town until I heard about it from Tommy. You see, I talked to him on the phone. I think I may have even been the last guy he ever spoke to. I don't much like to think about that because I sort of laughed at him at the time. Didn't really give a shit about him or his story. He wanted me to write down some things for his brother and his family—and for me, I think. I never did write any of it down, but for some reason, I can remember all of it.

To be honest, I never really knew if he was bullshitting me or not till I saw some stuff in the papers a few days later. Then I just took off, you know. Split out west for a while, moving around trying to catch a break, but I could never put it out of my mind. I've been so caught up in my own shit for so long, I just never cared. He was just a loser to me then— a dirty druggie—and now here I am, living on the same streets, maybe in just as bad a shape as he was."

And on Joe went. He told them the whole story of Tommy Boyle: how he had been the last call Tommy was to make before jumping in front of a train. He told them how Tommy had wanted to make it right with his brother Billy, how he had begged Joe to pass his words on to his younger brother. Something Joe had never done. Joe remembered how he had laughed at Tommy, how Tommy had tried to tell him not to let his family go. He told them everything and, for the first time in his life, told the truth about his addiction. He told them his story right up to the moment Hank was beating on his chest and breathing life into his lungs.

"So that's it, man. That's why I recognized your names. That's why I was surprised Rhonda was your girlfriend—because I never knew that part of the story. You know, I've been standing over here in the dark a couple of times a week for months now, watching you all over there at that meeting, wanting to come over, but I've been afraid to. I think I'm ready to come now. Will you guys take me over?"

Hank and Rhonda looked at Joe in disbelief and then looked at each other, breaking into laughter. Joe watched them, uncertain of what to think, as the two fell into each other's arms in a deep embrace. Through laughter and tears, Hank began to speak.

"Oh my God, and praise the Lord! Joe, my new friend in sobriety, Rhonda and I would be thrilled to go with you over to that meeting—most especially that meeting! This is going to be the first day of the rest of your life, my friend, and I'm pretty sure it'll be an evening you'll never forget. Come on now, let's get over there. There are some people you're going to want to meet and a whole bunch of folks who are going to want to meet you. God is good!"

Hank laughed, and Rhonda snickered as they each circled a hand around Joe's elbows and led him off to the Friday Night Late meeting at Mercy Mission.

THE MEETING

The smoke lay heavy in the air at the front door of the mission as eight or ten members huddled in the night air and talked amongst themselves. There was every kind of person there in the dim light; some were sick and shaking, clinging to the words of those who appeared at ease and self-assured. Others had darting eyes as they worked feverishly to avoid locking vision with any one person. Some were obviously still close to the street, while others were well-dressed and groomed, but all of them stood as one.

In the center, looming above them all, was Armist Hancock. Polly Anne stood at his side, and the two of them spoke to and acknowledged everyone present, greeting people and shaking their hands as they made their way into the Late Night Meeting. The calm and love that existed between them somehow permeated those nearby, and as Hank and Rhonda made their way through the small group toward the door, Joe felt a little closer to that feeling of peace he had experienced in the awesome presence of the Man.

"Armist, Polly!" Hank called out. "I want you to meet someone, someone special I think. This here is Joe; he is in a bad way and has been watching from the shadows for a while now. He's ready to get some help, and he's got quite a story to tell."

"Well, we all got a story to tell, brother, and they're all good to hear. Name's Armist." He stretched out a massive, worn, knurled hand, and Joe took it in his own. "This here is Polly," he said, smiling. "So you're the guy who's been standing in the dark over there for a while now, eh? I've been keeping an eye that way and praying you'd make the walk over."

Polly was reaching out her hand toward Joe when she stopped midway and turned her gaze to Armist.

"You mean to tell me you knew this man has been standing over there hurting for a while now, and you never walked over to see if he needed our help? Well, Armist, I just don't know what to say about that."

"Polly dear, I knew he needed our help. But I also know I stood many a night in that same spot, looking over here at your pretty face, but I wasn't able to make that journey. And if you'd known I was there and walked over to see me, I never would have come in. And if I had, I never would have made it. I needed the miracle, Polly, and I think Joe here needed it too. I'm thinking by the look on his face right now, he may have had it."

"Well, Armist Hancock, when did you get so smart, I wonder?" Polly dropped her cigarette and stamped it out under her foot as she raised her arm up and looked at Joe. "Well, let's all go in, Joe. The meeting is about to start, and it is going to be a dandy. Let's go get a coffee, and I'll introduce you to some folks."

Amidst the light laughter and conversation of the small crowd, they moved toward the door, and for the first time in his recent memory, Joe felt at home. They passed through the double doors and down a narrow stairway to a low-ceilinged basement room, which was full of chatter and chairs. On the walls, there were signs hanging like beacons of hope for those who had given up on their lives: **YOU**

ARE NOT ALONE! KEEP COMING BACK! LET GO AND LET GOD! EASY DOES IT! BUT FOR THE GRACE OF GOD! They hung like signposts to a better way of life, and Joe felt drawn in and encouraged as he made his way to the open area inside the door where people lined up for coffee. Polly reached in and poured Joe a half cup of the hot black coffee, which he took in his shaking hand.

As he began to drink, Armist called out a smiling warning, "Careful now, Joe. That there is probably the worst coffee you ever tasted. Here in this group, we are known for half cups of bad coffee. What you've got to look forward to, if you keep coming back, is full cups of bad coffee!"

Light laughter lilted through the gathering crowd as two uniformed officers approached Armist from the back of the room.

"Well, well, well, I never thought I'd ever see the day when Armist Hancock was telling folks what was good and what was bad!" said Bob Gideon.

"And I never thought I'd see the day I'd be standing in front of instead of running away from two of the city's finest!" As Armist spoke, he spread open his long arms and, with genuine affection, encircled the necks of Bob Gideon and Jim McCaskey. The three men fell into comfortable banter as Joe slowly moved away and began to mingle through the walking lost and found.

People were sitting and standing; some were laughing, some were crying, and Joe took it all in, trying to imprint all he observed on his memory. There was no distinction between them and no judgment among them. He saw women wearing expensive jewelry in conversation with women who had been used badly by the world, men in dry-cleaned suits in conversation with men whose apparel was in tatters.

Throughout his life, Joe had joined many churches and clubs, social activist groups, and neighborhood action committees, always seeking that place of acceptance—that place where he would not be judged, where he would find unconditional love. He had felt that love when he had met the Man, and now he felt it here again, in this room filled with society's cast-offs.

He turned slowly in the center aisle, taking it all in, and his eyes fell upon a row of chairs three or four rows back from the front. The people there seemed familiar to him in a way he could not define, and as he watched them intently, it occurred to him that they were out of place. The old man fussed over the woman, who gazed about the room with a look of contented confusion. He held her hand, spoke softly to her, occasionally stroked her hair, and smiled broadly.

Next to him was a little boy who looked to be five or six years old, kneeling, facing backward on his chair, his eyes wide and wandering from face to face as he took in all the commotion of people chattering while they took their seats. In the two chairs next to the small boy were two teenagers, a girl and a boy, both with heads down and thumbs working feverishly on iPhones, oblivious to anything in the world beyond the perimeter of the three-by-five screen. They could not appreciate the miracle of community as it unfolded in their presence.

Beside them sat a man and a woman, both looking uncomfortable but not entirely unaware of their surroundings. She looked worried, possibly frightened, and he looked concerned and protective, his focus shifting easily from this woman beside him to the room around him, ready to comfort or react as the situation demanded.

They were in love, deeply, thought Joe, and he remembered what that was like. He remembered the moments in his life he had shared with his wife, similar to these two people he watched from a distance—folded into each other in an unshakable bond. He remembered the night at the hospital when his wife's mother had died. How Teresa had sat beside him in silence for hours. There had been no spoken words but incredible communication as he had held her and been there for her in that moment of complete vulnerability. He remembered and was momentarily filled with sorrow over the decisions he had made which had broken that bond.

He remembered the day their oldest had been hit by a car and the state he had been in as they waited for word of her condition. He had been unable to cope, uncertain if there was something he could have done to protect her. He was weeping and losing his hope when suddenly she was there beside him. His strong wife Teresa was holding him close, telling him it would all be okay. Whispering in her soothing tones into his ear, letting him know that whatever happened, they were a team—together, they would get through; they would survive.

And it was true! They had been a team—unstoppable, unbreakable, and able to withstand an onslaught from any outside situation. But addiction does not attack from the outside. Addiction moves in with you, a little at a time, and slowly takes residence in your soul. It sleeps in between you and your wife each night, it goes along to the little league game with you and your kids, it sits at the table with your family for every meal, slipping outside words into private conversation. Eventually and unapologetically, it dominates every discussion, every activity, every moment of your life. And then it takes everything away. Every intimate moment, every cherished memory, every aspect of life and love that gave you joy. And like a coward, you just let it happen.

He felt tears begin to well behind his newly opened eyes as he realized he did not even know where they were. His family had moved on out of an instinct to survive, and Joe had not bothered to wonder where they went. Then he remembered the Man, he remembered His words and His love as He had sent Joe back with a mission—a mission to make it right. And Joe knew that he would. He fought back the tears and carried himself off the battlefield of his mind and emotion, refocusing on the room around him.

The little boy was fidgeting up and down on the chair now, his eyes darting in every direction, then falling on the old man at his side. "When will it all start, Grandpa John?" he asked.

"Soon, Tommy, just be patient a while longer," came the reply.

"Tommy?" said the old woman as she looked over at the smiling old man and past him to the boy.

"Yes Murial, dear, little Tommy, you remember!" he said, smiling as he encircled her shoulders with a protective arm, knowing that she did not.

Joe just stood and watched. He drifted into his own thoughts concerning what was to be done. "Make it right," the Man had said, but how on earth could he do that? Where to even begin? An overwhelming sense of his own inability to cope was creeping into the corners of Joe's mind, misting the memory of the Man ever so slightly when Joe was jolted back into the present.

A woman was standing before him, short, well-kept, with long flowing chestnut hair and a beautiful smile. Joe was taken by her beauty, and his mind began to take in all her features. The teeth were perfect—probably fake, thought Joe—but it was not the teeth that gave the girl a beautiful smile. There was a genuine quality that shone through her smile and settled into his heart. The girl's eyes were kind, but Joe noticed one eye moved slightly out of sync with the other, and he thought to himself, *The eye is also false.* But still, there was sincerity in her gaze that was slightly unsettling. Joe believed this woman could see into his heart and understand his deepest thoughts with only a mere glimpse.

The nose was a bit too straight, and the skin a bit too tight, and Joe suspected this woman had been made over. But the serenity she exuded seemed out of place in a woman who would redo herself out of vanity, and Joe suspected, like so many others in the room, that this woman would weave into his story.

"I'm sorry," said Joe. "Did you say something?"

"I did," replied the young girl as she extended her hand to Joe. Hanging from her wrist was a small circle of wooden beads attached to a crudely carved wooden cross.

"I said, *One Day at a Time.* You looked as though you were a thousand miles away, lost in thought, so it seemed to me an appropriate slogan for the moment. Are you new here?"

"Yes," said Joe. "I've been around the area for a while, but this is my first meeting. I am not really sure what I'm supposed to do."

"Well, right now, we are supposed to get a seat because things are about to get started. Beyond that, you really don't have to do anything tonight but listen. You did all that was required of you this evening by just walking through the door. And if I may say so, you picked a grand night to begin your journey."

Holding Joe's hand, the beautiful young girl with chestnut hair and a perfect smile led them to their seats.

The commotion in the room calmed slightly as the big form of Armist Hancock walked to the table at the front of the room. He looked with disdain at the gavel upon the table and, with a swift and alarming motion, slammed his knurled hand hard down upon the tabletop. Books fell over, a pile of monthly chips slid to the floor, and the room fell silent. Everyone looked in anticipatory silence toward the big man at the front of the room.

Armist smiled as he looked upon the gathering, these handpicked misfits he called his family.

"Sorry about that, folks. I guess old Armist just doesn't know his own strength."

An anonymous voice from the back of the room sang out in reply, "Well, I don't know why that would be, Armist. We all know about your incredible strength and legendary deeds because every chance you get, you tell us about it!"

The room erupted in genuine laughter—the kind that is only heard in a place where people feel at home and loved. Armist looked on, amazed that these people, the worst of the worst, now sat and shared such fellowship. He could not stop the broadening of his smile.

"All right, all right, I guess I had that coming. One day at a time, people, one day at a time. Humility is something I'm working on. But tonight is not about me. We have a special night tonight, an awesome speaker with an incredible story to share. We also have an old friend here tonight to chair our meeting. As far as I know, these two hombres have not seen each other in some time, both have been on their own journey. On top of that, we got a new guy here tonight. His name is Joe, and he is sitting right there with our dear Sister Petra. Make sure you say hello to him later on. I've got a feeling you may want to talk to him. So sit down and clam up! We will start in the usual way and then get right to it."

Armist cleared his throat and bowed his head, and hats were removed throughout the room as, in unison, this fellowship of previously lost and broken folks called out in prayer.

"God, grant me the serenity to accept the things I cannot

change, courage to change the things I can, and the wisdom to know the difference."

The Friday night meeting at the Fifth Street Mission was officially called to order.

Chairs scraped along the floor in the front row of the hall as a young man and woman rose to their feet. Both extended an arm to the older gentleman who had been sitting between them, and slowly, with some effort, the gentleman rose to his feet. On his head, he wore a ball cap tilted rakishly to one side, the crest on the front reading **'NEVER SAY DIE.'** The man was thin and pale, but in his eyes, there was a glint of joy, and his jaw was set in steely determination.

The young man and woman by his side reached out toward his elbows to steady him, but he quickly shook off their grasp. He looked at them both with a proud and loving smile and softly told them they could both be seated.

For a moment, he just looked out over the crowd, a smile on his face, deep in thought. Then, when he felt a steadiness beneath him, he leaned slightly forward and retrieved two canes that had been hung from the back of his chair. The room was completely silent as he moved forward on two prosthetic legs. Moving slowly and slightly awkwardly, he made his journey to the front table and turned to face the crowd.

He looked back upon hundreds of faces: some smiling broadly, others dabbing at tears in the corners of their eyes, and still others who had no knowledge of the event they were witnessing.

The man leaned his canes on the edge of the table and held tightly to the podium as he began to speak.

"I would like to welcome you all here tonight for this here meeting. It's been a while since I have been in these parts, and this here is my first meeting in the borough. My name is James Montgomery Patterson, and I am an alcoholic."

The room responded with the customary murmur, 'Hello, James.'

"Now, some of you folks hereabouts have heard tell of me, and some of you have maybe even known me, but none of you have ever seen me sober. Except for my boy and girl sitting there, who have kept me going these past seven years. For those of you who have known me in another life, I am going to start again. My name is Trip, and I am an alcoholic!"

The room exploded in whistles and catcalls and a thunderous reply: **"HELLO, TRIP!"**

Trip continued, "You know, folks, we all have a row to hoe in this world, and sometimes the rows are hard and rocky. Sometimes, we get them crooked, and sometimes—well, sometimes, we just can't get through, and we go in a whole other direction. That's the way it has been for lots of us here.

"But you know, if we live through it, and if we do the right things, and most important of all, if we call out to our Lord God in that time of the deepest despair, we can get help.

We can get clean and sober, and we can turn our lives around by the Grace of God.

"That's the story for all of us here tonight—maybe even more so for our speaker tonight. I would not be standing here in front of you on store-bought legs without the help of lots of folks. Maybe none of us would be here at this meeting tonight were it not for old Armist there. That's the way it is for us. We need each other, and we need help. But I am not the man sharing a message tonight. So please, help me to welcome our Speaker.

The room erupted in applause, people rising to their feet as, out of the side wings of the basement room at the Fifth Street Mission, a man walked toward the front table. His head was bowed, his face looked solemn, and he was clearly uncomfortable with the accolades of the crowd.

Silently, he took his place at the podium and waited as the din of the crowd transformed in seconds to absolute silence. He looked out at the faces—faces he recognized, many of which he had not seen in such a long time—and marveled that they were here. Here for him, after all he had done.

He thanked God under his breath, threw back his shoulders and, looked into the eyes of the people in the room, and began, "Hello, I am Tommy, and I am an alcoholic."

www.ingramcontent.com/pod-product-compliance
Lightning Source LLC
Chambersburg PA
CBHW060424310726
48977CB00001B/34